Dear Reader,

If you are holding this book in your hand (and I'm going to be presumptuous and assume that you are), that means that the little girl who dreamed of becoming a writer has made it.

She didn't think she would make it when she sat down to write *Vicious* almost a decade ago. By then, she was no longer a girl. A young, tired mom, yes. One who was just crazy and sleep-deprived enough to think that maybe, somewhere, anywhere, someone shared her love for delicious, decadent, morally cinder alpha males who are unapologetically themselves.

Vicious, Jaime, Dean, Trent, and Roman grow on you like fungus. Slowly but steadily, and without you noticing until it is too late. Unlike fungus, though, they age quite well as the books progress, and grow into the men they strive to be.

If I could go back to that girl who dreamed of writing books, who dared to imagine said books would be in bookstores, I would tell her not to worry. That she would turn out all right. Because that girl? She is me.

And to you, the reader, I say thank you. For giving her a chance. For making dreams come true. Most of all—for sharing her passion for a good, steamy romance novel with a lot of heart and (hopefully) just as much soul.

All my love, always,

xoxo

ALSO BY L.J. SHEN

Sinners of Saint
Vicious
Ruckus
Scandalous
Bane

All Saints
Pretty Reckless
Broken Knight
Angry God
Damaged Goods

BANE

L.J. SHEN

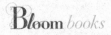

Published by Bloom Books, an imprint of Sourcebooks
P.O. Box 4410, Naperville, Illinois 60567-4410
(630) 961-3900
sourcebooks.com

Originally self-published in 2018 by L.J. Shen.

Cataloging-in-Publication data is on file with the Library of Congress.

Printed and bound in the United States of America.
WOZ 10 9 8 7 6 5 4 3 2 1

For Tijuana Turner and Amy Halter

PLAYLIST

"Can You Feel My Heart"—Bring Me the Horizon

"If You Can't Hang"—Sleeping With Sirens

"Time to Dance"—Panic! at the Disco

"Roadgame"—Kravinsky

"Iris"—Goo Goo Dolls

"Bite My Tongue"—You Me at Six

"My Own Summer"—Deftones

"Famous Last Words"—My Chemical Romance

"Hideaway"—KYKO

NOTE

It is said that no two snowflakes are alike. Each snowflake is beautiful and hypnotizing in its own unique silhouette. Snowflakes symbolize purity.

But every snowflake that's lucky enough to settle on the ground is destined to be blemished by dirt. Snowflakes teach us the lesson that if you live long enough, you will eventually get soiled.

But even your stains won't tarnish your beauty.

PROLOGUE
BANE

A liar.

A con.

A godless thief.

My reputation was a big wave that I rode, one that swallowed everyone around me, drowning every attempt to fuck with what was mine.

I'd been known as a stoner, but power was my real drug of choice. Money meant nothing. It was tangible and therefore easy to lose. See, to me, people were a game. One I'd always known how to win.

Move the rooks around.

Change the queen when necessary.

Guard the king at all fucking times.

I was never distracted, never deterred, and never jealous.

So imagine my surprise when I found myself being all three at once.

It was a siren with coal-black hair who robbed me of riding the biggest wave I'd seen that summer. Of my precious attention. Of my goddamn breath.

She glided from the ocean to the beach like nightfall.

I crouched down, straddling my surfboard, gawking.

Edie and Beck stopped beside me, floating on their boards in my periphery.

"This one's taken by Emery Wallace," Edie had warned. *Thief.*

"This one's the hottest masterpiece in town." Beck had chuckled. *Con.*

"More importantly, she only dates rich bastards." *Liar.*

I had all the ingredients to pull her in.

Her body was a patch of fresh snow. White, fair, like the sun shone through her, never quite soaking in. Her skin defied nature, her ass defied my sanity, but it was the words on her back that made my logic rebel.

It wasn't her curves or the way she swayed her hips like a dangling, poisonous apple that warranted my reaction to her.

It was that tattoo I had noticed when she swam close to me earlier, the words trickling down the nape of her neck and back in a straight arrow.

My Whole Life Has Been Pledged to This Meeting with You
Pushkin.

I only knew one person who went gaga over the Russian poet, and like the famous Alexander, he was currently six feet under.

My friends began to paddle back to shore. I couldn't move. It felt like my balls were ten tons heavy. I didn't believe in love at first sight. Lust, maybe, but even that wasn't the word I was looking for. No. This girl fucking *intrigued* me.

"What's her name?" I snatched Beck's ankle, yanking him back to me. Edie stopped paddling and looked back, her gaze ping-ponging between us.

"Doesn't matter, bro."

"What's. Her. Name?" I repeated through a locked jaw.

"Dude, she's, like, way young."

"I will not repeat myself a third time."

Beck's throat bobbed with a swallow. He knew damn well that I didn't mess around. If she was legal, it was on.

"Jesse Carter."

Jesse Carter was going to be mine before she even knew me.

Before I even knew *her*.

Before her life turned upside down and her fate rewrote itself with her blood.

So here was the truth that even my lying ass wouldn't admit later on in our story—I wanted her before.

Before she became business.

Before the truth caged her in.

Before the secrets gushed out.

I never did get to surf that day.

My surfboard broke.

Should have known it was an omen.

My heart was going to be next in line.

And for a small chick, she did one hell of a fucking job obliterating it.

JESSE

THEN

The moon was full that night.

It was chuckle-worthy if not completely tacky. What a freaking cliché, right? A pregnant, fat, ghostly white moon sparkling in triumph, shining over the night that carved my destiny, my identity, my *stomach*, with deep, gleaming gashes.

I stared at it, so still and tranquil. Beautiful things were often so useless.

Don't just hang there. Call the cops. Call an ambulance. Save me.

I wondered if I was going to die. If so, how long would it take Pam to notice my absence? How long before Darren would assure her I'd always been troubled? *"Thweet,"* he'd console with his lisp, *"but troubled."* How long before she'd agree with him? How long before the KitKat on Dad's tombstone melted under the punishing sun?

"What a shame. Such a good kid," they'd mourn. Nothing like a dead teenager to make the entire community come together. Especially in the town of Todos Santos, where tragedies only happened in the newspapers and on CNN. Oh yes. This would give them something to talk about. A forbidden and delicious tale about the fall from grace of the current It Girl.

Realization trickled into me like a leaking faucet. Emery, Henry, and Nolan wouldn't even get a slap on the wrist. Community service? In my dreams. The public embarrassment in the form of scowls and canceled invitations to the country club's events next year was reserved for me. I was the outsider. The mortal idiot who mixed with the blue-blooded royals of Todos Santos.

They'd get away with it, I knew. They'd go to college and attend parties. They would graduate and throw their stupid hats in the stupid air. They'd get married and have babies and reunions and take annual skiing trips with their friends. And they'd live. *God, they'd live.* It was maddening to think that their heritage and money would buy their way out of justice. Because whether anyone bothered to scrape me off the road with or without a pulse tonight, I knew that I was dead. Dead in all the places that mattered.

For a passing moment, I was still the old Jesse. I tried to look at the flip side of things. The weather was nice for February. Not too hot, not too cold. Whatever desert heat clung onto my flesh was diluted by the chill of the asphalt underneath me. A lot of victims bounced back. I could go to college abroad. Darren was an expert at throwing money at problems and making them go away. I could reinvent myself. Forget it ever happened. Didn't they use hypnosis to suppress things like that? I could ask Mayra, the shrink my parents had sent me to ever since I'd started having nightmares. Science was limitless. Case in point: My forty-year-old mom looked twenty-three thanks to Botox.

Little stones dug at my bare back. My pink lacy bra and panties were lying torn somewhere beside me, and even though my groin was numb, I felt something slithering down my thigh. Blood? Semen? Didn't really matter at this point.

Steadfast, I blinked back at the moon, hung high in the inky sky like a chandelier, sneering at my heartbreakingly mortal existence.

I needed to try to get up. Call for help. Save myself. But the prospect of trying to move and failing was far more paralyzing than the pain. My legs felt frozen, my hip bones crushed.

Sirens wailed in the distance.

I squeezed my eyes shut. Often, I'd see my dad on the other side, like his face was permanently inked to my eyelids. That's where he lived now. In my dreams. More vivid than the woman he'd left behind. Pam always faded to the sidelines of my story, more occupied with writing her own plot.

The sirens got closer. Louder. My heart scurried to my stomach, curling like a battered puppy.

A few more minutes, and you'll become a piece of gossip. A cautionary tale.

The old Jesse would cry. She would scream and tell the police everything. Act normal, given the abnormal circumstances. The old Jesse would declare vengeance and do the right thing. The feminist thing. She wouldn't let them get away with it.

The old Jesse would *feel*.

The ambulance sputtered at the curb, close enough for the heat to roll off the tires and the scent of scalded rubber to stick to my nostrils. Somehow, knowing they'd called for help was even more infuriating than being left for dead, like they knew they were untouchable even after doing this to me. A stretcher opened beside me. I remembered the last words I heard before they'd left me in the alleyway, a lone tear free-falling down my cheek.

My Whole Life Has Been Pledged to This Meeting with You

"And what a meeting it was, whore. You gave a good fight." Nolan kicked my ribs.

I'd inked this sentence thinking Emery was the man I'd been waiting for. Now the back of my neck burned. I wanted to tear the flesh off my neck and dump it right next to my ruined clothes.

With agonizing effort, I moved my left arm to cover my chest, my right arm dragging across my bare stomach, hiding what they'd carved onto my torso like I was a Halloween pumpkin. They'd made me watch as they did it. Held my jaw in their clean, smooth hands, my neck bending unnaturally to accommodate the awkward position. A punishment for my discreditable sin.

The word shone like a neon billboard on my skin for the whole world to see and to judge and to laugh at, the letters bleeding red into my pink designer skirt.

Slut

The old Jesse would explain and bargain and argue.

The old Jesse would try to save face.

The old Jesse was dead.

CHAPTER ONE
BANE

NOW

I suppose at the end of the day, I really didn't give a shit.

Not about people and not about the whole popularity contest rich people were so neck-deep in because they didn't have the usual pain-in-the-ass problems of paying bills and functioning as responsible adults.

I was the beach bum, the stoner, the dopehead—and the drug dealer on probation. I wasn't Mr. Popular, but people feared me enough to stay out of my way. It wasn't a conscious choice to become a crook. My mom was not rich, and my dad was never in the picture, so I had to do what I had to do to survive in the richest town in California and have a little more than basic cable and frozen meals for lunch.

Then there was the whole pro-surfing gig I got into when I was fifteen. That cost a pretty penny too. It was also the only thing I cared about beyond my mom. I otherwise found myself pretty apathetic toward life. So that's how I ended up dealing drugs early on. Pot, mainly. It was easier than you'd think. Buy burner phones at Walmart. One for suppliers. One for clients. Change them often. Never deal with people you don't know. Never talk about your shit. Stay nice and positive. I'd paid my way through my surfing journey and high school doing it, with the exception of pickpocketing every now and then when I'd needed a new surfboard. I tended to abuse mine.

This was how I got by, until the probation, anyway, but then I figured out the whole jail gig was not really for me and had to expand my business. That was around five years ago, but I never thought I'd be sitting here, in front of the most formidable dude in Todos Santos, conducting…well, *business*. Legitimate business, at that.

"About your nickname." Baron Spencer, dubbed Vicious by everyone who was unfortunate enough to know him, smirked. He poured four fingers of Macallan into two glasses, staring at the golden liquid with the kind of admiration people usually reserve for their kids.

I had come all the way from Todos Santos to Los Angeles to meet Spencer at his office. It made zero logistical sense. We lived ten minutes from one another. But if there was one thing I'd learned about rich assholes, it was that they liked *the act*. The whole enchilada. This was not a social call, so we needed to meet at his workplace, where I'd see how big his corner office was, how fuckable his secretary was, and how expensive his whiskey was.

Truth was, I couldn't care less if we were meeting on Mars, as long as I got what I'd come here for. I crossed my ankles under his desk, my unlaced boots knocking against one another, and ignored the drink he slid across his desk toward me. I preferred vodka. I also preferred not to get shit-faced before climbing on my Harley. Unlike Mr. Spencer, I didn't have a personal driver to chauffeur me around like a legless prick. But first things first. He'd asked a question.

"My nickname?" I stroked my beard thoughtfully.

He gave me a curt don't-fuck-with-me nod. "Bane is awfully similar to Vicious, wouldn't you agree?"

No, I wouldn't, dipshit.

"Weren't you the creator of the game Defy?" I pushed my chair off the floor, tipping it back on two legs and chewing on my cinnamon gum loudly. I should probably explain: Defy was an old school tradition at All Saints High, where students challenged other students to a fistfight. This clusterfuck was founded by the HotHoles, four kids who ruled the school like it belonged to their parents. Appropriately, it sort of did. Baron Spencer's ancestors built half the town, including the high school, and Jaime Followhill's mom had been the principal up until six years ago.

Vicious angled his chin down, inspecting me. Dickwad had the kind of smirk that would make women moan his name even when he was on another continent. He was happily married to Emilia LeBlanc-Spencer and strictly off the market. Shame they rocked the happily-in-love vibe. Married women were a favorite flavor of mine. They never asked for more than a dirty fuck.

"Correct."

"Well, you got the name Vicious for starting the game. I got the name Bane for killing it." I produced a joint from my pocket. I figured Vicious smoked in his office because his workspace bled into an open patio and there were more ashtrays than pens on the desk. Not a job for Sherlock, apparently.

I told Spencer about the first time I was invited for a fight in my freshman year. How I hadn't known the rules because I'd been too busy finding creative ways to pay for my backpack and tuition to get all the ins and outs of All Saints High. How I'd broken a lunch tray on a guy's head when he got in my face. How he'd suffered from a concussion and been saddled with the nickname SpongeBob FlatHead. How, two weeks later, he'd ambushed me outside school, armed with six senior jocks and three baseball bats. How I'd beaten the crap out of them, too, and broken the bats for good measure. Then I told him about the trouble we'd all gotten into. The pussies whined that I'd fought too hard and hadn't followed the rules. The name "Bane" stuck because the principal, Mrs. Followhill, accidentally pressed her elbow to the loudspeaker when she discussed my behavior with a counselor, calling me the "bane of her existence."

Principal Followhill took the opportunity to kill the tradition her son, Jaime, had helped make.

It didn't help that a month prior to the cafeteria incident, a private school in Washington had a Columbine 2.0 massacre on their hands. Everybody was scared of rich kids. But then I'd be the first one to admit everyone was even more scared of *me*.

Call me a people pleaser, but I'd provided them with good reasons to steer clear.

They'd given me a nickname, and I'd become it, lived it and breathed it.

Way I looked at it, I was a Russian immigrant bastard living in one of the richest towns in the States. I never stood a chance to fit in in the first place. So what was really the harm in standing out?

Vicious relaxed into his leather seat, his grin unwavering. He didn't care that I'd killed Defy. I doubted if he cared much about anything. He was richer than God, married to one of the most beautiful women in our zip code, and a doting father. He won the battle and the war and conquered every obstacle that had stood in his way. He had nothing to prove and reeked of contentment.

He was smug, but I was hungry. Hunger was dangerous.

"All right, *Bane*. Why are you here?"

"I'd like your investment," I said, taking a hit from the joint and passing it to him. He barely moved his head in a no gesture, but his smirk widened an inch, morphing into a patronizing smile.

"Easy there. We're not friends, kid. Barely even acquaintances."

I fanned smoke through my nostrils in a long, white stream.

"As you know, they're bulldozing the old hotel on the edge of Tobago Beach. The acres will be available for commercial use, and the general idea is to open a shopping center there. There's an auction at the end of the year. All the external companies who are planning to bid don't know what they're dealing with. They don't know Todos

Santos's social fabric or the local contractors. I do. I'm offering you twenty-five percent equity for a six-million-dollar investment on a surfing park there consisting of a surfing school, surfing shops, a food court, and some touristy bullshit stores. The acquisition of the land and demolition costs will fall solely on me, so consider this my one and final offer."

I was going to lose a lot of money in that deal, but I needed to attach Vicious's name to my proposal. Stapling Spencer's name to my bid would sweeten it in the eyes of the county. As you might imagine, I didn't have the best reputation.

"I already own a mall in Todos Santos." Vicious emptied his whiskey glass and slammed it against the desk, staring at the Los Angeles landscape through the open patio windows. "The only mall in Todos Santos, to be exact. Why would I help build another one?"

"You own a high-end shopping center. Prada, Armani, Chanel, and their ilk. The type of shit teenagers and tourists can't afford. I'm building a surfing park. It's like apples and oranges."

"There'll still be stores there."

"Yeah, surfing-related stores. Beach stores. I'm not your competition."

Vicious poured himself a second glass, his eyes hard on the liquid. "Every person with a pulse is my competition. Yours too. Never forget that."

I let smoke crawl out of my mouth upward, trying a different tactic. "Fine. Maybe the surf park will bite into your shit. If you can't beat them, join them, right?"

"Who said I can't beat you?" Vicious crossed his legs at the ankles on top of his desk. I stared at the clean soles of his shoes. He had no idea who he was dealing with. Sure, he knew *about* me. It was hard not to at this point. At twenty-five, I owned the most successful coffee shop in Todos Santos—Café Diem. I had recently purchased an inn on the outskirts of town. I was in the process of gutting it and making it a boutique hotel. In addition, I charged protection money from every store and shop on the promenade and split it with my friend Hale Rourke fifty-fifty. It sounded like a lot, but really, I was spending more than I was earning on both places, and for all intents and purposes, I was still the same broke bastard. I just had more shit under my name to take care of.

My rise to power was slow, steady, and unstoppable. My mother's family was affluent, but just enough to send us to the States when I was a toddler and leave us to fend for ourselves. Every penny I made was through pot-dealing, extortion, and fucking the wrong women for the right price. Sometimes the men, if I was really hard up for cash. Every connection I'd made to get ahead in the game was through a string of illicit, short-term affairs and sexual favors. This left me with a less-than-squeaky-clean reputation, which was fine by me. I wasn't here to run for office.

"I have to admit, Mr. Protsenko, I'm inclined to say no."

"And from where, pray tell, does your inclination stem?"

"Your reputation precedes you."

"Enlighten me as to what it says."

He uncrossed his legs and leaned forward, cocking his head sideways, his eyes a blazing ice storm. "That you're a con artist, a bad egg—the kind that gives you food poisoning—and a goddamn thief."

There was no point in disputing those facts. Call me a Renaissance man, but I checked every single fucking box on that list.

"For all I know, you may plan to use this place to launder money." His jaw twitched in annoyance. I wasn't planning to do that, but dude was definitely sharp.

"Nah, too risky. Money laundering is an art." I blew out another plume of thick smoke.

"It is also a federal offense."

"Can I ask you something?" I tapped the ash into the glass of whiskey he'd served me, showing him exactly what I thought about his sixty-thousand-dollar spirits. He arched an eyebrow sardonically, waiting for me to continue.

"Why did you invite me here if you knew you were going to say no? I'm one of the main runners for buying the lot. That's public knowledge. You knew I wasn't coming here to admire your pretty eyes."

Vicious tapped his chin with his laced index fingers, his lower lip poking out. "What's wrong with my eyes?"

"For one thing, they're not attached to someone with a pussy and a rack."

"According to the rumors, you don't limit yourself to one gender. Either way, I wanted to see for myself."

"See what?" I ignored his dig. Homophobia was beneath me. Besides, he wanted to get a rise out of me. It wasn't my first or last rodeo with a pompous prick. I always came out on top (all puns intended).

"What my successor looks like."

"Your successor? Color me confused, blushing, and deafened by my ringing bullshit radar." I smirked, scratching my face with my middle finger.

We were polar opposites. A single-parented, middle-class spawn sitting across from a trust-fund baby. I had a blond man-bun and enough tattoos to cover the better half of North America, and today's attire consisted of a Primitive shirt, black cargo pants, and muddy boots. He was wrapped head to toe in Brioni, with sleek black hair and porcelain-white skin. He looked like a Michelin-starred steak, and I looked like a greasy drive-through cheeseburger. Didn't bother me one bit. I loved cheeseburgers. Most people would opt for a McGreasy double cheeseburger over a tiny piece of tartar.

Vicious stretched in his seat. "You do understand that I cannot, in good conscience, help you build a shopping center—focused around surfing or otherwise—in Todos Santos? You'll nibble at my business." He ignored my question, and I didn't like it. I dropped the joint into the whiskey glass and got to my feet.

He stared up at me. Serene, sincere, and utterly blasé. "But that doesn't mean I'm not rooting for you, Bane. I'm just not going to equip you for the war you're planning to enter. Because I'll also have an army in this battle. Whoever is opening a shopping center there is going to bite into my shit, and when people bite into my shit, I devour what's theirs too."

I scratched my beard, allowing it to sink in. Of course Vicious and his like didn't care for me. He was at the top. I was getting there. Squashing me was survival instinct.

Spencer looked down, jotting something in a golden notepad with the logo of Fiscal Heights Holdings, his company's name. "But here's someone who could help you. He's been trying to lay down roots in Todos Santos for years now. He needs to build a rep here and is getting pretty desperate. He might not have the street cred, but he's got a clean name and the Benjamins." He glided the note across the black-and-gold-chrome desk, and I reached for it with my inked, callused fingers.

Darren Morgansen followed by a phone number.

"Oil money." He smoothed his tie over his dress shirt. "Even more important—he'll actually hear you out, unlike the vast majority of businessmen in this town."

He was right, and that irritated me.

"Why are you helping me?" I asked. I liked Baron Spencer. He was my first choice of business partner when I'd decided to make a bid on those acres. I knew other rich, influential people in this town, but no one was quite as ruthless as he was.

"I'm merely giving you a head start. It makes things interesting, and I like the element of surprise," he said, twirling his wedding band on his finger. "Open this surf park, Bane. I dare you. It'd be nice to finally meet my match."

Before I left his office building, I made it a point to take a shit in the restroom and tuck a few of the fancy Fiscal Heights Holdings pens into my pocket, just for funsies. Oh, and I might have fucked his secretary, Sue. She emailed me the contact details of all the service providers working for her boss's mall. They'd become handy when I opened the surf park. The one that was supposed to rid me of the bullshit and pay for my mom's mortgage.

Baron Spencer thought he was going to war with me.

He was about to find out that I *was* the war.

———————

I met Darren Morgansen that same evening.

First cue that he was overly eager? He invited me to his house. As I said, business tycoons rarely ever meet with you in their private domain. Morgansen completely ignored *the act*. Said on the phone that he was excited for the opportunity to get to know a key player like me, which almost made me cancel on his ass. I was the one who needed to wine and dine his ego, not vice versa. But I was willing to overlook the weird dynamics if it meant putting together the world's biggest surf park and making Todos Santos the next Huntington Beach.

Mostly, I saw an opening with the potential to make me as rich as the people who looked at me like I was trash, and I was happy to have a go at it. Not gonna lie—I hadn't expected to get half this far in my journey to buying the lot. People actually paid attention to what I was saying, and that surprised me a little.

Morgansen lived in El Dorado, a gated community on the hills of Todos Santos overlooking the ocean. The neighborhood was home to most of the heavily loaded brats in town. The Spencers. The Coles. The Followhills. The Wallaces. The kind of money one couldn't make in a lifetime but rather inherited.

The Morgansen house was a colonial mansion sprawled across a mountainside. Nothing like living on a cliff to inspire you to want to jump off it. There were a small pond and cascading fountain with (real) swans and (fake) angels shooting arrows of water at the front driveway, a garden, a hammam and a sauna next to the kidney-shaped pool, and a load of other crap I'd bet my right nut no one in the house had ever used. He had huge-ass plants lining up each side of his double-door entrance. This asshole's gardening bill for a month is probably what I'd paid for my entire houseboat when I purchased it.

Morgansen greeted me at the gate of the neighborhood, and I pretended to not already have an electronic key for it. He then showed me around his mansion like I was contemplating buying the place. We strolled through his front lawn, his backyard, and the *two* downstairs kitchens. Then we climbed up the curved staircase to the second floor. "Let me show you my offith"—he had a lisp. I inwardly let out a *thank fuck* breath. Finally, we were going in the right direction. We walked past a closed door, and he stopped, brushing his knuckles over the wooden door with a hesitant knock, pressing his forehead to it.

"Honey?" he whispered. He was lanky, crouched like a beatdown teenager, and morbidly WASP-y. Everything about him was mediocre. Brown, lemur-like eyes, bony nose that stood out like a weakness, lips narrow and pursed, salt-and-pepper hair, and a bland suit that gave him the unfortunate look of a bar mitzvah boy. He looked like an extra in someone else's story. I almost felt sorry for him. He had the kind of inborn averageness no money in the world was going to fix.

There was no answer from the other side of the door.

"Thweetheart, I'm in my offith. Let me know if you need anything. Or...or tell Hannah."

Breaking news: Rich guy has a spoiled stepdaughter.

"Okay. Going now." He stalled, loitering against the sound of silence. "Jutht down the hall..."

Morgansen was a peculiar creature in the three-comma club. He was submissive and contrite, two things that inspired my inner bloodthirsty bulldog to chew him like a squeaky toy. We walked into his office, the door closing shut behind us on a hiss. Darren pushed his hair back and then proceeded to wipe his palms over his dress pants and laugh nervously as he asked me what I wanted to drink. I told him I'd have vodka. He pressed a switchboard button on his oak desk and sank into his cashmere seat. "Hannah, vodka pleath."

I was seriously starting to second-guess why Baron Spencer had given me this clown's number. Maybe it was a joke at my expense. This dude may have been rich—correction, he was swimming in it and had a house the size of the marina to prove it—but he was also a goddamn wreck. I doubted a scaredy-cat like him would shell out a cool six mil for 25 percent equity to a total stranger with a dubious reputation. I made myself comfortable in my chair, trying not to think about it. His eyes trailed my movement. I knew what he was staring at and what I looked like.

People often asked me *why*. Why did I insist on looking like I was auditioning for *Sons of Anarchy*, with tattoos covering a good portion of my body? Why the man-bun? Why the beard? Why the fuck-you attire of a beach bum, with pants still stained with surfboard wax? Honestly, I didn't see the point in making an effort to look like them. I wasn't *them*. I was *me*. I was an outsider, with no lineage, fancy last name, or historic legacy.

Looking like every father's nightmare was my way of saying I was out of the rat race.

"You're quite the character in Todoth Thantoth." Morgansen fiddled with the edges of his thick planner. I wasn't sure whether he was referring to my professional reputation or my personal one. The rumor around town was that Café Diem and the hotel had been bought so I could smurf my protection money, and they weren't exactly wrong. I porked every chick with a pulse, sometimes venturing to blow jobs from guys when I was feeling drunk and adventurous, and then proceeded to engage in paid-for affairs with whomever could get me an inch closer to the total domination of Todos Santos's recreational venues. I entertained the forty-year-old wives of men I looked up to professionally for the sole purpose of pissing them off and was the shameless arm candy of even older women whom I knew could sponsor my brand and me. I was a man-whore in the biblical sense of the word, and people viewed me as about as trustworthy and loyal as an ounce of coke.

"I'll take that as a compliment," I said, just as Darren's house-keeper pushed the door open, entering with a tray, two glasses, and a Waterford vodka decanter in hand. She poured me a glass and then whiskey for Darren from the bar behind him, all meek silence and bowed head.

"P-pleath do," Darren stuttered. "I've been meaning to network with you for quite thome time. My family moved here four yearth ago."

Like I didn't know. Todos Santos was known as an upper-cruster: a morosely white town that put one's pedigree above their morals and reputation. Every time someone moved in, people knew. Every time someone moved out, people jumped on the gossip train, wondering what they were trying to hide. The Morgansens had managed to fly under the radar thus far. Not necessarily a good thing. It meant that they hadn't managed to form strong connections despite coming from oil money, and that was suspicious.

"How are you liking it here?" I snapped my gum, looking around in boredom.

"It'th…intereth-ting. Very hierarchical."

I grabbed my drink, knocked it back in one gulp, and placed the glass back on the tray in front of a thoroughly shocked Morgansen. I produced a joint from a small tin box in my front pocket.

"Neat. Shall we get to business?"

Darren's forehead wrinkled once again.

He motioned with his hand for me to start pitching. I did.

I told him about the prospect. About the piece of beach that was going to make a fantastic SurfCity center. Then I told him about my plan and took out blueprints one of the finest architects in LA had made for me. I told Darren about my vision for it and then pulled out some statistics about the ever-growing population of teenagers in Todos Santos—rich people loved popping out kids, and kids in SoCal were into either skateboarding or surfing, plus we were close enough to Huntington Beach, San Clemente, and San Diego to hijack their hard-core surfers. Not to mention the amount of pro competitions it was going to attract to Todos Santos. I explained how I needed a nice bowtie name to put on my proposal to make sure someone took it seriously and how he would be able to sit back and watch his money grow. I refrained from adding that sticking it to Baron Spencer, with his luxurious, half-dead mall downtown, would raise us to the position of deities. It was the truth, but Morgansen looked like the kind of person who'd crap his pants from the prospect of pissing someone off. Least of all Baron "Vicious" Spencer.

I'd sniffed around before I'd called Darren. His grandfather had bought oil fields in Kuwait before all the cool kids did it. Morgansen was barely keeping the family business alive. He didn't know what the fuck he was doing. He had a wife and a stepdaughter and a shit ton of people with mustaches telling him what to do.

"And how much do you need from me?" he asked.

"Six mill," I said, unblinking. He rubbed the back of his neck. For a second, I thought he was going to tell me to get the fuck out of there and throw something sharp at me. But he didn't. He glanced around. Scratched his face. Downed his bullshit-expensive scotch like a champ, wincing afterward, and then—and only then—met my gaze, defeat shining in his eyes.

"Fine."

"Fine?" I echoed, almost dumbly. That was it? *Fine?* Whatever this guy was high on, I wished I could sell it.

"Fine, I will shell out the money. You can have three mil up front."

"I don't need three mil up front. There is no guarantee I will get the land," I spat out. My instincts told me there was a catch, but Darren looked as harmless as a fucking Teletubby. Dude couldn't play Twister, let alone someone like me.

"You will, when they thee my name on it. Anyway, conthider it a gethture of goodwill. I don't need your equity."

"Are you on something right now? Because we can't have business together if you're a junkie. Pot is fine, but if you're on meth, I need to know." I scratched my cheek with the edge of my joint, one eyebrow raised in amusement.

He gave me his version of a sneer, and I've seen more character on faces of goddamn goats. "I don't need your equity. It'th not money I'm after. I have enough of it. I want thomething elth from you. As I thaid before, I heard all about you, Bane. I know who you are and what you do. What I need from you ith not to make me richer. I need you to help my thtepdaughter."

What you are.

What you do.

Holy hairy shit balls, Stepdaddy Darren wants his kid to get laid.

The first question I had in mind was how ugly was this daughter of his, exactly? Was she Quasimodo ugly? With the amount of money and resources this chick had, hopefully she could at least pass as cute. Maybe not hot as shit, but surely fuckable to someone. *Anyone.* Luckily, I was twenty-five, and when you're twenty-five, you find everything bone-able, pencil sharpeners included. If he wanted me to screw his stepdaughter for six million dollars, I would get my lawyer to draft this shit tonight, and by morning, she'd be so thoroughly fucked she'd have a few extra holes and orgasm-induced foggy brain for days. I'd even throw in oral and after-sex spooning for good measure because it wouldn't feel right not to give her a little extra for all this cash.

"That's fine." I waved him off. "I usually do a six-month contract, no exclusivity clause. Twice a week. Condom is nonnegotiable, and I want her tested before I touch her." I'd been told I was a good-looking son of a bitch, and I never knew when I'd need to stick my dick in someone as a favor or to gain something. As it was, I stopped taking on new clients for money. Cash simply stopped being an incentive once all my bills were paid and my mom was taken care of. But no one told me my dick was worth so much. The Morgansen kid's stepdaddy sure knew how to spoil her.

Darren shook his head, panic smeared all over his face.

"Wait, what? Oh, Lord. No. No. No, no, no." He flapped his hands around frantically, coughing. I straightened in my seat, not really sure how this guy was not dead from a heart attack already. "I didn't mean it like that. I don't want you to thleep with her. In fact, if there *ith* one clauth I want in, it'th one where you promith not to make a move on her. I want you becauth you're for hire and you do ath you're paid to do, nothing leth, nothing more. Jethy doethn't have many friendth. She'th been through a lot, and she jutht needth thomeone. A companion. I want you to help her gain her confidenth back and make thome friends. To hire her for your café tho that she will have to leave the house every day. It will be thtrictly platonic. Jethy ith untouchable. She doethn't *let* people touch her."

Jesse. But of course his stepdaughter has a name he can't properly pronounce. Poor bastard.

What was this Jesse girl's deal? She didn't even bother answering her stepdad, even though she was obviously there. It was tough luck that she sounded like a spoiled princess because I was going to take the job even if I needed to hear about her shopping sprees with mommy dearest until my ears fell off. For a few hundred thousand dollars, I wouldn't have bothered. But there was so much money on the line and such a lucrative investment, Jesse had just bought my attention. And, to an extent, my affection, too.

"What does this job entail?" I asked, fingering my beard.

"Her therapitht thays she needth a job. Any job. Hire her. Humor her. Court her. But don't touch her." His quivering fingers danced across the edges of his planner again. "Breathe life into her."

"Is she…" I didn't know how to articulate it without sounding like a politically incorrect dick. *Slow? Impaired in any way?* Not that it mattered, but I needed to know what I was dealing with here. Darren shifted in his seat.

"She'th a very bright kid. She jutht needth a little push back into thothiety."

"Why?"

"Why?" he echoed, blinking rapidly, like the question had never occurred to him. His jaw twitched, and he pinched the bridge of his nose. He looked on the verge of tears. Dude was about as put-together as a coked-up teenager at Coachella. He obviously needed a backbone transplant, and for the right price, I was a willing donor. If he needed help with his kid, I was going to give it to him. I wouldn't even have to feel like a dick because it would just be taking her to the movies or whatever. It wasn't like I was going to stick my dick in her and whisper love declarations in her ear. "I'll tell you why, but you'll have to thign a nondithclothure agreement."

Rich people had the craziest stories. She was probably into bestiality or some shit. Money makes you bored, and being bored makes you an asshole.

"I've signed so many NDAs in my life, at this point I don't talk to anyone about anything other than the weather." I eased back into my chair, suddenly feeling very smug about getting into business with this dude.

His eyes darted to me, glistening with hope. He loved her. I'd always been embarrassed by love. It was such an uncomfortable feeling. People did a lot of stupid stuff in the name of it.

"Right. Right. Tho...do we have a deal?" he piped, taking a greedy hit of air. I looked around, scanning his office for the first time. Traditional. Dark oak and floor-to-ceiling shelves with hundreds of thick, pristine books. A Persian carpet and camel-hued silk armchairs. The bar was the only thing that looked used, the bottles half-empty, sad, and riddled with his fingerprints. Everything else was for show. This man was lost, and I was the lucky bastard who'd found him.

Like taking candy from a fucking baby.

"I'll give her six months, and I want to know her story."

Morgansen poured himself another glass of whiskey, stared into it as one would into an abyss, gulped the whole thing as one would when they jumped to their death, and let the glass dangle between his fingertips before it fell to the carpeted floor.

"You want her thtory?"

I hitched one shoulder up. I never repeated myself and wasn't going to make a habit of it because of this fucker.

When the first words left his mouth, my fingers clutched my seat.

When the first sentences dug through my skull, my throat went dry.

And after ninety minutes of listening, I had only one response to spare. It was one word, actually. And it summarized what I was feeling pretty accurately.

Fuck.

CHAPTER TWO
BANE

"It's a good day for a hang eleven." Beck laughed wildly, his long, wet brown hair flipping in the wind as he lay stomach-down on his surfboard while riding a bomb wave. It was called dick-drag. Though fun, it was the equivalent of wasting a gorgeous supermodel on a drunken hand job. Truth was, every day when the beach was mostly empty was a good day to surf naked. That's why every sea creature in SoCal knew the shape of my dick by heart. I laughed and watched as Beck pulled his shorts down, wrapping them around his wrist like a bracelet. My high school friend, Hale, was a few feet away, busting through the break zone, and my high school girlfriend, Edie, was right beside me, sitting on her surfboard, staring at the beach in a lull.

I followed her gaze and spotted her husband, Trent, and his daughter, Luna, building elaborate sandcastles with their shapers. Edie was my favorite, and consequently only, ex. She was also one of my best friends. That sounded complicated, but it really wasn't. I liked people for who they were, regardless of my likelihood to fuck them. Edie—or Gidget, as I'd called her since high school—was unfuckable for me, but she was still Edie. Her forehead was creased in concern. I squatted down, straddling my Firewire Evo, and flicked her ear.

"You're doing it again."

"What?"

"Overthinking."

Gidget scrunched her nose. "I'm just a little dizzy." She sleeked her blond hair back, squinting to the golden shore.

"You look pale." It was an understatement, but not a very gentlemanly thing to point out. "Go home. The waves ain't going anywhere."

She twisted her head back. "Hey, Beck! My daughter is on the beach. Put your trunks back on, you creeper."

I loved how she referred to her stepdaughter as her daughter. They'd only known each other for a few years, but this family was the realest thing I'd seen.

"What about you? Are you okay?" Edie moved her fingertips across the water.

"Never been better."

"Still using a condom?" She arched a wet eyebrow. She'd been asking me this a lot ever since I decided I was open for business five years ago. I fought an eye roll and gave her surfboard a push with my foot. "You're breaking the waves, Gidget. Surf or get the fuck out."

I watched Edie paddling back to shore before I turned around to deal with Beck and Hale, only to find they were both straddling their surfboards mere feet from me.

"Show's over." I spat into the water. Beck jumped on his board—fucker had the core of a yoga instructor—and did the annoying groin-thrust dance douchebags do when they want to sexually harass everyone in their radius. He kind of looked like a young Matt Damon with long brown hair. He started singing "The Show Must Go On" by Queen, clutching his fist dramatically.

I'd taken Beck under my wing in hopes of making him the pro surfer everyone would drag their asses to competitions to see. He was Kelly Slater good, but he was also Homer Simpson lazy, so I was training him for his next competition in late September.

I was pretty much the only person he was afraid of, so I figured if anyone could drag his ass out of bed every morning at five, it'd be me.

Hale shook his head. "Get a trim, asshole. Your crotch looks like Phil Spector." He motioned to Beck's dick. The latter laughed, his dong flipping like hair in a shampoo commercial. Hale turned back to me, and now the three of us were sitting like assholes, killing the waves. Peachy.

"This month's my round, right?" The round was what we called paying visits to the shops at the promenade, collecting protection money.

"Right."

"Anything else I can do?" He plastered his abs to his stick. Hale had red hair, green eyes, and the soul of a self-destructive Holden Caulfield who'd been injected into the synthetic town of Todos Santos. Another thing he had that I didn't: helicopter parents. He was getting close to finishing his master's degree in philosophy and following in his parents' footsteps to becoming a professor. They wanted him to turn SoCal's plastic souls into thinking individuals. But Hale didn't want to be a professor or even a teacher. He wanted to be a professional fuckboy, like me.

"Be good and finish all your homework." I laughed.

He splashed me like a five-year-old. "I want more responsibility. I want to be a part of SurfCity."

Hale and I split the protection money fifty-fifty, which worked for me because he did all the legwork. But he always pushed for more. SurfCity was my idea, my baby, my dream. I wasn't going to share it with anyone.

"I don't need more help."

He groaned. "I'm serious."

I looked up and watched naked Beck paddling away, taking his hairy crotch with him. "So am I."

"I have money. I can invest in SurfCity."

"You can invest in getting the fuck out of my way and letting me surf."

"Why not? You need the money, obviously. Did you find anyone yet?"

I wasn't going to tell him about Darren and Jesse because I wasn't sure how shit was going to pan out, and anyway I wouldn't put it past Hale to try to fuck it up a little just for funsies. He was made out of the same cloth as the infamous HotHoles. Sometimes he liked to break shit for the simple reason of loving the sound of it cracking in his ears.

"None of your business."

"It's really hard to read you, Protsenko."

"Or"—I tilted my chin down, smiling—"maybe you're just illiterate at reading people, *Hale.*" His nostrils were comically wide. He took off on his surfboard, his own version of slamming the door in my face. I laughed. Beck appeared by my side a few minutes later, his chest rising and falling with adrenaline.

"What's up with everyone? Gidget is acting like a chick, and Hale is acting like a pussy. It's like you're everyone's abusive daddy."

I smirked, staring at the disappearing figure of Hale, my mind on SurfCity.

"So. Same time tomorrow?" Beck pretended to punch my arm but didn't actually have the balls to do it.

"Yeah. Let's make it early. I have a plan for the afternoon."

My plan had a name, a description, and an endgame.

My plan was a nineteen-year-old girl.

What I didn't know was my plan was about to blow up in my face in a spectacular fashion, making the same breaking sound that made Hale's balls tingle.

The first thing I did was learn Jesse Carter's routine. I use the term "routine" loosely because weirdo wasn't hot on leaving her house or room or…bed. Her name gave me déjà vu, but I didn't think much of it. It was a small town. I'd probably run into her at some point. Maybe I was even *in* her at some point.

That would be a whole other brand of awkward.

Darren told me Jesse's dad had died when she was twelve and that had fucked her up even before those boys finished the job. He also said that meeting her seemingly spontaneously was going to be a task akin to teaching a pig how to waltz.

"You're going to have to worm your path into her world becauth she doethn't leave here often," he said on the phone. "She goeth to therapy every Thurthday, that'th in downtown Todoth Santoth, and runth the track around El Dorado every noon and every night at around three."

Twice a fucking day? Still, none of my business.

"Interesting hours," I commented, my eyes on the paper.

"Leth human traffic." *Of course.*

I wrote everything down on a piece of paper, trying to figure out where in the fresh hell I fit in.

"What else?" I snapped my gum in his ear.

"She visith our neighbor, Mitheth Belfort, often. Eighty-thomething. Thufferth from Althheimer'th."

Jesse Carter sure led an interesting lifestyle. And I was the lucky bastard who was going to lure her back to the outside world.

"That's it?" I asked.

"That'th it." He sighed.

"No one else? Boyfriend? Best friend? Shopping sprees with Mommy at Balmain?" It left me very little room for action. I couldn't exactly drop by her neighbor's house unannounced and pretend to bump into her. Well, I could, if I was in the mood for getting arrested.

"Nothing." Darren gulped. "She'th got no one."

I squinted at the paper I held in my hand. At how little I had to work with. It's like the girl didn't want to exist outside the realm of her house. There was one more thing I needed from Darren. He'd already signed the contract, and everything was set and in motion. There were two clauses he insisted on that were highlighted in bold letters. One—Jesse Carter should never, ever, *ever* in her life know about this deal. And two—I would never, ever, *ever* have a sexual relationship with her. *"Break one or both, and the deal ith off."*

Truth was, I skimmed the motherfucker because Darren struck me as such an impotent man, I didn't really think he was capable of hurting a fly.

"Email me a recent picture of her. I need to know what she looks like, you know, so I don't hit on a rando."

"You're not hitting on her," he enunciated. "You're helping her."

Semantics, the Western society's favorite mistress. It didn't matter how I did it—all that mattered was that Jesse Carter would leave her fucking house. I didn't bother to search for her online. If I read this chick correctly, and I thought I did, she wouldn't have Facebook, Snapchat, or Instagram. She wanted to disappear from earth, so she had.

I was about to drag her back to society.

She could come alone or with her demons.

I really didn't fucking care.

―――――――

The photo Darren sent me was grainier than Tobago Beach, and I couldn't make out much of Jesse. It looked like he'd taken a picture of her when she wasn't looking, which made my Creep-O-Meter ding a few times. She was sitting on a tapestry bench, a copy of *The Captain's Daughter* by Alexander Pushkin clasped between her hands. Her face was buried inside. All I could make out was her raven hair, snowy skin, and long lashes. I had a weird feeling that I'd already seen her, but I shoved it to the back of my mind. Even if I had, she was business now.

Strictly business.

The kind of business I didn't want to lose.

Especially after using five hundred thousand dollars of the three million Darren had transferred to my account for importing Italian furniture to my new boutique hotel. *Oops.*

I decided the best course of action was to corner Jesse when she visited her therapist. I waited across from the glitzy building where the clinic was located. I sat in a coffee shop at Liberty Park and gawked through the glass wall. She parked her Range Rover in front of the building and stepped out. Her slumped shoulders looked like broken wings; her overcast eyes were where your soul went to fucking die.

My first thought seeing her was that she was nowhere near Quasimodo-ugly. She was beautiful, and that was the understatement of the fucking century.

The second thought was that I'd already seen her. I didn't need her to gather those inky strands of hair up to see the Pushkin tattoo. A girl like that you don't forget. It was years ago, on the beach, but I remember how carnal the need to conquer her had been. How pissed I'd been when I'd seen her pasty-ass teenage boyfriend fondling her as soon as she'd collapsed on the sand in her little red bikini next to him. Luckily, I'd held myself back from stealing her out from under his nose.

Now that she was collateral, there was no way I'd ever touch her with a ten-foot pole.

Jesse was wearing a pair of shapeless jeans in an attempt to hide her banging long legs, a tangerine shirt—long, baggy, and depressingly modest—and an open black hoodie over top. She had a ball cap on—Raiders, my kind of chick—and the shades she clutched in her fist were the size of her entire face. She clearly wanted to fly off the radar as much as possible. Unfortunately for her, for six mill, I was going to not only notice her existence but celebrate and build a shrine to it. So to speak.

She disappeared inside the building, her head ducked down, the

no-eye-contact policy in full effect. She had an hour at the therapist's. That was plenty of time for me to saunter over, unscrew the
core from the valve stem of her back tire, and watch as it slowly
hissed out air. After I did that, I walked two blocks down to get
my vehicle—a billion-year-old red Ford truck I'd rarely used—and
parked it directly behind her Range Rover.

As expected, Jesse reemerged from the building an hour later,
power walking to her Range Rover. A perceptive little thing, she
noticed the flat tire before she climbed into the car. She squatted,
sighed, and then shook her head. I pushed my driver's door open,
hopping to the ground a good few feet from her. Darren mentioned
she wasn't hot on men getting near her. *No problemo.*

"Everything good?" I asked. She snapped her head up and
scowled, like my talking to her broke approximately seven hundred
social rules. She didn't answer, bringing her small hand to the tire
and feeling for the valve stem frantically. She knew what she was
looking for, and that surprised me. Not that it mattered. To change
a tire, Jesse needed someone to grab her spare one, and not to be a
sexist pig but that shit weighed a ton. She was tiny. It was simple
physics.

Such a lucky coincidence that I was there, right?

"Your tire is flat." I stated the fucking obvious, taking a tenta-
tive step toward her. She nearly jumped out of her skin treading backward. The look in her eyes was of pure horror. It was my
educated guess that the beard, the tats, and my six-two frame didn't
help matters much.

"Don't," she barked, her voice shaking.

"Don't what?"

"Don't touch me."

"Wasn't planning on it," I said. And man, was that the truth. She
could have paid me 5,999,999 dollars and I still wouldn't give her
a peck on the cheek. I stepped back, raising my palms in surrender.
"Let's try again. Can I help you change that tire? I have a jack in

my truck." I jerked my thumb behind my shoulder. "You can stand a good five feet from me. I promise not to touch you. Hell, I promise not to look at you, either. I hate orange." I cocked my head to her shirt. Another truth. The color reminded me of that fucker Hale and his auburn hair.

She stared at me long and hard, like my real intentions were going to seep from my eyes on my next blink. I gawked right back, using every ounce of my self-control not to turn around and walk away. I got it, she had her reasons, but she was goddamn strange. I didn't do difficult or different or weird. I kept things simple on that front. Don't get me wrong—she was beautiful, but she looked like a dazzling tragedy, specially designed to fuck you up.

"My insurance covers it," she stumbled over her own words. Like she wasn't used to talking to strangers. I popped my cinnamon gum loudly.

"They're also going to take an hour. I can get you going in fifteen minutes and spare you the paperwork and headache."

"I'm fine with paperwork and headaches. Leave."

"Fair enough. Call your insurance company." I folded my arms over my chest.

She could search for their number online, but it would probably take her twenty minutes. There was close to zero reception in that part of downtown Todos Santos. It was located in a valley so low, we were practically neighbors with hell. She tried searching for the number, squinting at her cell phone, huffing at the scrutiny she was under. Then she stamped her foot.

"What's in it for you?" Jesse tilted her chin toward me, giving up on her spotty internet. Talk about complete opposite from her stepfather. While they were both anxious, he was passive and weak. She was a spitfire, ready to claw your eyes out if you got anywhere near her.

"A cup of coffee. Black. None of that soy shit," I said, rolling my sleeves up to my elbows and turning my back to her to grab the toolbox from my truck. I swaggered back to find her rooted to the ground, her expression caked with distrust. I dumped the toolbox on the sidewalk and popped her trunk open, feeling her eyes on my face like the barrel of a gun.

She didn't want to talk to me.

But she didn't want to spend the afternoon baking under the SoCal sun and waiting for the tow company to arrive even more.

"Feel free to get me that coffee any minute now." I didn't even spare her a look, pretending to feel the tire to see what went wrong. Did I mention I didn't like coffee? Because that shit was poison, and I was a semi-pro surfer with very clean-eating habits. She shifted, looking around, like I was going to tackle her into an alleyway.

"How do you take your coffee again?" *With a shot of vodka. And no coffee.*

"Surprise me."

"Surprise you?"

"Yeah. It's when you do something shocking and spontaneous. Like, you know, smile."

"Who are you to judge me?"

"I'm your new best friend. Now, go."

She shook her head gravely and started toward the Starbucks across the street. Downtown Todos Santos was dead for a Thursday evening. Another blessing for yours truly. I didn't need people recognizing either of us. Jesse was as uptight as a tampon as it was. I did my thing, pushing to the back of my mind the fact that she was like a siren calling to my desires.

She is also a rape victim.

She is also a lucrative business deal.

Oh, and she is also a fucking teenager, you twenty-five-year-old perv.

Jesse came back with a steaming cup of coffee and held it out to me like it was a dead body.

"Leave it on the hood."

My greasy hands were busy plucking the scissor jack and placing it under the frame rail. Being an only child to a single mom, I'd learned how to do everything short of performing open-heart surgery by myself. I could change all of Jesse's tires and make *okroshka* soup from scratch while she filed her fucking nails. Right now, I needed her to see that she could trust me. She was still staring at me, bewildered, like she herself had no idea why she was letting me help her.

Then, as if to confirm my suspicion, she blurted, "Why are you helping me again?"

"I wanted coffee."

"You can afford coffee."

"How do you know that? Do you have laser vision that goes straight through my pocket and into my wallet?" I grunted while lifting her spare tire. Couldn't she have a little fuck-me-missionary-style Mini Cooper like all the other rich chicks in town?

"Do I know you from somewhere?"

I hope not because if so it's from being either a beach bum or the unofficial town whore.

I looked up at her, wiping my forehead and smearing grease over it in the process. "Do you?"

"You're Roman Protsenko." She rubbed her worried brow, and there it was—the look of sheer fear and disgust.

My heart beat faster, even though it shouldn't have. I reminded myself that I didn't care…only I did because I'd already spent some of Darren's money. "So you do know who I am. What do you make of that?"

"I make nothing of that. It doesn't matter if you're the pope or Harry Styles. I don't date."

"Me neither, so stop acting like I'm hitting on you," I said honestly. Her spine relaxed a little, and she gave me a curt nod. I had a feeling that was her version of a smile, and I didn't hate it. California girls smiled like the whole world was watching. Jesse's movements were private, quiet.

"And what's your name?" I asked because I wasn't really supposed to know.

"No one. Are you done?" She nodded toward her tire.

"Almost, No One."

I was, in fact, nearly done. But I wanted to prolong her departure because she was about as compliant as a toaster. I wasn't sure when the next time I'd see her would be. I also knew that, in some fucked-up, fate-ish way, I *wanted* to help her. I had a dog in this fight. I knew a thing or two about rape. Hell, maybe that's why I was such a whore. It didn't feel right to say no when so many women hadn't had the choice. Then again, I couldn't leave Jesse hanging there for hours.

"All yours, Snowflake." I stood up, wiping the grease on my cargo pants. She nodded, still several feet away from me, pointing at the coffee sitting on her hood so she didn't have to come closer.

"Snowflake?"

"Your name can't be No One, so I choose Snowflake."

"Is that some political commentary on me?" She narrowed her eyes.

I tried not to roll mine. "No political assumptions here. You just look like a snowflake."

"Why?"

"Because you're pasty as fuck."

Because I found you in the dirt that's called life and you stood out. Like an opportunity I cannot miss.

Her gaze flicked to my face for the first time. Her eyes were terrifyingly expressive. The color of the ocean. I realized how corny that sounded, but shit, it didn't make it any less true. "I... Well, thanks, I guess."

"Wait," I said, dumping the toolbox to the ground with a thud. "Now I owe *you* a coffee."

She stared at me like I'd grown a second head, one that was green and had a hat in the shape of a dick. "That's not how things work." She frowned, incredulous.

"Who are you to say how things work?" I parked my hip over her vehicle, squinting under the sun.

"Who are *you* to say how things work?" She widened her eyes, her anger outweighing her distress.

"I own a coffee shop. I know more about coffee etiquette than you, and I owe you a coffee. Let's have it tomorrow."

She grabbed the untouched coffee from her hood, walked over to the nearest trash bin, and threw it with purpose. Then she sauntered to her SUV and yanked the driver's door open. "There. Now you don't owe me anything."

"You still paid for it," I said, not entirely sure I wasn't fucking it up, but not having much choice, either. She was a hard nut to crack. I was so used to charming my way into women's panties, I forgot how to worm my way into their hearts. Normally, it was embarrassingly easy.

I would flex my tatted arms, picking up my surfboard.

Gather my wild blond hair into a bun.

Curl my fingers and stretch on a yawn, displaying my six-pack.

Stick a fork in them. *Boom.* They were fucking done.

With her, I was off my game.

She slid into her seat and reached to slam the door in my face. I had to do something, *anything*, because I was feeling less and less in control of the situation and I hated it. Jesse Carter wasn't responding well to my advances, and wasn't that an ice-cold bucket of shit right into my face? I slid my foot between her door and her car.

"Wait."

Note to self: Never put your limbs anywhere near Jesse Carter when there's a door in the vicinity. She slammed the door on my foot. *Fuck.*

I pulled my leg away at the same time she yelped in disbelief. What was I thinking? I wasn't. Instead of jumping up and down and praying to hell she hadn't broken any bones, I simply flashed her my cocky grin.

"I didn't mean to slam it that hard." She winced, and I think she meant it. The contrast between her black hair and fair skin was shocking. She looked like a painting. Not a weird-ass, provocative painting like a Peter Paul Rubens. Rather, like a Disney princess. One that was drawn by a horny sixteen-year-old who gave her a pair of fantastic tits.

"Yeah? Make it up to me. Coffee. Tomorrow. Call it a job interview. I need a new barista, Snowflake." I hissed out the words, knowing they were desperate and not giving much of a shit.

"I'm not looking for a job."

"Do you have one?"

"It's not really any of your business."

"Good point. Let's establish a friendship first. I'll lure you into the position later. For now—coffee."

"No."

"What would it take for you to say yes?"

"Nothing."

"Bullshit. There's always something."

"Nope. Nothing would make me have coffee with you, *Bane*."

"Think harder. You seem like a bright girl. I'm sure we can come up with an idea."

She sighed, staring up at the sky like the answer was there in skywriting. "Maybe if you saved my life and I owed you in some fundamental way. Otherwise, I don't date."

"You're not listening. I want you to work for me. And to be your friend."

"I'll never work for you. And *why* would you want to be my friend?"

Because your daddy will pay me six million bucks for the pleasure.

"Because you seem like a cool chick. Because you're funny. And quick-witted. And not the worst to look at despite that shirt. But I don't date. And I'm not interested in sleeping with you, either."

Told you I was a goddamn liar.

"Are you gay?" Her eyes lit up. I might as well have pretended to be gay. I let plenty of guys suck my cock when I was younger, to see if I liked it. Then again, there was no point in lying to her more than absolutely necessary. She looked almost hopeful, chewing on a lock of her hair nervously. Like what was standing in our way of friendship was my lack of love for dick.

"No. But my job doesn't allow for a girlfriend. It's a long story." I wiped my forehead again, knowing I was sweaty and greasy and ruggedly delicious to every single woman in the universe who *wasn't* Jesse Carter.

"So you just want to be friends?" she asked. She was sitting in her car, and I was trying hard not to look down at my foot to see if it had fallen off, and it was goddamn sweltering. I didn't want to be her friend at that moment. I wanted to shove my foot into a bucket of ice and curse her into next week.

"And a barista," I added. "Two birds, one stone."

Jesse mulled the idea for a few seconds, worrying her lip, before saying, "No."

Then she threw her SUV into drive and bolted down the road, toward Main Street, probably up to El Dorado. I watched the back of her Rover in the same way I'd watched her ass all those years ago, with a mixture of longing, annoyance, and awe.

She really did remind me of the snow.

Just like it, she was going to melt on my tongue.

CHAPTER THREE
JESSE

Always part ways with people you love like you'll never see them again.

That's the advice my dad had given me when I was nine, and I'd mulled it over in my head since. I didn't know why his words made me think of Bane. Maybe because I remembered the last words I told my father so vividly before his death.

I never want to see you, ever again.

We had just found out about his affair, Pam and I. Back then, she used to let me call her Mom. His betrayal cut through every layer of confidence and happiness I'd been wrapped in throughout my life. I halfway blamed him for everything else that happened afterward. Even Emery. After all, if it weren't for his affair, Pam wouldn't have tried to reinvent herself and found Darren. I would still call her Mom. I wouldn't live in Todos Santos but in Anaheim. I wouldn't have a Range Rover, but at least I'd be happy.

I wouldn't have had to befriend Mrs. Belfort.

I wouldn't have to hide away in El Dorado.

I would be me. Poor and content and *myself.*

Stop whining, Jesse. Self-loathing isn't so bad when you settle into it.

"Hi, Imane! Is this a good time?" I dumped my backpack in Mrs. Belfort's foyer.

"In the dining room." Imane, her housekeeper, bowed her head, clearing the way for me.

I walked over to the royal-blue dining room, complete with high golden arches, red curtains, and a bronze chandelier. A French provincial dining set that could fit no fewer than thirty diners graced the center of the room. I saw Mrs. Belfort sitting at the end of the table, all by herself, clad in an emerald-satin dress with a gold neckline, bright-red lipstick, and a hairdo from the movies. She stared at the empty chair across from her, all the way on the other side of the table, willing it to fill itself with her late husband, Fred. My heart shriveled inside its bony cage, every beat burning against my ribs.

"Mrs. B?" I whispered, not too loudly to startle her.

She ignored me. "Fred, do try the oysters. They're marvelous."

Fred didn't respond because he wasn't there. For the sake of argument, the oysters weren't there, either. Mrs. Belfort had had lunch hours ago, I'm sure. Probably in the form of a soup or casserole her cook, Ula, made for her.

Your one and only friend is drifting, a little voice inside my head *tsk*ed. I'd like to believe that voice was the old Jesse. That she still lived somewhere inside me and was a constant companion. Which, of course, was monumentally pathetic.

Roman Protsenko slipped into my mind again.

Snowflake.

I remembered the intensity of his gaze as he'd looked at me. It dripped sex, even if his words were completely innocent. I appreciated his proposition. I even half-believed him about not wanting to get into my pants. But I didn't do socializing, and I sure as hell wasn't going to start now. Not with him, and not at all.

"Mrs. B," I repeated, stepping deeper into the room and pressing a hand over her back. "Let's go outside and look at the rosebushes. Maybe take a walk in the maze." She hadn't agreed to go in there for months now.

Juliette Belfort jerked away from me and looked up. Her face was marred with experience and heartache. The most fatal disease in the world was time, and her tired expression was proof of that. Juliette had two children. Both Ryan and Kacey lived on the East Coast, and she wasn't hot on joining them in the cold. Not that they ever offered. Mrs. B had brittle bone disease, so she usually wore three layers of clothes whenever she was out and had her thermostat set somewhere between a bonfire and hell. "Jesse, I can't spend time with you today, sweetheart. I'm having lunch with my husband."

At least she remembered my name this time. Mrs. Belfort wasn't always clear. That's why she had a full-time nurse, a housekeeper, and a cook. That's why she didn't understand why I kept declining meeting her sweet nephew, who was around my age, for a blind date.

I stopped telling her the skinny on my situation because she would ask all over again the next day.

I don't date.

I don't do boys.

I'm the Untouchable.

And Mrs. B would always reply—*stop being so afraid of love. It can't kill you!*

Only it had.

"Is it okay if I wait until you guys are finished?" I mustered a weak smile, inwardly begging for her company.

She shrugged, sipping tea from the fine china next to her. "Suit yourself."

I returned to the foyer and plopped on an upholstered bench, digging out a book from my backpack and riffling through the free hugs pamphlet some girl handed me on the street last time I visited Mayra. I smiled at the irony as I stared at the words, not really deciphering any of them.

Why did Bane want to hire me? I was about as customer friendly as pneumonia.

Had he heard about my story?

Stupid question. Of course he had. Everyone in town had heard a version or two of my story. I was the town's slut. Jezebel. The whore of Babylon. I'd asked for it, so they'd given it to me.

Emery Wallace was the poor victim. And I was the leg-spreading witch.

Maybe Bane thought I was going to put out easily.

Or perhaps he really did pity me.

It made little to no difference. The only thing I had going for me was that, despite everything I'd been through, I wasn't the charity case he tried to make me. I didn't need his mercy or job or affection. I didn't.

Crap, I hope Mrs. B will spend some time with me today.

I read a few pages, willing Bane out of my mind. Sometimes Mrs. B was clear as the August sky. I confided in her, more often than I'd like to admit. It was easier than talking to Mayra, my therapist, because Mayra always took notes and made suggestions. Mrs. Belfort very rarely remembered our conversations.

Twenty minutes after I walked in, Imane stepped out of the dining room with her arms behind her back, her expression downcast. "I'm sorry, Jesse. Not today. Fred wasn't..." Her throat bobbed. She gnawed on the inside of her cheek, unable to look me in the eye. "Fred wasn't feeling well."

I stood up, heading for the door, when Mrs. Belfort came out of the dining room, hugging the doorframe to support herself. She looked like a stranger, her eyes wearing an expression I'd never seen before. *Clarity.* "You can't be afraid of love, my dear. It's like being afraid of death. It is inevitable."

Love is like death. It's inevitable.

The words chased my thoughts long after I'd left Mrs. B's house. It was a good thing I was going for a run because I needed to declutter my head after the weird day I'd had.

Anything north of the witching hour was my favorite.

Time soaked into your skin like a kiss at three o'clock in the

morning, slow and seductive. I was always awake at night—that's
when the nightmares crept in. They were so bad that at some point,
I stopped falling asleep. Catnaps during the day kept me going. But
sleeping through a whole night? Yeah. No, thanks. That was practically inviting a rerun of the Incident. In loop.

I must have been under some kind of a spell tonight. I felt brave
from talking to a stranger—to a *male* stranger—and the limitations
and red lines I'd made for myself faded to the background. I shoved
my earbuds into my ears. "Time to Dance" by Panic! At The Disco
blasted in my ears as I headed toward El Dorado's track at 3:00 a.m.
I had a finger Taser and a little Swiss Army knife shoved inside my
sock. Plus, it was a gated neighborhood, with patrols driving around
in carts every hour. I took my Labrador, Shadow, with me because he
practically begged when I was at the door. He was probably the only
creature alive I still cared about pleasing.

The Untouchable, I thought as my feet hit the concrete trail,
Shadow on a leash, lagging behind me like the fourteen-year-old
veteran that he was. It had a nice ring to it. Even I had to admit it.

Only it wasn't a compliment. I'd gotten the nickname because
I wouldn't allow anyone to touch me. Ever. At all. *Thwack, thwack,
thwack.* I ran like my life depended on it. Three years ago, it had.
And I'd failed. They'd caught me.

I'd been running ever since, twice a day. Five miles on the edges
of the gated neighborhood I'd lived in.

Running to exhaust myself, physically and mentally, so I could
sleep.

Running so I wouldn't have to stand still and ponder and think
and crumble.

Running from my problems and my reality and the emptiness that nibbled at the edges of my gut like acid. Burning, eating,
destroying.

My routine had somewhat put me in an oxygen-thief status. Even
I had to admit that my life was aimless. I slept during the days and

lived in the dead of the night. I worked out obsessively in the basement and got out of Pam's and Darren's hair as much as humanly possible. They begged for me to come back to the world, but I never did. Then they took my treadmill, so I started running outside. They threatened to cut my allowance if I didn't get a job, so I simply stopped spending money. I read books instead, took Shadow on long strolls, and lived off the odd Kit Kat bar, mainly to keep myself alive. Sometimes I paid Mrs. B a visit. I never left El Dorado with the exception of weekly visits to Mayra.

I'd been with Mayra ever since I was twelve and can honestly say she hadn't contributed to making me feel better or reaching a fundamental conclusion even once. The only reason I kept going was because Pam had threatened to kick me out if I stopped, and I actually believed her.

People, as a concept, were starting to feel blurry and unfamiliar. Fuzzy, like black-and-white static flakes playing on an old-school TV. I'd been caught off guard when Bane started talking to me because no one ever did.

The soles of my feet burned, and my thighs quivered with the strain I was putting them through. I'd always been athletic, but it was only after what had happened to me senior year that I became obsessed with running, and not in a good way. Pam—she didn't like it when I called her Mom, claimed she looked too young for the title—said I looked "hot" since the Incident, and I tried not to hate her every time that she did.

Jesse, look at your legs. That's your silver lining right there. Just open up and try to be less weird, and everything will be fine.

Running at butt crack o'clock meant it was only Shadow and me on the track. Just as well. Whenever people recognized me, they either looked at me like I was trash or averted their gaze, making sure I didn't see the pity in their eyes. Loneliness was an old friend. So much so that, ironically, it became my company.

Shadow was beginning to pant loudly behind me, so I stopped, bending down and stretching my hamstrings, my fingers pressing my toes.

"Take your time, Old Sport." I patted his head, waiting for the next song on my iPod to start.

"Jesse? Jesse Carter?" a woman chirped behind me. My heart slammed against my rib cage at the sudden noise. I whipped my head around, tearing the earbuds from my ears. Wren, a girl I went to school with, waved at me as she jogged toward my spot. She was wearing clubbing attire consisting of a little red dress that could barely cover a freckle, let alone the two silicone balloons she'd been gifted on her seventeenth birthday. She wore slippers and looked drunk, which made me wonder what idiot had let this twenty-year-old girl party at their bar until the middle of the night. I wheezed out the remainder of the oxygen. Wren lived in El Dorado. She'd probably been stumbling home, s me, and decided to say hi. Why she decided that was beyond me.

"I knew it was you," she gasped, aligning her drunken, loose body in front of my tense, anxious one. "Ohmigosh, I *told* them it was you."

Them? Who were they? I was about to ask when Wren decided to abuse the nonexistent word "ohmigosh" once again. "Ohmigosh, and I can't believe your dog is still alive. He must be, like, twenty or something, right?"

The old Jesse would tell her not everyone was as young as her new tits and nose. The new Jesse avoided confrontation at almost any cost. Wren sized me up, raking her eyes over me, head to toe. Her gaze was like a bright spotlight aimed at a hibernating animal. I wanted to coil into myself and die.

She smirked. "You look hot, Jesse. Are you on the Dukan diet or something?"

I rubbed Shadow behind the ears and resumed my jogging, hoping she'd get the hint and give up on the one-sided conversation. To my disappointment, she sprinted forward, catching my step.

"Don't be a bitch. Share your secret."

Get gang-raped by your boyfriend and his friends. That would make you either lose your appetite completely or eat your feelings away.

"I'm not on any diet," I finally gritted out.

"Well, you look great! I mean, you've always looked great. Obvs," she abbreviated the word "obviously" because it was just too long for her holy mouth. For the first three years of high school, I'd been one of the popular girls. The designated queen bee. *Devastating blue eyes and legs for miles.* They called me Snow White: dark hair, fair skin, witch-bitch mother. It helped that I had been born and raised in Anaheim. My mom was freshly wed to an oil tycoon, and everyone at All Saints High had thought I was trash. "Classy but trash," Emery corrected whenever someone asked me if I'd ever seen someone getting stabbed or shot. After the Incident, my status took a nosedive. In fact, by the end of senior year, I'd been outranked by pretty much everyone, including the toilet seats and peeling cafeteria tables of All Saints High. Wren and her friends were the first to cough the word "slut" in the hallways, the first to whine about STDs when asked to take a seat next to me in chemistry or calc.

"That really means a lot," I said sarcastically, refraining from asking her about her life. I didn't want to know.

"I wish I had it in me to put so much effort into my body." Wren sighed dramatically, barely keeping up with my pace. The sound of her after-party flip-flops slapping against the ground made me want to tear my hair from my skull. "But I'm just so busy with school and friends and my new boyfriend. You know I'm dating Justin Finn now, right?"

I didn't know that. I'd pretty much stopped talking to the entire world after what happened. The only thing I remembered about Justin Finn was the way his brother Henry's teeth had felt against my thigh when I'd finally come to, dizzy and nauseous, after they'd beaten me senseless. His laughter into my sex as he tasted me, defenseless, against my will. I remembered it so clearly, in fact, I could still feel him on my body, even after two years and countless showers. I bit my lip hard, stifling a scream.

They're not here.

They can't hurt you.

"What the hell are you doing here, Wren? It's three in the morning."

"Aw. She talks! Exciting." She golf-clapped on another vicious smile. "So what have you been doing with your life?"

The idea that I could be in real danger trickled into my consciousness slowly. Wren's house was on the other side of the neighborhood. The track was located by a small park with swings and a slide. Teenagers often came here at night to get tanked during summer vacations. That meant that she wasn't alone. Already, I had the disadvantage.

"You look a little pale, Jesse. Or maybe it's just you never leave the house." She snort-laughed. I picked up my pace, watching from my peripheral as her arms flailed beside her body with exhaustion. Shadow wheezed behind me. I inwardly begged him not to hate me for what I was doing. But I was panicking. I wanted to flee back home, but who the hell knew what waited for me by the playground?

"No one's seen you in a while. People said you were in a mental institution. I was like, ohmigosh, Jesse? No way. But really, Jesse, where were you?"

Wren tried to catch up, but her body was failing her. Shadow and I had the stamina. We were pro joggers. That's what we did.

Bits and pieces from high school came back to me, falling clumsily into a wonky picture I tried hard to unsee. Wren and I had been cool before the Incident—frenemies who'd played the school hierarchy game. Then she became one of *them*. One of the people who stuffed my locker with condoms and sprayed the word "whore"

across it and exchanged horrified looks whenever a teacher paired
me up with them in lab or PE. My legs sprinted faster.

Shadow was yelping. My brain finally caught up with my heart.
I didn't want anything to happen to him, so I picked him up, all sixty
pounds of him, and veered off the course, jumping between the trees
lining the Spencers' estate.

"Hey! Where are you going?" I heard her whining behind me.
I knew I was going to regret it as soon as the branches slapped my
ankles and my Keds sank into the mud. I felt the sharp burn of new
cuts opening on my legs, but I kept on running.

"Bitch, you won't be able to hide for long!" Her voice became
muffled and weak, but there was one thing I heard good and loud. It
bled from my ears into the rest of my body, resting on my soul like
deadweight I was going to carry around with me like a scar for years
to come.

"Run all you want. No one will be chasing you anyway, you little
whore."

Another thing I didn't forget: Wren had always been a vindictive brat.

That's why I wasn't surprised to find a car parked by the
playground next to the track when Shadow and I limped our way
back toward the neighborhood, thoroughly muddy.

I couldn't recognize them from the distance, but they were
leaning against the hood of their vehicle, ankles crossed and arms
folded over their chests. The kiddie park by the track was deserted,
save for their car. A Camaro SS with a paint job made in car hell,
black with yellow flames, the headlights set on high.

I was about to turn around and head back to the track on limping
legs, but a loud whistle pierced the silence of the night.

"Well, well. If it isn't Todos Santos's favorite slut," one of the two
guys singsonged. "Good morning, Jesse."

Oh, God. Oh, no.

Fear had a scent. A pungent, rancid smell of cold sweat, and it surrounded me like fog, crawling into my slack mouth and sucking my soul out.

I put a face to the voice.

Looked up.

Then recognized the other guy who was beside him.

Henry and Nolan.

They wore their uniform of polo shirts and smug smirks. What the hell were they doing in El Dorado? In the middle of the freaking night? And even more importantly—was Emery here, too? *Wren.* Wren had let them in. She probably partied with them, they must've dropped her off, but then they spotted me and couldn't resist having some fun.

There was vomit lodged in the back of my throat as I tugged Shadow's leash toward the main road of the neighborhood, praying a patrol cart would breeze through but knowing that with my luck, it wouldn't.

"Come on, Old Sport." My voice was strangled, begging. Suddenly, I didn't feel the cuts on my ankles, the heavy mud caking my Keds.

"Man, even her dog is fucking handicapped." Nolan cackled, throwing an empty can of beer to roll on the concrete with a hollow echo. "How're them legs, Jesse? Still limping?"

I wasn't, but they'd nearly broken my hip bones when they'd attacked me senior year. A violent shiver licked my spine, my heart palpitating so fast I clapped a hand over my mouth from fear of vomiting it.

"White trash girl with a white trash dog." Henry laughed, pushing off the hood of the car and sauntering over to me. Fear cemented me to the ground like a statue, and a blush crept up my cheeks. I felt my whole body coming alive with red-hot rage. Behind him, Wren was pretending to do her makeup in the back seat of the Camaro, ignoring the scene like she had no part in it.

Shadow growled, exposing his yellow teeth to Henry. I tugged him close to my thigh, sucking in air. *Shit, shit, shit.*

"Where you headed, Jesse? Night shift at the brothel? Let's have some fun," Nolan hollered from the hood, flicking his cell phone flashlight on and aiming it at me.

"Yeah, Jesse. You looking for trouble? We can do a round two for old times' sake. Just don't tell Emery. Though, really, I'm sure he wouldn't mind. He has a nice, respectable girlfriend now. The kind who *doesn't* open her legs so often that she can't even remember who popped her cherry."

I didn't know which part felt worse: hearing Emery's name or knowing that he'd moved on without any consequences. Or maybe it was the reminder that the night in the alleyway really had happened. Though I had plenty of reasons to remember it, even beyond the physical damage. Weeks after, Pam had taken me to a clinic outside town to have an abortion. I'd begged her not to, but she was adamant that "it" would ruin our nonexistent image in Todos Santos.

I turned around and started running toward the main road.

"*Stop,*" Nolan snarled, charging after me, quicker than me on his long legs. His hand burned its pattern on my shoulder. He swiveled me around with enough force to remind me he was capable of much more. Shadow growled again, and Nolan kicked his front leg. My dog collapsed to the ground, whimpering.

Staring at Nolan, I tried to cut myself some slack for not realizing how sadistic he was sooner. He was boyishly good-looking, with soft blond curls and hazel eyes, now with crow's feet gathering like an elegant fan around them.

Wholesome. Handsome. *Fearsome.*

I jerked my arm like his touch was cold fire. I was about to swing my fist directly to his nose and pick up Shadow again when dark, violent energy crackled around me like electricity. A metal-hitting-metal thud and screech penetrated the air, and everything stopped like someone hit pause. We both twisted our heads back.

Bane. Clouds of playground sand dancing around his army boots.

Bane. His stony jaw set in anger I could feel all the way down to my toes.

Bane. Holding Henry in a headlock, the preppy boy on his knees, staring at Nolan with horror I could decipher even with only the poor lighting of the streetlamp. Wren was in the car, holding her face and screaming. That's when I noticed he'd smashed into the back of the Camaro with his truck, and not by accident. The car had slid to the concrete sidewalk bordering the playground. A swing swayed from the impact.

Up, down. Up, down.

I finally lowered myself to one knee, pressing Shadow to my chest and hugging him close.

"Well, this is awkward." Bane flashed a wolfish, badder-than-bad grin. "A sober dude crashing his truck into a bunch of sorry-ass tanked teenagers. Wonder who is gonna take the blame for that one?"

You could feel the atmosphere shifting. Nolan's body going slack. Wren bowing her head down in defeat. A terrified tear rolling down Henry's cheek. Nolan lifted both his hands in surrender, taking a step back.

"Stay where you are," Bane ordered.

He did.

"I believe a trade is in order. This dipshit is of no interest to me, and you have no business touching Jesse Carter," Bane said, tucking a joint between his lips and lighting it up with his free hand. He tilted his chin up, letting the smoke crawl upward in a curly ribbon.

Jesse Carter. He knew my name and probably everything else there was to know about me. Stupid me thought I could escape him by withholding information from him.

Wild relief washed over me when Nolan pivoted to face the big, blond surfer, forgetting all about me. I gathered Shadow into my arms again on the ground, watching the golden locks of Nolan's hair from behind, wondering if I had it in me to grip a handful of them and smash his head against the concrete under our feet.

"Bane Protsenko?" Nolan scratched his smooth forehead.

"C'mere." Bane curled his ringed fingers that held the blunt, beckoning. Henry was still on the ground, choking on a sob. Bane's jaw was locked so tight I thought his teeth were going to snap out of his mouth. Nolan walked over to them, coiling into himself as his posture caught up with his pulse.

"What's going on? We were just having fun." He sounded like the good boy his mother probably thought he was.

"Was it fun for Carter?"

"Yeah!" Henry yelled, gagging around Bane's arm. "We know her. We went to school together. R…right, Jesse?"

I shook my head. I may not have had the balls to kill them, but I would never protect them. "I went to school with them, yes, but they're harassing me."

I wasn't sure if Bane was trying to blackmail me or simply do the right thing by me, but it didn't matter. He was helping me, and I needed him there. Nolan stopped a good three feet away from Bane and Henry.

"What's up, man? Nothing to see here. I'm sure you have better things to do than to bang up our night." Nolan's voice was toneless. He was trying to swallow in the anger he'd felt for being interrupted.

"Snowflake, what should we do with them?" Bane said "Snowflake" like we had pet names for each other and "we" like it was a concept I was familiar and comfortable with. Like *we* did things together all the time. Like *we* were friends.

I don't date. My job doesn't allow it. Long story. Let's be friends.

A month after the Incident, I got back to school to complete my senior year and graduate. I saw Henry, Nolan, and Emery every day. I saw them in the cafeteria and in class and at whatever events

Pam and Darren dragged me to in town in their attempt to fit in. Emery, Nolan, and Henry acted as if I didn't exist, and they did such a thorough job that by the end of the year, even I'd bought into it. Point was, we always pretended we didn't know each other. I was tired of pretending it didn't happen.

It did, and it hurt. It still hurt, years after. It would always hurt, for as long as I lived.

I took a step forward. "What are you doing in Todos Santos?"

Nolan turned his head to me. Henry winced. The silence was pregnant with things I didn't want to hear.

"We're on a forced vacation." Henry's voice broke. He was always so much weaker than Nolan, than Emery. The frail, dangling link that was likely to snap first.

"What'd you do?"

"None of your business," Nolan snapped.

"What. Did. You. Do?" Bane's tenor was chilling. A cold knife gliding down your skin, its edge poking your flesh. Roman Protsenko was highly connected in Todos Santos. Even I knew that. He was the kind of person you really didn't want to mess with.

"Campus incident." The words sounded like they wanted to be swallowed back into Nolan's mouth. The three golden boys of All Saints High went to college together. East Coast. That was the deal their parents had made with Darren and Pam.

We want your kids as far away as possible from ours. Much good it had done me.

"Consisting of?"

"A girl…" Henry said through clenched teeth. My heart split into mosaic pieces. They'd assaulted someone else? "We didn't do anything. That's why it's just a week. She was sauced as hell. Anyway, we only messed around with her. Shit was under investigation for, like, a second, but we're good to go back."

Bane's eyes sought mine under the sad artificial light. He was no less dangerous than they were. If anything, they were hyenas, and he was a lion, quiet and deadly. "What're we gonna do with them, Jesse?"

"I don't want them anywhere near me ever again. No talking, no touching, no breathing in my direction." My teeth chattered, even though it wasn't cold. I wasn't proud of using Bane to make sure the boys were off my case, but the temptation was too much. Henry and Nolan were bullies. If they smelled weakness, they would strike. They'd continue to provoke me until the day I died if they didn't have an incentive not to.

Bane said, "You heard her. Consider this her official restraining order against you."

"I'm sorry, but who the hell are you to tell us what to do?" Nolan spat out. Bane released Henry from the chokehold, sauntering over to Nolan. The air was drenched with menace. The world seemed painfully mundane while wrapped up in Roman Protsenko's exceptional orbit. Like he was bigger than the place he was born in.

He captured Nolan's throat in his palm and squeezed, still reeking of bored stoicism. "If you get anywhere near her again, I will personally make sure it will be the last time you step foot in this town. Your family will be driven out of here. Your college dream will be dead. I will unleash every ounce of power I have in this town to make sure your lives are a continuous, Freddy Krueger–style nightmare. Fair warning: I'm very good at nightmares. I've lived a different life from yours and know what you rich kids can survive...*and what you cannot.*"

I'd have paid good money to see Nolan's face at that moment, but he had his back to me. What I did hear clearly was Henry choking on his own saliva. "Man, let's get the hell out of here! Let's go!" simultaneously with Wren, who wept out, "Nolan, don't be an idiot!"

Nolan stood like the Leaning Tower of Pisa, askew and unsteady, realizing for the first time the lesson he had taught me—that we were all fragile and breakable. Bane unlocked his hand from Nolan's neck and pushed him toward the car.

"You're trying my patience," the blond mammoth growled.

"Under any other circumstance, you wouldn't walk out of this park alive."

Nolan tossed me a narrowed-eyed look. "Fine. You're dead to us. Happy?"

Hardly. But I wanted them to finally let go of me so maybe, one day, someday, I could let go of them.

"You're a prick," I hissed, nuzzling my face into Shadow's fur.

"And you're a slut. Just remember that when the town's bully replaces your ass with someone who isn't crammed with STDs."

That awarded Nolan a punch to the face from Bane. It happened so fast, he staggered and fell down, his ass hitting the concrete. Bane kicked his face with the tip of his boot, and I heard something crack. I barked out a laugh, mainly from shock. Henry half-ran, half-stumbled to Nolan, picking him up by the collar of his shirt and galloping toward the Camaro. "Dude, we need to bail. Now!"

He shoved Nolan into the Camaro and bolted around to the driver's seat, attempting to start the car a few times before the engine roared to life. He reversed with a screech, bumping into Bane's truck slightly before fleeing the scene while peppering small bits of the car's wrecked hood in his wake. My eyes followed the vehicle, dancing in their sockets. I was so entranced by what had happened, I hadn't even noticed Bane was standing right in front of me. But he was.

There, with his long, muscled body.

Green eyes like winter mint, dark and frighteningly alive.

Under the harsh light, I could see the holes where his past piercings must have been. Lower lip. Nose. Eyebrow. He was tall and smooth and youthful. Regal in his beauty. The only things staining his noble good looks were his tattoos and beard.

My gaze swept down to his knuckles. They were individually inked, carefully hiding every inch of skin.

My eyes halted on the dark stain between them. *Nolan's blood.*

I looked up.

I didn't know if it was the air that smelled of grass and adrenaline or the allure of the night that promised to swallow what had passed between us into a secret or the fact that he'd saved me, but I didn't hate Bane like everyone else in that moment. My mouth opened of its own accord, and the words tumbled out. "Thank you."

"What would it take for you to have coffee with me?" He breathed hard, picking up where we'd left off. Last time, I told him he'd need to save my life.

I guess he just had.

"For you to tell me why you want to do this."

"I need to fix you," he said, his greens on my blues.

To. Fix. You.

Shadow stirred in my arms, trying to sniff Bane from a distance. I was surprised he didn't try to bite his head off like he normally would. He knew how weird I felt about men.

"I don't mean to sound rude, but who the hell are you to fix me, and who said I'm in need of fixing?" I tilted my chin down, aware of the fact I hadn't exchanged so many words with another man for years. I was on the verge of shoving him away. *How dare he?* But I was also on the verge of smashing my body against his, collapsing into a hug. *How good was he?* No one had ever tried to fix me. Even Darren and Pam merely wanted to get rid of me. Of course, I did neither. The Untouchable never touched anyone.

Bane took a step forward. I didn't take a step back.

"I heard about your story. I heard about what Emery, Nolan, and Henry did to you. And let's just say I have someone close to me who experienced something similar, so shit hit pretty close to home." He pointed to the space where the Camaro was no longer parked. I thought about what I knew of him. Of his bad reputation. But then I also remembered that he'd been the one to shut down the Defy game in All Saints High. That all he'd ever been to me was kind and helpful.

"I don't think you understand, Snowflake. You don't have any say in this shit. I'm going to help you whether you want my help or not. And I'm willing to punch every face in Todos Santos if it makes you feel safer, my own included. I don't want to fuck you, Jesse." He breathed hard, and in my mind, he was cupping my cheeks with his big, callused palms, and I didn't even flinch.

In my mind, his cinnamon breath skimmed over my face warmly.

In my mind, we didn't have all that dead space between us, and our voices didn't echo against the nothingness of the empty night because I wasn't so broken and scared. "I want to fucking save you."

"But—" I started.

He cut me off. "They called you a whore. What they did to you is inexcusable. You're going to be saved, hear me? You're going to be saved because the other girl couldn't be saved."

I didn't question it.

I didn't doubt it.

I just accepted it, the way you do the sky above your head, knowing he was a stronger force than my resistance ever would be.

Bane had helped me. He'd protected me.

And, sadly, it was more than anyone else had done in my life.

All he wanted was coffee. Somewhere public. Once. I could survive this. I could.

I thought about the wilting Mrs. Belfort and how loneliness drove me running from my memories and nightmares in the middle of the night and then nodded. He motioned for me to get into his truck, and I shook my head, standing up to my full height. We were going to walk. Bane threw his cell phone into my hands.

"Five, three, three, seven. Have 911 on speed dial. I'll drive slowly. Keep the passenger door open just in case. But you're not walking home with your feet looking like that." He motioned down, and I followed his gaze, finding my ankles and Keds beaten almost to death, the little pocketknife nearly falling out of my blood-soaked sock. I nodded slowly, tucking it back in. I then dialed 911 and kept my thumb hovering on the green button and got into his truck.

It was the shock that made me do it.

New Jesse never got into anyone's vehicle.

"Just one question, Bane," I said as we arrived at my house. "What were you doing here tonight? It's a gated community."

He cut his engine, sank back into his seat, and rolled his head to look at me. "I have a hookup in El Dorado every Thursday. I have the electronic key." He flashed the small black device between his fingers.

I swallowed hard as I tumbled out of the passenger's seat with Shadow in front of my house.

My ankle dragged, leaving a bloodstain on his old leather seat.

And I thought it to be ironic.

How he was the most powerful man I knew and yet I was the one to mark him before he marked me.

CHAPTER FOUR
BANE

The minute Darren texted me that Jesse went to the track for a jog, I was out of bed and in my truck, speeding in its direction.

Fine. I'll rephrase: I was out of Samantha's bed—an El Dorado local lay and a lawyer who gave me legal advice—and heading toward the track.

It was three thirty in the fucking morning. If Snowflake had a death wish, she worked hard on fulfilling it. I'd arrived just in time. In a classic deus ex machina, more-luck-than-brains scenario, there were two douchebags, one jaded girl, and Jesse and her dog in the middle of the shit show.

She'd been so disoriented and horrified that she'd accepted the excuse for my sudden arrival and hadn't even doubted me. She'd tripped on her ass bolting out of my truck when I dropped her off, and I'd pretended not to notice because I didn't want to embarrass her. It was a lie I didn't usually offer, but she had special circumstances.

Thin trails of her blood smeared on my passenger seat reminded me just how broken she was and how careful I needed to be with that one.

I fucked plenty of women for money. Unfucking them, though? That wasn't my expertise.

The flip side was I'd finally milked a coffee date out of her. Only, between surfing and taking care of business, I had very little time for coffee, so she was going to tag along for a business meeting.

And by a business meeting, I meant extortion. Same shit, really.

I met Jesse at Café Diem the next day at four o'clock. The fact that she showed up at all was a miracle. She glided between the busy tables and hectic bar, wearing her usual creeper-from-the-nineties attire of black ball cap, baggy jeans, and that damn black hoodie. The blandest outfit in the world to hide who she really was.

My Whole Life Has Been Pledged to This Meeting with You

A poet. An explorer. A romantic. A culture-loving, dragon-slaying princess.

Bonus points—she apparently had the ability to make me sound hella emo. So there was that, too.

Darren Morgansen gave me the gist of what had happened to her. Jesse had dated Emery Wallace, heir to Wallace, Walmart's main competition on the West Coast, all throughout high school. Emery was your typical spoiled fuck with too much money and zero grasp of what real life was about. The one with the right clothes, the right car, and the wrong friends. He loved the idea of dating the prettiest girl in school. A virgin, no less. On the night his jackpot of a girlfriend had supposedly lost her virginity to him, Emery installed a camera behind the PlayStation in his room to record the whole thing.

Only he never deflowered her.

There had been no blood.

There had been no signs of virginity being taken.

Jesse Carter had been about as virginal as a used condom.

If anything, Darren had said (or, rather, sniffed) that according to the rumors, the live camera showed that she'd been bored, on the verge of yawning at his thrusts.

Emery chose a questionable method to show her how he'd felt. A few weeks later, he'd snatched her from a junction where she'd been standing, waiting for the light to turn green, driven her to a deserted alley with his best friends, and marked her forever. Jesse knew the kids at her school would have a fucking field day if the truth came out, so the families struck a deal: The boys were to stay away from Jesse and leave town to attend an out-of-state college, and she was never to speak about the Incident. Ever. The idea that someone on Jesse's side had agreed to that deal made me want to strangle the life out of both of them.

That was her story. Sex tape. Gang rape. Stupid-ass parents.

Coming face-to-face with Nolan and Henry, knowing I couldn't smash their faces into a rock until their airways were clogged with blood, killed a piece of me I really cherished. The piece where my morals were safely locked away.

The worst part about our situation was that Jesse might not have wanted people to touch her, but deep inside she was a carnal little pixie. The stunning siren with powder-blue eyes I'd seen swimming to shore all those years ago still lived somewhere inside her. I couldn't overlook that fact, even with that hoodie and ball cap. She made her way to me, marching like a captured soldier—proud but defeated—her eyes fixed on an invisible spot behind my head. I was perched on a barstool, rolling myself a fat one. She stopped before we could smell each other. Before the ink at the nape of her neck reminded her that I, too, was a sin.

"I don't like coffee," she said flatly. No *hi*. No *how are you*. Social codes be damned.

"Me neither."

She fought a timid smirk, shooting her gaze down to her Keds. Seeing her teeth sinking into her lower lip made my dick jam its way against my surf shorts. I didn't even bother to hate myself for it. There were more chances of my making a move on a dead vampire bat than ever tapping her ass. Nonetheless—*damn*.

"You'll get a smoothie if you behave. I have some stuff to do first. Let's hit the road." I started making my way outside, tipping my head down as a farewell to Gail and Beck behind the counter.

Snowflake followed. "Where are we going?"

"I have business to transact."

"Sounds shady."

Couldn't argue with that one. "Some of us don't have rich parents to buy our way through life. C'mon, it'll be fun."

Or not. It's not like she had plenty of social calls to choose from, and I did have a job to do. Jesse matched my steps, light-jogging toward me. I was much taller and much faster, but she had good stamina on her. She didn't get an ass worthy of a thousand poems and a world war sitting on those fine cheeks all day. I slid a joint between my lips, mainly because I didn't know what to say to her.

"You smoke an awful lot of pot." She plucked a piece of her hair and brought it to her mouth, chewing on the tips.

"Legal in California," I said around my hippy stick, lighting it.

"Not if you do it in public. Are you begging to get arrested?"

"Begging—no. Trying, maybe." Brian Diaz, the local sheriff, was in my pocket. I fucked his wife every Tuesday as a favor for turning a blind eye to my shenanigans. I could do anything I wanted short of decapitating the mayor in the middle of Liberty Park and get away with it with little to no repercussions. Plus, Grier was kind of hot, so it wasn't exactly a torture.

We walked along the promenade, two very unlikely allies. I was the guy everyone knew, and she was a ghost desperate to be forgotten. A bunch of girls in bikini tops and Daisy Dukes passed by us, fist-bumping me with seductive grins while checking her out. At first, she didn't say anything. But then when Samantha the lawyer winked at me and laughed when our shoulders brushed while she hurried in her cream suit to a meeting or whatever, Jesse creased her forehead.

"Is there one woman in this town you haven't slept with?"

"Yeah. You."

"Is that why I'm here?"

"As I said, my job doesn't allow for a girlfriend, and you're not exactly giving me the one-night-stand vibes."

We were passing by a fast-food joint, a tattoo parlor, and a Sicilian ice cream place. The sun was dazzling, the sky liquid blue, and the smiles around us big and genuine. Life was a giant, fat sunray, but Jesse was shivering in a dark slice of shadow, refusing to join the fun.

"And why is that?"

In my periphery, I could see her fiddling with the straps of her backpack, just to do something with her hands. This was difficult for her. Going out. Being seen. I slowed down, giving her time to collect herself.

"Why is what?" I took a final hit of my joint before flicking it to the sand. Conversation went fine now. I didn't need it.

"Why does your job not allow you to date?"

"Because I fuck women I shouldn't be fucking to get away with fucked-up shit I shouldn't be doing."

There was no point hiding the truth from her. She was going to hear it from someone else sooner or later. When we stopped in front of a new shop that had been opened just days ago by an interloper from out of town, I knew I'd done the right thing being up-front. Her face transformed from annoyed to…what was it exactly? Fascination. Mischief. I might have even seen a little attraction thrown in. Jury's still out on that one.

My Whole Life Has Been Pledged to This Meeting with You

A sudden need—to break these walls and see who she was before what happened to her—slammed into me. This quote couldn't be about us, could it? I wasn't that person. I was the bastard who used her to get his surf park.

"You're an escort?" Her already large eyes widened further. I reached for one strap of her backpack and snapped it against her shoulder, careful not to touch her, and then smirked.

"I prefer the term 'sexual plumber.'"

She snorted. "Oh, God."

"Yeah. They sometimes call me that, too. Point is, you're definitely not getting for free what people pay good money and services for.

So you don't need to worry. Look, you need a friend, and I need a barista and someone to hang out with who doesn't see me as God. We make sense, ya know?"

She actually smiled a real smile for the first time, and holy fucking shit, Jesse Carter needed to smile for a goddamn living. She could very possibly bring about world peace, and I wasn't even entirely exaggerating. It was those dimples. They dented that smooth, pale face of hers like a patch of dirt in the snow.

"Wait here. I'll be back in ten minutes. Then I'll buy you a complimentary smoothie for allowing me to save your ass." I jerked my head to the store behind me.

"I'll come with you," she said, and I wasn't surprised. She wasn't a flickering candle. She was a blaze, but someone had put her flame out. Three someones. I was about to ignite her right the fuck back up, even if it was the last thing I did. I flattened my palm against an imaginary wall between us. "No way, Jose."

"Why not?"

"Because then you'll technically be an accessory to a crime, and no smoothie in the world is worth a criminal record. Trust me on that one."

Instead of asking me more questions, she nodded, turned around, and parked her ass on the first step leading to the shop. I watched the crown of her head for a few seconds before snapping out of it and pushing the glass door open.

I slammed the door behind me, feeling myself smile against my will.

No, she wasn't a snowflake.

She was a snowstorm.

———

The secret to being an asshole was to not be an asshole.

This probably warranted some kind of explanation. Sure, there were people like Vicious. They were outwardly crass. But people like him were born with the world at their feet. It wasn't so simple for people like me. I had to worm my way into people's good graces and hearts when I needed something. Winning people over became sort of an art. I had to compete for affection, be it from my colleagues, my enemies, my one-night stands. Hell, even from my mom.

Freeze frame.

Rewind: I was born in Saint Petersburg twenty-five years ago to Sonya, daughter of a semi-aristocratic family that fell from grace along with the Soviet Union and lost most of its wealth. My sperm donor was a Bratva soldier. If you ask yourself what a good girl like Mom wanted with a bad boy, the answer is—nothing. My mother had been raped. That's how I came into this world, and that was my disadvantage in winning her over. My mom decided to flee the country and study in the United States. She wasn't considered rich anymore by any stretch of the imagination, but she had enough for the both of us to stay afloat and to put herself through school. Barely. She became a child therapist. I always half-wondered if it was about me, if she wanted to make sure I wouldn't turn out like my dad, so she studied how to defuse fucked-up kids. Maybe I overthought it. My guess was, the truth lay somewhere in the middle.

We'd come to the States when I was three, so I didn't really remember much from Russia. My mom barely had money to buy a pair of sensible shoes, but she did have a fancy plan for out-of-country calls, and she talked to her family every day, twirling the curly phone cord, gossiping in Russian. Her face would light up like Christmas every time she'd hear a piece of hot gossip about her friends Luba or Sveta. For the longest time, I wondered what the fuck had made her move in the first place, since she was still so hung up on Saint Petersburg. But it was clear as fucking day.

Me. I was the reason. She wanted something good for me.

I may not have remembered Russia vividly, but I did remember America. Every piece of it. I remembered the looks, the glares, and the wrinkled noses whenever my mom opened her mouth in a new room for the first time. She would stutter, blush, and apologize for her heavy accent, which watered down with every passing year of living here.

I never forgot the way people's smiles dropped every time she struggled with explaining herself to customer service and at job interviews. So I vowed to be charming, sweet, and good-natured. To be nice and respectful and too alluring to resist. I might have been fearsome to men, but women were a different story. You see, I had a bit of a mommy issue, and putting women under my spell was a compulsion I carried out on autopilot.

Come. See. Conquer (then come again, but in a completely different way).

Unfreeze frame.

I silently locked the door to the store behind me and then sauntered over to the counter, my hand already brushing the shit on the display shelf. What were they selling, anyway? It looked like a souvenir place. Todos Santos snowballs and pens. Who needed that kind of stuff? It wasn't goddamn New York. Just a beach town in the anus of California. I dumped my ball cap on the counter and smirked.

"Nice place."

"Thank you." A woman—late twenties?—rose up from a chair behind the counter. A little stocky, with red-dyed hair and brown eyes. "Are you looking for something specific today, sir?"

"Yeah. My protection money."

"Excuse me?"

"Protection. Money," I said, loudly and slowly, like the entire issue was her hearing and not what came out of my mouth. "Twenty percent of your rent, to be exact. Which, I believe, is twelve hundred bucks. We only take cash at this time." I let loose a wolfish grin. "I'm Bane, by the way."

She gasped, slapping a hand over her chest and twisting a

necklace back and forth. "I–I don't get it. Who do I need to be protected from?"

"*Me.*"

"B-but why?"

"Because you're in my zone and therefore play by my rules." I loved giving that speech. It was very *Scarface*. "This is my beach. I brought the pro surfers here. I brought the annual competitions, the capital, and the tourists. The skaters outside your store? I brought them, too. I'm the reason why you wanted to open a shop here in the first place, so consider me a silent landlord. I have a business partner, Hale Rourke, and we alternate between months, just to keep things fresh and make sure you miss me."

She nodded jerkily, taking it all in. The look on her face was anger flirting with horror. But I was casual, smiling, and nice. So, *so* nice. For now.

She gulped. "What if I don't pay?"

I parked my elbows on her counter. She didn't lean back because she was attracted. I looked intimidating, but the kind you should be wary of in bed, not in an alleyway. "Accidents will happen. You've no idea how clumsy I can be."

"What accidents?"

"If I knew, they wouldn't be accidents. You feelin' me?"

"Will you… Will you hurt me?"

I clutched the fabric of my tattered, abused-by-bad-laundry Billabong shirt. "I will never lay a finger on a woman if the endgame is not making her come. The only thing that concerns me is your business, ma'am. Or lack of it, if you're late on rent."

"Do you ask everyone on the promenade for a cut?"

"Baby." I lifted her chin with my index finger, locking my gaze on hers and throwing away the fucking key for good measure. "Don't think for a second that you're singled out because you're new here. Everyone pays the same dues."

Maybe it's the Marxist in me, but I always liked the idea of true equality. I just never thought it was plausible. It's like loving the idea of coming for three hours straight—it sounds great, but it also sounds fucking impossible. Still, I wasn't lying. I charged protection from every single fucker on the promenade, save for Edie Rexroth. I liked Edie, but my not charging protection of her wasn't personal or anything. She was great, but she was business like everyone else. I chose to ignore Breakline because I didn't want to mess with her husband and his three friends. They had too much power over this town, and I was smarter than my ego.

Red blinked at me, finally coming to her senses. She stepped away from the counter, her quivering hand reaching for her cell phone. I cocked my head and *tsk*ed, making a show of sighing at her theatrics.

"I wouldn't do that if I were you. I've made some real good friends at the local police station. Comes with the territory of getting arrested twice a month between the ages of eighteen and twenty-one." Before I was Bane: Business Owner, I was Bane: Unhinged Asshole. Red got the diluted me. The post-probation dude who just came for what was his. This beach was dead before I stepped onto it. Fact.

"Who *are* you?"

I usually made a habit of never repeating myself, but for the sake of being polite and only because I'd come there out of the blue demanding shit, I indulged her.

"My name is Roman 'Bane' Protsenko, and I run this town. You pay up, or you get shut down. These are your only options. There is no secret third alternative. There is no way out. Don't worry. I've got your back. I'll send people your way, spread the word, and keep your shop safe and thriving. Payment is the second day of each month." I knocked my knuckles on her counter, winking as her mouth slowly fell open in what must've been the first enthralled scowl. "Nice doing business with you."

When I walked out, I found Jesse sitting on the step, right where

I'd left her. She looked up from a book, and I immediately realized two things:

1. She was supposedly reading a red hard copy of something. Something classic, by its cover.
2. She had another book tucked inside. And my eyes landed on a paragraph I was pretty sure I had no business seeing.

He slid his big palms down her thighs and spread them wide, pressing his hot tongue to her mound. "I hope you like it rough, my darling, because you're about to get pounded like the pavement."

CHAPTER FIVE
JESSE

Even though the old Jesse had died the night of the Incident, the leftovers of her were still in my system. Mainly, her carnal need to feel. That was one of the reasons I wasn't suicidal, I guess. I was never numb or anything. I was angry and sad and desperate, but I felt. Most of all, I was needy.

I'd always been needy for affection—wasn't that the entire point of hanging out with Emery's stupid crew, even though I'd known they hadn't cared about me? I just made sure I kept it to myself.

My needs were mine. No one was supposed to know about them. Least of all *him*.

"She was about to get pounded like the pavement? Like. The. Pavement?" Bane light-jogged behind me, the chuckle in his voice vibrating inside my chest for some reason. My ears were on fire. What was I thinking, reading smut in public? I was thinking no one was going to notice, since the book I was reading was tucked inside a perfectly respectable classic. I wasn't counting on Bane to reappear five minutes after he'd entered the shop. Hadn't he said ten? How good was he at extortion?

Pretty freaking amazing. You're here, aren't you?

"Shut up!" I covered my face with my palms. "God, this is so humiliating. Just let me go home, please."

He sprinted ahead, swiveled to face me, and walked backward

with his arms open, his smile so cocky I wanted to tear it off his brutally handsome face.

"What about the smoothie I promised you?"

"That was before you made fun of my literary preferences."

"Stop talking like that."

"Like what?"

"Like an eighty-year-old. What do you like in your smoothie?"

My knee-jerk reaction was to tell him I liked solitude in my smoothie, turn around, and walk away. Immature, I know, but I was so rusty when it came to socializing. Especially with boys. Especially with boys who looked like Bane—inked devils with quick wit and foreign beauty.

"Strawberries."

"What else?"

"Cantaloupe."

"And?"

"Banana?"

"Hmm. Banana." But it wasn't suggestive or disgusting, the way Nolan or Henry would say it.

"So subtle. Humor at its finest." I rolled my eyes, throwing my wallet at him. It was the only thing I had handy. He caught the wallet, unplastering it from his chest and opening it nonchalantly as he continued marching backward.

"You don't carry a lot of cash on you."

"Why should I?"

"You never know who you need to bribe not to tell about your literary preferences." His grin widened, making his face gleam with delight.

"I think you forget my reputation can't get any worse unless I start murdering puppies. The Untouchable whom everyone has already touched," I muttered, shoulders slumped. It was the naked truth, and the cold chill of it was already slithering down my spine when I thought about the looks I'd get if I walked into the coffee shop with him. We stopped in front of Café Diem. He tossed my wallet back to me, and I caught it in midair.

"Hmm. Pity party. Thanks for the invite, Jesse, but I'm busy tonight."

"You're an asshole." I sighed.

"Tell me something I don't know."

"Sean Connery wore a toupee in all his James Bond movies," I said.

Bane laughed. "The fuck?"

"You told me to tell you something you don't know. I bet you didn't know that."

He shook his head, his shoulders shaking with laughter now, his whole body radiating happiness like the sun. He motioned for me with his hand. "Come on. I'll buy you that smoothie."

"You own the place." That was my second eye roll in a minute. I was starting to sound like old Jesse again, sassing like there was no tomorrow.

Bane threw the glass door to Café Diem open and stepped in without even checking to see if I followed. His jerk tactic worked because after a brief pause, I did. I didn't know what it was about Bane that made talking to him so easy. I knew what he wanted to do. He wanted to throw me back into the cruel arms of the world. A world I resented but, at the same time, so terribly missed. And for some reason, despite the paralyzing fear of it, I was letting him.

Everybody was watching.

It wasn't a figure of speech. Literally, every single person stared.

It was as if the residents of Todos Santos had waited for me to step out of hiding so they could see if I really was a monster. If I'd gained fifty pounds or become anorexic. If I was on suicide watch or just plain old crazy. If I'd shaved my head, torn off my skin, and lost my striking all-American-girl features.

The rumors were endless, and they wanted at least some of them to be true.

Bane slowed his pace, walking in line with me. His expression was pissed yet bored, a combination that dared anyone to say something about us. About me. I had a feeling that he wanted to make an example out of someone, but no one took the bait. I felt my face so hot with embarrassment I thought I would ignite, but at the same time, I didn't not want to be there. I needed to face the world at some point, and today was as good a day as any, especially when I had the protection of Bane Protsenko at my side.

Bane sauntered behind the counter, and I leaned against the champagne-hued wooden counter, watching him. He washed his hands quietly and then dropped a banana, strawberries, and cantaloupe into a blender while I hopped onto a stool, burying my face inside my hoodie. People stared at him as if he were the Messiah, blazing into town on his donkey wearing a glittery thong. He lifted his head up from the tall glass he'd poured my smoothie into and barked, "Next person to gawk gets fired. Customers included. How 'bout them apples?"

I nearly laughed. Nearly. But it felt like betraying the new Jesse.

The new Jesse didn't make friends, and she sure as hell wasn't going to break bread with Roman "Bane" Protsenko, the most infamous bad boy in Todos Santos, just because he was showing mild interest in her. Bane jerked his head to a corner table, nestled between the glass walls overlooking the ocean.

"Go ahead. I'll be there in a sec."

There was nothing I wanted less than making the journey there on my own, but I couldn't chicken out of it. I followed his instructions, assuming he was making himself a smoothie, too. When he arrived at our table, he slid the smoothie toward me and set a glass on the table for himself, plopping down on the chair opposite mine. The stench was unmistakable. Vodka.

"To good friends and bad decisions." He saluted with his drink, tipping his chin down.

"Vodka in the middle of the day?" I arched an eyebrow, my brain skipping down memory lane as I remembered it was Dad's favorite drink.

"Who are you, the fun police?" He mimicked my curved brow. "If so, you'd probably get suspended for reading smut."

"I wish I could 'Men in Black' you and erase your memory of that paragraph." I stabbed my smoothie with the straw. It was lumpy as hell.

"'Men in Black' ain't a verb."

"Who are you, the grammar police? If so, you'd probably get jail time for saying 'ain't.'"

Bane chuckled, giving me his glorious profile. I bet he was used to getting what he wanted when he flaunted that cut-stone jaw and ungodly tall figure. I also bet the old Jesse would have given him her heart and her panties, had she been single. Hell, the new one was half-tempted to do it, too.

"I'm Russian, too, you know," I said out of nowhere, bringing the pink straw to my lips and tasting the smoothie. Bane raised one eyebrow but didn't say anything.

"Yeah." I cleared my throat, dropping my gaze to the vodka. "My dad came here with his family after the Soviet Union fell. Most of them are in Chicago, though. I don't speak Russian or anything. Pam said it would be useless since I'd never go there."

"Pam is an idiot," Bane said flatly. I couldn't argue with that, so I just shrugged.

"I know some words, though." I dipped the straw inside my smoothie and brought it to my lips for another taste. I never usually ate anything other than my stash of Kit Kats, so I considered it sort of progress. Pathetic, but still.

"Let's hear them."

"*Suka blyat. Horosho. Kak dela. Pizdets. Privet.*"

"Those are all curses and pleasantries. Your Russian family must be really fucking passive-aggressive."

I didn't know why it made me laugh so hard. Maybe the realization that we were just so normal together. Normal. God, I hadn't realized how much I'd missed that feeling.

"So tell me about Beavis and Butthead." He slumped forward on the table.

Poof! And the normal feeling was gone.

"You mean Henry and Nolan?" I stabbed a piece of strawberry with the straw and popped it between my lips. The way his eyes lingered on them made an electric shock shoot through my body, head to toe. I looked away, focusing on something safe: a piece of art on the stark-white wall behind him of Marilyn Monroe made out of coffee beans.

"The little fuckers with the Camaro." He cleared his throat. I took a deep breath. I'd only ever been honest and candid with Mrs. Belfort, and that didn't really count because she didn't remember most things. With Mayra, I cherry-picked my words. But with Bane…who knew how I was supposed to act around him? I still hadn't figured out whether he was an enemy or a friend.

"Well, I guess you know about the sex tape…and the orgy." I swallowed hard. Bane's jaw twitched under his thick beard, and he took a big gulp of his drink. "I never agreed to what they did to me."

"It was rape," he said matter-of-factly, but his eyes weren't so hard anymore.

My back stiffened. No one had called it that in…maybe ever.

Attack. Abuse. Violation. Sexual harassment. People sugarcoated the situation like I wasn't there, like it wasn't real. Rape. I'd been raped. I plucked a lock of hair from my ponytail and chewed it.

Bane shook his head, flattening his palm over the table. "I don't know many people who have an orgy in an alleyway and then treat themselves to a spontaneous trip to the ER afterward."

I ducked my chin down. "Nolan's dad works at the hospital. He was able to sweep my admittance under the carpet," I confessed, wondering why the hell I was telling Bane this—why the hell was I talking to him at all?—and hating myself for every spoken word and peeled layer. "I nursed myself back to health at home. By the time I got back to school, all that was left from the Incident was the limp." And the scars on my stomach. I still had them. A shudder rolled over my skin. New Jesse begged me: *Don't tell him. Don't open up to him.* But old Jesse pointed out: *He called it rape. No one else ever did. Take a chance.* I wondered since when was she talking to me?

"By the time I got back to school, people were hungry for the drama. The hushed whispers, the pitiful looks. Everyone already thought I was a slut because of that sex tape in which Emery found out I wasn't a…" I wasn't going to say the word "virgin." Because I had been. I'd never slept with anyone before him. But no one believed me. I hung my head down. "Anyway, that's how I became the Untouchable. Every time people tried to touch me, I ran away, or worse. It's like there's the old Jesse, the girl who used to be so fun and confident and friendly, and the new Jesse, the girl who sits in front of you right now. This girl is still waiting to see when you're going to pounce on her and rip her clothes off, just because you physically can."

Silence fell between us like a thick blanket. He didn't offer any condolences.

"That why you never leave your house?"

"I leave my house," I said defensively. The place was crowded, and a trickle of sweat crawled from the nape of my neck down to my spine. The noise. The laughter. People crammed together. It bothered me, but I tried to block it.

Bane leaned even closer to me. His scent drifted into my nostrils. I leaned backward.

"Yeah? Where to?" he asked.

"My therapist."

"That's once a week, two at most. What else?"

I curled my knuckles, tapping them against the table, looking anywhere but at him. "The maze."

"The maze?"

I nodded triumphantly. "My neighbor has a hedge maze. It's where I go when I don't want to deal with Darren and Pam's constant nagging about my getting a job and finding friends." Like those are so easy to find.

"How old are you, Jesse?"

"I'll be twenty in September."

"Do you like your life?"

"What kind of question is that?"

"One that I'd like an answer to. Life is about meeting your eyes in the mirror without flinching."

"Is that why you're extorting money from innocent people and whoring yourself out?" I lifted my chin defiantly. I hated that he was patronizing me. Hated that I'd opened up to him, just because he was the only one who seemed to remotely care. Hated that he was right. I wasn't living. Not really.

None of my reasons for being crude mattered, though, the minute I saw his face. His eyes narrowed, his nostrils flared, and his short nails bit into the trendy white wood of the table. There was ice in those veins. The thought trickled into my conscience. Bane was normally laid-back, but now, I saw him for who he was. He put that mask of bored and pissed on his face again, and I wished I could tear it off and see how he really felt about what I'd said, just so I could hurt for hurting him.

"It's true." I raised my quivering voice, straightening my spine. "That's what you are. A criminal and a whore."

Kick me out. Let me go. I'm no good, I inwardly begged. *You will ruin me, and there's not much left to ruin. Please let me keep whatever I have left.*

"You don't believe that," he said, his baritone voice taciturn and relaxed.

"That you're a whore? I do."

"Well, then, get the fuck out of here." He gestured for the door, still wearing the bored mask. "Now."

I stared at his face, debating my next move. It was his eyes that managed to scare me more than his words. To penetrate my soul. I grabbed my backpack from under my chair and stood up. Something stirred inside me. Something unsettling. I felt...heated. Suddenly intense. I wasn't used to this feeling. Was I anxious? Sure. Scared? More times than I wanted to admit. But rage was different. It was passionate.

It didn't even make any sense. I'd insulted him—so he'd kicked me out of his place. It was natural. Understandable, even. So why did I want to throw the smoothie in his face and defy every word that came out of his mouth? Anything to create more friction and taunt and drink up his attention and face and secrets.

Why do I want to fight this guy? Maybe because I knew, after today, without a shadow of a doubt, that he wouldn't use his physical advantage over me to try to win.

"Thanks for the smoothie." I turned around and stormed out, my relief at leaving the crowded place caked with irritation and a weird sense of loss. I clutched the handle of my Range Rover's door and jerked it open. His voice boomed behind me.

"Anyone ever tell you that you're a huge pain in the ass?"

I turned around, pointing at him with a trembling finger.

"You said life is about meeting your eyes in the mirror. I just wondered if you're at peace with sleeping with random people for favors."

He flashed me a look-at-this-little-naive-girl smirk. "Need I remind you that I'm young and healthy and this town is the home of a high percentage of very dickable people?"

"So now 'dick' is a verb but 'Men in Black' isn't?"

His face transformed from patronizing to surprised and then from surprised to bemused. He shook his head, taking another step toward me.

"You should know better than anyone that words have an impact."

"What's that supposed to mean?" I turned to him fully, yelling now. My palms itched to slap him across the face. Seagulls floated above us, eavesdropping.

"It means that you're impossible." He finally sighed, shaking his head.

"Maybe I am. So don't try to make me possible." I turned back to my vehicle, yanking my door open.

"Fine. Go ahead. Hide from the world."

"I'm not hiding."

"Whatever helps you sleep at night, Snowflake."

I don't sleep at night. Haven't for a long time now.

"Stop calling me that."

"Why not? It's a perfect fit, considering you're having a fucking meltdown."

I was waiting for him to say something more. I swiveled to him again, not exactly sure why it was so hard to just leave. We stood in front of each other on the busy promenade, panting hard, shooting daggers at each other. We made a scene, one that attracted the eyes and ears of beachgoers. I clutched the roots of my hair, realizing that sometime during that hour, I'd removed my ball cap and hood. People could see me. My face. My vulnerability. All of me.

I turned around, jumped into the car, and took off like the devil was at my heels.

When I got to the first red light, I punched my steering wheel and let out a scream.

It felt good.

I felt alive.

I let the delicious pain and anger swirl in me like a storm, knowing I was going to regret every single word I'd told Bane that afternoon.

Knowing what he probably knew, too.

I hadn't looked at myself in the mirror for months, maybe even years.

So much so that sometimes, I even forgot the color of my own eyes.

CHAPTER SIX
BANE

Life is about looking at yourself in the mirror without flinching.

Five minutes.

That's how long I stared at myself in the mirror just to make sure fucking Snowflake was wrong. And she was. I hardly even blinked.

I wasn't butthurt over her comments at Café Diem. It just rubbed me all wrong—and not in the right places—that Jesse Carter, of all people in Todos Santos, would label someone as a whore. People were allowed to fuck whomever they wanted, as long as it was legal and consensual. She'd probably cheated on her high school sweetheart and gotten deflowered by another. Pot and kettle, anyone?

Whatever. Fuck that and fuck her. Also, fuck this.

"'Kay, Grier, thanks for a wonderful time and a lovely blow job." I tossed my Tuesday girl's dress on my bed. I lived on a houseboat in the marina. I'd bought it when I was eighteen because I'd wanted to own something—anything, really, other than a bad reputation—and never saw the point in moving anywhere else over the years. I could probably afford more than a shitty mini-yacht at this point. But I liked the houseboat fine. It was nice and cozy, and I fed the fish under it every morning, my way to say thanks for sharing the ocean with me. Plus my bedroom was big enough for a queen-size bed, and that's all I really needed. A place to eat, shit, and sleep. Grier's blond mane spilled all over her back as she sat on the mattress, stretching lazily.

"Were you distracted today?" She yawned.

"Huh?" I kicked the door leading to the deck open. I was naked, save for my briefs. Even they were pulled half-down after a piss, my inked ass cheek on full display. Skulls with roses pouring from their eye sockets, monsters in battle, sea creatures crawling up my thigh. I looked like a human canvas because fucking Snowflake was right. About the eyes. About the mirror. About everything, really.

Hiding made me feel like shit.

"It seemed like your mind was elsewhere." Grier lit a cigarette and joined me on the deck, leaning against the banisters, wrapped in nothing but my white sheet. The roar of the ocean rising made her skin blossom into goose bumps. I angled my face toward hers.

"Is this your diplomatic way of saying I sucked?" I flicked her jawline softly, and she shivered in pleasure.

"You can never suck, Bane. That's why I keep you around." She winked. I smacked her ass.

"Tell Brian I need him to stall the health and safety inspectors," I instructed. "They are pushing to come check out Café Diem, but the faucets are leaking again." Another hundred grand I spent from Darren's advance on plumbing before fulfilling my part of the deal.

Brian Diaz, the county sheriff, struck a deal with me. I kept his wife happy, and he, in return, gave me access to police files and turned a blind eye to some stuff that probably didn't put me high on the Citizen of the Year list of Todos Santos. From the outside, it looked kind of fucked-up, but it wasn't, trust me. Brian was gay and came from a notoriously Catholic and rich family. The last thing he needed was to be disowned and stripped of his fat inheritance and badge. No one wanted a closeted sheriff who secretly liked picking up street workers at Redondo Beach. And it wasn't as if he was a bad husband, but Grier had needs. I took care of the Diazes' problem, and they, in return, took care of mine.

"I will. Anything else?" She nuzzled her nose to my shoulder.

She was warm and soft and wrong. Suddenly, I didn't want another rodeo. I wanted her gone.

"Nope."

A knock on the door saved me from the prospect of round two. I broke her cigarette in half and threw it in the water. "Say no to cancer."

"You smoke like a chimney." She laughed.

"Yeah, but you should know better." With that, I tilted my head to my bedroom, silently ordering her to make herself invisible. I grabbed some pants and opened the door.

Hale.

I propped my shoulder against the frame, folding my arms.

"Miss me?" The smirk on his face was the main reason they invented sucker punches.

"Like a bad case of crabs, baby." I tucked the joint I was about to smoke on the deck between my lips. Hale coerced his way into my living room like he owned the place. He wore Hawaiian board shorts and a black wet suit top. I closed the door behind us, inwardly cursing him for making Grier stay longer. Hale flopped down onto my couch and crossed his ankles on my coffee table, making himself at home.

"You're treading hot water, Captain Save-a-Ho," he warned, folding his arms behind his head and staring at my peeling ceiling with a smile.

"Is this the part where I pretend I know what you're talking about?" I strolled to my fridge, plucking out two beers and throwing one into his hands. I popped my bottle cap off on the edge of my breakfast nook.

"I'm not talking about you." Hale took a sip from his drink. "I'm talking about Jesse Carter. You were seen with her outside Café Diem, making a scene. A lover's quarrel?"

I didn't know how to answer that. Just the fact that he'd called her a whore made me want to smash my fist in his face so hard he would be unrecognizable, even to his own parents.

"Is she your angle?" Hale moved sideways on my sofa to turn his whole body toward mine, tilting his head. "Is Darren Morgansen your investor? I wish you'd tell me more about SurfCity."

"She's not an angle," I gritted out.

"Well, she is not a date, that's for sure. I mean, you don't do girlfriends. What is she then?"

"A toy." The word slid between my teeth angrily. Fine. I was mad at Jesse. I wanted to hurt her, but not enough to say this kind of shit to her face.

"Couldn't you find a better toy? One that hasn't been played with by every guy in Todos Santos?" He snorted.

I discarded my beer in the sink and walked over to him. "Get the fuck out of my house."

Hale stood up, smirking. "Easy there, tiger. Are you planning on keeping this one?"

"Jesus." I shook my head. "Why do you give a fuck?"

"I don't. But this piece of hot gossip has caught me off guard, so I thought I'd check for myself."

Dude seriously needed a girlfriend. And some life to go with her.

"Get out," I said.

"You've never spoken about any girl the way you do about the Morgansen chick."

"Her last name is not Morgansen."

"See!" His eyes widened, his smile gloating. "My point exactly."

I erased the space between us, standing toe to toe with him now. My breath mingled with his, our noses nearly brushing, and my eyes must have been blazing because for once in his miserable life, Hale looked less than keen to ruffle my feathers. "Bane…"

"One more word about Jesse Carter, Hale. I dare you. I don't want you anywhere near her. Consider this a warning—not as a business partner or a friend but as an enemy. We clear?"

We held each other's gaze for a long beat before Hale's jaw

twitched. Finally, he dragged his gaze to my bedroom door. "Tell the lady in your bedroom eavesdropping is grossly impolite." He grinned, sauntering out of my houseboat. The wooden door slapped in its frame.

I turned around to see Grier sloping against the doorframe of my bedroom, her eyes shimmering with something I was too much of an emotional fuck-up to decipher.

"Now I'll ask again, Bane—were you distracted this evening?"

I growled a sound that wasn't a yes or a no.

"Is she worth it?"

I thought about the six million bucks and gave her a half-shrug. "Yeah."

"Does she need you?"

The third question left me unprepared. Did Snowflake need me? Was it fucked-up to think that she did? Because she definitely needed someone. I didn't think I was the best choice she had, but I sure as hell was the only thing available currently.

"She needs me." I didn't just say the words. I felt them. They crushed into my chest. Because I needed her, too.

Not just because of the six million bucks.

The five minutes in front of the mirror felt like a lifetime.

I needed some kind of atonement. Closure. Something to separate me from him.

And that was one truth even a liar like me couldn't deny.

I waited for Jesse to pull her head out of her ass and make the first move. I gave her two days to show signs of life. A phone call, a text message, a goddamn carrier pigeon. Alas, the girl was quieter than a dead cheerleader in a horror flick. I half-missed our back and forth but carried on with my life as if she'd never happened. She was funny and unaffected, and I really liked that about her. And she used movie titles as verbs. That shit was sexier than an edible thong.

I spoke with Darren on the phone later that week, and he complained that I was slacking off and not doing my part of the deal. I wanted to argue with him, but at this point, I'd already spent four hundred thousand of his advance on Café Diem and the refurbished boutique hotel. It was small, but it was also fucking expensive. I was waist-deep in the quicksand, and I knew it.

That's how I ended up heading to Mrs. Belfort's. When I'd called Darren, he'd said Jesse would probably be there. Guess I was hanging out with an eighty-year-old today. I parked outside her mansion, hanging my helmet on the handle and shaking the desert sand off my combat boots before ringing her doorbell. No one answered. I punched it a few more times. Nada.

The house was framed by rosebushes and nothing else. None of the houses in El Dorado had any additional gates. The neighborhood was walled and hermetically locked by an electronic gate and artificial lake. I walked freely into Mrs. Belfort's backyard. There was a hedge maze at the center of the garden and a set of rocking chairs overlooking it on the massive porch with an elderly woman occupying one of them, sipping lemonade. The other seat was empty and rocking back and forth, telling me the person I was after was probably nearby.

"It's been a while," she mumbled to herself, her eyes glued to the maze like it was the most interesting thing in the world. I decided the best course of action was to make myself known. I did the whole awkward hi thing with my hand, even though I was a giant subhuman enveloped in ink and carved by brutality. "Oh, Fred, how I've missed you." She smiled at me with tears in her eyes.

And the plot thickens. Mrs. Belfort wasn't lucid. That, or I had a strong resemblance to a dude named Fred.

"I'm a friend of Jesse's. Do you know where she is?"

"Jesse doesn't have any friends. It's just Shadow and I."

"She does now. Where can I find her?"

Mrs. Belfort tilted her chin to the maze.

"She can be there for hours. Sometimes even days." She paused, sipping her lemonade with shaking hands. "The maze is enormous."

Mrs. Belfort wasn't kidding, either. It was the size of the average Target. I knew exactly why Carter liked getting lost there. It was because she didn't want to be found.

"Remember the maze, Fred? You and I used to go there all the time. It was our secret spot away from the children."

"Sure, sweetheart. Sure." I patted her knee distractedly, slowly walking toward the labyrinth. I stood at the edge.

"Jesse?" I took a step in, glancing left and right. All I saw were lush green shrubberies. They were all a few inches taller than me, which meant that I couldn't cheat my way to the exit.

No answer, but footfalls thumped on the ground. I tried to remember what shoes Jesse wore and surprised myself by recalling her dirty white Keds. Then an image of her slender white ankles popped into my head. They were almost as fair as her shoes. The mental image shot a missile of blood straight to my cock, making it swell and twitch.

Now would be a good time to focus, horndog.

"How well do you know this place?" I made conversation, even though I had no idea if she was anywhere near me. Didn't matter, as I couldn't turn back now. I was in too deep, and wasn't that a perfect fucking analogy for the clusterfuck that was our relationship? I was playing her. Using her. Toying with the frayed leftovers of her trust. If Jesse could hear me, I couldn't tell. She remained silent. She obviously wasn't sure about my angle yet, and I loved that I needed to earn her trust, even if I didn't deserve it.

"So you like getting lost." I listened to the silence, drinking it in. I stopped for a minute, thinking I'd already been in that same spot. Was I walking in circles?

I looked around me. "You like the thrill of it. I get it. I have the same thing with ink. It's the endorphins. Everybody chases their high."

"Some more than others," I heard her mutter somewhere in the distance, to my right. My cock swelled in an instant. I needed to keep myself in check when it came to her. It shouldn't have been difficult. Six million dollars and my beloved SurfCity were on the line. Bonus points: She'd sworn off men, and last I checked, I had a dick between my legs.

"See?" I grinned. "I knew you wouldn't pass up a chance to talk shit about me."

"Really, Bane? Mrs. Belfort, too?" Jesse sighed, her voice becoming more distant. She was running. I was chasing. It'd been a fucking while since I'd chased. Sex was readily available, like buying meat at a butcher's shop. I liked hunting more.

I liked it a lot.

I picked up my pace, realizing her implication, and let out a chuckle.

"I'm not porking your senior friend, Little Miss Sass."

I turned left, my fingers brushing the carefully cut bush. Her footfalls sounded to my right.

"Why are you here?"

"Because of you." The truth felt like a cotton ball in my mouth.

She turned sharply again, her steps becoming less prominent. Fuck, Jesse, fuck.

"When are you going to get tired of chasing me around?" Her breaths were fast, hard, desperate. I felt them in my own lungs.

"Never sounds like a good time to me."

"Bullshit. Even my mom gave up on me. So the town's bad boy? Yeah. Not holding my breath here."

"Hold your fucking breath, Jesse. I'm not a stereotype or a title or the town's bully. And I'm going to get you."

"Get me then."

"Give me a clue."

"The maze is the shape of a snowflake. I'm at the center."

It was? That was an odd coincidence. Then I remembered her tat.

My Whole Life Has Been Pledged to This Meeting with You

Maybe it wasn't. Maybe she really was my atonement.

I looked around. I was definitely on some kind of an edge. I knew that because if I jumped up in place, I could see the rosebushes on the other end. I charged in the opposite direction.

"Are you really looking for me?" Her voice was quiet.

"Nah. I'm taking a lengthy stroll in a stranger's maze in the middle of the fucking summer because sweating my own body weight is a favorite hobby," I quipped.

"No one else ever did, and I've been coming here for two and a half years now. Sometimes for entire days."

I sucked in a slow breath, ignoring the fact that my blood had migrated from my dick to my head, and now I was angry. Where the hell were her parents?

"I'm getting closer," I said.

"How do you know?"

"I can smell you."

"How do I smell?"

Like dessert.

"Green apples and the first rain after a dry spell."

She laughed and then sniffed. Was she crying? I didn't ask because I didn't want to do something stupid if she was. Already I sounded like a bad Valentine's postcard. Then she said, "Cedar wood and cinnamon."

"Huh?"

"That's what you smell like." I heard the grin in her voice and imagined her chewing the tip of her raven-black hair.

"I didn't think you were ever close enough to notice."

"It's a strong smell." She sniffed again. Definitely crying.

"Bet it smells delicious," I said, hating the beat that followed my statement.

"It does."

Warmth filled my chest. This was not good. My cock was one thing. Anything north of it was something else entirely. We were going to establish a few rules once I got to her. If I ever did. It occurred to me then that Jesse sounded sad but not stressed. She knew her way around this maze, probably better than anyone.

Step. Another step.

My eyes found her back like a light in the dark. Her silky hair. Her sweet, round, small, perky ass. I wanted to sink my teeth into one of the cheeks and dig a finger into that tight hole. Make her moan my name. Then suck on her pussy until I had pussy breath for the next week.

"Boo," I said dryly.

Jesse turned around, the red of her eyelids against the blue of her pupils sending me crashing back to planet Earth.

"I can't believe you looked for me."

"I can." Mother of all fucks, what was I saying? I took a step forward without meaning to. She didn't take a step back. Another calamity waiting to arise. "You called me a whore because you wanted me to give up on you like all those other motherfuckers, didn't you?"

She dropped her gaze to her Keds. "I don't trust men, Bane, but I guess you haven't given me a reason not to trust you yet." A truth. "Whatever your motives are about me, are they one hundred percent pure?"

"Yeah." A lie.

I liked her. I did. That was good—I needed to like her, I had six months to spend with her—but I didn't want to *like her* like her. I liked Jesse in the same way I used to like my ex-girlfriend, Edie. It was a long way from the L word, but it sat comfortably between caring about someone to wanting to fuck them so hard they couldn't walk straight for three days after.

"So. You've met Mrs. B." Jesse wiped her eyes quickly, breaking whatever spell we'd found ourselves entwined in.

I tousled my hair to do something with my hands. "Yeah. I wouldn't be surprised if she is calling the police right now, reporting the mammoth Viking stamped with tattoos who trudged into her hedge maze."

Jesse laughed, bringing a lock of dark hair to her lips and chewing on it. "How did you find me?"

Your stepdad tells me where you are twenty-four-fucking-seven.

"You told me about this place right before you decided to take a shit on our newfound friendship. I figured you'd be here, and I was in El Dorado with one of my usual hookups."

And the lies just kept on piling up like shitty food at an all-you-can-eat buffet.

She narrowed her eyes. "You're not stalking me, right? Because I've had my fair share of crazy for this lifetime."

I gave her a pitying look. "You barely leave your house and dress like a teenage nun. No offense, but you make a very unattractive stalkee."

"'Stalkee' isn't a word."

"But you have to admit it'd make a good one."

She could smile right now if she weren't so broken. But she was. So she nodded instead. "I came here to gather courage. Shadow hasn't been eating or drinking for two days now. I need to take him to the vet."

I vaguely remembered the furry dirtball from the playground. She'd clutched him to her chest like he was her newborn baby, even though he was kind of big.

"Okay. Let's go." I cocked my head to one of the many paths of the maze. She looked up, and there was hope in her eyes.

"You'll come with me?"

Her gratitude depressed me. What role did her parents play in her life, other than trying to get her to have a job so she could leave their home?

I shrugged. "I'm not meeting my evening piece till nine."

I didn't know why I said it. Well, actually, I did. I said it because I needed to remember it. Because Jesse Carter was a project, not a goddamn date. But that still didn't explain why I scanned her face for emotional clues. And definitely didn't explain why I fucking hated not finding any.

"Okay, so we'd better hurry. I know a way out of here that's not through the entrance." She quirked her lips up in a lopsided grin.

My logic flew out the window around the same second. That was a new expression on her face. A leftover from her former self was my guess.

"Follow me." She motioned with her hand.

My eyes clung to her ass, and I was no longer chasing her.

No, I was hunting her.

Waiting on her.

Knowing the pounce would never come.

Knowing no amount of tall stacks was going to make up for the damage I was about to create.

CHAPTER SEVEN
BANE

"Let me go grab Shadow's leash."

Remember those words because they were the ones leading to a shit show of epic proportions, sponsored by Pam Morgansen, directed by yours fucking truly.

Here's how it happened: I stood in the foyer next to the oldest dog in the world. Not an exaggeration. Shadow flashed me a tired I-don't-trust-your-ass glare, and I answered him with an I-wouldn't-trust-my-ass-either smirk. It was the first time I visited her house in daylight, and it was luxurious, silent, and empty. It was like putting a designer dress on a corpse. Beautifully depressing. I scanned the huge paintings on the walls and tried not to think about the fact that Jesse thought that I smelled good. Usually, I didn't give a shit. That's not to say I smelled like it. But I wasn't used to making an effort.

Anyway, I was trying not to think about that moment in the maze. Instead, I focused on how Shadow's breath smelled eerily similar to a dead body. Not a good sign. I heard rustling from the kitchen's direction. My ears perked. If Darren saw me here, he'd see the progress I'd made with Jesse. Only it wasn't Darren. It was, or should I say that was, a human Barbie doll.

The lady of the manor.

Her hair was too bleached, her skin too tanned, too leathery, too much. Her blue eyes were vacant. An overpainted marionette with the strings cut off. Pretty but hollow in all the important places. She wore wedge shoes and a bright-green caftan. Her fake tan was the exact shade of a KFC chicken thigh.

"A stranger in the house." Barbie slid her sunglasses down, gasping theatrically, but it was flirtatious. "I'm Pam. And you are?"

Not interested.

"Roman." I leaned back—boot against the swan-hued wall— my charming smirk on full display. She was of zero interest to me, but I didn't need her causing trouble with her daughter. Best to be civilized, for now.

Pam shifted closer, offering me the back of her hand for a kiss. I took her palm, lowered it, and then shook it. Her blindingly white beam collapsed an inch.

"That was not very chivalrous," she commented.

"It is also not the seventeenth century," I informed her, snapping my gum in her face.

"That's all right. I'm not too fond of gentlemen, anyway." Her pale eyes scanned my body with hunger I knew too well because I satisfied those cravings. "I didn't know Jesse hung out with the tattooed, tall, handsome types."

I was starting to feel increasingly sorry for Darren. His stepdaughter didn't care for him much, and his wife actively tried to screw men who weren't him. All the money in the world and not an ounce of respect. I refrained from answering Pam, lowering myself down to pat Shadow.

"How did you meet Jesse?" Her bare thigh was suddenly thrust in front of my eyes.

"She had a flat tire. I had hands. The rest is history."

"Classic Jesse. She's a total mess sometimes." Pam laughed, but there was no humor in her voice.

I kneaded Shadow's fur. How long did it take Jesse to grab a goddamn leash? I wanted to get out of there. Preferably before my potential investor found his wife trying to grind her groin all over my face, which was starting to look like a plausible scenario.

"So…are you guys…?" Pam left the question hanging in the air. It was time to smash her little black heart. I straightened my spine, looked her in the eye, and delivered the news.

"Dating? No."

"Oh." She licked her lips, staring at me through her extended eyelashes. "That's good to know."

"Not for my lack of trying," I said after a calculated pause, making sure the sentence left the desired impact I was looking for. I stared through her, the way I did when I wanted to dismantle people with egos bigger than their mansions. In my experience, the more insecure you were about holding on to what you had, the bigger your ego was. "She's not too hot on buying a cow that every farmer in town has already milked, and I can't blame her. I only attract a certain type of woman. Not the picky ones." I cocked my head sideways, giving her a thorough scan.

If Pam had balls, they would have shriveled in my fist. But she didn't, so she simply tilted her chin up in mock defiance, batted her eyelashes when she realized she'd chosen the wrong person to talk shit about her daughter with, and stepped back. Jesse selected the exact same moment to drag her ass back downstairs, skipping two steps at a time with a black leash in her hand. I successfully suppressed the mental image of collaring her with it and taking her on a nice, lengthy stroll inside her fancy bathroom before fucking her in front of what I bet was a Jack and Jill mirror. And by "successfully," I meant not really.

Same. Fucking. Difference.

"Ready?" I asked. Jesse's eyes darted from her mom to me, her face rippled with concern. I offered her an easy smile that hopefully conveyed she had nothing to worry about. It was the first time I truly felt sorry for Snowflake. Because even after everything she'd been through, she was tough as nails (and just about as friendly).

But being betrayed by your own parent…that's a whole new level of fucked-up. I knew because I wanted to be sick in my mouth every time I thought about who I came from.

Pam's eyes finally flickered to Jesse. "So. Bane Protsenko, huh? Least now we know you're my kid." She snort-laughed, shaking her head.

Of course Pam knew who I was. I was an official gigolo, the Lululemon housewives' favorite toy. I spun around to stare at Jesse's mom, this time without the coat of indifference and fake politeness, but with my real expression. The one I saved for people who overstepped their boundaries.

"Is there a problem, Pamela?" I didn't call her Mrs. Morgansen because I didn't want to show her respect, and "Pam" felt too friendly. Pamela was a nice fuck-you way to address her without using the b-word.

"You tell me." She took a step toward us. "I just want to make sure your intentions for my daughter are nice and pure." She tongued her lower lip again. "I would like to discuss your relationship with Jesse privately."

What she wanted was for me to dick her down until she was buried in orgasms. I smiled tightly. I was going to play her little game. I needed to make it perfectly clear to her that I'd never touch her. It would also put Jesse's mind at ease.

"Tomorrow afternoon," I said dryly.

"Perfect. I'll meet you at your café."

Bitch knew everything worth knowing about me, apparently. It was perfectly possible she'd tried to hire me sometime in the last couple of years and I'd just never noticed because I didn't take any unknown calls since I'd closed my list of clients.

"Perfect," I echoed, my tone implying it was anything but.

Jesse and I were out the door a minute later. She helped Shadow climb up to the back seat of the Rover and then rounded her vehicle and slipped in. I started walking over to my Harley across the street.

"Where to?" I asked over my shoulder. She rolled her window down, her brow worried and her eyes inquisitorial.

"What was all that about with Pam?" With Pam? What the fuck kind of family was that? My mom would club me with a jar of pickled cabbage if I referred to her as Sonya and not Mamul.

"Guess she's worried about you." I shrugged, turning to face her. I wasn't going to add that she'd hit on me. I was in the business of saving Jesse, not hurting her. And she was a smart girl. She didn't need me to spell it out for her.

"She is worried about getting laid." A flame kindled in Jesse's eyes. "If you take her on as a client, I won't hang out with you anymore. It's not an ultimatum. I know you have a business to run. I'm just letting you know." Her voice was firm and resolute.

"There you are." I grinned. She cocked one eyebrow, waiting for an explanation. "The old Jesse. I was waiting for her to make a cameo."

Snowflake shook her head, pretending to be exasperated, but I knew she secretly liked that I saw her as more than just her reputation.

"So. Where to?" I repeated. I wasn't going to address her question seriously. We were friends. We hung out. She was supposed to trust me not to bang her mom.

Snowflake gave me the address, but she still looked hesitant, tapping her fingers over the edge of her opened window.

I flipped my keys in my hand. "Meet you there."

"So. About my mom…?" She trailed off. I stared at her like she'd tried to rub a hedgehog on my cock.

"Of course I'm not going to fuck your mom, Jesse. What kind of asshole would do that?"

"Nolan would," she muttered, and then amended, "Did."

I stopped in my tracks. Nolan had been in high school when he and Jesse were still on speaking terms. Was he a senior or a junior when he'd sampled Mrs. Morgansen? I turned around to the girl with the Pushkin tattoo.

"Is that a figure of speech all the cool kids are using nowadays?"

"Nope, it's the figure zero in loyalty when it comes to Pam Carter. My mom likes them young. So please excuse my suspicion."

"You're shitting me."

She gave me a pointed look and then sighed. "I really hate men."

"As a species or as a concept? And does that include me?"

"As everything. And unless you have a secret vagina, yes, you're included."

"Pretty sure I'd know if I had one. It'd make a great place to stash pot." I groomed the tip of my beard with my fingers, something I did more and more when Jesse was around. Normally I didn't care what people thought of me. With her, I didn't not care.

"Too bad. That would mean eighty percent of the women of Todos Santos were gay, and that would explain why all the guys here are such angry douchebags."

I couldn't help but laugh. It was the lightest thing she'd ever said to me. In fact, I nearly toppled over laughing. Jesse Carter had been burned, but that only made her hotter than hell. She wasn't emo about what had happened to her. She was angry. And rightly fucking so. A weird, stupid regret slammed into me—for never properly meeting the girl she'd been before the attack.

She was good and funny and broken. But it was only the last part that defined her. In her eyes, anyway.

"Know what, Snowflake? I think you officially graduated from creeper to a mild weirdo. You're ready to give me a ride. Least you can do for dragging my ass through a fucking maze."

"Did I win you over with my girl-on-girl imagery?" She batted her eyelashes, plastering a hand to her cheek.

"Yes. I want to hear all about it the entire ride to the vet, please."

"Not happening, and no thank you."

"Look at us, bantering like old friends." I opened my arms wide. Shadow barked from the back, a gentle reminder that he was feeling like crap. "See? Even your dog agrees."

She reddened, and that was my cue. I circled her Rover, getting into her car, into her realm, and under her skin. She stared ahead as she reversed and slid back from the roundabout parking area. Shadow whimpered, and Jesse twisted slightly, reaching back and patting him. Her scent hit my nostrils and sent my head tipping back against the seat. Ever been punched in the face? I had. Plenty of times. The first few seconds, you're disoriented. Not really sure what time of the day it is. Where you are. That's what Jesse smelled like. Like a punch in the fucking face. And, honestly, women should find a way to bottle it as perfume. Very powerful stuff.

"What are you so happy about?" she asked, suspicious of my smirk.

I shook my head. "Green apples and fresh rain."

Experience had taught me that there were a few types of silence.

Embarrassed silence. Intense silence. Sexy silence. Mysterious silence. Sorry-I-fucked-your-wife-she-said-you-were-cool-with-it silence. Jesse and I had settled into a new type—companionable silence. It felt like her variation of small talk and sat between us like your favorite uncle who always made great fart jokes.

I got it. She was slowly getting used to hanging out with someone new. Not just someone new, but an actual man, who smelled and looked and acted like a guy. It couldn't have been easy. Her life story was like a bitter winter, one that covers everything in a thick layer of ice you need to crash your way through. It was in the air, crackling between us. I was working my way to the flame that danced inside the old Jesse.

After the ride, I carried Shadow out of the back seat because Old Sport, as she'd called him, was damn heavy and didn't seem to be getting around very well. The forty-something receptionist at the vet looked between us, obviously half-worried that I'd kidnapped

Jesse, before buzzing the intercom on her desk. Two minutes later, Snowflake walked into the examination room with Shadow. There was a glass window overlooking the reception area, so I could see them both, along with the vet, Dr. Wiese.

Dr. Wiese was a man.

A man who didn't know Snowflake.

A man who therefore tried to shake her hand and watched how she very awkwardly pretended not to notice, talking in fast spurts of words and turning fifty shades of red. She took desperate steps away from him as she helped Shadow hop onto the metal examination table, all while Dr. Wiese—oblivious to her condition—kept on getting closer to her to show her a batch of Shadow's fur that he plucked out or something in his ear. I paced the reception like a wild animal in captivity, trying not to think about how her discomfort resulted in me feeling like a pile of shit.

Not your problem.

Not your issue.

Step away from the crazy train, Bane. That shit is moving way too fast and doesn't have a return ticket.

Sometimes, when you know you're in too deep, you try to give yourself excuses. Mine was that it wasn't about Jesse. I wouldn't have wanted any girl to feel sexually harassed, even if by a handshake. I braced my arms over the back of a chair in the waiting room, shaking my head. The receptionist wrinkled her nose, her eyes still on her monitor.

"Sir, can I help you with anything?" She cleared her throat. The bright glows flicking against her face told me she was playing Candy Crush and that she really didn't give a damn about Jesse, Shadow, or even her job.

"I need to get in there." I raked my fingers through my hair.

"Why?"

"Because he doesn't know."

"Doesn't know what?"

That Jesse isn't like the rest. Dr. Wiese was going to touch her, and she was going to freak out, and everything was going to go down the shitter. That was my only angle, really. Dude was going to ruin my progress with Snowflake. I would be back to square one trying to lure her out to the land of the free and independent. Right? Right?

Whatever. Fuck. Yes. Of course that was it.

"I need to get in there." I slapped my palms over her desk, and she finally looked up from her screen, her fingers hovering over the mouse, her jaw slack.

"I'm not sure…"

"She doesn't let anyone touch her," I said, fast. "And he's trying to. He doesn't know, but she's freaking out." I was hoping I could communicate it to her with my gaze alone that Jesse could cock-punch Dr. Wiese if she felt too threatened.

Our eyes met, and she nodded, swallowing. "I…uh…"

I didn't bother to hear the rest. I stormed inside. The first thing I noticed was Jesse's posture when her head whipped to look at who it was. It relaxed at my presence, and that wasn't a stroke to my ego but a full-blown hand job. Dr. Wiese was a couple of feet away from her, explaining something about Shadow's teeth that she probably couldn't decipher because she was too busy having the mother of all internal meltdowns. I walked over to them, placing myself between her and the vet, leaning my entire body against a wall. A human shield.

"And you are…?" Dr. Wiese scratched his meaty cheek.

"Jesse's bodyguard," I said, reaching out to shake his hand. Dr. Wiese remained professional and got back to examining Shadow. I buried my hands in my pockets, and when Snowflake shot me a look, I answered back with a smirk. The old vet frowned and then said that he wanted to do blood work for Shadow, already washing his hands and putting his blue gloves on.

"Whatever for?" Jesse's back straightened, her eyes widening. Wiese shook his head, patting an apathetic Shadow, still on the steel table.

"It's just…here." He took her hand and directed it to Shadow's throat. Jesse's hand jolted violently, but I stepped in, removing Dr. Wiese's hand, placing mine on hers instead. Her palm was on Shadow's fur now, and mine was covering hers. My heart pounded so fast I thought it was going to jump out of my throat, and I didn't even know why. Her skin was hot and silky.

Perfectly gorgeous.

Perfectly damaged.

Perfectly ruined.

Did I mention perfectly forbidden? Because that shit should be at the top of the list. And since when did I care about how people's skin felt ? Seriously, what the hell was happening to me?

I knew I needed to remove my hand from hers, now that I'd saved her from Dr. Wiese and mostly from herself, but decided to wait for her to give me a cue. The cue that never came. I felt her fingers trembling with excitement and fear under mine. No one talked. No one moved. No one breathed.

The Untouchable had been touched. And she'd survived.

Dr. Wiese swallowed loudly beside us. He was finally picking up on the context clues. "That's it. Now, move her hand around so she can feel the lump. It might be nothing, but we don't want to take any chances. Shadow is not a pup anymore."

Her hand froze on Shadow's fur. I began to move it in circles under my palm. It felt…weird. Intimate. More intimate than fucking a girl to a near-death experience, somehow. I began to realize that maybe I wasn't as immune as I thought I was to illicit pussy. Because all I could think about was directing her hand into the inside of the waistband of her jeans and having her finger herself with my hand on top of hers.

"Blood work," she echoed, as we both found the lump Dr. Wiese was talking about. Her eyes fluttered shut, and I squeezed my fingers between hers, lacing them together, tightening my hold on her.

My mouth was nearly pressed to Jesse's ear. I was behind her, enveloping her almost.

"Is he going to be okay?" I asked.

Asshole pled the fifth. I wanted to leap on Dr. Wiese and strangle the words out of his throat, but I wanted to keep my hand on Jesse's more. Shadow began to move around, sniffing and whimpering, asking to be taken down. Jesse's hand went rigid under my own. She turned around and looked at Dr. Wiese.

"I can't lose him."

"He's in good shape, Jesse. We just need to run some tests." He tried soothing her, rubbing Shadow's cheek again. Must have been a nervous tic.

"No, no. I can't lose him," she repeated, her eyes filling with unshed tears.

"Jess…"

"He's my only true friend."

"Come on, sweetheart," he murmured nervously. "I'm sure that's not true."

But it was. There were Old Sport and Mrs. Belfort, and then there was me. And I didn't count because she was nothing but a business transaction to me. Sup-fucking-posedly.

Shadow was aimlessly pacing back and forth on the table, his nails making a click-click-click sound that matched the tic behind Jesse's left eyelid. Dr. Wiese gave me a look, and I pulled Jesse away from her dog, again surprised at how she had let me touch her, even though I kept shit as PG as possible, my fingers fluttering over her arm. Dr. Wiese took Shadow's blood—a few tubes of it, at that—while Jesse looked the other way and cried silently.

"When are we going to get the results?" I shoved my hands into my front pockets.

"It's pretty busy here this time of the year. We'll call and send the results by mail, so watch out for them," Dr. Wiese said as he placed all the tubes in the test tube rack. I gave Jesse a look to confirm she'd heard him, and she nodded faintly.

"What are we thinking about?" I walked over to stand by Dr.

Wiese, watching Shadow, who looked exhausted and kind of spent. I'd never had a pet. Not for lack of wanting. Money had been tight, and a pet meant spending more money. Also, my mom had worked ridiculous hours the first ten years of her career, and I'd learned early on that in order to survive, I needed to hang out at other people's places after school to eat home-cooked meals, so I hadn't been around much, either.

I didn't know what it felt like to lose a dog, but I had a feeling that for Jesse, it was also ten times worse because he was more than just a pet. He was another piece of old Jesse she was never going to get back.

"All done." Dr. Wiese snapped his elastic gloves off and dumped them into a stainless-steel trash bin, turning around to wash his hands again. "Give him plenty of water and make sure he eats. Wet food, if he doesn't have any appetite. I'll prescribe him antibiotics right now, but we'll be in touch."

"Okay," Jesse managed, still sniffing.

I grabbed Shadow and helped him down just when she turned to the doctor and said, "This is all my fault, you know."

The silence that followed made me want to throw up a little.

I thanked the doctor, booked the follow-up appointment for Shadow myself with Miss Candy Crush, and paid the bill because Jesse was busy shivering in the corner of the reception, mumbling empty promises and apologies to a lethargic Shadow. I carried the smelly furball to her Rover, put him in the back seat, and made sure that he was all curled up and comfortable. Then I turned around to face her.

I was going to say something. I wasn't really sure what. Usually, I just tossed a lie or two to make uncomfortable shit go away. But as I swiveled, I realized Jesse was right beside me, her green-apples-and-fresh-rain scent filling my nostrils once again.

"What?" My brow furrowed.

She shook her head, taking another step closer to me.

"You're entering creeper zone again," I said. She didn't smile. She didn't talk. It didn't register at first, when she rose on her tiptoes and pressed her lips to my cheek.

Now, here's the part I wasn't so crazy about admitting: I didn't do any of my usual moves. I didn't smirk or rake my eyes over her body or gather her into a one-arm hug like the tool they had taught me to be at All Saints High. I just stood there like a damn fool, feeling her kiss soaking into my cheek like poison. Why poison? Because it was going to kill me if I wasn't careful.

This girl was an apple, all right.

But it wasn't green. It was red and lethal and not worthy of six fucking million dollars.

Shadow broke the moment by barking from the back seat. Jesse stepped away. Old Sport cheek-blocked me. After everything I'd done for him. Now I knew generosity didn't pay off.

We both hurried into the vehicle, our seat belts clicking in unison. Jesse drove us back into downtown Todos Santos, and I tried to convince myself that I wasn't fucking up the deal because kissing on the cheek was like a shoulder punch in some cultures. There was nothing sexual about it, a statement that my throbbing dick didn't agree with, but since when was I listening to his opinions? He liked everyone. That fucker and his hippie mentality.

"Shadow is going to be fine." I said something aloud so that the voices in my head would stop urging me to do shit like putting my hand on hers again.

She answered, "I hope so because he is the only one I have."

"Flattered," I quipped.

She laughed. "Stop doing this."

"Doing what?"

"Offering me hope. Faith is a dangerous thing. It drives you to try, and when you try, you fail."

I wondered if she realized that our knees were nearly touching. That we were closer than we'd ever been. That not only could we smell each other, but we could also study every individual freckle and blemish on each other's skin.

"Aren't you a bundle of sunshine and unicorns," I remarked.

"My dad is dead, my mom is a bitch, and I have zero friends. My dog is dying because I was too much of a coward to take him to his annual checkups. I have no ties to this world. Setting up roots, getting out of the house..." She took a sharp breath, tapping her fingers against the steering wheel as she drove. "For the past two years, I've been waiting for the sky to fall on me. Wishing for it, really. I didn't plan on giving this whole life thing another shot. That's why I didn't want you to give me a job."

"But that's why you need one," I countered. She was rolling onto Main Street, heading toward El Dorado, and I wasn't ready to part ways. Not on that note. "A reason to wake up in the morning. I need a barista, Snowflake." I didn't, but someone was going to lose their job. Probably Beck. He needed to concentrate on his surfing, anyway, and the sponsorships had started pouring in, so it wasn't like he was going to go hungry. "It's the easiest job in the world. A chipmunk can do it. Even worse—Beck can."

"As much as the offer flatters me—and make no mistake, proposing I should do the job of a chipmunk flatters me beyond belief"—she paused for a second, allowing the fact she'd handed me my own ass to seep in—"I'm not going to work for you. Have you been to Darren's house? Money is hardly an issue in my family."

"Don't work for the money. Work for the sweat. Work for the power. Work to feel needed and independent and goddamn fucking productive. Work to show the motherfuckers who did what they did to you that you're strong. *Illegitimi non carborundum.*"

"Is that a Kama Sutra position?" She sighed loudly. I chuckled. She was slowly peeling off her layers of fear. Now she was just annoyed, and I could work with that.

"It means 'Don't let the bastards grind you down.'"

For a second there, it looked like I'd gotten to her. She nodded, agreeing with the sentiment. Then she said, "I don't even know how to make smoothies."

"Neither do I," I answered. "What's the worst you can do?"

I put my hand on the wheel and steered it to the left, toward the promenade, toward Café Diem. Jesse swiveled her head and stared at me hard.

"Don't be late to your own job interview. Officially, we started five minutes ago, and you're already sassing."

She smiled to herself.

This time it reached her eyes.

Another win for me.

Another win I didn't want to share with Darren.

I let Jesse park in my spot since I didn't have the truck or the Harley. Then I helped Shadow out on autopilot. He seemed in better spirits but still looked like he needed a dog spa retreat or something. Jesse trailed behind us into the coffee shop because even though she didn't mind my proximity, she was much more comfortable without me all up in her business. Side bonus: Shadow had stopped looking at me like I was the Gestapo, so I guess we were getting places.

You still cheek-blocked me, asshole.

We got in.

Skateboarding teenagers, young professionals, tattooed MacBooks, skinny lattes, and green shakes. Café Diem was hipster heaven, and it was full of regulars, so I knew a lot of people here had witnessed the shit show that was Jesse storming out on me mid-date a couple of days ago. Date, hangout. Whatever. Darren said I could date her but not fuck her. Wasn't that the definition of marriage?

I waltzed behind the counter before Jesse had the time to object. She was going to get the job. It was in my contract with Darren. She could pretty much burn the place down trying to make coffee, and

I'd still hire her. Not that it was that bad a deal, to be honest. I hated to admit that it wouldn't be the worst thing to look at her tight little body, luscious raven hair, and ocean eyes.

Ocean eyes.

Okay, now I was 99 percent sure I'd lost my faculties completely. In fact, it was possible me and said faculties weren't even on the same continent. And Snowflake wasn't only nice to look at it. She was one funny chick, too.

"This is Jesse and Shadow. Don't shake her hand or pet him. They're both rabid." I jerked my thumb toward them, my voice as grave and serious as always. "Jesse, this is Beck and Gail." I motioned to my bald-by-choice emo chick and surfer friend baristas. Jesse snickered, and I didn't turn around to see it, even though it was rare. I knew better than to fuck myself over like that. I sauntered toward the smoothie blender and tapped it.

"Hi!" Gail chirped. I wasn't sure what she was trying to prove with the shiny, shaved head. If it was an attempt to look a little less girlie, Beck didn't get the memo because he nudged her away with his ass, doing a little wave of his own.

"And I'm Gail's better half, Callum Beck."

"You're not half of me. You're not even half a man," Gail retorted.

Beck snickered. "I could easily prove you wrong, if you'd just go on a date with me."

"Anyway," I stressed, not wanting Jesse to think this was some kind of a hormone hub where everybody fucked everybody, even though it wasn't that far from the truth. "Most of our customers are surfers, skateboarders, or beach bums, so we mainly focus on smoothies, not coffee. Make me one now and we'll see how we go from there."

"I don't want the job," she repeated for the thousandth time. To make her point, she stayed rooted to the floor, but it was on the business side of the counter, right along with us. I was the first one to admit my experience with the other sex was usually just that—sex.

I'd only had one girlfriend in my life, Edie, and although she was feisty and brave, she was never so angry. I seemed to have brought out the red in Jesse, and I couldn't lie—it turned me the fuck on and lit me up like Christmas at Bethlehem.

"But you do want me to take Shadow for his follow-up appointment. Correct?" I asked, smiling nonchalantly.

She opened her mouth to say something and then snapped it shut.

"That's what I thought. I'm happy to play Nurse Protsenko to Old Sport as long as I gain a new employee."

She shifted her gaze, swallowing hard. I knew I'd won this one, and it felt good.

Snowflake marched over to the blender. She waved her little hand at me, her face a brewing storm. "If I make you a smoothie, do you promise to drink it?"

My eyebrows dove down with suspicion. "Are you gonna put jizz in it or something?"

She rolled her eyes. "Yeah. I have it handy in my purse."

I grinned. Like it mattered. I'd lick the sweat between her ass cheeks after a hot yoga class if it wasn't for the contract I'd signed.

"I promise everything I put in there is legit. I'm just not sure if the combination will be to your liking."

I humored her. "I like my employees innovative. Let's see what you got."

Now she was smiling. Really smiling. I looked away and led Shadow to the far corner of the café, giving him a bowl with fresh water. It was going to be a long-ass six months if every time she grinned, my dick wanted to give her mouth-to-mouth.

I leaned against the counter, Gail and Beck by my side, as we all watched Jesse dumping banana pieces, strawberries, vanilla yogurt, coconut water…then spinach, kale, avocado, cream cheese, ginger, cayenne, tofu…

"Easy there, Jesse," Gail said, taking a step toward Carter. I watched closely for any signs of distress from the latter but found none. She was less uncomfortable with women. "I'm not sure everything goes together."

Jesse slammed the blender shut and offered Gail a sweet smile. "You think? Gee, I can't imagine what would happen if I don't get this job."

"There's no way Bane's gonna drink that." Beck chortled from behind me, and I imagined him blowing his stupid, long brown hair away. Stupid because I had long hair, too, but at least I kept mine in a bun.

It was only then—with Beck behind me and Gail lined up with me, but not anywhere near Jesse—that I noticed that I was blocking people from Jesse. It had become second nature to me at this point.

See a person that's not me, put myself between him/her and Snowflake, make sure he/she doesn't get anywhere near her until we are out of the room.

Jesse started the blender, and I watched in disgust as every single thing we had in stock swirled together into a smoothie from hell. Once she was done, she made a show of biting her lower lip, leaning forward, plucking a large slushie cup from the pyramid of cups, and pouring the smoothie into it as the entire room watched her with awe mixed with disbelief. I guessed she was oblivious to the fact that everyone was watching her. Or maybe she knew, and for a moment there, she was the Jesse prior to what had happened to her. Confident and feisty and a lot of fucking fun. She slid the cup across the counter and tilted her head sideways, batting her eyelashes.

"Here, Mr. Protsenko. I truly hope this will be to your satisfaction and will result in my employment."

Silence. A guy at the far end of the room stood up from his chair and slapped his table repeatedly, shouting, "Drink. Drink. Drink. Drink."

Seconds later, everyone was standing, balling their fists, urging me on to down that fucking nightmare of a smoothie. Take it from someone who'd visited Russia often enough to remember the small details—this shit could only happen in America. The way people unite to see someone do something completely stupid is uplifting, if not downright inspirational. Hell, *Jackass* made millions off that concept.

"You're funny," I said flatly.

"And you're stalling." She grinned.

Hot. Fucking. Damn.

But, really—was that my thank-you for dragging her ass back to civilization? At the same time, I couldn't ignore how fun it was to finally be challenged and, yes, even ridiculed. Beck drummed the counter, and Gail clapped her hands excitedly, woohoo-ing like an extra in a nineties high school movie. Jesse's eyes clung to my face, so I picked up the cup, my eyes locked on hers as it touched my lips.

"You're going to regret it," I hissed into the brown foam on my lips.

"So are you," she whispered, her eyes holding mine.

I downed the whole disgusting thing without breathing through my nose once.

People burst into applause, like kernels of popcorn exploding in a microwave bag, and Jesse laughed so hard she had to brace herself against the counter. I pretended to launch at her, and she pretended to run, her shoulder brushing mine. Instead of flinching or running, she just straightened back up, wiped a happy tear off her face, and smiled at the brownish-greenish foam that clung to my upper lip.

"You're hired," I growled into her face.

For a second, it looked like she might just wipe the foam off with her thumb.

For a second, it looked like old Jesse would bulldoze her way into the room.

But in reality, she turned around and moved away, calling for Shadow.

That was fine by me because even though I didn't get the old Jesse, I'd still managed to do something monumental that day.

I'd touched the Untouchable. And for the first time in a long time, her sky wasn't going to fall.

CHAPTER EIGHT
JESSE

That night, I skipped my usual nighttime jog.

My head was reeling from the day. From Shadow's upcoming blood work results. The new job. From kissing Bane on the cheek.

Habits and repetition were the only things that kept me from throwing myself off a cliff, and I still needed a physical outlet, so I went to the outside pool for a quick swim. I did a few laps and then stopped in the middle of the pool, floating face down with my arms stretched and eyes wide. I held my breath, my lungs burning with the last deep breath I'd taken.

The only lights visible were reflecting on the water from the outdoor lamps. It looked and felt like I was floating in the atmosphere, with nothing to anchor me back home. It reminded me of the days after the Incident, when I'd contemplated suicide. I wasn't sure how serious I'd been—deep down, the concept still seemed so crazy, but sometimes in the dead of the night, when it was really quiet, I waited for the tears to come out, and all I felt was emptiness.

I didn't feel so empty now. Scared, yes, and very unsure. But there was excitement there, too. Roman "Bane" Protsenko was a paid escort. But funnily enough, that took the pressure off. We weren't a boy and a girl. We were two lonely, fucked-up souls. It made wanting Bane in my life acceptable. I wanted him to fix me.

To cure me.

To hold me.

To make me laugh.

To make the pain go away.

More than anything, I wanted him to lift my shirt, see the scar, kiss it better, and tell me that I was beautiful. I could almost imagine it if I tried really hard—his beard on my marred flesh. His crinkly, soothing eyes on my sore memories.

Soft.

Warm.

Good.

Breathe.

I needed to breathe.

I snapped my head up from the water and took a greedy breath, gasping for air. My arms flailed around me, and I swam in place, looking around, before paddling frantically to the edge of the pool.

Maybe that was the difference between Bane and all the others.

I didn't want him.

I needed him to remind me how to breathe.

I liked to think of my memories as a graveyard for my thoughts.

Moments that were already dead, so I didn't have to worry about them happening again.

I remembered a lot of things I wished I hadn't, and maybe that was my problem. For instance, I remembered the moment Emery yanked my shirt and jerked me into that car. The moment I realized I was in danger. I remembered the first rip of fabric in my ear—that was Emery, too, who started everything before the other two followed.

I remembered the first dry thrust into me. Nolan.

The first punch to the face. Henry.

I remembered how it felt on the operating table when they

sucked my fetus out of me. Those were all crisp, clear memories. Sharp like knives. But then there was the moment I couldn't remember at all.

The one prior to Emery trying to take my virginity.

The one when I'd already lost it.

"If only I could remember." I clutched the roots of my hair. I could feel Mayra's soft gaze flickering on my skin. She always gaped at me with a mixture of hopelessness and pity. My therapist looked like the classic loving grandma. White-cotton hair on tan skin. Deep wrinkles and big dangling jewelry.

"Remember what?" she coaxed.

"When did it happen? When did I lose my virginity?"

I worried my lower lip, my fingers twisting together. I'd been happy with Emery. And I hadn't slept with anyone else before him. I would remember if I had. He was my first, but when we got to business, there was no blood. No pain. His shocked face hovered over mine as he'd thrust into me, his pelvic movements becoming more punishing and desperate with every second that passed. Emery's brows knitted as I'd grown anxious and exasperated, writhing underneath him in unwarranted remorse. I wondered if I should fake the discomfort he craved to see in my eyes.

Some girls needed to fake pleasure. With Emery, I needed to give him my pain.

Then his gaze shifted to his PlayStation device, and mine followed.

Then I noticed the camera, blinking a red dot at me.

Then I threw a fist in his face, scrambling up, wrapping my torso with his sheet.

Then I sealed my fate.

"How do you mean?" Mayra scratched her temple with her pen.

"What if I'm suppressing something? Forgetting something?" I stood up from the seat in front of her, pacing back and forth. Mayra's office looked nothing like her so-called personality. White on beige.

Pottery Barn on West Elm. Rich on prudish. It often made me wonder which one of them was fake—the office or the persona?

"Do you think you might be trying to find a reason for why such a horrid thing happened to you? Perhaps you'd like to convince yourself that there is something for you to atone for. But the truth is Emery, Nolan, and Henry are the ones who have wronged you. Not the other way around."

"No." I shook my head, feeling like the room wasn't big enough to contain all my anger. "What I'm saying is…"

"You could have broken your hymen falling from a bike or inserting a tampon. Some girls are born with no hymen at all. I'm worried that looking for reasons why this has happened to you might pull you away from the road you should be taking to recovery. Acceptance and rehabilitation will come when you realize nothing bad happened before. You did nothing to invite such behavior." She burst into my thoughts, quiet but stern. Her eyes followed my movements, but I knew her butt would never leave the couch. I stopped in front of her window, glancing down toward the street. Something made me look for Bane's red truck. He was probably at Café Diem, getting hit on by every person with a pulse. Pam included. I hated that he drew so much attention. I hated that he'd slept with people for money and connections. And I hated that I was secretly excited to start working for him.

Most of all, I hated that I'd been with Mayra ever since I was twelve, shortly after Pam and I had moved in with Darren, and I still counted every minute of every session, waiting for it to be over.

But Bane…he was a different story. Today I'd woken up feeling different than yesterday. Maybe I'd had time to digest everything that had happened, but I felt slightly possessive of Bane, and that was worrisome.

He made me feel normal, and that was more than I could say about most people I came across. My curiosity toward him bothered me, too. But talking to Mayra about him or about my mom hitting on him made me feel...weird. For one thing, Mayra was a longtime friend of Darren's family. I couldn't trust her not to pay it forward. Ethics codes be damned. I pressed my fingertips to the cold window glass.

"There's a chunk of memory missing from my brain," I gritted out. It was during the year Pam and Darren had gotten married, shortly after Dad had died. Everything had happened so fast and all at once. Mayra said it was a natural reaction. So much had happened to me in such a short time, I'd created an abyss in my memory to cope with all the changes.

"We don't remember every single day of our lives." I watched Mayra play with one of the many necklaces on her chest through the reflection of the window. "And that's a good thing, Jesse."

The clock next to Mayra's couch chimed with glee—not the subtlest signal that our session was over, I'd once pointed out, and Mayra had even agreed but had never changed it—and that was our cue. We gave each other respectful nods.

"By the way, I got a job." I dropped the bomb a second before we were done.

"Jesse!" Mayra smiled from her couch, and as always, it didn't reach her eyes. "That's wonderful! I want to hear all about it next week."

Now it was my turn to grin. I sometimes did that. Dropped important stuff at the end of my meetings with Mayra just to see her shutting me down and kicking me out. It reminded me she wasn't a friend. She was a paid ally, the worst thing a person could have, and call me paranoid but reminding myself that she was Team Benjamins and not Team Jesse helped.

"Yeah." I grabbed my backpack and slung it over my shoulder, one foot already on the threshold. I zipped my hoodie all the way up before I went out to face the world. "Can hardly wait."

———

I once read that people often mistake infatuation for love and that the best way to distinguish between the two is to look at the time it took you from the moment you met the person to the moment you realized you couldn't let them go even if you tried.

Falling in love is when you lose yourself slowly, piece by piece.

Infatuation is when you lose yourself all at once.

Love is like ivy. It wraps around you, chokes every part of you quietly. It is not patient or kind or gentle. It is needy, cunning, and suffocating.

When I made my way to Café Diem, I genuinely thought I was doing Bane a favor by warning him about Pam. But that's because the ivy was only tickling my feet at that point, not yet gripping my ankles and rooting me to the ground. Bane and Pam were scheduled to meet there, and an overwhelming notion of loathing toward my own mother filled my chest. I had one friend. She'd had at least four lovers. Not only had she slept with Nolan while I was dating Emery at the beginning of my senior year—a fact Nolan enjoyed sharing with me the night when he took me against my will—but there had been others, too.

Her married plastic surgeon.

Her young personal trainer.

She even had a dating app called NoToNosy where she'd met other married men. I didn't get why Darren turned a blind eye to all the bullshit she threw in his face. He owed her nothing. A different man would have kicked us to the curb long ago.

I parked at the promenade and strode with purpose, hyperaware of the stares and looks. Walking in the middle of summer wearing a hoodie was odd. Being known as the girl who was into orgies and suicide? Even odder. One guy in particular made my steps falter. He wore a gray beanie, a white tank with the word "FREE" scribbled on it, and flowery board shorts. He didn't look much older than me, leaning against a Mercedes, loitering in the way cool SoCal young people did. Like time was of no significance and youth was eternal. I thought he was going to talk to me. Luckily, it was just my overworked imagination and thriving paranoia. He smiled, gesturing with his hand to say hi. I ignored him, my pulse hammering against my eyelids. I descended the stairs leading to the café that was right on the beach, below the promenade. I couldn't breeze in, knowing Pam and Bane would notice me. So I stayed outside, lurking by the chained bikes, until I spotted them from the glass windows, sitting in the same corner Bane and I had sat in when he'd made me that smoothie. My heart rebelled inside my chest. I felt cheated by both of them, when in truth neither of them had promised me loyalty.

The thing was, one of them owed it to me, anyway.

I watched as Pam threw her head back and laughed at something Bane had said, fluffing her bleached-blond hair and pushing down the fabric of her pink cocktail dress. She swirled a manicured bubblegum-pink finger around the rim of her wine glass and nodded at what he'd said as if he'd just shared the cure to cancer with her.

Bane was slouched on the chair in front of her, talking low and looking blissfully bored. I'd learned his facial expressions by now. There weren't that many. When he was invested, his eyes glittered like he was high on something. On life. But right now, he looked like he was on the verge of yawning.

Pam reached across the table and put her palm on his, pressing her free one to her heart. He withdrew his hand without as much as a blink, tucking it into his pocket.

It was a tango of push and pull for the next ten minutes.

She flipped her hair. He pressed a button on his cell phone to check the time. She giggled. He craned his neck and glanced over her shoulder, barking something at Gail and Beck. She squeezed her arms together to show her ample cleavage. He leaned down to pet a dog that sat under the seat of the customer next to him. I was partly relieved at Bane's rejection of her advances and partly furious that she had pretended to care about me when actually all she wanted was to sleep with the guy who'd tried to befriend me. Most of all,

I felt unequipped to deal with all the sudden changes in my life. So much so that it took me a few seconds to register that they had gotten up from their seats. By the time I snapped back into reality, Pam was already heading toward the door. I leaped behind the café, hiding behind a concrete wall. They both stepped out, and I could hear them chatting.

The flick of the lighter as Bane lit himself a joint. The suggestive purr Pam unleashed after he did.

"Sharing is caring," she drawled.

"Spare me the bullshit, Pamela. You're one of the most capitalist people I've ever met. You wouldn't share a pile of shit if you thought someone else truly wanted it."

"You don't have to be so harsh."

"You don't have to be so desperate."

Pause. My heart swelled, and I was pretty sure I meant it in the literal sense of the word. I felt it spreading inside me, almost too big to carry.

"So what are your intentions with my daughter?" Her voice thickened as she took a hit of his joint. Bane's answer came after a calculated pause.

"It's not her panties that I'm after."

"Good. Because she'll never sleep with you."

My cheeks flamed. It wasn't that she was wrong. It was that she chose to tell him the truth because the underlying message was *But I will.*

"I don't look at her that way."

"Like what?"

"Like a cum-soaked hole. Besides, she's too young for me," he snapped. My jaw tensed. He was only five years older. We'd both be in our twenties in a few weeks. Another invisible ivy branch curled around my leg, rising higher, toward my knee. *Why does it bother you?*

"Well, as long as you know..." Pam trailed off.

"Nice meeting you, Pamela. I hope to see a lot of you while

hanging out—not sleeping—with your daughter." And that was it. I watched from my hidden spot as Pam climbed up the stairs from the beach to the promenade. I gave Bane a few more minutes to finish his joint and get back inside before I stepped out of hiding, only to find that he was still standing there.

Peachy.

Making a direct move toward the stairs without allowing any eye contact, I heard him sigh melodramatically behind my back.

"Next time you miss me, just give me a call. Although stalking is definitely a preferred method if your goal is to stroke my ego."

I froze mid-step, a blush heating my face in an instant. I was doing a lot of blushing lately. That was another thing the new Jesse didn't approve of.

"I was just..." I looked around me, searching for...what, exactly? A comfortable slice of sand I could stick my head into?

"You were just...?" He cocked an eyebrow, walking toward me. Each time I met him, I was knocked off-balance by his sheer maleness. And not in a good way. Even in my memories, in which Bane was carved handsomely, I still couldn't fully capture his sharp bone structure and bright-green eyes. "Let me guess—you were just in the neighborhood and decided to drop by and see if I'd hit on your mom?" He leaned his shoulder against the glass wall of his café, his hands shoved deep inside his pockets. I kicked a little stone, sending it to the other side of the road, my eyes hard on my Keds. "I told you, Snowflake. I ain't gonna fuck up what we have."

"So you keep saying," I said.

"And so you keep not listening. Change of topic. What do you wanna do on the last day of your freedom?"

"Freedom?" I sounded dumb, even to my own ears. It was the cinnamon breath mixed with the ocean salt of his hair that did it. Standing so close to the man without running for my life felt like an accomplishment, but it didn't leave me unaffected.

"Yeah." He kicked his joint with his boot, shooting it to the sand like a soccer player. "Before you start gainful employment tomorrow."

"Don't you have any poor unfortunate souls to embezzle?" I tilted my chin up, crossing my arms over my chest. Bane laughed.

"Happy to report all the unfortunate souls I'm in charge of are blissfully embezzled. Have you done your ten-mile run for today?"

"How do you know about my ten-mile runs?" My forehead creased. Sure, he'd seen me jogging the night he scared away Henry and Nolan—but that seemed a particularly specific number. Ten miles. Bane's eyes widened before his casual smirk returned.

"Mother Dearest told me a little about you today."

"There's nothing dear about her."

"Looks like we're in agreement on that one." He unleashed his devil's smile and then snapped his fingers and pointed at me. "Italian ice cream."

"People will think it's a date." I bit my lower lip, hating that I cared. I was allowed to get out of El Dorado. I was allowed to date, if I wanted, not that I did. And I was allowed to go on an ice cream run with a male friend. I knew, logically, that all of those things were true, but it didn't make them any less frightening.

"Right." Bane patted his back pockets to make sure his wallet was intact. He was already striding toward the stairs. "Remind me who cares?"

"I do." I stayed cemented in place. "I have a bad reputation."

He stopped, staring at me. "Mine's worse."

"Wanna bet?" I snorted bitterly. He smiled one of his relaxed smiles that felt like a lullaby. His next sentence came as a hushed whisper.

"Already told you. I heard all the rumors about you, Jesse. Fuck 'em. Fuck 'em to death. Fuck this town and its preppy, judgmental residents and every idiot who looks at us funny. Don't you get it? We're the outliers. The rejects. We're free. Free to do whatever the hell we want because it won't matter. We'll never fit in here, so we don't have to try. We're liberated from all this bullshit." He motioned around us with his hand. "They can't hurt you if you don't give them permission to. So don't."

I took a step toward him, hesitant. People were coming in and out of Café Diem, and no one looked at us funny. Maybe that was part of the reason I liked hanging out with Bane. People weren't quick to disrespect him. I still found it hard to believe that he wanted to hang out with me after all the rumors.

They'd said the night in the alley was not really in an alley but in Henry's house and that it had been a consensual orgy. The abortion news also leaked into the eager ears of townsfolk. I once heard Wren's friend Kandi say, "The baby probably died of embarrassment. Could you imagine? Being conceived in a mass orgy?"

But Bane didn't care.

He screwed for a living, for God's sake.

No wonder he was the only one here to accept me.

He said it was personal, and maybe that's what he meant. Maybe he just hated slut shaming so much, I was a pet project for him. The worst part was that I didn't even care. I was still grateful for the friendship.

"All right," I said, the words so heavy in my mouth I said them again, this time louder. "All right, let's go."

We walked silently to the ice cream parlor, basking in the glorious sun. Our hands almost brushed when he opened the door to the shop for me, prompting something inside me to rise like a tide and then soar like a tsunami. I ordered two scoops—two more than I would have eaten any other day.

There was something about Bane that made me want to reinvent myself. To try something fresh. I went for pistachio and Alaskan ice cream. And for the first time in a long time, the food I was eating actually had a taste.

It tasted new.

I liked it.

When we got out of the ice cream parlor, I turned around and told him, "About us holding hands in Dr. Wiese's clinic…"

I was feeling brave, but then he stopped, turned around, and looked at me seriously. "Yeah. Wasn't thinking. Won't happen again."

"No," I said, stopping too. We were now the only people standing in a busy promenade, disrupting the rest of the crowd and not giving much of a damn. "I was wondering if we could do that again sometime. Not, like, in a weird capacity or anything. I just want to know that I, um…" I swallowed, glancing around. "Can."

I couldn't stop thinking about his inked hand on mine. About the moment my lips fluttered on his surprisingly smooth cheek. His nostrils flared, and something I couldn't decipher zinged in his eyes. Whatever it was, he weighed his words carefully before he said them. "Yeah." He looked around us, as if someone was watching, tugging at his beard. "Sure. You want me to surprise you or just do it now?"

I thought about it for a second, resuming our walk. We were in sync now.

"Surprise me."

We reached the end of the promenade and waited for the light to turn green before we crossed it. His palm found mine, but he kept looking at the traffic light, as though nothing was happening, all bored and indifferent.

"Okay?" he whispered under his breath.

"Okay."

CHAPTER NINE
BANE

My mother's doorbell was the color of vomit.

Dirty, overused. Kind of like me. It gave me a strange sense of familiarity. People came. People went. Sonya Protsenko always stayed, her shoulder always ready for me to put my head on it. Her fridge always full of homemade potato dumplings and cabbage soup. There was comfort in that. In having a functioning mom. Not that shit between us was simple—I wasn't the best son in the world.

I wasn't the worst, either.

For instance, I always did as I was told because I felt a sense of gratitude that she hadn't scraped my ass out with a hanger, which I wouldn't have blamed her for. Raped at eighteen by a Russian mafia *vor*, she'd fled the country with me when I was a few months short of three. Mom had attended college here. Graduated as a therapist. Found the time to come to my bullshit school stuff and to buy me a surfboard and to sit on the sand all by herself—because she didn't know anyone and was much too shy to talk to people—and watch me compete.

So I'd always done the dishes. Taken out the trash. Helped the neighbors fix their roof. Kept my grades up and played the whole perfect-kid charade in front of her friends and colleagues.

But I had the bad gene in me. The one that craved power. I could feel it running through my veins, making my blood hotter.

That's where my being a not-so-good kid came into play. I didn't rape or murder or do any of the nasty shit my piece-of-busted-condom father had done, but I still stole.

And sold pot.

And fucked women who weren't mine to fuck.

Loving my mom the way I did—unequivocally—reminded me that I was human. Intimacy scared the shit out of me otherwise. That's why I'd never gone bareback with anyone. Not even my ex-girlfriend. I didn't mind missing out on some of the pleasure if it meant not giving them my all.

But let's not talk about fucking and my mom in the same sentence. Point was, I had a good relationship with Mamul. I loved that we spoke Russian with each other. It put a wall between us and them. Gave us another layer of closeness other kids didn't have with their parents. And I loved her take on English because that was fun, too.

Such as when she'd written endless letters to my teachers and principals when I'd gotten into trouble, she would always refer to me as "my sun." "My sun didn't do this." "My sun didn't say that." She'd been right most of the time. I was scapegoated a lot for being the Russian, single-parent kid. Still, I would slap the letter onto the kitchen table with my palm and growl, "Mom, it's *s-o-n*, not *s-u-n*," and she would yell back, "I know exactly what I meant. You are my sun. Why do you think the words are so similar?"

I walked into her house, bringing the sand and saline scent of the ocean with me, wearing nothing but my surf shorts. Today, Jesse had started her job at Café Diem, and I had Gail guide her through it. I chose not to be there because I knew I was already in too deep with the girl, especially considering I'd nearly jizzed my pants holding her hand. Yeah, spending more time with her than necessary was a hard pass for me. So I'd gone surfing instead.

"Mamul," I barked, heading into the kitchen. She was standing over the stove, boiling beets and talking on the phone in Russian.

Loudly. Mom motioned for me to wait with her hand. She was talking to Aunt Luba about…oh, who the fuck knew? Probably gossip. My mom still went back to Saint Petersburg whenever she could afford it. Everything was crazy expensive in Russia, and she would buy me the most useless shit, like coats that could protect you from an apocalypse even though I lived in a place where people got hysterical when it started to drizzle.

"Roman!" Her eyes lit up, and she muttered a quick goodbye before turning off the stove and pulling a chair for me to sit down. My childhood house was very…Russian, from the flowery pale wallpaper, heavy curtains, and quilted everything to the kind of heavy carpets you could roll bodies in. In her defense, Sonya Protsenko gave everything a modern twist, so our house looked like a funky IKEA display room. "How are you doing, my darling sun?"

I took the glass of vodka she offered me, planting a soft kiss on her head. She was dwarfed by my six-two frame, the top of her head barely reaching my shoulders. "I'm drinking vodka in the middle of the day with no shirt on and hanging with my favorite girl. 'Nuff said. You?"

"Couldn't be better." She took a seat across from me, leaning forward and cradling her drink between her fine fingers. "What's new?"

"I met a girl."

"You met a girl?"

"I met a girl." I couldn't really talk about Jesse with anyone. Beck was an idiot, Hale was a frenemy, and Gail and Edie were chicks, and it just felt like a whole new level of pussy to consult them. Mom was a safe bet because she'd never say shit to anyone else. Other than Aunt Luba, and I guess I could live with a few relatives on the other side of the planet knowing about Snowflake.

Mom asked more questions, and I ended up telling her everything. About the gang rape and the sex tape and all the other shit that made Jesse's life sound like a Netflix show.

Thirteen Reasons Why I'm Going to Kill Emery and Co.

I was telling Mom how I was helping Jesse get out of the house more when she put her hand on my bearded cheek and looked deep into my eyes.

"I love you," she said, and I went *uh-oh* in my head because that sounded like the beginning of a speech that I'd hate.

I rubbed my index finger over my front teeth. "You're not too bad, either."

"But," her voice rose, cutting through my shitty joke, "for the sake of being honest and as a rape victim—please don't take this the wrong way. I'd never replace you, never not have you. You're my fate, my blood, the sunshine upon my skin." She took a shaky breath, closing her eyes. "If you get into this girl's life, you cannot leave without a trace. You know that. Right, Roman?"

I blinked at her with a mixture of annoyance and rage. "I'm not an idiot."

But did I really know that? I had a six-month contract with Darren. A month of it was already gone. I'd never stopped to think about the consequences of my deal with Darren because I figured I would just continue my relationship with Jesse as if nothing had happened. But it wasn't so simple, was it? I was deceiving her, lying to her, and, in a sense, really fucking her over, making her put her hard-earned trust in someone who didn't deserve it. It was the first time it dawned on me that I would have probably done this favor to Darren even if there weren't a huge chunk of money involved. It was sobering, but hell, it was also very fucking depressing. I didn't do emotions. There is little to no room for them when you fuck for a living.

"Make me proud, Roman. Do the right thing by her."

I promised her that I would, and when I came out of her house, my heart cracked open. I felt the blood of a rapist mafia rat pumping in my veins. It felt like snakes beneath my skin. I wanted to tear them out of my body and dump them on the ground. To fall on my knees and bleed to death.

Because most of the time, I didn't feel like a good person.

But today, I felt like a bad person.

The kind of bad Jesse didn't need in her life.

The kind of sun that didn't caress and nourish life but burned shit to the ground, turning everything to ash.

The next thing I did was pretty goddamn stupid, even by my standards, and trust me when I say I'd done some stupid shit in my lifetime.

I went to see her after her shift.

If you're trying to find the logic in that—don't.

Everything in the situation screamed for me to take a step back. I needed to gather my wits and try not to be pussy-whipped by a girl whose pussy was more forbidden than incest. But, of course, what do you expect from a dude who sold his cock to the highest bidder? Exactly.

I contemplated texting Jesse beforehand, but she never checked her cell phone. So I went to her house after taking a shower and a piss, bypassing my weekly hookup with a forty-two-year-old realtor who'd helped me with my hotel refurbishment. I punched her doorbell a dozen times, walking back and forth, waiting for her to answer. I wanted to make sure she'd had a good first day. Gail said she was quiet and attentive—wasn't that the definition of Jesse?— but the overwhelming, out-of-nowhere notion that I should have been there for her consumed me.

Guilty. I felt guilty. And I never felt guilty in my life.

"Bane," Pam answered, hugging the door, her smile borderline arsenic. My face fell. At this point I was happy to fuck a goddamn tuna can before I laid a hand on her. The lights were dimmed behind her, and I wondered if Jesse was even there. Maybe I should have started my search at Mrs. Belfort's.

"Is Jesse around?"

She cocked her head to the side, pouting. "Maybe."

I parked my elbow on the doorframe. "I wouldn't fuck with me, Pam."

"But I would." Her voice was lace and lust and that damp thing between them that I had no interest touching.

I pushed my way into her house, bulldozing in like a hostile army, knowing she had little to no say about this shit. Darren had hired me. He would have my back if need be. "I want your daughter," I told her because a part of me no longer cared about hiding it.

"You're kidding me." She followed me across the landing of her house.

"Fucking wish I was. But I know better than to go after her, so don't worry your little head. At the same time—I'm never going to dick you. Not in this lifetime and probably not in the next one. So do us both a favor and pretend to be a decent mom."

Her mouth dropped open, and she stood in front of me, probably waiting for an apology that would never come. I turned around and climbed up the stairs to Jesse's room, feeling the weight of my words on my shoulders.

I wanted Snowflake. I did. I wanted to feast on her pussy and fuck her tight little body senseless and kiss that tattoo on the back of her neck, telling her that I'd seen it before and liked it. That I saw her before and wanted her. That she wasn't just a goddamn sob story for me.

I knocked on her door. No response.

Then did it again. Nothing.

Third time. "Go away," she yawned from the other side of the door.

"Not happening. Open up."

"Bane?" I liked that she was still naive enough to be surprised.

"We need to talk." I was pacing again. Why the fuck was I pacing again? Silence rang in my ears before her door slid open. I drank her face through the gap. She was so beautiful, it nearly hurt to see. I dated a lot of beautiful women. I fucked a ton of them, too. No one was pretty the way Snowflake was. Everything around her faded, like a poem with burned edges. She was the lyrics inside it, so focused and sharp. I pushed my shoulder against her door, moving into her room, and it nearly knocked the hell out of my breath.

Hanging from her ceiling was a chandelier made out of small memorabilia: old-school CD-ROMs, pens, remotes, postcards, letters, keychains of her favorite indie bands. It looked like her soul had exploded and poured down between us. The wall behind her queen-size bed was covered with Polaroid pictures of people's backs. I recognized her mom. A dark-haired man who was probably her dad. Darren and a bunch of cheerleaders and maybe even a bunch of strangers. Some pushpins clung on to nothing. My guess was that they used to hold on to the pictures of the people from her previous life before they'd fucked her over in every sense of the word. Though I did notice one picture curled under a pin. The back of a young man, his hair light brown and full. Emery was my guess. His neck was stabbed a hundred times with the pin that was holding it up until there was almost a pea-shaped hole in the middle.

A mason jar filled with fairy lights sat on her windowsill, making me wonder how many dreams she still had that were trapped inside. Smutty books scattered on the floor. She had black-and-white-striped Beetlejuice linens and a rusty "No trespassing, we're tired of hiding the bodies" sign hanging on her door. Her room had character. Personality. And lots of it.

"Who did all this?" I asked, acutely aware of how close our bodies were and how her chest went up and down like she was feeling what I was feeling, even though I had no idea what the fuck that was.

"I did," she said quietly. Her hair was still wet from the shower she must've taken after coming home from the shift. She wore tiny pajama bottoms—again, orange—and a baggy Sleeping with Sirens black top. I didn't know why, but it was the sexiest thing I'd ever seen.

She was a person.

She was a teenager, on the verge of breaking twenty.

She was a fucking girl, a woman, an in-betweener, with tits and hormones and sass, and that layer of ice was melting too fast, and I wanted to fucking drink every drop of it while it did.

My toes touched hers. The proximity made both of us sway a little. My eyes on hers. Green on blue. Tough on soft. A dirty liar on the purest, kindest girl I ever knew.

"How was your first day?" I asked.

"Uneventful. Where were you?" Her voice was small, but the meaning behind her words was colossal.

I couldn't face you without breaking a six-million-dollar contract.

"Surfing." I took a step back, popping my gum. "I'm training Beck for a competition at the end of the month. That's why I looked for a new barista. He quit." I was bending the truth so much it was about to snap.

"Okay."

"But is it really okay?"

"No. It was my first day working. The first day I faced the world again. I thought you were going to check on me." Her voice shook. I'd betrayed her, and she was pissed. "I thought you were my friend."

"I am your friend."

"Friends care."

"I care." And that was becoming a fucking problem. Case in point, the next thing to come out of my mouth made me want to punch myself. "Have dinner with me." What the fuck was I saying? Asking?

She nearly leaned on me—nearly—and I smelled her everywhere. Even the musky sweet scent of her pussy. And it killed me that I couldn't help her with what she really needed to see. That she could enjoy sex again. With me.

My reckless moments were piling up quickly. The next thing I did was stupid, too. I clasped her chin between my thumb and my index finger to guide her face up so that our lips were aligned. The door was still half ajar, and I knew how much I was putting on the line. But I needed to do this with eye contact. Because my mom was right. I couldn't fuck it up.

"You need to say no. I'm a bastard," I whispered.

Kick me out of here. Before I'll be the one who won't be able to let you go.

She looked up and shook her head. "Yes."

"No, Snowflake, you don't understand. I am literally a bastard. My sperm donor was married, but not to my mom. Of course, it wasn't her choice. She was brutally raped by him. And I'm the constant fucking reminder of that. I have his hair. His eyes. His lips. I have his height and his build. I've never met him, but I've a feeling that if I ever did, I would tear my fucking limbs apart just to make sure I'd never be capable of doing what he did to her. That's why the tattoos. And the beard. That's why I'm hiding. I don't want to be him, understand?"

I'd never told that to anyone before, and whoever said the truth will set you free needed to have their head examined. The truth felt like a five-ton chain around my neck. The truth was, the beard was my armor. I'd started growing it when I started getting paid for sex. Less of my face to look at in the mirror.

And for my next trick, ladies and gents, I will become the whore my father pegged my mother to be. Only worse. She didn't ask for it. For the right price—I will.

Jesse's eyes widened at my confession, and I hated what I saw there. Pity swam in her pupils. I wanted her to blink and give me anything else instead. Lust. Anger. Confusion. Hate. I'd take anything, really, other than fucking pity.

"That's why you said my story was personal to you. That's why you said your mom couldn't be saved."

I didn't nod—wasn't really capable of doing anything other than shrugging—but she continued. "That's why you don't want to sleep with me." Her fingertips fluttered across her lips.

"Among other reasons. Look, you're not a tragedy to me, okay? You're a person. An adorable, talented, funny—hotter-than-fire— person. But that's the thing. I can't touch you. I won't touch you. As long as we keep this shit platonic, we'll be gold. I just can't have this on my conscience." It was already soaked with deceit. I owed Darren more than I'd ever have in my bank account. Even if I wanted to break the contract, I'd already spent a quarter of the money.

She took a step forward. There was no more space between us, so her inner thigh pressed against my outer thigh through my surf shorts. My eyes dropped to her milky flesh. She pressed harder. I looked up, my pulse thrumming on my eyelids.

"I don't care what your father did. He is the bastard. Not you. And you're the only man I'm not afraid of. You make me feel brave. Powerful. You make staring at myself in the mirror without flinching slightly easier. And I want to, Bane. I want those things I read about in the books." She licked her lips fast, shifting her gaze so I wouldn't see all of her through her eyes. "So, by all means, kiss me."

I wanted so badly to twist the collar of her shirt, pull her into me, crash my lips on hers, and fuck her against the wall. More than that—I knew that it was what she probably needed.

"Snowflake," I warned, my voice a soft growl. She squeezed both her thighs together against my leg, riding it, her eyes cool and daring, her movements so subtle I wasn't sure whether I was imagin- ing them. I swallowed hard as she found a hesitant, slow rhythm. I couldn't push her away. Other than the very simple fact I didn't want to, she was also a rape victim. Shutting her down would be the kiss of death to our relationship. The choice was mine to make. Six million bucks or her pussy. It sounded like an easy choice, though it was anything but.

"Bane," she breathed, so close to my mouth, and my dick twitched between us, slapping her stomach. Fuck. Fuck. Fuck.

I pulled my face away, but just to show her she was not alone in this attraction, I pressed my thigh against her pussy, pushing my knee north, putting pressure on her clit. I felt her slit open through her jammies. Her eyes rolled inside their sockets, and pre-cum glued my hard-on to my briefs.

"Kiss me."

"No."

"Why?"

"I told you why. You deserve better than a bastard like me."

"But you're my bastard."

I *tsk*ed. "I'm everyone's bastard, Jesse, and therein lies the problem."

"I don't mind sharing. It's not about you. It's about me." She was grinding against me so hard, and I was pushing into her more and more, my back against the wall. Technically, I wasn't breaking any rules. I wasn't kissing her. I wasn't fucking her, and I sure as hell wasn't seducing her. But in every other sense, I was neck-deep in shit, and it was the first time I actually acknowledged it. Because whether it was in the contract or not, the way my knee kept rubbing and pushing against her puffy clit was anything but professional.

"If you don't kiss me now, I'll stop," she whispered into my neck, so much smaller than me.

I breathed through my nose, my lips pinched.

Don't say it. Don't say it. Don't you dare say it.

"Don't stop." The words fell from my mouth, strangled.

"Cut the beard."

"Dafuq?"

"You heard me. Cut the beard, Bane. You're not your father. Stop hiding." Her thighs clamped against my leg, and I knew that she was close. I might as well have shot my load straight into her pj's because that shit was more erotic than any fuck I'd had in the last three years.

"No," I grunted.

"Then I'll stop."

"Do what you have to do." I pretended to smirk. I wasn't one to negotiate with terrorists, no matter how hot they were and how hard they made my dick. But when her thighs left mine and I felt how damp and warm my leg was, how I missed her stomach pressing against my cock, I jerked her back in to me.

"I'll cut the beard." What the fuck? Where were my balls? Probably in the same place I'd left my brain because I was very clearly shitting all over six million dollars.

Her thighs were about to clasp my leg again when the door flew open and I almost stumbled down. That's what you get for letting a borderline-teenager dry hump you into oblivion and back. Jesse straightened her posture, her cheeks all flushed mid-orgasm-y, when Darren peeked sheepishly from the corridor.

"Jethy?"

I wanted to yank his tongue out for ruining one of the hottest moments of my life with his lisp and lemur eyes. Snowflake gathered her hair and blinked away the lust from her eyes, tilting her chin up.

"Yeah, Darren?"

"Dinner ith almost ready. I wondered if…oh. Ah, Bane."

Now he was inside the room, facing me, with Jesse in the middle, which meant that there was still some space between us because apparently she didn't allow her stepdad to come anywhere close to her, either.

"Do you guys know each other?" Jesse looked between us, her face falling. I didn't know whether Darren figured out what we were doing or not. I was too busy mentally smashing his head against a rock for having the discretion of a fucking brick.

"Yeah. Darren and I met at city hall. I recently purchased a hotel, and he was there doing the usual rich asshole paperwork." I recovered quickly, especially considering 85 percent of my blood was still in my dick.

That seemed to pacify her, and her posture eased. Ironically, that only made me feel like even more of a bastard. She turned around back to him.

"Thank you, Darren, but the answer is—as always—no. Now

excuse me while I go to the ladies' room." Her cheeks pinked, and my fucked-up mind convinced me that she was going to go rub her clit to take the edge off. Also, this just in: I was going to jerk off tonight until my dick fell off. For the first time in years.

Darren leaned over the door, essentially shutting it and leaving us together in a closed room. For the first time since I'd met him, he looked less than contrite. Arms crossed, brows crashing, he looked about ready for a war.

"What were you doing?" he demanded.

I shrugged, my unofficial mind-your-own-fucking-business statement.

"Thee looked close to you."

"She is getting more comfortable with me. She started work at the shop today. And you're standing here, shitting all over my work by acting like we know each other when we're not supposed to." I pushed off Snowflake's wall, walking over to her Juliette balcony and cracking the window open while lighting a joint. I observed the view, realizing that her window overlooked Mrs. Belfort's maze. The pieces of the puzzle came together with a satisfied click.

That's why she knew her way around it by heart. Little devil.

"What'th that?"

"What's what?" I took a hit.

"Why are you thmiling?"

Was I? Maybe I was. So what?

"I'm fulfilling my part of the deal," I said, thinking about Jesse rubbing her little clit in circles in the bathroom, her mouth falling open in pleasure. Having a raging boner in the company of a sweaty, lanky oil tycoon was not my finest hour.

"You're altho thpending a lot of money." He took a step toward me, bracing an elbow on Jesse's bookshelf and knocking down a row of Jane Austen books. He seemed to have drunk from the confidence well because I swear the fucker hadn't been that nonchalant the last time I'd seen him. "Gutting and refurbithing the hotel? Breaking ground on the water park before the money ith even yourth? Do you know thomething that I don't?"

The answer was yes. I did know. I knew that I was in deep shit.

The reason why I'd started spending the money was simple: I didn't want to fail. My wanting to fail had nothing to do with the money. It had to do with Jesse. She needed to get away from this place because her parents were as constructive to her future as fucking herpes.

I blew smoke out the window, fingering my beard. "Don't pretend like I don't own this money. She's working for me and is already hanging outside more than she has the entire previous year combined. But if what makes you sleep well at night is me completing the entire six months, that's not a problem, either."

"Thtick to the plan if you want to get the retht of the money. It'th not yourth yet."

"It is mine," I gritted out.

"What's yours?" a small voice chirped from the doorway. Both our gazes darted toward the door. Snowflake was there, looking thoroughly orgasmed and oh so pissed.

Son of a fucking bitch.

CHAPTER TEN
JESSE

Thirty seconds.

I forced myself to stare back in the mirror after making myself come.

The first time I'd come since before the Incident.

The first time I'd masturbated since that night.

At first, I wasn't sure I'd be able to at all. It wasn't that I was not attracted to men because I was. But it was in the same way you admired paintings and sculptures: from afar, knowing they were heartless, soulless, not to have, and definitely not to hold. As I propped my butt against the sink and spread my legs, however, the surge of heat and excitement I'd felt before the Incident came crashing into my body like a wave. I pushed my lips apart, looking down at my clit.

Swollen, throbbing, begging.

It's been a long time. Touch me.

I did, but it didn't feel as good as Bane's thigh. His body was rough and callused, lithe and male. My fingers didn't hold a candle to his strong leg. Frustrated, I pulled a towel from the steam cabinet and dumped it across the bathtub edge. I hoisted one leg and straddled it, riding the edge like it was a mechanical bull.

I closed my eyes, imagining Bane.

The hard planes of muscles under his thin, over-washed Billabong shirt.

His rough fingers finding my clit. Big, dirty, and inky.

His cinnamon breath and ocean scent as my thighs straddled his bearded face while I rode his mouth, my juices dripping down his chin. I moaned, squeezing my thighs against the bathtub, biting my arm to stifle my little yelps of joy—sheer, newfound bliss—as the first flood of pleasure washed my inhibitions and anxiety away. I was coming. Feeling. Falling. Breaking the chains of misery that anchored me down.

It wasn't about my physical needs. Not all of it, anyway. It was about taking my power back. It was about reconquering my sexuality, a piece of land that had always belonged to no one else but me.

It was about finding my way back to the world.

I nearly skipped back to my room after washing my face and hands. Darren was still there, and that surprised me because he usually barely had the guts to knock, let alone step inside.

"It is mine," Bane said conversationally, but his posture, tense and commanding, suggested that he was a breath away from tackling Darren.

"What's yours?" I leaned against the door, folding my arms over my chest.

"The boutique hotel on the promenade. The one that's being gutted," Bane bit out, his voice manufactured and detached. His eyes were still hard on Darren, and the threat was there, stark clear and shining in his pupils. "Your stepdad has some very elaborate ideas of what I should do about it, even though I never asked for advice."

Bane grabbed my hoodie from my bed and walked over to me, tossing it into my hands and looking back to my stepdad, who stood there, in the middle of my room, looking like a wounded soldier who'd come back home to find out that everything he knew and loved had been consumed in flames.

"Come on, Snowflake. Food, and then we'll take Old Sport for a walk."

"Shadow is sleeping," I muttered, still confused by the entire exchange.

"Dogs are always sleeping. We'll wake him up." He mussed my hair, like I was an adorable kid.

The way he touched me, so casually, as if it was okay, as if I was normal, made my heart skip several beats.

I stole one last look at Darren, trying to find the pity I had usually felt for him. His eyes were blank, his jaw tight.

Usually, looking at him losing another battle made my heart pinch.

This time it didn't.

We didn't talk about what had happened in my room.

Something told me that the minute I addressed it, it wouldn't happen again, and that was a scenario I didn't want to entertain. We put Shadow—who was looking slightly better—on a leash and then grabbed some pizza downtown. I ate two slices and whimpered at the first bite, surprised by how much flavor it had.

Then we sat in his rusty red truck and called Dr. Wiese's office. The receptionist yawned a generic don't call us we'll call you, adding that it had been hectic at the clinic, so we might need to wait a few extra days. Then we dropped Old Sport back home and headed to the beach. Bane had promised Beck he'd surf with him, and I didn't care what we did. The sky was dusky, and for the first time in a long time, I felt liberated.

Liberated from the idea that Bane would think my "slut" scar was ugly.

Liberated from worrying about Shadow's blood work.

There was a perfect moment on that beach, right after Bane introduced me to his friends, Beck—whom I'd already met at Café Diem—and Edie, a blond surfer who was every insecure woman's worst nightmare. Petite, pretty, and approachable. It was when they were paddling deep into the water while I settled against my backpack, drowning in the words of *The Princess Bride*. The feeling of solitude holding hands with intimacy. I was hanging out with Bane without really hanging out with him.

I looked up every now and again and smiled.

Sometimes he didn't notice me.

Sometimes he smiled back.

When he took me back home, the thought that he might be going to one of his clients slammed into me, hard, and suddenly, prolonging our time together as much as I could, in some half-baked plan to make him cancel on whoever this woman might be, took the wheel.

"Edie is nice." I opened his glove compartment to find a mountain of cinnamon gum and a small plastic bag with weed. I took two pieces of gum and closed it.

Bane shrugged but didn't answer.

"And she's a surfer, so she's obviously your type." I searched his face.

His mouth curved into a comma-like smirk, his eyes still hard on the road. "Obviously."

"Come on, Bane. You wanna tell me you've never considered dating her?"

"I have. And I did. For a year. Ish," he said, so casually, though I guessed for him, it was. My mouth went dry. Up until then, I'd suspected I was jealous of Bane's clients. But I wasn't. Because this was jealousy. The thought that Edie—whom I'd enjoyed hanging out with and actually shared a joke or two with—was the devil and public enemy number one. My head swam, and I curled my fists beside my body.

Bane took a left turn, tipping his chin down.

"Don't get your panties in a twist. It was in high school." I hate high school.

"Who ended it?" I tried to sound chipper, but it came off a little manic.

He pushed his lower lip out, giving it some thought. "I don't know. It was never serious. We mainly fucked, and I took her to prom. Guess we stopped dating when we started fucking other people, too. Then she met her husband, Trent, and we just stopped completely."

I love Trent.

Seriously. It was getting pathetic, how relieved I was to hear Edie was married.

Bane used the neighborhood's remote nonchalantly—like it wasn't illegal for him to have one—and eased his truck in front of my house, cutting the engine. I stayed put in my seat, half-wishing he'd forget that I was there and decide to take a spontaneous nap.

Yeah. That was very likely.

"Umm…" He looked at me incredulously, silently questioning why the hell I was still there.

"Will you be at Café Diem tomorrow?" I asked. He turned fully toward me, resting his elbow on the steering wheel. His hair was messily thrown into a bun, and he looked so youthful and so gorgeous I wanted to cry.

"Maybe."

I swallowed, changing the subject. "You know, I have a tattoo, too."

I was blabbing. But I didn't want him to go. I didn't want him to roll someone else between his sheets. Didn't want his hard inked thigh pressing against someone else's sex. I could have died just thinking of his full lips skimming the jawline of a paying customer.

He smirked. "Show me."

I turned around, gathering my long hair up into a ponytail. I felt his eyes on my neck. My eyelashes fluttered, my eyes hard on the row of palm trees facing the Morgansen estate through the passenger window. I waited for Bane to react. I felt his fingers brushing my ink. Trailing down to my spine, further south to my waist. He clutched my hip bone, and not gently. His mouth pressed against my tattoo, and it was warm and perfect against the roughness of his beard on my skin, just like I'd imagined earlier in the bathroom. A breathy grunt escaped me the moment his lips touched my flesh.

"Saw it before," he whispered.

"You did?"

He nodded into the curve between my shoulder and neck. "At the beach. A few years ago. Red bikini. Cherry-patterned."

I remembered that day. What surprised me was that he remembered me. I licked my lips, waiting for him to continue.

"I was going through some shit that got me thinking. On the brink of stopping the whole escort bullshit for a hot second. I thought that quote was aimed at me. I've always been a Pushkin fan. Well, actually, my mom and wannabe stepdad—they were never married—liked him. They're, like, mega-Russian. Anyway, it seemed like a sign. Like the universe was screaming something at me, and I didn't speak the language. I was gonna hit on you, but then you crawled into this pasty fuck's arms, and I realized it wasn't a sign. It was a big fuck-you from God for thinking I could be something else. Or, you know, someone else's."

I twisted back to face him, inwardly inviting, praying, begging for him to break his rules and ruin this. Ruin us. Because once his lips were on mine, it was on. We were no longer friends. Or enemies. Or two lonely skies—one empty and starless like me, one full of lights. One hidden by walls and the other by ink and a beard. We'd just be free to be.

We were looking at each other now. He was inching closer into surrender, and I wanted his defeat.

"You're poisoned. Sheltered. Yet you're no Snow White. Wanna know why?"

"Why?"

"Snow White waited for the prince. You'll be the one saving yourself in this story."

I blinked at him, thinking about what my dad used to say, his accent thick, almost as strong as his words.

"You don't need a prince, princess. You need a sword."

Bane had my back. He believed in me, and that made me believe in myself. My body was saturated with hope. "You can be my sword," I said quietly. God. That was pathetic. What if he couldn't? What if he didn't want to be?

He brushed my cheek with his thumb. His eyes crinkled. They were expressive. Real. Older with his experience. "I'm afraid I'm going to wound you if I'm not careful."

"You're not your father, Roman."

"Maybe I'm not, but it still doesn't make us right for each other. I'm your boss and one of your only friends. I'd be taking advantage of you if I laid a finger on you. Tell me you understand that, Jesse."

I knew he was holding my faith in his callused hands, and I understood where he was coming from. I needed to gain independence for us to be equal.

"I'm going to make this job my bitch," I said.

"I don't doubt you."

"But I haven't been kissed in…" Nine hundred and three days, four hours, and twenty-four seconds. Since my eyes had met the red dot of the recorder while I lay underneath Emery. Since my fate had been sealed. I cleared my throat. "In a long time."

"You will be kissed by a lot of men. A lot of men I'd love to punch in the face. A lot of men who aren't me."

Recognizing that I was begging, I scooted away from him, my butt touching the passenger door. I needed to leave, and I was going to despite not wanting to. I didn't want him to go to anyone else. It was greedy and selfish and uncalled for, but it was the truth. I wanted Bane for myself.

"I don't want you to sleep with anyone else."

He smiled bitterly. "You can't always get what you want."

"I know," I grumbled, waiting one more minute for him to say something more. To take it back. He didn't. I threw the door open and hopped out. I wanted to be mad at him for the way he'd reacted, but he was right. From the outside, it might look like he was using me, had I slept with him. I raced toward my house, refusing to look back. Maybe it was for the best if he didn't show up at Café Diem tomorrow morning.

"Hey, Snowflake," he hollered from behind me. I stopped but didn't turn around.

"Care to explain why you came out of that bathroom all flustered today?"

I put my hand on the door handle, twisted it, and walked in, leaving him high and dry. I thought I heard the thump of his head hitting the leather headrest behind him before I slammed the door and wasn't surprised.

He wanted me to feel empowered.

And that's what I was going to be.

That night was the first in months when sleep came. And with it, the nightmare I'd been avoiding.

It felt like a memory more than a dream.

A black, empty room. A figure of my slightly younger self, curled in a corner, on a couch. I watched the entire thing like I was watching TV, outside my own body.

Young Jesse was reading a book. She flipped the pages, munching on a lock of her hair. Then the scent came to me. Alcohol. The kind my dad used to drink. Vodka. And with that scent, an intense fear that intensified in my gut.

A shadow floated over my figure. A man. I couldn't get a good look at him. His back was to me, but he was facing young Jesse.

His back.

His back.

His back.

That's why I did it. That's why I took pictures of backs.

It was because of this man.

But who was he?

The Jesse in my dream dropped the book to her lap and stared back at him. She looked about ready to jump up and run away, and I wanted her to. Badly.

The man took a step toward me. Her. Us.

She dragged my body to the corner of the couch.

"No," she said. "Please. I know I shouldn't be here, but I promise I won't come back if you let me go."

My brain ordered my body to move. For my eyes to open. I wanted to get out of the dream before it consumed me. I wanted to get out before I remembered something I was pretty sure there was a good reason for me to forget. The only thing I could feel was my eyelids fluttering in REM. My body was frozen, my mind reeling.

Move. Wake up. Get the hell out of bed right now.

The man inched closer, and she curled inside herself, much like I had after what Emery, Nolan, and Henry did to me.

I wanted to kick my legs. To fall off the bed.

The scent of vodka pierced my nose, settling in my gut.

I finally managed to open my mouth, but nothing came out. Not a whisper, not a scream.

Somehow, I managed to grip one post of the bed and straighten myself up, gulping the morning sun and cracking my eyes open. Panting hard and dripping cold sweat, all I could do was turn around to the pin board behind me and flatten my hands around it, frantically looking for this man's back. I couldn't find it.

I put on my Keds, finger Taser, and black hoodie and went out for a run.

This time, I didn't stop until my knees hit the concrete.

CHAPTER ELEVEN
BANE

I spent the next few days dragging my ass to business meetings, surfing with Beck, and sulking like a little bitch. Everything and everyone annoyed the shit out of me. My friends. My mom. My beard. I was even pissy at Edie just because she reminded me of my last conversation with Jesse.

Jesse, whom I'd been ignoring religiously for the past couple of days; I'd been avoiding Café Diem just because I knew seeing her would make me start a world war.

I knew it was a dick move, but now that she was getting better at the whole life-ing gig, I definitely needed to put some space between us to make sure it wasn't my cock she was riding the next time her crayon-blue eyes flicked at me beguilingly. As it was, I was entering dangerous territory by spending the advance Darren gave me like that shit was guaranteed.

New furniture for the hotel? Ka-ching.

New plumbing for Café Diem? Ka-ching.

New asshole Darren's lawyers were going to tear me if they found out I broke our deal, touched the Untouchable, and was now around a million bucks indebted to him? Ka-ching, ka-ching, ka-fucking-ching.

Truth was I didn't think I had more power over Jesse than she had over me.

She had plenty of power over my ass. I was just a damn good con who knew how to hide it.

And power was a game I knew all too well. Once upon a time, my mom had dated a dude who'd stuck around long enough for me to actually remember his name. Artem. Russian. Well, obviously. Artem was not a piece of shit in the grand scheme of things. Maybe I'm not giving him enough credit. He was actually a father to me without doing the whole parenting crap. One thing he did was teach me how to play chess. The rules of chess were very simple: While it was true that the king was the most important piece in the game, he was also the weakest. The queen was the most powerful, and you best not forget that if you wanted to get ahead in life.

Jesse was pretty much the only pussy in this town that was completely forbidden to me, and yet I found myself craving her more and more. It was a combination of a few things. Her defiance, her quiet strength, her wit, and her compassion toward others.

I found myself trudging to Café Diem despite my best efforts because I wanted to make up for not checking on her on her first day. And the day after. And the one after it.

It's okay to judge me. I'm fucking judging myself, too.

It was surreal. Opening the door to my café without wanting to. Strolling between the busy tables without meaning to. Parking my ass on the stool by the counter, in front of Jesse and Gail, knowing I should be somewhere—hell, anywhere—else.

Gail's bald head was shining like a marble, totally in contrast with her feminine, round face, and she wore a Stay Weird black T-shirt, red Chucks, and matching nail polish. Her lips were powder-pink against dramatic makeup. Jesse was wearing something, too, though I was too mesmerized by her moving, pouty lips to notice what it was.

"Tell me more about him," Jesse probed, so focused on Gail she didn't notice me. But Gail sure did. And she did that little let's-fuck-things-up smirk of hers before she turned around back to Snowflake for an answer.

"He's nice, I guess. Kind of strange, but that's hardly a fault in my book." Gail wiped steamy mugs fresh out of the dishwasher with a cloth and arranged them neatly behind her against the white, exposed-brick wall. She'd better not have been referring to me because not only was I not nice or strange, but I also was her fucking boss.

"Hale is super hot, though. Plus he's like this crazy philosopher dude. And he never hits on anyone, so he obviously likes you," Gail singsonged, her words shooting straight to my veins, heating my bloodstream.

Hale? Fucking Hale was here? Hitting on my Jesse? I mean, Jesse. Not mine. She wasn't mine. But the small hole that opened in my chest didn't agree with that last statement.

"Oh, I don't date. I was just wondering what his story was. I caught him staring at me the other day. He wore the same FREE tank today. I just wondered what his deal was." Jesse used her hip to shut a stainless-steel fridge underneath her where we kept the crushed ice. She prepared a smoothie for a surfer chick at the cash register. I was in awe of how natural Jesse looked behind the counter. A part of me had still believed that Snowflake wouldn't be able to fully settle into her job, and it was still early, but damn, she looked… normal. Although I was happy for her, a small, crazy, petty-ass part of me was pissed. Pissed that she no longer needed me like she'd thought she did.

I mentally started listing reasons why she needed to stay in the picture. My picture.

I gave her a job with flexible hours. I gave her security. I humored her with whatever she needed. But I also told her I was going to fuck other people. She not only accepted that but also seemed to fit right into her role as a barista. Not that it bothered me that she didn't need me as much as she thought.

Okay, yeah, it did bother me.

And it bothered me that it bothered me because what kind of

asshole wants others to be dependent on them simply to keep them close?

Me. That's who.

"Famous Last Words" by My Chemical Romance played over "Crystallize" by Lindsey Stirling (we had a DJ drop ready-made music weekly because we couldn't decide on playlists we liked), and Gail dug her phone out of her back pocket.

"Whoa!" My super emo employee held her cell phone in the air, her mouth forming into an O. I was still pretending to browse through my phone, pinching my eyebrows like it was important, and cursing Hale for figuring my shit out. I was 99 percent sure he'd worked out my so-called angle and had decided to piss me off by hitting on the girl I had my eye on.

"Dude! Hale just texted me. He asked for your number. What do I do?" Gail squealed. Jesse's eyes widened, as did her smile, and I wanted to die a thousand deaths.

You stab him in the face and then hand him over to me to finish the job.

Snowflake punched the blender's button to buy time. I wanted so badly to kiss her for it. She was flattered, sure, but she wasn't going to hand over her number so fast. Hell, she'd barely given it to me, and I'd courted her ass for weeks. But that didn't change the fact that there would be more Hales. More good-looking, smooth-talking assholes who would try to hit on her now that she was in plain sight, looking delicious and alive.

Snow White had woken up, and a prince was on his way, probably riding in a white Tesla.

There was always a fucking prince to rain on the villain's parade.

The blender stopped. Jesse plucked it out of its hub and slapped the bottom as she poured the pink smoothie into a tall cup.

"Jesse? Should I give him your number?" Gail's thumbs were already moving on her screen, and I wondered how much she would hate me if I broke them.

Say no.

"Sure."

Fuck.

At the risk of becoming the douchiest dipshit to ever set foot in Todos Santos—a goddamn mission, considering the average income per household and number of entitled teenagers in this place—I decided to stay the fuck out of this conversation and actually found it in me to allow Jesse the time to give Gail her number. Not only did I successfully manage not to detonate with anger while Gail repeated it aloud while typing it back to Hale, but I also chose the moment after Gail tucked her phone into her jeans to make myself known.

By the way, did I mention that Hale was a dead man? No? Because that was the case.

"How are my favorite ladies?" I flashed my come-hither smirk. See? Casual. What was that twitch in my eyelid? Not a stroke, that's for sure.

"Good question. That's roughly eighty-five percent of the female population of SoCal, so you better start an online questionnaire to save time," Jesse said sweetly, sliding the smoothie to the girl in the wet suit. I'd walked right into that one, so I permitted her the moment to bask in Gail's giggles.

One point to the girl with the Pushkin tattoo, zero to the asshole who was pissing all over her hard-earned trust.

The surfer chick rolled two dollars into the tip jar and then winked at me, sucking hard on her straw. Jesse followed that silent exchange, and that made me feel better about shit. Kind of.

"Work's good so far?" I ignored Jesse's spunk. She placed her elbows on the counter from the other side, and it didn't escape me that she looked confident and radiant and fucking edible. I zoned in on her again, realizing she wasn't wearing her usual black hoodie. She must've pulled shit from the depth of her closet because she looked…fresh. Colorful, even, with plaid red leggings that were tight everywhere, her trademark Keds, and a long yellow T-shirt with two skeleton hands giving the finger. She looked delicious and alive, and I suddenly felt both possessive and protective of her.

"Great. Thank you. Did you surf today?"

"Did you breathe today?" I challenged.

She smiled. "Yes."

"Yeah, I surfed today." I grabbed a bottle of sparkling water from behind the counter and unscrewed the cap, taking a swig. "You should learn how to surf. You'll love it. It's a lonely sport. A lot of shutting up involved."

The thought occurred to me out of nowhere. It meant more time with Jesse and—even more important—more time with her while she was wearing either a bikini or a wet suit. A huge win for my libido, a terrible loss for my balls. It only took one look at her to know that plan had flushed down the drain. She looked like I'd offered her a threesome with Shadow.

"No, thanks."

"'Cause?" I snapped my gum in faked boredom.

She looked down at her shoes, clutched her stomach through the yellow fabric of her shirt, and then shook her head. "It really doesn't matter, Bane."

"Call me Roman."

"Why?"

Because no one else does, and I need something about us to feel different.

Of course, I didn't actually entertain myself with the idea of saying something quite so Kate Hudson film-ish. I shrugged. "I don't know. Just sounds weird coming from your mouth. You didn't know me in high school."

Bull, meet shit.

I stuck around for the remainder of her shift. I tried to tell myself that I needed to supervise my own coffee shop, but the truth of the matter was I didn't want any more Hales to show up and hit on her ass. I didn't actually think for a second that she was going to go out with him. But Hale, like his hair, was a red flag. Another guy would come, soon. He would look wholesome, and she would take a chance. Why wouldn't she?

I sat in the corner for a while and pretended to work on some numbers. I hated numbers, though I was good with them. Every time I looked up, Jesse was busy. Finally—fucking finally—at one in the afternoon, she loitered by the coffee machine, flipping songs in our playlist. I moved my ass in her direction, watching her back, her neck, that tattoo that peeked back at me now that her hair was gathered into a messy bun on top of her head.

"No one touches the playlist," I said coolly. "That shit is cherry-picked by a Swedish indie music producer. No one wants to hear your Taylor Swift songs."

I was an asshole. She didn't like Taylor Swift, and I knew it.

"Jesus H, dude!" She turned around, jumping at the sudden intrusion. She'd said "dude." She never said "dude." Hell, I sometimes forgot Jesse was a twenty-year-old. Actually, not really. Her birthday was next week, and I was hyperaware of that. Because of the deal and everything, of course.

"Come with me." I motioned with my head to the storage room. I wasn't going to risk another public meltdown. Jesse was good at handing me my own ass in public. And I wanted to talk to her about something sensitive. Namely—how we couldn't be rubbing each other's privates anymore.

She followed me silently. I felt her steps a foot from mine. Darren was going to shish-kebab my head *Game of Thrones*–style if I touched her. Besides, there was a bigger plan.

A bigger endgame.

The door behind us closed, and because my dick didn't get the memo that I was not sixteen anymore, I had some serious wood to take care of. My cock was so hard the slit stared directly at my face, only Jesse couldn't see it because I still wore surf shorts. But it was just shorts, and I was normally morally opposed to any kind of underwear on men or women, so she could make out my hard-on if she simply looked.

Which she didn't.

Thank fuck.

She hopped on top of a crate of orange juice gallons and folded her arms over her chest, dangling her legs. The light was murky and shitty, and she looked even more beautiful now that I could clearly see her imperfections under the harsh-yellow bulb. Her eyes were tired and red. Her mouth was curved in sad dissatisfaction with life. And the freckle under her left eye stained her otherwise pristine skin.

I needed to stop fixating and start fixing. I took her hand in mine. Wasn't that supposed to be the thing you did when you wanted to be sympathetic? Hold someone's hand? I'd never been in this position before. I mean, I'd broken plenty of bad news, but I never felt bad about breaking it, if that made sense.

Okay, now I was definitely stalling.

"Repeat after me, Snowflake: The queen is more powerful than the king."

Her eyes were on mine, and the passion in them surprised me. It was like she knew what I was talking about. Maybe she was good at chess, too.

"The queen is more powerful than the king."

I took her face in my hands, knowing the natural thing to do was to crash my lips against hers and see my plans and dreams bursting into flames.

We can't touch each other anymore. Not even a peck on the cheek.

Only I didn't say that. I didn't even think that all the way. Instead, I asked, "What's the story with the surfing? You won't do it?"

I thought she was going to tell me she didn't like displaying her body after what had happened—which was fair enough—but I never expected her to silently lift her shirt and show me that.

"That" being her scars.

Purple and deep and taunting.

Slut

I felt my throat bobbing but couldn't feel the swallow. Her top was bunched up around her tits. I wanted to yank her to me and hug her. I wanted to kiss that damn scar better. I wanted to lick it and bite it and show her that she was still sexy, with or without it. Actually, especially with it. What's sexier than a goddamn survivor?

But I couldn't touch her, not like that, so I just rubbed her cheek with my thumb and said through my locked jaw, "I'm going to kill those bastards."

As I said that, the realization that I could and should crashed into me. I knew their names. Who they were. Getting their addresses would be embarrassingly easy. The only thing stopping me was my conscience, and that fucker was flaky to begin with, which didn't bode well for them.

She dragged her shirt back down, her eyes searching mine, looking for disgust and disapproval. When she didn't find any, she rubbed her forehead tiredly. "So that's why I don't want to go. I don't want anyone to see this."

"I understand." There were suits that would cover it completely, but even I wasn't emotionally dumb enough to realize the general sentiment. Her whole body repulsed her.

Jesse released a disbelieving laugh, rolling her eyes so I wouldn't see the tears hanging on her lower eyelashes. "It's disgusting, huh? I know."

"Don't," I said, wanting to elaborate but not wanting to admit aloud what I was already beginning to come to terms with—she was gorgeous in the way a lot of girls were, but the demons inside her made her beautiful in a unique, once-in-a-lifetime way.

"But it's the truth." She bit her inner cheek, wiping her eyes quickly. The boom of the bass outside hammered against the door. "My Own Summer" by Deftones. "That's why I'm not really mad about you not wanting me. I get it, Ba…Roman. I get why you wouldn't want messy and scarred."

What the fuck was she talking about?

"Who said I…"

"Did you enjoy whoever you were with last night? And the night before? You must like the variety." She sniffed, jerking her chin up. I'd actually bailed on yesterday's client in favor of getting high with Beck and watching porn. But, of course, I couldn't admit it because then she'd ask why, and then I'd have to answer, and the answer was very fucking clear, even to a liar like me.

She was still sitting on that crate when I turned around, walking toward a tall table where the boxes of coffee capsules stood.

"You want the truth?" I asked, bracing my hands on the surface. Now I needed a goddamn shield to talk to her without fucking her. Great. Things were going just great.

A sound that was closer to a yelp but supposed to be a groan left her mouth. "I'm definitely getting tired of the lies."

"I want your ass. Happy? Want it with the scars. With the fucked-up, tragic story. With every fiber of my body. I want to fuck you and own you and bruise you and save you. But I can't do any of those things. Why? Because you'd hate me afterward, and that's a fact, not a speculation. Mark my words. For reasons I can't tell you right now, fucking you will break you and ruin me. And I may be a bastard, but I'm not the fucking villain."

That was the closest to the truth I was willing to offer her. "So here's the truth, Snowflake—whatever this is, we're going to have to fight it."

I was so tempted to say fuck this shit.

So what if I didn't build the surf park? Mikayla, my cousin, never got a unicorn for her birthday. She'd survived. So would I. Thing was, it was too late for me to back out because I had been busy spending a shit ton of that money on the hotel and fixing stuff at Café Diem, and now I was in debt to Darren. And I really was in no position to be in debt to anyone. I was already drowning in businesses and endeavors, trying to prove God knows what to Lord knows who.

I stared at her face, waiting for her to tell me that she got it. That she understood. She slid down from the crate and shimmied out of her leggings, sliding them all the way to her ankles and then kicking them off, along with her shoes. Her black cotton underwear was next in line. She stood in front of me, her pussy shaved and slick and mouthwateringly delicious, on full display. Then Jesse sauntered to the door flippantly, her round ass swaying from side to side, turned the lock, made the same casual walk to the crate, hopped back on it, and spread her legs, flashing a pink slit of heaven.

"You don't have to touch me to ruin me," she croaked, her tongue sweeping her lower lip.

Let the record show that I tried to resist. Sort of.

I responded in the only way I saw fit.

"Oh, shit."

Over and out.

CHAPTER TWELVE
JESSE

"Oh, shit" sounded about right.

I didn't know where my lack of inhibitions came from. Maybe it was because of the way he'd looked at my stomach, so differently from anyone else. I'd had a handful of people stare at it after the Incident. The doctors. The nurses. Pam. Darren. All of them were horrified and sickened. It was the exact opposite of what I wanted to see on people's faces. I was hoping for an "it's not so bad" look, as opposed to "someone pass the emesis bag." But Roman looked at me like I was still pretty. I could see in the bob of his throat under his bushy beard that he thought more about my flat stomach and curvy waist than he did about the scars that covered them.

And that gave me strength.

I wasn't proud of what I had done—seducing him against his will. But it made some kind of backward logic in my mind that I was the one chasing sex with the most sexual man on the planet, who happened to think us sleeping together was a bad idea.

Maybe it was.

But no one said we needed to touch each other to get off.

Bane looked tortured. I'd never seen him look that way before. He was always assertive, ruthless, and confident beyond belief. Dark energy crackled around him, like he'd been struck by lightning, split in half, and filled with rage. He was simmering, shimmering, and glowing.

He was lusting.

His desire for me empowered me because he didn't take, like all the rest.

Hell, he didn't even ask.

Another reason why he was the perfect sexual partner.

I circled my clit with my index finger, feeling anxious, elated, turned on, and on fire. Yes. On fire. Him watching me ignited every match in the pit of my stomach and had me burning for him like the brightest torch.

I'd seen him around women. They had to be surgically removed from his environment. And I knew all about his affairs. His married and influential lovers. I told him I didn't care, and to an extent it was true. I cared more about healing than about what he did in his recreational time. About being able to writhe under a man without panic tightening around my throat like a coarse rope and my limbs flailing, begging for me to flee.

I needed him inside me with a passion that scared me. A need so basic I wasn't above begging for it.

I slanted my chin up, rubbing my sensitive bud faster and faster. At first, he didn't react. Just stared, like he was trying to calculate his next move, his palms frozen on the table, his eyes ablaze. My heart flipped inside my chest, a warning that this was more than sex for me. I chose not to listen.

I needed him to fix me.

I needed him to make me come.

"What the fuck are you doing, Jesse?" He moaned, his voice so thick with sex that lust dripped between us.

"Seducing you," I said simply. I opened my thighs wider and moaned, knowing that he liked what he saw. Agony colored his face. I looked down, watching his cock swelling in his surf shorts behind the small table. I waited for fear to grip my body, but it never came.

I wanted to slip his shorts off with my teeth, take his thick ridge into my mouth, and show him I wasn't broken. Not beyond repair, anyway. Not like I'd previously thought.

What are you thinking? What are you saying? Do you even know yourself anymore?

But it was exactly who I was. The old Jesse took. She'd demanded and claimed the things she had wanted.

And she came out to play in the storage room.

I pinched my nipple through my shirt, knowing it was puckered and visible even through my sports bra. Normally, I gulped the space Bane allowed me with thirst. He didn't try to change who I was. The Untouchable. But today, I wanted to be taken, to be possessed and devoured. I wanted to show myself that I could do it.

I could be touched.

I could feel.

I could break in someone's arms without feeling broken.

"Jesse," he growled, his forehead falling to the table on a sigh. His breaths were deep, heavy. Like he was losing an inner battle. His knuckles whitened as he tried his best not to flip the table aside and charge toward me. I wanted him to. I didn't care about all those people outside.

"Do you want me?" I coaxed.

"Want you?" The table nearly flew to the other side of the room from the impact of his slap on it. "I'm way beyond want. I'm somewhere between need and desperate. And I don't like that place, Jesse. I don't like it at all."

"Take me, then."

He stared deep into my eyes, like he was trying to communicate something to me, a thought that even sounded stupid in my own head. What would he try to tell me?

"You're not ready." Emotionless. Indifferent. Too bad I didn't buy it for one second.

"Who the hell are you to say?" I grinned.

"Your only lucid friend," he deadpanned, blinking at me slowly. "And I'm not fucking up what we have for a fuck."

"You're a jerk," I groaned.

"Yeah," he said.

"Bane."

"What part of the word 'no' don't you fucking understand?"

All of it, apparently. I didn't understand why we couldn't do it. The attraction was obviously there—I saw it in his eyes. And he was the only man I wanted. The only man I felt safe with. If it wouldn't be him, it wouldn't be anyone—and that thought scared me.

Everyone needed someone. Even the Untouchable.

Lust sizzled between us like fire, hot and heavy and red. I pushed two fingers into myself, spreading my lips and showing him how pink and normal and unscarred I was from within.

His throat bobbed again.

"Tell me you don't want to be the one doing this to me," I hissed, a knot of pleasure tightening in my belly. I trailed my index finger around my clit, watching his eyes sparkle as the pink bud swelled under my touch.

"Jesse…"

I didn't answer, licking my lips as I brushed my fingertips up and down my slit. I did it a few times and then opened my palm and offered it to him from across the room. He stared at my fingers, glistening with my need for him.

"I'm ready," I whispered.

He shook his head but didn't have it in him to utter the rejection aloud.

"Fine. I'm sure Hale will do what you are hesitant to."

I didn't know where it came from. Maybe it stemmed from the fact that I saw Bane's jaw jerking every time Gail mentioned Hale's name. In all honesty, I knew I would never date Hale or lead him on, but I felt like all Bane needed was a push. If he really didn't want me, he'd be happy for me to move on with his friend.

But if he wanted me for himself…

"It's okay if you don't want to touch me, Roman." I dipped a third finger into myself, rolling my head against the wall behind me. "I can already feel you everywhere."

Bane straightened up, pushed his surf shorts down just enough to take out his cock, and squeezed it hard. Something glinted, and I almost fell off the crate. He was pierced. The Prince Albert on the tip twinkled like a royal diamond. He began to pump himself punishingly, and I noticed how his shaft was fat and big everywhere. And beautiful. Jesus, he was beautiful. I wanted it in my mouth, and I didn't even care that I'd never agreed to do that to Emery. I didn't care about anything at all other than Bane.

"Let's start over. Take your fingers out, and push one in very. Fucking. Slowly. Now." His voice changed from pissed off to commanding and cruel. I did as I was told, pushing one finger into myself and rubbing my clit back and forth with my thumb.

"No one said anything about your clit. Fuck yourself for me, but not enough to come. Because this is how I feel, Jesse, when you torture me."

"I don't enjoy torturing you." Our eyes met, and what passed between them was pure magic, like fireworks exploding all at once in multicolor. I was going back to watching his beautiful cock being milked in his iron fist in just a second, but I needed this message to hit home. "I'm inviting you to do anything you want to with my body."

"Fuck." He pumped harder, squeezing his eyes shut. "How wet are you?"

"Soaking."

"Show me."

He opened his eyes, and I pulled my finger out slowly. It was coated with my heat.

"Suck on it."

"You suck on it."

"If I come over there, I'll bite it off. Just—" He sucked in a sharp breath, nearly begging. "For once in your life, do something you're asked to do, Jesse."

I did, but only because it felt good to see him like that, dangling off the cliff of self-control, ready to crash and burn with me.

"Oh, Snowflake. What the fuck am I going to do with you?"

"Pounding me like the pavement would be a good start." I grinned, and he let out a tortured laugh. The base of my spine tingled at the sound of his coarse voice. This man could slice you into ribbons with his words alone. I wanted so badly to know what he could do with his hands and arms and teeth. With his entire gorgeous body.

"Three fingers," he ordered. I complied, dipping three fingers into myself, the stretch painful and delicious at the same time. He pumped himself harder, one hand bracing the table—the coffee capsules on top of it dancing in rhythm with his thrusts—and the bulgy bicep of his other arm flexing with every stroke.

I bit down on my lower lip and pushed four fingers into myself, knuckle-deep, teasing the hell out of him.

"Jesse." I saw his resolve not to touch me as it unraveled, string by string, tattered between us on the floor.

"I'm so wet." I arched my back until it hurt, fingers still inside me, the base of my palm squeezing into my sex.

He darted toward me, still stroking himself furiously. I loved seeing him this way, vulnerable with need. And it was when he showed me his weakness for the very first time that I realized I was already halfway in love with him. With us. That the only thing I needed to push me off the edge and into the arms of complete obsession was for him to just…touch me. Feel me. Claim me.

Bane positioned himself between my legs, stroking his cock inches from my hand, plastering his sticky forehead to my damp one. His fine blond hair mixed with my thick raven locks, and the tips of our noses brushed, but we didn't kiss. We wouldn't kiss. Not because I couldn't bring him to it, but because I chose not to break him all the way.

And having that choice? It felt good.

"I can smell your pussy on your breath." He licked his lips, his hot tongue almost touching my mouth.

"Yeah?" I croaked.

"Yeah." He stared down at my mouth, his eyes heavy, his lashes thick. "It doesn't smell like green apples or rain. It smells like a needy cunt, my favorite food category in the entire world. And I can't have you."

The way he said that made me want to laugh. Like he'd made a promise. Like I was forbidden. Maybe to him, I was. I couldn't fault him for that. People said that I was damaged. Fragile. Complicated. They weren't wrong.

"But you want to." I slid the tip of my nose down the length of his, and he let out a shaky breath. Our knuckles touched every time I pushed my fingers into myself and he stroked his cock, roughly pulling the PA as he ran his hand over the tip. My hand briefly brushed the velvety length, and my eyes rolled in their sockets. One time, our fingers lingered together a second longer, sending jolts of electricity to the back of my skull.

"I need to," he said.

"What do you have to lose, then?"

"Too fucking much. Come for me, Snowflake."

We were thrusting, panting, breathing into each other's mouths without crossing an invisible line. The room around us was cluttered with cardboard boxes and beverages and industrial fridges, and yet my soul felt light at that moment. A shudder ran through my spine down to my toes when my orgasm hit me for the second time in a week. I felt it bone-deep, slicing through me, reminding me what sex was all about.

Pleasure. Power. Control.

"Shit, I'm coming, too," he panted. We were so close. Physically and otherwise. I pushed against him at the same time his cock began to jerk in his hand, and he found his release. He yanked my shirt up and came all over my scar, strings of white cum decorating the word I wished I could forget.

And yet I didn't feel dirty.

Our eyes met, his cum between us, my fingers wet with my arousal. He took my hand, brought it to his hot lips, and kissed my knuckles, never breaking eye contact. The way he held me—clutched my fist in his, almost brutally—showed me how he felt. He was no longer calculated, good-natured Bane. He was the devil I'd heard about. The man I was supposed to fear.

"The queen is the most powerful piece," he hissed. "Don't let the pawns bring you down."

I wanted to ask him if he was my king.

Because I knew how to play chess very well.

But the answer was crystal clear to me.

Roman "Bane" Protsenko was my knight. The piece of the chess game that needed to be moved sooner than the pawns, the bishops, and the queens.

The piece that could have saved me, had he just approached me on that beach the day he'd seen me with Emery.

The day Emery had pulled me close and whispered into my ear, "And for my next trick, baby, I'm going to take your virginity."

CHAPTER THIRTEEN
BANE

I took my mom out for lunch the next day.

The entire time, she stared at me across the table like I had an ulterior motive or some shit. We were at a seafood restaurant, sitting on the balcony overlooking the golden, pulsating sand and endless ocean. She had the lobster, and I opted for fish tacos and a scowl from hell. I couldn't erase it even if I tried, which, for the sake of full disclosure, I didn't.

"What's going on?" she asked with her mouth full when my frown deepened. "What's up?" I flicked my Wayfarers down and watched the water with the kind of longing only surfers could relate to.

"Nothing's up." Other than my cock every time Jesse breathed in my direction. Naturally, I chose to omit that from my answer. Mamul and I were close. But not, thank God, that close.

"Is everything okay?" She patted the corners of her mouth with a napkin.

"That's another version of 'What's going on?' I'm still fine."

"I'm just wondering why you took me out for lunch," Mamul said honestly, pushing her half-full plate toward me and patting an invisible bump in her flat belly. She took another sip of her wine. I was about to tell her just what it was about when she added, "Oh, Roman. Please tell me you didn't get anyone pregnant."

"Fuck, Mamul, are you ever gonna stop asking that?"

"Don't curse."

"Don't be insane, then."

"You still haven't answered my question." The entire conversation was in Russian. At least I had this going for me. My mom didn't know my dick was for hire—or if she did, she hadn't said anything—but she was always worried I'd end up getting someone pregnant. I was half-tempted to tell her I needed to buy shares at Durex I was being so safe. I finished the last bite off my plate and took whatever she'd left. I could hoover two more plates without batting an eyelash. I washed the food down with my beer.

"I didn't get anyone pregnant." Although it should be said that coming on Jesse's stomach and watching my cum drip right down her slit wasn't exactly Family Planning 101.

"What is it, then?"

The waiter appeared with the bill, and I took the opportunity to tuck my credit card in and stall. Normally, I had designated my Friday evenings for takeout with Mom. It was the one evening where I didn't entertain anyone and focused on pursuing the heart of the one woman I actually gave a fuck about. It was easier to chill at home and watch one of her weird Russian shows than to book a place and see all the desperate wannabes of Todos Santos flocking to the local restaurants and bars. Her crack was the Russian version of *Big Brother*. That shit was crazier than a condomless party at an unlicensed brothel. Every five minutes, a huge fight would break out. My mom would *tsk* in horror, but I knew she secretly enjoyed it. And I enjoyed watching her enjoy it. Anyway, we rarely hung out in public together, so her suspicion wasn't completely unwarranted.

We stood up, and I laced her arm in mine. "I need help."

"Is it drugs?" She gasped, going for the next best thing after surprise pregnancy. I let my jaw clench without snapping at her last comment. Yes, I was a saint. And yes, she was forgiven.

"Actually, I need help choosing a gift, but thank you for the vote of confidence."

"A gift for who?"

"That girl I told you about. It's her birthday."

"The rape victim?"

The word almost made me flinch. I hated that Jesse was reduced to this. Least of all by my mother. A flashback of that scar zinged through my mind. The bastards were going to pay. It wasn't a promise but a simple fact.

"Yeah. Her."

"Do you have an idea what she likes? Where to start?"

I did, and that worried the hell out of me.

We went to Vicious's fancy-ass mall and browsed the stores, which, any man could tell you, is the equivalent of throwing your time down the shitter after kissing it goodbye. I'd never shopped for a gift before. I mean, I had. I wasn't a crappy boyfriend. I got Edie gifts all the time. But I always did the usual thing of getting her gear or a new surfboard whenever it was time to celebrate whatever shit date society deemed as important. With Jesse, it was different. I didn't want to give her something she needed; I wanted to give her something that would show her that she didn't need anyone but herself.

Jesus, what?

By the time I escorted Mom back to her car, she looked like she needed a two-week vacation on a Caribbean island. I may have taken the task a little too seriously, but since I couldn't exactly show Jesse how I felt about her with my dick, I figured a gift was a good place to start.

"You chose the perfect present." Mom swiveled to face me, flattening her palm over my chest and smiling up at me. Her sensible Prius was parked behind her, ready to take her back to the office building where she accepted clients as a star child therapist. "I'm so proud of you, my sun."

"Damn straight you are. You thought I was a drug-addicted, deadbeat dad just an hour ago. Bet you're feeling pretty awful about yourself right now."

She swatted my chest and laughed. "Does that mean I get to meet her soon?"

I gave it a second of thought. "She is not big on people. I'll ask."

"Neither are you. Maybe that's why you like each other so much."

"Maybe."

Maybe it's because I promised to like her, didn't understand just how much I would, and now was in too deep.

"By the way, how's the hotel going? And the surf park? Are you going to bid on that?" Mamul fished her sunglasses from her handbag, her hand already on the door handle of her car. I very rarely talked business with my mom. First of all, she didn't particularly care for the specifics. She was just happy I owned something that was not a contagious STD or a lengthy criminal record at the age of twenty-five. Second of all, I dreaded the day my mom would ask me how, exactly, I funded all of my business ventures because the answer was less than impressive. I shoved my hand inside my pocket, fingering the joint I knew I was going to smoke the minute she turned around. I'd fucking earned it, gift-shopping for a chick I hadn't even slept with.

But you came close, asshole. And also: all over her stomach.

"It's going well. I'm refurbishing the hotel and will probably put an offer on the land when it's available for auction. Why're you asking?"

"Now who's the skeptical one between us?" Her smile stroked my cheek. I swear it did. "Just wanted to see how you are doing."

"Are you going to see Luna Rexroth today?" Luna was Edie's stepdaughter. Edie was crazy about her. Luna had come to my mom twice a week since she was practically a baby. She'd decided the whole talking gig wasn't for her early on, but it was my understanding that she was talking to Edie, Trent, and my mom. Only a handful of words, so I guessed she still classified as a basket case at her school. Poor kid.

"Be good to your girlfriend." Mom smoothed my wrinkled shirt, tucking my shark-tooth necklace into it. The doctor–patient privilege did not extend to the therapist's son, apparently.

"She's not my girlfriend," I spat, watching her slipping into her car and sliding her sunglasses on with a smile.

She looked up to the sun, pointed at it, and said, "Sometimes the sun is a liar. Sometimes it's out, even though it is cold."

I opened my mouth to say something, but nothing came out.

Later that day, I headed to the beach to train Beck.

I'd like to say it was solely for the purpose of preparing him for the looming competition I was sponsoring, but I was trying the whole honesty thing to better myself and such, so I should probably mention that I knew that Hale was going to be there and I had some unfinished business with the fucker. Namely: Jesse.

I found Beck, Hale, and Edie sitting outside Breakline, her surf shop. She was waxing her surfboard on the sand in a little white bikini, and from afar, I could see the uncanny bulge peeking above her bikini line. Pregnant.

Every now and again I asked myself how come Gidget wasn't knocked up yet, and honestly, I was surprised they'd lasted seven years before deciding to give Luna a sibling. Edie was a nurturer by nature. Either way, I was happy for her. I knew she hadn't said anything to anyone because I would be the first person outside her immediate family she'd tell, so I kept my mouth shut. Hale was painting old surfboards shirtless, and Beck was already in his wet suit, reading something on his phone—it better had been his competitors' stats because the asshole was too chill and I'd put some big money on his gig.

"Douchebags, Dudette," I greeted, dumping my surfboard on the sand next to Beck's Firewire. He had the sickest surfboards, but that came with the territory of spending his entire paycheck on them.

Edie looked up from her board and smiled, squinting her eyes under the sun. "What's in the bag?"

I was dangling the bag with Jesse's present in my hand absent-mindedly and hadn't even noticed. Damn. "The necessary tools to castrate Hale."

Beck and Edie laughed. Hale didn't. He knew exactly why I was pissed at him. I cocked my head sideways, my smirk sending an arrow of venom all the way across to him.

"A word," I said.

"I have a feeling I'll be hearing a lot more than one and none of them will be to my liking," Hale groaned but followed me into the store. I sauntered to the mini fridge behind Edie's counter and took out a beer. He fell into a donut-shaped beanbag, flicking dirt from his fingernails and looking skyward, as if I was a melodramatic cheerleader who'd just found out he'd liked some other chick's photo on Instagram. I placed Jesse's present on the counter carefully and turned to face him.

"Have you texted her yet?"

"Texted who?"

"Don't fuck with me. I fuck harder. Comes with the territory of doing it for a living."

"I'm not fucking with you. I'm genuinely wondering what you are talking about." He blinked, still playing coy. I didn't know why Hale wanted to get a rise out of me or people in general. It was my personal suspicion that he was bored out of his mind and looking to antagonize people because the two people he wanted so badly to piss off—his own parents—controlled his every move, including his future. He wanted to become an entrepreneur and spend his days bumming around, but it so happened he couldn't have what I had—his hand was twisted into becoming a professor like his dad, so that's what he was going to be.

"What do you think I'm talking about?" Okay, now I was beginning to sound like a cheerleader. *What did you do to me, Jesse? I want my balls back.*

He made a show of rubbing the back of his neck, exhaling loudly. "I don't know. I collected all the protection money a day early. I'm helping Gidget with her shop. I'm just a nice guy doing nice things." He flashed me a toothy, wolfish smirk I wanted to wipe off his face with my boot. "Guess you'll have to enlighten me."

"Jesse Carter." I splayed my fingers over the counter, standing behind it so I wouldn't launch myself at Hale accidentally. Or not so accidentally.

"Hmm. Your new barista, right? Fuck hot." He whistled and then proceeded to bite his fist. I wanted to kill him. But in a mean way. Not a clean bullet to the head. Maybe choke him or throw him into a pit of snakes.

"Have you texted her yet?" I asked again.

"I have."

Where am I going to find so many snakes? "And what did you say?"

"I asked her if she wanted to grab a coffee later. Not at Café Diem, obviously. Somewhere cool." His voice was calm and calculated, as if pissing me off was his mission in life. Did he have any idea what he was messing with? Whom he was messing with? No. Of course not. I'd never been half as possessive of any woman in my life. Even with Edie, whom I very much liked, I didn't particularly care. I'd let her slip through my fingers right into Trent's arms without a fight, knowing they'd needed each other and that I didn't need anyone. Whenever men hit on her, I'd watched with a mixture of pity and amusement. Not in Jesse's case. This felt personal.

"Did she answer?" I never asked questions, let alone that many, but I couldn't stop myself, and that was a problem.

"Not yet."

"She won't," I deadpanned, tossing the beer in the trash without even touching it. "Delete her number from your contacts and never talk to her again."

"What?" He laughed.

"Did I fucking stutter?" My jaw stiffened, and I kicked a can of fresh paint sideways, ready to march over to him and plant a fist in his face.

"Says who?" His smile evaporated.

"Says me."

"And you are…?"

"Are you having an amnesia episode? I'm your fucking boss."

Hale shook his head. "What I mean is, what are you to her? What gives you the right to warn me off? Are you her boyfriend? Brother? Daddy?"

Let the record show that he asked for it.

I rounded the counter toward him, fisted the collar of his shirt, and yanked him so that we were nose to nose.

"She's mine."

"Does she know that?" He searched my eyes, his expression tranquil.

"Yeah." Told you I was a liar.

"Guess I'll have to hear it from her, then."

I released him, letting his body fall like a stone on the beanbag. "Drop it."

"Or what?"

"Or I'm kicking you out of the business and your game will be over. No more Mr. Tough Guy and back to folding shirts at the Gap. Of course, cutting ties with me would mean less pussy and surfing time, but at least you'll get a fifty percent employee discount and can finally stop wearing these fucking Hawaiian shirts."

Yes. I went there. I insulted his clothes. I was officially a chick.

Hale narrowed his eyes, the gravity of my threat sinking in. "You can't do that."

I grabbed his phone next to him and punched in his code—his ex-girlfriend's birthday he was too lazy to change—looking for Jesse's contact as I spoke. "News flash: I can do whatever I want. People come and go. It was Edie in your shoes seven years ago. Then she married a millionaire, and I took Robbie on. Then he moved, and

I employed Ashford. There's always a Hale in the background—an errand boy I split my money with to make sure everything's in check. Don't be fooled by my generosity. I don't need you, and the minute I drop you, you're done here. Stay away from Jesse Carter. I'll ask again—am. I. Clear?" I threw his phone onto his chest after I was done removing her number from its memory.

His jaw locked, and he got up from the beanbag, zigzagging his way back outside. He was blind with rage. I looked up to see Gidget and Beck standing there, looking less than impressed. I'd always been harsh on Hale, but I never went as far as threatening to fuck him over. But things were beginning to change, and not only because of Jesse.

"Was that really necessary?" Beck crossed his arms over his chest, shaking his head.

I ignored him. "Get your surfboard. Time to kill some waves."

When I came out, Edie pulled me by the arm to a corner behind her shack-like shop, and I let her, even though I knew she was going to annoy the crap out of me with whatever was going to fall out of her mouth.

"Is this about Jesse?" She was so annoyed her nostrils were as wide as her eyes.

"Why?"

"Because you act all weird about her. I've seen you with her, Bane. I'm not blind. And I'm wondering…" She licked her lips, staring up at me in a way I couldn't decode. Hopeful? Yeah. She looked kind of hopeful.

"Go on. That's not technically a fucking sentence," I grumbled.

"I was wondering if she knew about your job."

Oh.

Oh.

"She knows," I said. And she did. She also hated it. That was why Hale had her number in the first place. "Don't be dramatic. Everything is under control." Wasn't that what people whose lives were a big, hot mess said? I shook my arm away, flashing a confident smile I couldn't feel, let alone believe. I knew I had no fucking right blocking other guys from dating Jesse when I couldn't do it myself. Nonetheless, I just couldn't stop myself.

"Hale should stay away from Jesse if he wants to keep his dick intact. Actually, feel free to pass this message on to the rest of the male population in this town. By the way"—I leaned down, my mouth on her cheek—"you're showing. Congratulations."

Later that evening, I stared at myself in my bathroom mirror, trying not to flinch.

I gripped the sink to a point of white knuckles, asking myself if I had it in me to do what I supposed I should have done a long time ago.

To let go of the bad shit.

I looked down. Clutched the scissors next to the faucet.

Looked back up.

You're not the bastard who raped your mom, Jesse had said to me this week. But Jesse didn't know all there was to know about me, so really, did her opinion count for shit?

I grabbed the bun on top of my head and cut it, throwing it to the sink and turning on the water with the elastic band still on.

Looked back up. Didn't flinch.

Proceeded with the rest of my task.

Looked up.

Flinched.

CHAPTER FOURTEEN
JESSE

There's an evolution to birthdays. The older you got, the less eager you were to celebrate them. In my case, the Incident had aged me a dozen decades. For the past couple of years, I'd tried to act like it didn't exist. Like I didn't exist. It was easier to pretend nothing was happening because if life happened, I had to take control of it, and I didn't have it in me to do it.

Not until now.

Three years ago, Pam had gotten me a bow bracelet from Tiffany's for my seventeenth birthday, and Darren had shelled out the big bucks for a weekend on a yacht for my friends and me. I invited fifty kids to the party, and some of their parents attended as chaperones, too. "For mingling and networking purposes, although making sure no one gets pregnant is also a priority"—Pam had giggled plastically, feeling blue-blooded like the people of Todos Santos for a hot minute. I was dating Emery back then, and I remember how triumphant she'd felt. She even went back to letting me call her Mom.

It was the year when, for the first time, I skipped visiting my dad's grave and placing the Kit Kat we used to share every morning on his tombstone.

It was the first and last year I truly felt normal, accepted, and popular.

Now, for my twentieth birthday, I decided to go back to the

basics and celebrate by munching on a Kit Kat bar in my room, reading a book that Mrs. B had loaned me.

I opted for not leaving my room, since I didn't have a shift at Café Diem today. Pam and Darren texted me their banal happy birthday wishes. Their messages remained unanswered.

Hannah slid her annual birthday card under my door, and Mayra called. I answered, but only because she monitored my moves so closely, I was afraid she was going to tell Darren and Pam I wasn't making progress, and they would insist on upping my sessions with her.

Bane hadn't called, and I tried not to let it affect me. I tried, but I failed.

At 9:00 p.m., I was already in my bed, my face buried in *Whitney, My Love* by Judith McNaught. I thought I heard something—a soft thud. I looked up from the page. I'd been stuck on the same paragraph for half an hour because my mind kept on drifting toward Roman. How I'd let him drag me back into the world too quickly, too recklessly, and he hadn't even bothered to wish me a happy birthday. I listened closely to the silence. Nothing. My eyes dropped back to the page.

Click.

I glanced at the window. The usual oak tree stood there, staring back at me. I flipped a page, knowing I should pay more attention and that the juicy part was unfolding in front of my eyes, when…

Click.

This time I stood up.

Click. Click.

I paced to the window, climbed onto the seat on my knees, and yanked my window up, slanting my gaze to the back of our garden, which was overlooking Mrs. Belfort's maze. I saw a shadow of a man standing under the tree. His face was turned down, and he was wearing a ball cap. But the stance, height, and attire seemed familiar: cargo pants and a faded black surfer shirt with holes in it.

"Roman?" My eyebrows collapsed into a frown.

"You asleep?"

His voice in my ears felt like a sweet promise, and that's when I realized how much I'd missed him. How much I'd needed him to acknowledge my existence today of all days, even though most of the time I didn't want to remember I was still alive.

"Reading." I cleared my throat, trying to sound indifferent.

"On your birthday? Very rock 'n' roll."

My heart began to drum faster. He'd remembered.

I noticed he was swinging a bag in his hand but didn't want to be presumptuous.

"Why don't you go back to bed? All this rebelling must be exhausting." He was bouncing on the balls of his feet, looking less than his pissed-off, take-no-prisoners self. I wanted him to look up and drink me in with his green eyes no less than I wanted my next breath.

"What?" I snorted.

"Go back to what you were doing, Jesse, and pretend I'm not here. I just wanted to make sure you were in your room. Giving you a heart attack for your birthday is memorable but kind of crappy, even by my very low standards." His face was still down, and that damn ball cap denied me my current favorite view.

I knew I needed to keep my emotions in check with him, but it was easy to slip into infatuation with Bane. All the ingredients were there: funny, charming, confident, and hot as sin.

"You're weird," I grumbled, walking backward, my butt hitting my bed.

I heard him hop onto the metal barbecue grill outside, his boots producing a thump Pam and Darren would never hear because their room was on the other side of the house. I bit back my smile and settled in bed, picking up my book despite knowing I'd never be able to concentrate.

A boot slid against the glass of the kitchen window. I realized that he was climbing up to my room, and my heart was doing an insane dance in my chest, completely drunk, and I wanted to yell at it to stop before we were both going to be sorry.

"Oh, shit." He chuckled breathlessly, and the exclamation was followed by the sound of scrabbling hands against the side of the house.

My smile crumbled. I set the book down. "Are you okay?"

Another puff and scrape. "Fine. My pants are slipping down, though, and my ass is making a grand appearance. Hopefully Mrs. Belfort is not in the mood for some maze watching."

I giggled. "Classy."

"Hey, you haven't seen my ass, lady. Don't slam it before you try it."

"Was trying your ass ever an option?" My heart somersaulted a thousand times a minute. Maybe I was having a heart attack after all. What was happening in my chest didn't seem natural or familiar.

"Close your eyes," he commanded, his voice booming all over my room, so I knew that he was close. I did as I was told. This year, I'd told Pam and Darren not to get me anything. They hadn't. I couldn't fault them for following my request. Besides, last year Darren had tried to give me something—a new flat-screen TV for my room—and I couldn't bear to keep it. I'd called Hannah's son and had him pick it up, since I knew she'd never accept the gift. But whatever Roman wanted to give me—I eagerly wanted to own it.

My eyes were squeezed shut when I heard his boots land on my carpeted floor. My pulse skyrocketed, thudding against every inch of my skin. There was a special thrill in knowing he could be doing anything to me. And that he wouldn't. Because he was decent and fair. Because no matter what he thought about himself, he was good.

"Open." His breath fanned across my face.

I blinked, adjusting to what I was seeing and not entirely believing it was truth. The ball cap was gone.

So was his beard.

And his man-bun.

Bane. All of Bane. His entire beautiful, silky, boyish face in front of me. Clean-shaven and mesmerizing, like Leonardo DiCaprio as Romeo the very first time you see him through the aquarium, and it feels like someone is pinching your heart from within, twisting it evilly on a taunting smirk.

I knew Roman was attractive, but this was different. It was *more*. His jaw was square and strong, but everything about him was utterly youthful. His bee-stung lips and Grecian nose. It was like he was invented to destroy me.

Then it dawned on me.

He'd shaved for me.

Last week I was standing here, in my room, telling him to shave.

So he had. He'd stopped hiding. For me. Gifting me the most important thing in the world on my birthday—his acceptance of who he was and from whom he came.

Realizing it had been at least a full minute and I still hadn't said anything, I opened my mouth. He stared at me expectantly, like I was holding the sky in my hands.

"Is that…a new shirt?"

He raised one eyebrow. "Now who's being an asshole here?"

I fell into my bed, laughing. Roman pretended to punch my shoulder, mounting my body and pinning me to the mattress, while I desperately clung to the waistband of his pants, yanking them back up.

"You said your ass was showing. I didn't think you meant the one that was on your neck." I giggled breathlessly.

"Don't do that." He straddled me fully now, his erection grinding against my stomach, and not by accident. The air swelled between us, full of heavy breaths and hormones and need. I glanced at my door. Locked. Boy, I wanted to do a lot more things that involved gasping.

"Why?"

"Because I have an erection from hell and you almost sliced my balls into pastrami."

I snorted, rolling my groin once, my navel hitting the crown of his cock through our clothes. He flinched and quickly moved away from me, standing up and walking over to the window, pushing it shut. He turned back to me, and we stared at each other.

We'd helped each other tear down the walls, and I hoped, with every fiber of my body, that what we'd find underneath them wasn't rotten.

"I'll ask again—what do you think?" He gestured to his face before grabbing the mysterious bag he'd come with from my window seat.

I scrunched my nose. "I liked you better with the beard and the man-bun."

"Well, too bad because you're going to see this nasty-ass face for a very long time, every day." He plopped down on my bed and handed me the bag. "Happy birthday, Snowflake."

"How do you know that it's my birthday?" I held the bag, wondering if it felt so heavy because it held so many of my hopes and dreams.

"You told me."

"Once. In passing. I didn't mention the date." My gaze clung to the bag like it was going to dissolve into thin air. It was a simple, purple plastic bag. No name or brand on it. I knew Bane, and he wasn't the type to buy a girl jewelry, even if he could afford it. I'd never really liked that Tiffany's bracelet, anyway. Best thing I ever got was the Kit Kat my dad and I shared every morning at the bus stop before I went to school.

"Fine. I looked at your paperwork after I hired you because you'd mentioned it was in September." He rolled his eyes, his head hitting my pillow. Now that he was clean-shaven, he didn't look a day over twenty. I wondered if he knew that and if it bothered him. I ran a hand over his jaw. Velvet and honey.

"I do like it," I whispered. He covered his face with his inked hands, as if the whole situation was mortifying for him, and nudged my knee with his foot.

"Just open your present."

When I shoved my hand in the bag, my fingers found wrapping paper, something round and hard swathed inside it. I tore it apart and stared, awestruck.

A snow globe with a Labrador puppy inside, one that looked just like young Shadow. Flakes raining down on him, fat and lazy and fake and mine. This gift was all mine, and it meant something. Tears filled my eyes.

"Wow. It's…"

"There's more." He cut me off, sitting up straight. His foot bounced on the bed. He cleared his throat, rubbing the tip of his chin and jerking it in my direction. "Look again. There's more than just a snow globe."

I pulled the second present out of the bag. A…wet suit? I examined it with a frown. The room was dim, but I could still see the little details. The waves that adorned the cuffs, the setting sun printed across the chest. It was a full-piece one that was going to cover me head to toe.

He grabbed my wrist and pulled me into his chest, his eyes hard on mine.

"You will never not do something because of the scars they left. Never. You will surf. You will live. Why didn't you report them? Why the fuck are they not in jail right now? They were eighteen when it happened."

My eyes widened. This had taken a wrong turn, fast. I didn't want to get into the story. I didn't even want to know how Bane knew they weren't minors and how deep he'd dug into my case.

"The case is closed, Officer Villegas. Nothing to talk about anymore. Let's go, Jesse."

Pam's words came back to haunt me. I shook my head, trying to swallow the bitter lump in my throat.

"Can we not talk about it?"

"No. We kind of have to."

"Really, Bane? On my birthday?"

"It's Roman. And will you talk about it tomorrow?"

No. "Maybe."

"You let them get away with it."

"I didn't have a choice," I growled. The way I said that, with my eyes burning holes through his newly shaven skin, must have told him he was in no position to talk to me about it. He narrowed his eyes, the fire in them promising the retaliation I was reluctant to seek for myself, and then wiped the anger from his face completely and smiled.

"So how did I do?"

I looked back to the wet suit and the snow globe.

"Great," I bit out, still angry about the sudden change of topic. "Thank you."

"Anything else you want for your birthday?"

I smoothed a hand over the wet suit, smiling at it absentmindedly. "It's more than enough, really. You made my day." *My year.*

He leaned forward, and we were close. Too close. Close enough for me to fantasize about what might happen. Close enough for me to get the wrong idea. I leaned back, afraid I'd kiss him and make a fool of myself.

"What?" I swallowed. His eyes were heavy in the same way they'd been in the storage room, but also different. The agony was deeper, more profound.

We're just a helium balloon waiting to pop, every breath bringing us a step closer.

"You could ask for anything," he enunciated, and I knew what he was shooting for. A kiss. But I was done begging. My father had once said that affection shouldn't be asked for. It is not a reward, but a necessity.

"Anything?" I batted my eyelashes. He leaned closer still, the heat of his body seeping into mine. My chest was tight, my limbs jelly. Everything was backward and weird. Illogical yet made perfect sense.

"Anything." His voice was a soft snarl, his lips inches from mine. And it was tempting, but I had to do it. For my self-esteem. For the way the power was distributed between us in our relationship.

"Then I want you to show me your ass. Seems unfair that the maze got to see it, but I didn't."

It took him a few seconds to recover, jerk away, and stand up, but to Roman's credit, he did it without as much as a grumble.

He lifted a warning finger in my direction before twisting to show me his back. "Is this going to turn into a case where you'll fall so deeply in love with my ass, I will have to file a restraining order against you?"

I braced myself on my forearms, a cocky smile on my face. "I can't commit to an answer, but I'll try my best not to become a stalker."

He shrugged. "Worst-case scenario—it'd be nice to have someone tell me a day before I run out of beer."

He turned around and pulled his cargo pants down, not bothering to twist his head and see my reaction. I gulped. His tight, muscular ass had a skull dripping blood down to his thigh, three skeletons holdings surfboards and smiling, and a third tattoo that said, "Cool Story, Bro."

"Tell me the story," I said. He tugged his pants up and rounded my bed, sliding in again, fitting perfectly next to me like that's where he belonged. We were tucked next to each other.

"I lost a bet."

"You're kidding me." My jaw dropped, but he just pulled one shoulder in an I-fucking-wish shrug.

I blinked, giving him a soft shove. "Who inks something like that on their ass because their friends told them to?"

"Someone who doesn't give two shits and never misses an opportunity to do something stupid," he quipped, tucking a lock of hair behind my ear. I grabbed his hand, dragged it to my mouth, and kissed his open palm. He nearly flinched, and it saddened me. He'd slept with so many women, but I wondered when the last time he'd been kissed on the knuckles, hugged in the rain, or loved the way everyone deserved to be loved.

"You need to respect your body more, Roman. The tattoos. The women. You can say no. You're so screwed up over this." This was his father. This was like the Incident. Mental scars are like Lord Voldemort. They shall not be spoken.

He pretended to flatten the collar of my oversize shirt with his hand, looking down at it when he said, "Tell you what. I'll stop treating my body like it's a frat house if you promise to stop treating yours like it's made of marshmallow and sin. Come surf with me tomorrow."

I laughed. "And if I do?"

"Then I won't get any more stupid-ass tattoos. Pun intended."

"Not fair. You don't have any more space for them, anyway."

He stroked his chin and then pointed at his smooth, shaven face. "I do now."

I swatted his chest. "I'll kill you."

"Trust me, baby. You're already halfway there."

"What does that mean?" I purred.

He looked serious as hell. "It means I can't stay away from you, and at this point, I know I fucking should."

I swallowed but didn't reply.

I was walking the tightrope of not wanting to beg and not wanting him to leave.

Roman asked me to get back to reading, and I did. We were tucked together like sardines while I read the book aloud, finishing the chapter; then I turned off the light, twisted to my corner of the bed, and closed my eyes.

He wrapped his arm around me, and I grinned into the darkness when his cock met my ass again, grinding very slowly, torturing the both of us. My skin tingled and my sex felt achingly empty as his hard six-pack brushed along my back. He was rubbing all against me, and my mouth watered with need.

"Roman…"

He snaked his inked palm around me and muffled my voice by dipping his middle finger between my lips. I sucked hard, hungry for the sweet taste of his last hashish joint and salty manhood. His lips trailed the shell of my ear from behind. "Shh."

My whole body quivered as his hard length dug deeper and deeper between the clothed slit of my ass, and my knees knocked against one another. I was on the brink of the most frustrating orgasm to ever be experienced on earth.

"Fuck me." My voice shook around his finger, the words falling from my mouth before I could stop them. It wasn't me. Not the old Jesse and definitely not the new one. It was a girl who seemed to have been born especially for Bane. Reckless and needy. Desperate and deprived. "Please, just…I feel so empty." Even that wasn't true anymore. Alone, I was empty. With Roman, I burst at the seams.

His callused palm left my mouth, tugging at my nipple through my pj's, and he was touching me, and I was burning like a witch, alive in the fire, my body screaming as I bit my lip to suppress a hard moan.

I reached for the waistband of my pj's, the need for friction tingling between my legs. Bane captured my wrist in his palm and brought it to his lips. I could feel his smile. He whispered, "Bet I can make you come without even touching you."

I snorted. "Cocky much?"

"Evidently." He thrust into my clothed ass.

My eyelids dropped on a heavy sigh as he traced his lips along my ear.

"Can you feel me fucking you with my words?"

I rubbed my thighs together, begging for any kind of roughness between them. It was the sweetest torture, and a part of me was enjoying his cruelty.

"I'd rather you fuck me with something else." Was I really saying those things? I couldn't tell if my heated face was due to embarrassment or because I was simply sweltering under his touch.

"Everybody got the something else. You're getting the never-seen-before version. The one where I actually try to do the right thing. Can you feel me sucking on your swollen pink clit?"

He swirled his cock between my butt cheeks, and I rocked into him, every muscle in my body spasming involuntarily. He was still rubbing against me persistently, in a rhythm I wanted to tattoo into my brain and write into a melody.

Little pants of pleasure began to escape me involuntarily.

"Don't patronize me, Roman. I know what's good for me."

"I'm pinching your clit."

Groan. "Roman."

"Your pussy juice is all over my chin."

Why was he doing this?

The orgasm started at my curling toes, shooting upward like a bullet and exploding between my legs. I tried to loosen my trapped hands from his grip, but to no avail. I came on nothing, barely touched, just from his words. It took me a few minutes to calm down, my pulse floating down slowly like a feather, before I noticed the warm, damp cum sticking my top to my lower back.

He'd come, too. From rubbing off against me.

"I hate you," I muttered, my voice shaking. I'd never known how empty my sex was until I met Roman and realized that I wanted him there. All the time.

"Good night, birthday girl." He planted a soft kiss on the back of my head, dropping his heavy arm on my waist.

For the first time in years, I didn't want to put on my Keds and run from the demons that lurked under my bed at night.

For the first time in my life, I let them sleep with us, inside my bed, in my room, knowing that they were just ghosts of my past.

That they couldn't touch me.

CHAPTER FIFTEEN
JESSE

By the time I cracked a reluctant eye open, Bane was gone.

The space where he'd slept was cold and empty. I blinked away the cobwebs of sleep and felt for the cell phone on my nightstand. It was a new move, one I hadn't practiced in two and a half years. As a teenager, that was the first thing I'd done every morning: check my phone for messages, Snapchat, and Facebook posts. After the Incident, I'd migrated my cell phone to one of my desk's drawers. That's until Roman barged into my life.

He'd left me one message, probably a few minutes after he'd climbed his way down my window.

Roman: Let's talk tonight.

I tried to read it in a casual way. Bane was a casual guy. But I was so pathetically dependent on him that fear trickled into my system. I tried to tell myself no true friend would break a friendship with you the day after your birthday. I replied with a curt "sure" and hopped downstairs, taking two steps at a time.

I was starving. It felt like I hadn't eaten in years. And in a way, that was sort of the case.

"Good morning," Hannah sang from the kitchen, slicing root vegetables for Pam's gross shakes. My mom lived off vegetables,

Botox, and wine. A diet made in Hollywood hell. If Hannah was surprised to see me—which she should have been as I never left my room during the mornings because I slept away the night run's exhaustion—she didn't let it show. "Hungry?" She peered under her lashes.

"Famished." I opened our glass fridge, sticking my head in.

"Pancakes it is, then." I heard her cluck her tongue behind me. Hannah was nice. Too nice for Pam. Darren treated her well, but Pam had conveniently forgotten that she'd been waiting tables not too long ago before Darren had found us, his pretty little strays.

"Please don't bother." I put a reassuring hand on her shoulder, realizing I wouldn't have done that weeks ago, before I met Bane. The forty-something-year-old used her waist to butt me out of the way in front of the fridge. "It's your birthday. Well, technically a day after, but birthday girls deserve pancakes. It's a rule."

It was a rule I was happy not to break.

I sat at the breakfast nook, watching Hannah doing her thing while twisting a lock of hair around my finger and chewing on it. I needed a haircut. No. I'll rephrase—I wanted a haircut. For the first time in years, I wanted to look pretty. Or maybe I was simply ready to be seen. Hannah squatted down to take out a measuring cup from a drawer, and when she turned around, holding the stainless-steel thing in her hand, my jaw went slack.

Me. Sitting on a couch. Reading a book. Everything around me black.

Him. His back to me, just like all the pictures I took ever since the day it happened.

Backs.

Heads.

Necks.

Faceless people.

He held something made out of stainless steel in his hand. Cup? Shaker? It smelled of vodka. His vodka.

"Dad?" I asked. But, of course, it couldn't have been. I loved my dad. I put my half-eaten Kit Kat bar on the table beside me and rose to my feet. "I want to leave."

"No." His hand locked on my wrist. He was sweating. He still had no face. Why didn't he have a face? "No, baby."

I watched the younger version of me as her face twisted with realization. She was not going to get out of that room. Not the same way she'd walked in, anyway.

"Please, I don't want to…"

She didn't get to finish the sentence. He pinned her to the wall like the masterpiece that she was and tarnished her into something empty and hollow.

"Jesse? Jesse? Honey?" Hannah shook my shoulders, and I finally snapped out of it. In front of me was a plate full of thick, fluffy, hot pancakes and maple syrup poured generously on top. Blueberries and cut strawberries made out the number twenty. And I'd officially lost my appetite.

"I made you the good stuff with the Sparrow Brennan mix that costs two bucks more, but your parents can afford it. What's wrong? You seemed out of it." Hannah wiped her hands on her apron, leaning against the counter and pouring herself a glass of OJ.

"Yes. I'm sorry." I smiled, hurrying to stab a fork into the mountain of pancakes and bring a bite to my lips.

I forced myself to eat at least two, knowing how hard Hannah had worked on them, but for the life of me couldn't taste their sweetness.

Something in me told me Mayra could not know about this.

I washed my plate, gave Hannah a hug, and, when she wasn't looking, grabbed the stainless-steel cup and carried it to my room. I put it on my desk, staring at it, lost in thought.

What happened to me?

———

Since I didn't have a shift and Roman hadn't answered me, I decided to pester Dr. Wiese. I called him twice, but he didn't answer. Reluctantly, I walked over to Mrs. Belfort's, my mind still on Shadow. I felt like I'd been neglecting Mrs. Belfort ever since I got a job, and I promised myself I wouldn't be that person. The person all my high school friends turned out to be after the Incident. A user. A leaver. An asshole.

First, I took a lengthy trip by myself in the maze, trying to decode my most recent flashback. Yes, flashback. A chunk of my memory was missing from my brain, and I didn't know how or what had happened to me exactly, but I knew that it had snowballed into a catastrophe that had ended up ruining my life.

I hadn't been a virgin when I'd met Emery.

And whoever took my virginity did it by force.

My dad died around the same time it had happened. I knew, because in all the flashbacks, I looked to be on the verge of adolescence. Twelve, maybe thirteen. Although I loved my father dearly, I couldn't help but wonder—what did I know about him, really?

I knew that he'd cheated on my mom with another woman. That he'd had a lengthy affair. That's why my mom had kicked him out the day he died. But I also knew he'd been nothing but amazing to me. He was the one to teach me how to ride a bike. To take me to school every day. He was the one to wipe my tears when I was sad and make me laugh when I was angry and tuck me back into bed when I had nightmares.

He read me stories about princesses and castles and dragons and always changed the plot so that the princesses saved themselves from the fire-breathing villains.

He spent the extra buck on Band-Aids with the Wonder Woman branding. He made me his special mac and cheese with crushed Doritos whenever I had the flu because he thought I liked it, when really I liked the attention. I liked his standing in the kitchen doing something silly for me.

I liked being loved.

Yes, he was a drunk, with vodka being his drink of choice. I remembered the bite of alcohol when he'd pressed his lips to my forehead when he'd kissed me goodnight.

I'd liked the sharp bite of it. It smelled like home. And I refused to believe that my home had become my hell. That he'd done something to me.

By the time I emerged back from the maze, my head pounded with unsolved questions.

Mrs. B was waiting for me in her usual rocking chair, swaying back and forth, her lips curved in a smile. She was wearing two coats in September, but that was brittle bone disease for you. She seemed lucid, exceptionally calm. She handed me a pair of tweezers, tapping her cheek silently.

"Want me to weed out your whiskers?" I dragged my chair close to hers, waggling my brows. It was best to pluck Mrs. Belfort's chin whiskers under bright sunlight. She said that I'd be getting them too when I became her age, but the thing about being twenty is that you don't actually understand the concept of getting old. You know it's going to happen to you eventually, but you don't believe it. Not really.

I plucked her hair for a while before she said, "Love is art. Some people shut their eyes and refuse to see it. Others visit every museum in the world. Which type do you fall under, Jesse, my dear?"

I blinked, staring at the maze. "I think I'm capable of seeing the beauty in art." I swallowed, looking up at her and plucking another misplaced white hair floating from her chin.

"Good. Good. Because that's the only way you'll get to my age with no qualms. I know what you see when you look at me, Jesse, and I know it mustn't look appealing to you. But understand this—I have no regrets. I lived life fully. Wholly. I loved freely, without doubt or jealousy. Whoever that boy was…" She tilted her newly smooth chin to the maze, her smile spreading to her cheeks. My heart lodged in my throat—she remembered Bane? "That boy cares for you. Be smart and care for him back. No one should live a lonely life."

She looked down at me and smoothed my hair lovingly. Like a mother would. Like Pam should. "Yes, I remember him, Jesse. I have a condition, but I'm still here," she said softly.

I nodded. I was going to tell her I would not let him go. That I would keep Roman for as long as he'd stick around. But then she opened her mouth again.

"I know I have Alzheimer's."

Her words rattled something inside me. Maybe I wanted to believe that there was no connection between the Mrs. Belfort I knew and loved and the woman who had lengthy conversations with her dead husband at an empty dining table.

I swallowed before I answered, "I'm so sorry, Mrs. Belfort."

"I also know that I'm dying. I'm not well, Jesse. Yet no one talks to me about it. They think I don't understand, but I do."

Tears filled my eyes, but I didn't let them loose. It wasn't fair to Mrs. B.

I remembered how much I hated it when people stole my tragedy thunder. After the Incident, I despised every single person I came across who cried for me. If I didn't cry for myself, neither should they. I remembered Detective Madison Villegas at the police station, the night I got out of the hospital and was supposed to give my official statement.

She'd stood in the corner of the room with tears in her eyes, watching as I'd fed them laconic lies that didn't match the mountain of evidence, as if it was her I was hurting.

"What can I do to make it easier for you?" I asked, plucking another stray hair and letting it fall on Mrs. B's wooden porch. I put the tweezers aside and took both her cold hands in my warm ones.

"Call my children. Tell them to come here. Every time I call them, they think I'm crazy. When Imane calls them, they say she is overdramatic. I need to say goodbye."

"You're not going to die," I said. I wasn't sure of what I was saying. I just couldn't bear the idea that she would. Especially with Shadow's blood work still in the lab. There was so much potential of losing everything that had kept me alive the last two years.

"Nobody lives forever." She smiled at me, her eyes glistening. The sun was shining above us fiercely, and she was shivering inside her coats. Her blue-veined hand patted my own. "Don't worry. By the time you're my age, you're tired. I'm ready. I just want to see my children. Please."

I knew right then and there that her kids were going to come to California, even if I had to drag them by their goddamn ears. "Of course. I will call them."

I left shortly after, pretending like everything was okay but internally screaming at her kids. Stomping over to my house, I dialed Dr. Wiese's clinic number again. If they didn't pick up soon, I'd have to pay the office a visit myself. I jammed my key into the keyhole, ready to open the door, when a hand snaked from a monstrous plant and jerked me into a big rough body.

Bane.

I mean, Roman. It was difficult to wrap my head around him asking me to refer to him by his real name. His real name. He'd given me the real him.

"Christ!" I was so surprised, I accidentally bit my tongue. The taste of warm copper filled my mouth. Every time I saw his face it felt like someone punched my heart from the inside. I wondered if it was a normal reaction when you loved someone before realizing that, yes, I was in love with Roman "Bane" Protsenko. All of him. The thief, the con, the whore. He was cracking my heart with every touch, shattering it with every smile, and it didn't make any sense because how could he break something that was already broken? Still, I felt his presence in my bones. His newly shaven face, so promising, so misleading. His mouth was wide, sexy, and pouty. I wished it was hidden by the beard so I could think straight again.

I opened my mouth, and he clamped his hand over it, crowding me against the wall. My breath shook against his hot palm. A surge of adrenaline ran through my system.

"In the interest of full disclosure, I have no idea what the fuck I am doing here."

All I could do was nod, slowly, telling him that I understood. He plastered his body to mine, his erection digging into my stomach. Every muscle in his body was tight, his skin hot with sun and lust.

"Kiss me." My voice came out muffled under his hand.

Love freely, Mrs. Belfort had said. *I want to, Mrs. B. And that scares me. A lot.*

"You kiss me," he said, rolling his forehead against mine in frustration. He removed his hand from my lips.

I grinned. "Why?"

"Because I need you to be proactive about this shit, Jesse. I want the old Jesse, baby. The one who made decisions. The new one just won't fucking cut it."

Something ignited inside me. I'd like to think that it was her. The old Jesse accepted the challenge, rose within me like a hurricane, and came out in a rush of need and determination.

Whether it was because I was a rape victim.

A woman who knew he was an escort.

Or just because he wasn't sure whether I was going to regret it didn't matter.

I swallowed hard and realized that I was looking at the man I was in love with. The man who was set to ruin me.

It was in that moment I realized that I'd survived many things, but Roman Protsenko was probably not going to be one of them.

CHAPTER SIXTEEN
BANE

She stared.

I stared.

This was bad. Six million bucks kind of bad. So bad it ought to be really fucking good for me to stand there like an idiot and let Jesse rise on her tiptoes, her lashes, thick and long, fanning across her cheeks. I wanted to kiss the curve of her lips and dip my tongue between them and conquer her inch by inch, like a hidden continent. Mine to explore and reign. Mine to rule. Mine to hold. She tipped her chin up, her lips a breath from mine. I liked Jesse a lot, but watching her make the first move was killing my fucking balls, and I wasn't too keen on kids, but I liked having the option, you know?

Finally—Jesus, fucking *finally*—her lips locked on mine, and the urge to grab her face and kiss her the way I knew, the way I was used to, the way I wanted to, burned every cell in my body. I itched. I burned. Yet I stood there, still as a brick, giving her the power as her mouth shyly explored mine.

"Is this… Am I doing it okay?"

I nodded slowly. Moses on a cracker, yeah. It was more than okay. More than okay for her to fuck up my deal with her stepdaddy. It was more than okay for her to fuck up my plans. And my dreams. And my life. It was more than okay because it was I who'd come to her. Who'd crawled to her, really, sporting zero self-control.

I inched down, closing the space between us. My blood pounded between my ears, and I wanted to punch my own face for feeling the way I'd felt about a closed-mouth kiss. I needed to get laid. Soon. Shit, right now. We kissed like kids. One peck. Two pecks. Three pecks. Again and again and again, the world around us vanishing into a thick cloud of nothing until the kisses became one long kiss.

And then she opened her mouth. Gently. Timidly. A baby's first step in the world. Her tongue swept my lips, silently asking for permission, which I granted. She tasted warm and coconutty, and we stroked for a while, just kissing, just fucking kissing, before I realized I'd wrapped her hair in my fist like the devil that I was and yanked her into me. Her body responded, wrapping around me like ivy. She bobbed her head into our kiss, as if giving me permission to go ahead, and that's all I needed to open my mouth all the way and demolish her. I ate her face, and I might be talking literally here. I licked the corners of her lips, biting and tugging until they became puffy and sensitive. Our foreheads crashed as I sucked her tongue into my mouth, until it stopped being a kiss and ventured deep into tongue-fucking territory. She whimpered into my mouth, and I nearly let go of her, worried that it was too much, but then her little fists balled around my neckline, and I grabbed her by the back of her thigh and curled it against my waist, grinding against her in a mixture of agony and need I'd never felt before.

As I boxed her in with my arms against the wall, I realized that I didn't have anyone to blame but myself. I'd sprinted past every single red line and broken every rule on my way to so-called healing her, all while creating the biggest junkie to walk on earth.

Yeah, that would be me.

My hard-on was aligned with her pussy, and I bent my knees a little, fucking her through her clothes. She clawed into my shoulders as I ground against her like I was trying to drill her into the wall. Her pussy against my cock felt like dark magic.

I was fucking her through our clothes. Literally fucking her without a condom. My dick was halfway inside her pussy; the only things separating us were her yoga pants and my trunks. I was going to remove my lips from hers for the first time in forty minutes when her little hand slipped into my waistband and grabbed my shaft. My dick jerked in her fist and sprang out of my trunks, and even though this was the definition of stupid—fucking the girl you signed a six-million-dollar contract not to fuck mere feet from the front door of the man who'd made you sign it—Jesse inspired the idiot in me. I was about to protest and mumble something about needing to calm down a little before my dick exploded when she slipped my cock between her clothed thighs and rubbed them together.

Dumb Bane: fuck our dick. Let's do it.

It was delicious and dirty and the kind of thing to make the new Jesse heave, which prompted me to believe I was getting the old one. The pre-Emery one.

"Snowflake…" I said. That was it. I didn't really think beyond that. I wasn't even sure what I was asking. Maybe for her to take mercy on my balls.

"Let's come," she moaned into our kiss. "Finger me." She moved her hand back to my cock and began to stroke it, thumbing my PA and sending shivers up my spine.

Since I knew Darren's security cameras didn't point at the oversize plants decorating his entrance from each side—I'd checked—I knew we were in the clear. I shoved my hand into her yoga pants and found her silky and warm and so fucking tight I wanted to die right then and there, knowing no moment in my life was going to top this one. I slipped two fingers between her thighs and played with her a little. With any other woman, I'd get straight to the punch line, rub her clit and make her come so we could move on to the important part—me. With Jesse, she was the important part, and while a few months ago I'd have found this idea unnerving, I couldn't give two shits about me when it came to her.

I grazed the walls of her wet pussy, fingering her old-school, thrusting two fingers into her and making sure her clit and pussy were thoroughly wet. My hand teased her with a come-hither motion that slammed into her G-spot again and again and a-fucking-gain, slowly enough to build her orgasm gradually, like never-ending foreplay. Her head rolled from side to side on the wall, and I had to chase her for every kiss and bite.

"Touch my clit," she begged, hooking her finger in the titanium ring and tugging. I was so close I could feel the cum rushing through my dick. I laughed into our kiss because it was such a trip, having Jesse talk like that. The old or the new or anything in between.

"Ask nicely."

"Please touch my clit."

"Will you go surfing with me tomorrow morning?"

"Maybe."

I dragged two fingers below her clit and pressed them to her core. She chased my touch with her pussy, but I withdrew quickly. She groaned.

"Will Edie be there?"

"Who the fuck cares about Edie? Maybe she will. Maybe she won't. She's married. And irrelevant. You're my girl."

My girl.

My girl.

My girl.

The sentence echoed in my apparently otherwise empty head. I didn't know what made me say that. Maybe the crazy need for it to be real. Truth was, it drove me crazy that Hale had even looked at her. I wanted to tear his eyeballs out and make a smoothie with them for even noticing she existed.

She squeezed me harder, and I bit down on her lip out of instinct, reopening a recent small cut that made her bleed. I sucked her pain into my mouth.

"I'm your girl?" she asked. My heart raced like a wild horse, galloping straight into her little fists. Break it and I'll fuck you up, I wanted to warn. But that was bullshit, and I knew it.

"Not to be messed with, not to be touched. So what's it going to be?"

Pause. "I'll surf with you tomorrow."

"That's my girl." I pushed my fingers into her clit and rubbed until she choked on her breath. She pumped me until her hand began to shake and her legs gave out. Her orgasm was like a domino, the fall long and steady and epic.

She dropped to her knees, writhing and panting, just as I said, "I'm coming, too."

She wrapped her lips around my cock and looked up to me, her blue eyes shining. I fisted her hair, realizing what needed to be done to save both of us.

Giving up my dream.

"I want you to swallow every drop, Snowflake," I said as I shot my load into her mouth. I made it messy, not going straight for her throat, but pulling out halfway through so she could taste me on her tongue. Marking her in all the ways I could.

She swallowed. I tucked myself back in.

"What did you want to talk to me about in the text message?" She wiped her mouth with the back of her hand, looking up at me. I took her hand and helped her get to her feet. What I wanted to tell her was that we needed to stop doing this couple bullshit. But now I had a solution. It was going to make me hate myself forever, but I would also get to keep Jesse.

"I wanted to tell you that you snore."

She punched my arm.

I smiled.

She bought it.

"Bane?" a soft voice probed, forcing me to open my eyes.

It took me a second to figure out where I was. Flung over my messy bed, catching up on some sleep. I looked up and saw Grier pulling an elastic off of her hair, letting her blond locks fall down all the way to her ass. She was wearing a summer dress I'd once told her made me want to eat her ass. Yellow with cornflower-blue daisies. It did nothing for me now.

"Shit," I croaked, jerking up to my forearms and rubbing a hand over my face. "What's the time?"

"Eight o'clock. You didn't open the door, so I let myself in." Her fingers grazed the strap of her bra. Eight o'clock. I was supposed to meet Darren at six at his Newport Beach office. I'd even set my alarm, not wanting to miss the meeting for obvious reasons, but I must've crashed. I looked down and saw the nightstand clock broken into pieces on the floor. Shit. Goddamn Beck was going to be the end of me with those long surfing sessions. Asshole better get third place or above; otherwise, I was going to kick his ass all the way back to Hermosa Beach.

I jerked upright, tossing a shirt on, when a shriek left Grier's mouth.

"Oh my God, you shaved! Roman, you are gorgeous!"

I wished people would stop saying that. No real man wanted to be described as gorgeous or beautiful. I wasn't a fucking cocktail dress. But seeing the look on Jesse's face last night when I'd climbed through her window was enough to make me stand by my decision. She'd looked at me with soft eyes, and her sudden submission was worth waxing the rest of my body, too.

Without sparing Grier an answer, I flung my sheet back and darted to the kitchenette, where I charged my phone. I had a few text messages, and I dreaded almost all of them.

Darren: Are you here?

Darren: Of course you are not here. You called me asking for an urgent meeting, which you didn't even show up to. I waited for you. Now I'm going to be stuck in traffic for hours.

Darren: It better not be about Jesse. I know she has a new
job with you and that she is making friends with a bald girl
who came to pick her up for the mall today. But you still
need to get her to meet more people, make more friends.
The six months are not up yet.

I hadn't even known about Gail and Jesse, but I was happy they'd
hit it off. Gail was a solid chick. Then there was another message.
One I didn't dread.

Snowflake: At the mall with Gail. I thought I'd treat you to this
beauty because I know you like orange.

She sent me a picture of her with an orange onesie. Not only the
color, but the fruit. I snort-laughed, shaking my head. I shot her a
quick message before returning my gaze to a confused Grier.

Bane: Delicious to a fault, but we're gonna do something
about this orange onesie. For one thing: take it off you
once I see you. x

Yeah. I ended a message with an x. I really was a special kind of
fucked.

Grier tapped her foot nervously, her arms crossed over her chest,
glancing at her Cartier. She kept her clothes on, which told me that
she already knew what was up. I'd bailed on our hookup last week,
and frankly, I was about to ditch this one, too, and would have if I
hadn't crashed like a goddamn meteor. I plucked two beers from
the fridge and handed her one. It was time for an uncomfortable
conversation.

She took a sip and looked down at her shoes. "Jesse Carter,"
she said.

I walked over to the door leading to the deck, parking my

forearms on the rusty railways. She mirrored my movements, doing the same. We both stared at the waves crashing on rocks by the shore.

"Brian said you asked for him to pull out her case file and sniffed around who worked on it."

I had, a second after I'd cleaned my cum-coated dick the day Jesse and I had fooled around in the storage room. Maybe she didn't want to retaliate, but I wasn't going to go on pretending these assholes hadn't done anything to her. They had. And they were going to pay. The fact that I had to chase two of them away not too long ago meant they did not understand the error of their ways. And nothing, and no one, was going to harm Jesse.

I shrugged. "This whole goddamn town knows what happened, but the little dipshits are still free. How is that okay?"

Grier's eyes sparkled like the water underneath us. Even in my periphery, I saw that she was emotional, but not about Jesse.

"You know, I never thought you'd fall in love. That's what made you such a safe bet," she said, wiping the cold mist of her beer bottle on her dress. "There was something so detached about you when I met you. Like you were here, but not really. It made sleeping with you so easy. So…uncomplicated. And I know a lot of other women share this sentiment. Yes, you were paid. Yes, you were an escort. But you were decent. Discreet and cool and nice to talk to. You didn't make us feel cheap or tacky or like freaks. You were always a true gentleman, Bane."

I didn't really know how to respond to this. I noticed that she talked about me in past tense, and that was a relief. She knew that we were over. I swiveled my body to face her, resting my hip on the railway.

"You'll find someone better. Someone who'll give you more than a quickie once a week."

"Maybe I can have a full-blown affair this time." She smiled bitterly. "With feelings and all."

I made a gagging sound. "Ugh. Feelings."

"How would you know what they're like?" she teased.

Because I've been ambushed by the fuckers and can't seem to shake them off.

We shared one of the most awkward hugs in the history of embraces. It was only when she let go of me that I realized I was relieved. I was done with the bullshit, with or without Snowflake. Really, she was the kick in the ass I'd needed all this time. And what a fucking kick that was. My tailbone was still sore.

"I'm a little jealous of Jesse Carter," Grier said to me when I walked her to my door. I rubbed the back of my neck.

Don't worry. I'll fuck it up at some point, I'm sure.

When Grier left, I walked over to my kitchen nook, plucked my phone out of the charger, and started going over every single client on my contact list. I decided to go for something laconic, firm, and polite. Thing was, I wasn't much of a diplomat, so after much thinking, I came up with this:

Hi. It's Bane. I'm writing to let you know that I'm hereby terminating our professional relationship. I'm officially retired and will not be making a comeback anytime soon. If you owe me money, consider it paid. If I owe you dick—I suggest you go look for it somewhere else.

So long and thanks for all the fish.—Bane.

I sent it to all forty-six women I had worked with at once, thinking in retrospect that the fish reference could probably have been omitted. All I knew was that I'd just killed the business that had helped me rise to power in this town and that I was about to kill my dream next time I spoke to Darren.

Grier described what I felt toward Jesse as love. But I wasn't so sure what actually existed between us, which made all this rash decision-making even crazier. If Jesse found out about my deal with Darren, she'd kill me. And I wouldn't blame her. I needed to terminate it immediately and come clean if I wanted half a chance to make it right.

But do you want to make it right?

Along the years, I'd watched as plenty of idiots around me formed long-lasting relationships. Maybe I could, too. All I needed was to remind myself that I was not my father, that I was worthy, and that I deserved her. Even if the mere deal I'd struck to get to her in the first place suggested otherwise.

I texted Snowflake one more time before I dragged my ass back to bed.

Bane: Still can't unsee that orange onesie. Send a pic w/o it.

She responded back with a faceless selfie of her tits pressed together inside her black My Bloody Valentine tank top, a smutty book open on her bent legs. I bit my fist.

Bane: Is that My Bloody Valentine? I hate them, too. Remove.
Snowflake: Is there something you don't hate?
Bane: Yes. You.
Snowflake: Interesting. So you don't hate me?
Bane: Not even close. Not even close to close. What's the antonym of hate?
Snowflake: No way I'll be the first one to say the word.
Bane: Sleep tight, Snowflake. Big day tomorrow.

I stared at my peeling ceiling for the remainder of that night, ignoring the chiming cell phone beside me as a stream of messages from clients started pouring in, from irate to panicked to mildly offended.

Maybe love wasn't about feeling happy and whole.

Maybe love was about breaking so the person you cared for would feel a little more whole.

CHAPTER SEVENTEEN
JESSE

Things were tense at the dinner table that evening.

The only reason I'd decided to show up at all was because I was feeling increasingly normal and thought I could handle it. I tried not to think about how attached I'd suddenly become to my own life. How things and people and events around me had begun to matter. How Roman reshaped the way I looked at men—not completely, but enough for me not to be scared of them. How Gail had reminded me that good friends are worth having.

Earlier, she and I had raided Hot Topic like we were twelve again, then had ice cream, and then sat by the ramp on the promenade and rated random guys on skateboards from one to ten based on hotness, even though they were all sixteen. It just felt so real, so simple, so normal, I even managed to shove away all the bad stuff. The flashback, Shadow's blood work, and even Mrs. Belfort's request. I left another message on Dr. Wiese's answering machine and decided that tomorrow I would deal with Mrs. B's kids and pay Wiese a visit after I finished my shift at Café Diem.

Hannah clocked out for the day but left us some grilled asparagus and sautéed potatoes along with her mouthwatering lemon-garlic chicken. I carved the chicken and served the food while Pam read something on her cell phone and Darren drummed his fingers on the table. Shadow was all but tap-dancing under the table. It'd been a while since I'd seen him like this. Back when I was still the old Jesse, I used to eat dinner at the table every evening and slip him food when no one was watching. It was our own little secret. We had a few of those. Making him happy again was the one thing that kept me positive about this whole scenario.

When I sat down, both pairs of eyes flicked to me.

I looked between them. "Anything interesting about myself I should know?"

"Nothing." Pam snapped open her napkin theatrically, resting it on her thighs. Darren didn't answer.

"Did you get a phone call from Dr. Wiese by any chance?" I asked no one in particular. It was odd that I hadn't heard from him yet, but I read on the internet that sometimes it could take weeks. I slipped Shadow a piece of lemon chicken, and he chewed so loudly, I had to fake a cough. They both looked at each other, puzzled.

"No."

"Hey, honey." Pam stabbed a piece of chicken and brought it to her mouth. She would eat her own foot before touching potatoes or anything else with carbs. By the term of endearment, I gathered she was talking to Darren and not me. "Did you know that Jesse started hanging out with Bane Protsenko? Do you know him?"

"I do," Darren said conversationally, cutting his potatoes into tiny pieces. The aggression in his movements suggested he was annoyed either with Bane or with the potatoes. My money was on the former. "He'th bad newth."

"Not to mention he's got a name for himself as the town's escort," Pam added, chewing on a piece of chicken twenty-seven times. She'd read about it in a women's magazine once and had been eating like a toothless turtle ever since. It was abnormal on so many levels. I refrained from mentioning how Pam didn't seem too bothered by Bane's reputation when she'd wanted to get into his pants, and a flame of jealousy immediately licked at my core. She'd tried to hit on Roman. My Roman. And now she was acting like he was dirt.

"Well, whatever his reputation is, I accepted a job at his café," I said, and, because I knew timing was everything, brought an asparagus spear to my mouth, biting the tip and patting Shadow underneath with my socked foot. Pam's eyebrows nosedived, and Darren put his utensils next to his plate, trying hard not to slam them.

"I wanted to talk to you about it. I'm tho happy you've dethided to find yourthelf a job. How about you come work for me? I'll offer a nithe paycheck, a daily ride, and, of courth, you can take ath much time off ath you need."

There was an apology in his smile, and his eyes clung to mine.

"I'm happy at Café Diem. Thanks, Darren."

"Stop being so ungrateful," Pam snipped from across the table. "Darren is offering you a once-in-a-lifetime opportunity. I think you should take it."

"You took it." I grinned. "Didn't make you too happy, did it?"

She stood up, throwing her napkin on her plate. Guess she was done with her tiny piece of chicken. "How dare you!"

"How dare I?" I asked, still seated, my pulse slow and calm. "How dare you. You conveniently forgot about my existence until Bane walked into the picture, and we both know why you're interested in my life now."

"Jethy!" It was Darren's turn to stand up and slap the edge of the table. "Don't talk to your mother like thith!"

For the sake of good, synchronized choreography, I stood up, too. "Grow some eyes, Dar. She is sleeping with the better half of Todos Santos and not even hiding it."

"I don't care about her!" he snapped, his face red, his eyes bloodshot. "I care about you. Are you and Bane friendth or more?"

"More," I chirped. "So much more, Darren. You have no idea."

This was directed at Pam, a clear back-off statement, but it was Darren who looked about ready to explode.

"You're thleeping with him?"

"Sheesh!" I shook my head, laughing. "It's none of your business who I sleep with. You're not my real dad, remember?"

"In that case, you're not my daughter!" Pam yelled from across the table. God, I wished it were the truth. Unfortunately, the resemblance between us prior to her plastic surgeries was uncanny.

I shrugged. "I would tell you to sue me, but I have nothing to my name other than a rich stepdaddy."

"That'th not true. You will inherit everything I have, Jethy. You know I care about you. When I die, everything will go to you."

Actually, I had not known that. Pam hadn't known it, either, based on the way her eyes widened and searched for his, but he was still looking at me.

I pushed my chair back and rounded the table. "I know you're protective of me, Dar, and I understand why, because my mom isn't, but please know Bane is not the issue. He is the only person who really understands me."

"He doethn't underthtand you." Darren gripped the back of his chair, his face reddening further. What the hell was up with him? Sometimes I wished he'd just man up. Stand his ground and say what he needed to say. It was sad, but if he were to divorce Pam and find a nice woman who wasn't turned off by his submissive nature, I'd be really happy for him.

"Hmm, yes, he does."

"He'th... Thweetheart, your mom thaid it right. He ith an ethcort. He thouldn't be mething with you. He thould be helping you."

"You don't know him," I gritted out.

"Neither do you."

I wasn't proud of what I did next, but it needed to be done. I stormed out of the kitchen and went up to my room, where I slammed the door like a moody teenager and dove headfirst into a sea of fluffy pillows. It took me minutes to finally catch my breath and look up at the pinboard wall. At all the backs of all the faceless people I'd taken pictures of.

I'm losing my mind trying to find out what happened. But I will. I will solve this riddle.

Then Roman sent me a text (or maybe it was a sext?) asking for an orange onesie-less picture, so I complied.

At some point, he stopped texting and just called me.

"I needed to hear your voice."

"Why?"

"Because I had a feeling you were touching yourself, and I would pay good money to listen to that shit."

"How romantic," I said, a smile on my face. "You know, sex is not about money."

"My little grasshopper. Everything is about money. Are you gonna touch yourself?"

"Are you gonna touch yourself?" I taunted.

He was silent for a moment. "I'm a dude, and I'm talking to my girlfriend in the middle of the night. I've been playing with my dick like it's Nintendo for the past ten minutes now."

I snickered, allowing the conversation to take a very sharp, unexpected turn. Most of the time I wasn't really sure of what Roman was doing. I simply enjoyed tagging along for the ride. For a while, we just panted, taunted, and described what we were going to do to one another. My whole body was clenched before it loosened with a tsunami of an orgasm.

After that, Roman told me, "Good night, Snowflake."

"Wait," I choked on the word, feeling needy, too needy, but then again, he had called me his girlfriend, and my heart was about to burst every time I replayed his voice saying that word. "I can't fall asleep. That's why I jog at night. I always have nightmares."

Another meaningful pause.

"Try. I promise I won't hang up until I hear your gross snores."

I fell asleep with my phone pressed against my ear.

When I woke up, the top of the touch screen was still green, and the call was still going.

"Good morning, SnortyPants."

Neptune.

Dark. Cold. Blue. The ocean seemed morbid at six in the morning. I shuddered in my wet suit, jogging in place without really feeling my toes. The sand was cold and tight, stretching like canvas beneath my feet, and I felt like I was ruining Roman's art by being there. We were nearly done with our session. Beck, Edie, and Hale—whom Bane had reintroduced to me as "my real asshole, the source of all the shit in my life"—went on surfing while Roman stayed ashore with me, teaching me how to paddle with my stomach flat against the surfboard on the sand. I felt like an idiot. Like I was slowing him down. Then we moved to the water and he stayed by my side. Hale and Beck were laughing and coughing "pussy-whipped" every time we got near them, and Edie smiled at us, shaking her head. I felt bad hating on her for no reason. She was actually pretty cool. Not Gail-cool, but still good people. Not to mention the bump of her lower stomach was unmistakable. She spent her time sitting on her surfboard, letting the first rays of morning sun braid her yellow hair with fresh highlights.

She wasn't after Roman.

She was after the ocean, nature, and everything it had to give.

After we were done, Roman invited me to take a shower at his place. It was the first time I'd set foot in his houseboat. Small, neat, basic. I knew Roman probably made enough to live in one of the candy-colored condos of the promenade, and I loved that he didn't. I loved a lot of things about him.

What's the antonym of hate?

Love. It is love, and maybe I should be the one to say it first.

"I can't believe your place is so tidy." I ran a hand over his coffee table, eager to leave a mark. His place was small and old-ish, almost like a sailor's pad. He stood behind me, dumping his surfing gear by the door.

"Might've tidied up for you," he said around a freshly rolled joint.

"Might've?" I turned around, beaming at him.

"Please let me keep my balls for a little longer, Snowflake. See, I'm kind of attached to them. Also: literally."

He'd made me laugh more in a few short weeks than I had in three years. I shrugged. "If you behave."

Before I headed out to the promenade this morning, I'd packed a duffel bag with a change of clothes, knowing my shift started at 9:00 a.m. and I might not have time for a shower. I pulled out burgundy corduroys and a cute tank top the color of my eyes. I'd ransacked my closet earlier this morning to find something that wasn't emo black hoodies and pants loose enough to fit three clowns and a convertible. I walked over to where I presumed Roman's shower was, swaying my hips and knowing that he was watching.

I wanted to have sex with him.

I wanted to have lots and lots of sex with him.

I wanted him to make me feel the way only he could. Like I was beautiful, lethal, and strong. Like the old Jesse.

"And where do you think you're going?" He snaked his arm around my waist and pulled my ass into his erection. I was still wearing the wet suit, and my nipples puckered in my red bikini under it. He buried his face in my neck, dragging his hot lips to kiss the tattoo on my nape.

"I'm going to take a shower. I don't want to be late for work."

"Gail can cover for you."

"She'll kill me. Morning shifts are busier than hell."

"You say 'shift.' I hear 'shaft.'" He gave me a shove with his dick, and I skipped into his bathroom. I peeled off my wet suit alone, knowing that he'd stayed behind. That yet again, he would deprive me of what I really wanted. Him. Inside me. Making me feel desired and whole again. I dumped the heavy wet suit on the floor with a thud and stared into the mirror. My eyes were defiant, lit. A monsoon of emotions swirled inside them.

Bane stepped behind me, our gazes meeting in the slightly cracked mirror. There was a hunter in there, and I wanted to pull him out. Wanted him to chase me. His wet suit was pulled down to his V-cut, his tattoos glistening against his tan. His blond, wavy hair was a rumpled mess. He stared at my stomach.

"I hate it," he said simply.

I swallowed. "Fuck you."

"I also love it," he added. "This scar gave you claws. Can't fucking wait for you to use them on me."

I turned around, smiling sweetly. I was done playing games. I wanted him, all of him, the parts he reserved only for me and the parts that were communal property. Bane stared at my puckered nipples, his green eyes gleaming like morning dew on fresh grass. It was time for a good dose of reality.

"I got pregnant. I wanted to keep the baby. Stupid, huh? But I did. It was like the silver lining of the Incident. I was going to have someone for my own. Someone who would be faithful and loyal to me. Someone who would love me, no matter what. We could take care of each other, and she or he would never take their father's side because they wouldn't even know them. It felt almost like revenge, as sick as it may sound. They took something of mine—my will, my power, my innocence—so I took something of theirs. But Pam forced me to have an abortion. I didn't want to, but I was weak. I was too weak to scrape myself off the bed, let alone fight her on this."

He pushed my wet hair away from my face. Bane had pressed me to talk about it the other night. Now he got his wish and, oh, how ugly was the truth.

"The truth is I wasn't a virgin when Emery tried to take my virginity, Roman, but something happened before. Something I can't remember. The Incident wasn't the first time I'd been raped."

Bane's nostrils flared, and his eyes leveled with mine. They breathed fire, and I was afraid he was going to tear the whole bathroom apart. I kept talking, knowing I was going to lose momentum if I dared to take a breath. "After what happened in the alleyway, I was so confused that I panicked. I didn't know what to say or think. Pam solved this issue by walking through every sentence that left my mouth. She said if I screwed it up, we'd be forced to leave and Darren would dump us on the streets. The boys' parents were breathing down my neck. Pam and Darren thought it was an orgy gone wrong and that I was ashamed to admit it. Hell, even I didn't believe myself for a while. I thought—maybe I did cheat on Emery. It took me a lot of time to understand just how played I was, and by the time I figured it out, it was too late. Everyone had already moved on. Well, everyone other than me."

His thumbs pressed my cheeks, and he pulled me into a hug. I wanted to curl into his strong body and live there.

"For the past two years, time did not move. Technically, it did, but not for me. Not really. That night in the alleyway still chases me like it was yesterday. And in walks you. At first, I didn't want you in the picture. My grief was still so fresh and pristine—I didn't want anyone tarnishing it with hope. But you didn't just walk into my life, Roman. You stormed into it. You left me no choice but to heal. Now I want everything. I want the job and the friends and my sexuality back. If you don't fuck me, someone else will, Bane." I purposely used the name he didn't want me using. "I need this. Need this to heal me. To break me and to put me back together. To kill me and resurrect me. This is not about sex. Not all of it, anyway." I gulped in a breath. "It's about me."

Bane swallowed but didn't say anything.

I shook my head, dropping my gaze down to my toes. Then I turned around and charged for the door, ready to flee his boathouse, even half-naked. I was done asking and begging and bargaining. I was done seducing and luring and hoping. If he didn't want me after this admission, we were done.

I didn't even want him to be my friend. Like I could really be friends with Bane Goddamn Protsenko. Every word to leave his mouth was foreplay.

"Jesse," he growled. I ignored him, making a U-turn and yanking my duffel bag to get my clothes. Before I could unzip it and pluck them out, Bane slammed me against the wall of his kitchen. The thud of my back crashing against it pounded between my ears. I was ready to slap his stupidly gorgeous face when I felt his cock springing free from his wet suit, hot and velvety against my opening. He wrapped my legs around his waist and crashed his fist to the wall above my head. "Fucking dammit, Jesse!"

"Leave me alone, then," I yelled in his face. "Just let me leave."

"Never," he snarled, biting my neck. Hard. "And ever." He dragged his nose down to my shoulder, sucking a sensitive spot on the curve of my collarbone. "And fucking ever." He thrust into me, nailing me to the wall and filling me to the hilt.

A moan escaped between my lips. He was big and long...and bare.

"You want to be fucked?" He spat out the words, his face so intense I shivered under his touch. "Just remember, Snowflake—you fucking begged for it."

He pounded into me, each stroke harder and deeper and more punishing. My body felt like a dormant nest of fireflies lighting up together in batches. I felt their lights flicking, their wings zapping over every inch of my flesh. I felt every inch of him inside me, the titanium hoop of his piercing scraping my walls, and it still wasn't enough.

I was desperate. I was feral.

I clawed at his face, tears streaming down my cheeks and onto my neck, and he licked them, laughing as he fucked me harder, not giving much of a damn about who or what I was, just like he'd said he would. Taking me the way I wanted to be taken. Not gently or apologetically. Like an equal. Like a captured soldier, in a war where pleasantries and fake condolences weren't necessary.

"Harder," he taunted. "I'm denting your ass from the inside. Least you can do is leave a pretty little mark on me." Roman laughed, smashing his lips to mine with a kiss that made it clear that he owned my body—every inch of it—and all the things inside it. Every thought and heartbeat. Every painful breath. His.

I raked my fingernails down his back, returning the violence when his tongue went to war with mine. Heat pooled in my lower stomach, his cock stretching me out and swelling inside me, twitching, circling, pounding.

"That's my fighter." He chuckled, adjusting our position by hoisting me upward by my ass with his rough fingers with one hand while twisting my nipple with the other. I squeaked, watching as he lowered his beautiful face to suck the pain away, so hard yet so delicate, and even though there was nothing I wanted more than to run my hand through his strings of golden mane, I held myself back.

This time, the trembling started from my fingertips, working its way up and heating my body like a blanket. I was coming, but this time it felt different. Like an epiphany. I reached for his ass to squeeze as I shuddered between him and the wall, but he swatted my hands away, pushing me off and splaying his fingers over my neck, pinning me to the wall.

"I'm not your goddamn girlfriend, Jesse. You don't get to squeeze my ass unless it's to hold back a choke from my cock pounding into your mouth. We clear about that?"

I didn't know what it was about his dirty brazen words that completely unraveled the old Jesse, but she was back, and she was clasping his cock in her sex in a vise, like a fist, laughing into his face with wild abandon.

"Jesus," came from somewhere in the back of my throat as I came around his shaft, shaking violently. He only pumped harder, and my back was burning from the friction against the wall.

"Coming," he said, just one word, and I nodded, thinking he was going to finish inside me, but he pulled out instead, his swift movement radiating self-control, and angled his tip so that he came all over my clit. White spurts of cum grazed the delicate flesh of my sex, and he swirled the cum with his cock, rubbing it into my already sensitive yet neglected clit. The second orgasm burst out of me like fireworks. I sifted through his hair and brought him closer for a greedy kiss, biting his lower lip and tugging way too hard.

"Roman." Again. One word. Not a request, not a plea, and not a statement. Rather, a spell I was falling deeper and deeper under, not bothering to go back up for a quick breath.

He pulled away from me, narrowing his eyes and tugging his wet suit back up, his cock still half-erect between us.

He turned around, leaving me to slide down to my ass against his wall, sagging with post-climax bliss. He walked over to his coffee table, retrieved a blunt, and lit it casually, like we hadn't just done what we had. Like we hadn't broken any rules or promises or even—potentially—my heart.

"What's the antonym of hate?" I blurted, drunk on pleasure.

He collapsed to his couch, cupping the blunt with his thumb and forefinger and sucking hard. "Jesse."

———

We managed to squeeze in one more quickie in the shower after the kitchenette sex. Again, Roman showed zero mercy on me, which explained why he'd held back for so long on touching me. He had a take-no-prisoners approach to sex, and not only was missionary not on the menu for him, but I doubted it was even in his vocabulary. The shower sex involved me bent over, holding onto the faucet, while he pounded into me from behind, playing with my sex and letting me taste myself on his fingers every now and again. I was surprised by how open and uninhibited he was with me, but I shouldn't have been. Just because Roman was a nice guy didn't mean he wasn't the devil himself. He was both. And it was part of his charm.

As we finally got dressed in his tiny, humid bathroom, I took it upon myself to iron his wrinkled, flimsy California Republic tank with my hands.

"Do I get the invoice in the mail, or do I pay you in Café Diem shifts?" My voice was playful, but the actual comment was snarky. I couldn't help it, though. A part of me was pissed that I wasn't the only one. That what we did was probably an appetizer for a tour de force involving a married couple, their dog, and a dildo. Okay. Maybe not all of them, but still.

Roman flipped his car keys with his forefinger, shooting me a bored look. "I should drop you as a client for that wise mouth alone."

"So do." I waltzed past him to the living room. His big strides echoed behind me.

"I can't."

"Why?"

"Because I quit."

I turned around, blinking rapidly. "Come again?"

"Planning to. This time between your tits." He smacked my ass, moving forward, casually grabbing a can of beer from the fridge and popping it open. It was not even ten in the morning. Jesus. "I quit," he repeated, taking a gulp. "My dick is officially retired and closed for business."

"When?" I gulped, pretty proud of myself for not stuttering.

"Yesterday."

"Before or after our sexting?" I leaned a shoulder against the same wall we'd screwed against earlier that morning. There was a damp spot of cum gracing the chipped yellow surface, and it took everything in me not to slide back on my knees and scrub it clean.

Roman finished the beer in a gulp and slam-dunked it to the sink. "Before. Remember my whole speech about looking at yourself in the mirror without flinching?"

"Yeah."

"Couldn't do that anymore."

"Do what?"

"Fuck other women when I had a girlfriend."

It was the second time he had called me that, but this time, there was a question mark at the end of the sentence. It felt like a proposal. It felt like a thousand caterpillars turning into dazzling butterflies all at the same time in my stomach, hopeful and alive. I searched his face, trying to find doubt. Humor. Deceit. Anything that would make it less real and anchor me back to earth. His face was blank. The perfect poker expression.

"I am?" I grinned.

"You tell me." He hitched one shoulder up, his defensive wall rising, almost reaching his eyes.

"I mean, you quit your glamorous job for me. Can't really say no to you now."

"You can always say no to me," he countered, meaning it.

"I want to be your girlfriend, Roman."

"Good. Because there's a list of things I want to do to you, and none of them fall into the friend-zone category." He walked over to me, dropping three kisses on my mouth, nose, and chin.

My heart felt mossy. Soft-walled. So easy to break in his big hands.

"About this morning…" he started.

"I'm on the pill." I stood on my tiptoes, brushing my lips against his. They were both cracked and sore, and he winced a little before I pulled away.

"I know." He trailed a finger down my arm.

I didn't even need to ask how he knew. I was religious about taking my pills ever since the abortion. Ever since I was too scared to tell the doctors what happened, so they'd never offered me the morning-after pill. The foil package sat on my nightstand, next to a bottle of Fiji water. I took one every morning before brushing my teeth.

We marched through the door, heading for his truck, and maybe he was the same old infamous Bane Protsenko, but I walked out of there different from the person I'd been when I'd first walked in.

Alive.

Alert.

In bloom.

Old Jesse was no longer knocking on my soul's door. She'd kicked that thing down.

And all the light streamed in.

"Well, someone looks thoroughly fucked." Gail snickered as she pushed the ice fridge shut with her ass, flinging a kitchen towel over her shoulder. Roman had said he had to go to city hall for a business meeting—something about SurfCity—and I actually didn't mind spending some time away from him. I'd enjoyed our morning together, but I also enjoyed being my own person. Facing the world independently, even if from behind Café Diem's trendy counter. I liked this job, and that made me happy because it made me the opposite of Pam. She frowned upon jobs in general, thought life was meant for shopping and socializing.

Turning scarlet red, I grinned, slicing the strawberries on the board in front of me into minuscule pieces. "Shut up."

"It's okay. There's not one girl in this room who can't relate to wanting to screw Bane Protsenko senseless. I'm guessing you got a free sample? Does he offer a weekly pass?" Gail elbowed my ribs, her eyes scanning me up and down. I flipped her the bird and then proceeded to wash my hands to get rid of the stickiness from the fruit I cut for the smoothies.

"Seriously, Gail, you need professional help. And dick. Perhaps especially that. I'll see if Beck is available."

"No, thanks. I'd rather rub myself against an iceberg. And I'll take that as a no."

It felt so normal talking to someone like that. Like a friend. My grin spread wider over my face.

"Ding ding, what's that? Yup, it's my lunch break. See you in half an hour." I grabbed my phone and the smoothie I'd made for myself and dodged the scene. I waved the device in my hand. "I'll be outside if you need me."

"Hey, you just got here! His jerk-ism is rubbing off on you, and I bet it's not the only thing." She laughed, wiping coffee beans off the surface in front of her.

"You're funny." I pushed my shoulder to the glass door. "Keep it up."

"Probably not. Don't wanna mess with boyfriend dearest and find myself in the ER."

"Huh?" I blinked. Gail leaned her elbows on the counter, whisper-shouting for everyone to hear. "Rumor has it Bane almost kicked Hale's ass for hitting on you. I think you have an admirer, Jesse."

I slipped out of Café Diem, wondering what else I didn't know about Roman and his behavior. If he'd touched Hale for flirting with me, I wasn't sure how he was going to react when Emery, Henry, and Nolan finally dragged their butts back to Todos Santos. I didn't want to know, either. I appreciated his protective ways, but I wanted to take care of myself. In fact, it seemed mandatory after everything that had gone down.

Outside, I called Mrs. Belfort's daughter, Kacey. She was a New Yorker with a husband and kids, and I'd once seen her at Mrs. B's, which was more than I could say about her Bostonian brother. Kacey answered after the third ring and sounded less than happy when I told her who I was. When I explained that Mrs. Belfort wasn't feeling very well, I heard a steel cabinet slam in the background and an animalistic growl.

"So. My overdramatic mother finally resorted to getting her teenage neighbor to call me? Jesus Christ. Get a life." Then she hung up.

I sat there, staring at the ocean for a long minute, trying to figure out what had just happened. Then I shook off my anger and dialed Ryan, Mrs. Belfort's son. It went straight to voicemail. I called again. Same. Maybe his phone was turned off. Or maybe he was at a meeting. Or maybe he didn't want to deal with me, just like his sister. Anger sizzled in my blood as I wrote him a quick text message.

> This is Juliette Belfort's neighbor. I'm calling because your mother is not doing well. She needs you and your sister to come home.

He wrote back a minute later.

> Don't call me again.

Exasperation made my breathing labored and hard. I thought about how I would have reacted had my own father still been alive and in need. I would drop everything to be with him. Of course, I didn't have that privilege, and that annoyed me, too.

> Your mother is still alive, but you deem her a drama queen, even though you know she is slipping in and out of lucidity.

His second text came a minute later.

> This is not a kiddie game, sweetheart.

Yeah, I thought. *Professional oxygen wasters.*

I went back into the café, finished my shift, and drove home. On my way there, an unsettled feeling of a pending disaster formed in my gut. It was brewing, I could tell, because I wanted to be sick. I tried to call Roman, but he didn't pick up, and I had to remind myself once again that everything was okay. I parked and pushed the entrance door open, feeling my mouth going dry before I even heard the yelp coming from the kitchen.

"Jesse? Jesse, is that you?"

Pam was heaving, her voice panicky and uneven. I dumped my backpack by the door and tucked my cell phone into my back pocket, heading over to the kitchen. Had she broken a nail or something?

"Nope. It's the pope."

"You need to come here, sweetie!" she called.

Sweetie? That was new. And worrying. The knot in my stomach tightened, and the need to turn around and run took hold of my legs, but I fought it. I rounded the corner into the kitchen and found Pam standing above the kitchen sink, sniffing. I arched an eyebrow.

"Are you sick? Do you need Tylenol?" Ever since Pam had twisted my arm into having an abortion, I tried very hard to generally ignore her existence. It was almost going against my nature to offer her help, but it was stronger than me.

Some part of me, albeit small and quiet, still wanted us to be close.

"I already took two and washed them down with water. You need to see something." She grabbed my hand, and I nearly jolted. Another bad sign. Pam never touched me if she could help it. She slid the glass door leading to the patio open and nearly dragged me outside to the backyard with the oak tree, lush grass, and Olympic-size pool.

"I found him like that this morning, a little after you left." She rounded a red Moroccan-style sunbed and pointed at the grass. Shadow lay there, his eyes open, staring at the sun unnaturally. He was still, so very still.

I cupped my mouth, trying not to throw up. It looked all wrong. Him, staring at the scalding sun instead of squinting. A fly trailed along his unmoving ribs, and it occurred to me that he would try to bite it if he were alive.

But he wasn't.

My dog wasn't alive.

My dog was very, very dead.

I crouched down and gathered him in my arms, feeling the tears streaming down like a broken fountain. It took time. Years, to be exact, but it had finally happened. After everything I'd been through—I cried.

"Goddammit, Old Sport," I snuffled, pressing his head to my thighs. He felt heavier than usual. Slack but stiff. Pam was standing behind me, motionless, and I wanted to turn around and throw something sharp at her. "You said he was like this since this morning."

"Yeah."

"Why didn't you tell me, Pam? Why didn't you call?" I jumped up to my feet, my grief interrupted by sudden anger. Anger was easier to digest. Easier to pour out. Loss was crippling, breathtaking, chaining.

Pam ran a hand over her bleached hair, her acrylic pink nails making an unbearable sound along her scalp. "I've been throwing up all morning. You know I liked that dog, too. But he was old, Jesse. Besides, he had cancer. There was nothing we could do."

"Wait." I lifted my palm up. "What cancer? What are you talking about?"

As far as my knowledge went, the blood work never came back, and last time I'd asked about it, Pam had said Dr. Wiese had never called. I'd been meaning to drop by his clinic today after lunch, but...

Pam scrunched her nose, like I was being unreasonable. Tiresome, even. I wanted to push her into the pool and watch her flail helplessly. More than that, I knew that I could. That I had it in me. I was no longer lethargic and sad. I was burning with rage, the kind of flame that sparked fast, consuming everything around it in seconds.

She threw her arms in the air. "Look, I'm sorry, but you're a mess, okay? We didn't want to tell you because we knew you'd make a scene. Guess what? Here you are, making a scene. I don't need this in my life. My life coach says you're messing up my zen."

"We? Darren knew, too?" I advanced toward her. She took a step back. I realized that I didn't have to throw her into the pool. She was going to fall into it all on her own.

"Fine. It was me. Sue me, Jesse! You're a weird, unpredictable girl. I don't want to deal with you if I can help it."

"I'm the girl you forced into having an abortion after you made me pretend I hadn't been gang-raped. What do you expect, cocktails at the Ivy?" I snapped. "I'm messing with your zen? You messed up my life!"

"Really? This again?" She stumbled back another step, waving a dismissive hand in my face. "You were a kid! You'd have popped out that baby and left it for me to take care of. All I've ever wanted was to do my thing."

I plunged forward, recognizing, perhaps for the first time, that maybe I wasn't totally sane, but Pam wasn't, either. She still couldn't admit the simple fact that I'd been raped, and she was self-absorbed to a point of madness.

"When did you find out about the cancer, Pam?"

I needed her to tell me it was this morning so I could look at her face again without wanting to do something horrible to her. But she lifted her hands in surrender and took another step back, her posture already defensive.

"A couple of days after the test."

My stomach churned. I'd had time to tell him goodbye. I hadn't gotten to hold him when he took his last breath. I hadn't even been there to comfort him. Couldn't make sure that he felt comfortable and loved. That he was lying down on one of my hoodies—he loved sleeping on my clothes—and looking up at me, and I would have said something soothing he would somehow have understood. I hadn't even had the chance to give him what no one else in this house deserved—the respect you give to a family member who'd been there for you when no one else had.

When Shadow had taken his last breath, I'd probably been messing around with Roman in his shower, grunting and clawing at his flesh.

This is what happens when you take a chance on life.

"I hate you! I fucking hate you!" I screamed, launching at Pam out of nowhere. She tripped backward and fell into the deep end of the pool. Pam wasn't a good swimmer. For all the sunbathing she did, she never bothered to dip her toe inside the pool.

Her arms flailed hysterically, and she gasped for air, swallowing water in the process. She shrieked, looking like an ant in sticky honey, and although I knew she would get out of there eventually, I enjoyed the first time in our relationship where she did the squirming.

I crouched down, staring at her emotionlessly. "But you know what the worst part is?"

"Jesse!" She gulped more water. "Je-ssse! Help me out!"

"I can't drown my demons. They know how to swim."

CHAPTER EIGHTEEN
BANE

I love you, but you chose the worst fucking time to call.

Like all thoughts, it was mundane, spontaneous, and gratuitous. It flashed through my mind as I waited outside Darren Morgansen's office to tell him thanks for the six million bucks, but I'd really rather bury my dick in his stepdaughter. In-fucking-definitely. Problem was, the person calling me was said stepdaughter.

And I'd just said that I loved her.

Or at least thought it.

Yes. I'd thought it.

No, wait, I was sure of it.

Shit, I loved Jesse Carter.

Was in love with Jesse Carter.

But of course you are, little prick. Do you make a habit of impulsively pissing over six million bucks from an oil tycoon and breaking a contract with him?

This morning, in my dingy kitchenette, I'd known that I wasn't just fucking Snowflake. I was also fucking SurfCity to death because I would never come up with the money for the investment, and more than that, I was fucking myself over because, holy shit, I was about to be one million dollars indebted to someone. Wasn't that the ultimate irony, though? I made so much money fucking people for a living, but in the end, it was one fuck that would cost me a million bucks.

Darren opened his office door and motioned for me to come in, so I let the call die rather than send it to voicemail. For the first time in a long time I didn't feel cocky as a rooster. I was actually nervous. Not about the breaking-the-deal part. Fuck him. But about owing someone so much money. Usually, I was on the owed-to side, not vice versa. I could come up with the money, but not right away. I needed twelve months. Minimum. No one said he was going to give them to me.

"How are you feeling?" Darren asked as he led me to his underwhelming office. The thought occurred to me, for the first time, that Darren designed everything around him—himself included—to come off as unthreatening and harmless. A red alert started flashing inside my head. Ding, ding, ding.

He never wore expensive suits.

Always stood crouched, his chin down.

His lips. His offices. His relationships. He was almost conveniently weak.

"Please don't pretend like you give a fuck." I dumped my wallet and cell phone onto his desk, taking a seat. "Life's too short for that."

"Fair enough." He watched me carefully, making his way to his seat. This time he didn't offer me a drink or a cigar or his left lung. He offered me a pissed look that told me that he already knew I'd come bearing bad news.

Then he actually beat me to it. "You thlept with her."

The gentleman code dictated that I shouldn't deny or confirm this statement, but the contract I'd signed indicated that I'd better speak up, unless getting slapped with a lawsuit was a turn-on. I settled for somewhere in between. I wasn't ready to throw Jesse under the bus in case she hadn't told him. And I strongly wanted to believe Jesse hadn't shared her sexual exploits with her stepdaddy because: Super. Fucking. Gross.

"Whether I did or not is irrelevant. Circumstances change. I want out." I lit up a joint coolly, throwing the still-lit match onto the desk between us. I did it mainly to spite him and to remind him that he was not the boss of me. Though I wasn't entirely sure if that was true. The match sizzled and died, and I wished Darren would follow suit.

"You have a few more months left, I believe." Darren cracked his neck, glancing at the time on my phone. He looked oddly at ease, and I wondered what kind of Xanax he was popping these days.

"She has a job. She's got friends. She's got me. None of that is going to change in the next six months or years, if she decides to stay in Todos Santos." The thought she might not made me want to break someone's nose. "So the whole timeline issue is irrelevant. I'm not asking for the remainder of the money. I'm letting you walk away after paying me three million dollars for way more than six months." For a lifetime. But, of course, I didn't utter this shit aloud because one, it was pathetic, and two, I knew Jesse was going to wise up sooner or later and go for a guy who deserved her. Life doesn't stop for anyone. Even not for a low-bending asshole like me.

"The time limit was the reason we had a contract," Darren argued, his left eye twitching, before adding, "but that was before you broke the contract. You're right about one thing, Bane. Circumstances have changed."

I leaned forward. "Don't give me this bullshit. I helped your stepdaughter more than her therapist and the two of you have, combined."

"Still broke a contract," he said dryly.

I realized I didn't have the time nor the interest to bicker with this clown, so I just waved him off. "Know what? Whatever. I spent around a mil of what you gave me. I'll wire you the remaining two million back. We'll call it even. Move on with your life and put that wife of yours on a shorter leash."

"Bane." He splayed his bony fingers on the desk, grinning. "You're not listening carefully to this entire conversation."

I cocked my head to the side. "Huh?"

"You're seriously, stupidly fucked."

Darren opened a locked drawer in his desk, not sparing me a look. He took out a pile of documents from it and slapped it on the surface between us before taking a steady breath, his expression blasé and foreign on his face, and said, "Why don't you read clause number seventy-seven, point seven, Mr. Protsenko? Maybe the damages clause will make the penny drop."

Then I finally got it.

The lisp.

It was gone.

It was gone, and so was the man I thought I'd read so well. Darren Morgansen straightened in his seat. He looked sharper, more alert. Not the same god the tycoons of Todos Santos were, but closer. Warmer.

What the fuck are you playing at, old man?

He slid the signed contract my way, and my eyes searched frantically for that goddamn clause I hadn't bothered reading. I didn't even have to ask why he'd faked a goddamn lisp. It was to throw people like me off. That's why I'd skimmed the contract. Because he acted like a weak-chinned chicken. He wasn't. He was something else entirely, and the worst part was that I had yet to figure out what. My eyes landed on the clause, and I could almost feel the chuckle Darren produced from his mouth inside my own throat, choking me.

77.7 In the case of termination or breach of the contract for any reason whatsoever by Roman Protsenko (the Entrepreneur) and with respect to the time, effort, and resources of Darren Morgansen (the Investor), the Entrepreneur shall compensate the Investor with $1.5 million USD, which is a readily ascertainable sum certain of damages suffered by the Investor.

My eyes kept on reading and reading and re-fucking-reading the same paragraph over and over again because it didn't make any sense. How had I signed something like this? I was savvy. Every move I made was calculated to a fault. I may have looked like the easygoing pothead, and I certainly played the part—just like Darren played his—but I was a chess player, for fuck's sake. Artem would kill me if he knew. If he was alive. Which he wasn't.

Shit. Oh, God. Shit, shit, shit.

Darren propped his elbows on his desk, his smirk widening. He was having a great time. He pressed his index finger to the middle of the page and dragged it slowly back to his side of the desk, making a show of sighing. "Looks like you're in a bit of a pickle."

I stared him down, feeling the air inside my body turning into fuel, burning with anger. "What's your fucking angle?"

He raised one eyebrow, poking his lower lip out. "Angle?"

"You didn't go through all this trouble for nothing. What was your endgame, Morgansen? And don't fuck with me."

He rubbed his chin in circles, thinking about it. "Fair enough. Seeing as you are indebted to me for a sum of money you can never repay—two and a half million dollars, I believe—and your relationship with Jesse is pretty much over, I guess I can tell you. It was about Artem."

"Huh?" I wasn't following him.

"Artem," he repeated, "was my angle. See, I knew you wouldn't be able to keep your hands off Jesse, and I never liked you, Bane. Even before I knew you, I hated you. I hated you because I hated him."

"What business did you have with fucking Artem?" I spat out. I'd liked my mother's former boyfriend, but he was a distant memory at this point. Mostly, I was sad for my mom. She'd really liked him.

Darren threw his head back and laughed. I wanted to punch his face but wanted to hear his explanation even more.

Finally, he calmed down. "Artem Omeniski was Jesse's dad."

Here's the thing about life: Most of the time you're in motion, so you don't really know what's happening around you. You are simply reacting to situations, and that's why it is said that your life is actually nothing but a collection of your decisions. But sometimes, life is more than that. Sometimes, it's a puzzle that falls into place with a click. Everything made sense now.

Pam and Artem had never been married. Therefore, Jesse was a Carter, not an Omeniski.

Artem had cheated on Pam with my mother, tearing Jesse's family apart.

Artem was loved and adored by Jesse, and Darren hated him or the idea of him. Consequently, he knew that I was the bastard child Artem had taken under his wing all those years ago. That's actually how my mom and Artem had met. Around middle school, he'd gotten assigned to make sure I wasn't going to grow up to be a serial killer or something, and we had weekly meetings. They'd wanted a Russian-speaking social worker I'd feel comfortable with, and I did. We hit it off. He'd come to our house. Eaten from our plates. Taught me shit. And my mother was always warm, perceptive, beautiful, and soft-spoken. They had similar values and thoughts and culture. I couldn't fault him for cheating on Pam. Hell, he'd probably stuck around just to be in Jesse's life. Who knew what Pam would have been capable of if he'd left?

"So you wanted to get back at Artem through me?" I rubbed my chin. "Are you aware of the fact that you can't hurt dead people? They're kind of beyond that."

Darren shrugged. "Still. Jesse loved the bastard so much. He didn't deserve all this admiration."

"Did you kill him?" As far as everyone knew, Artem had fallen down the stairs and died in the office building where he'd worked. Broken neck. His death sounded too convenient.

Darren stared at me with confusion. "I'm not a killer."

"So Vicious was a part of this plan," I said, trying to make sure all the pieces of the puzzle were neatly placed. "He helped you get to me."

I thought about the meeting with Vicious all those months ago. About how he'd directed me to Darren. The latter shook his head.

"I met Baron at the country club a few months ago. Knew you were going to ask him if he wanted in on the deal because you look up to him. Everyone in this rancid town knows that you're the next heir in line for the title of king. So I casually mentioned that I was looking to invest in local business. He didn't know of my plan for you—he simply took the bait."

"And how do you think Jesse is going to react when she finds out about this?" I gritted out.

"That's the beauty of our situation." He smiled, stretching his arms wide. "You would never tell her anything unless you want to be drowning in debt for the rest of your miserable life. Everything I did was for Jesse. Artem was a vile man. I knew that from the moment I laid my eyes on Pam and Jesse all those years ago. I wanted to give Jesse the life she never would have gotten. And I did. But after Jesse was attacked by those boys, I needed to find a way to lure her back into reality. You were perfect. Beautiful, boyish, and most importantly—openly for sale."

He stopped, his eyes darting to my face. I didn't even offer a twitch of a jaw, looking blasé as ever. He continued cautiously. "I knew you'd be able to slay her demons for the right price, and I was eager to pay it. I thought it could go two ways—either you would fulfill your part of the deal and let her go quietly because, let's admit it, a girl like Jesse is simply too good for a punk like you." He hitched a shoulder, smirking. "Or you would break the contract, in which case not only would I be preventing Artem's favorite bastard from getting his precious SurfCity, but I would also be owed some serious money.

"Now, here is what's going to happen—you are going to walk out of my office and end it with Jesse. Tell her you don't want a relationship and that she can still keep the job at Café Diem. Erase her contact from your phone. Ignore her texts. Leave her alone. Do all this and consider us square. Disobey, and you're in big trouble. Millions of problems, to be exact."

There was an unwritten rule about confrontation. The last one to speak usually won. Or, at the very least, the last one to speak normally didn't lose. I wanted to be that person, so I did the only thing I saw fit. I smiled, like he'd just offered me a deal that was way too easy to refuse, when in reality, I knew that I was no longer drowning in deep shit. I was already half-dead.

I sent a hand to his neck, running my fingers through his tie and then yanking the tip. Hard. Not to choke him, but enough to show him that I could. And that I would, if need be. My face was so close to his, I saw the panic swimming in his pupils. He may have faked a lisp, but he couldn't fake bravery. He was scared. Rightly so.

"I think you didn't take one thing into consideration, Morgansen. I grew up here. I know this place. I am the place. You may have the money, but not the respect. Or the friends. Or the connections. You have zero power over me, and if you think I will cower and bow down to you, get lawyered up right now." I let go of his tie, letting him drop like a sack of potatoes back to his executive chair, gagging a little. I paced to the door, easy, unconcerned, and smiling, though I felt none of those things. I stopped at the threshold and turned around. "You messed with the wrong motherfucker, Darren."

"Dump her."

"I'm sorry. Are you deaf now? Did you not hear my last sentence?"

"You'll regret it, son."

I hadn't had the best history with dads in general, but I was pretty sure I'd rather pluck off my balls than ever hear Darren refer to me as his son. I slammed the door in his face, letting it rattle on its hinges in my wake.

Like hell I will.

———

I barely made the trip down in the elevator before bile glazed my throat. I threw my breakfast up into a manicured rosebush outside

Darren's corporate building and then wobbled my way to the nearest BevMo and bought a bottle of vodka to wash down a couple of Tylenol. Class before ass. After washing down two pills with a swig of the good stuff and discarding the rest of the bottle into a trash can, I leaned against my Harley, elbows on handles, trying to figure out what the hell I was going to say to Jesse.

The truth, you liar. How about you start being honest?

But the truth was complicated. It was messy and uncomfortable. And even I couldn't fathom it all the way. For one thing, Jesse and I were kind of stepsiblings. Artem and I didn't share any genes. In fact, he hadn't even married my mom, but he'd played Daddy when I'd needed him to, which was more often than not. Even though my mother hadn't known he had a family until it was too late—I'm sure she figured it out when she went to his funeral and was too much of a saint to share with me, not wanting to tarnish his reputation in my eyes—she felt close to him. Bright side to this bombshell: At least now I had a definite answer to my mom's question whether she was going to meet Jesse anytime soon. The verdict—hard pass.

I was pretty sure Jesse would want nothing to do with my mother and me, and even if she could overcome the twisted misfortune of our connection, there was still the deceit factor. I was going to have to own up to signing a contract where she was pretty much nothing more than a pawn. A means to an end. Then, finally, there was the money issue. I was officially indebted to Darren—millions of dollars I did not have. I could sell Café Diem, and the new hotel definitely had to go. Without a doubt, I was going to lose my pants in the upcoming months—probably the houseboat, too. I tried to tell myself that I would eventually reinvent myself. I always had.

The liar. The con. The thief. The escort.

I wore many hats, playing people like they were my favorite instrument. They say you win some, you lose some, but the latter, I'd never really experienced. Not until I'd gained something that actually mattered.

Fuck it. I would lose my pants and my properties and my business, but not her. Not Jesse.

With that in mind, I hopped on my bike and headed toward her house. The plan was to come clean and maybe try to convince her not to kill me. I was hoping my pissing all over Darren's threats and choosing her over the money was going to earn me some bonus points. Of course, I'd never been fucked by a guy who agreed to take me out for money, so what the fuck did I know?

Shit.

When I arrived at El Dorado, I pushed the automatic button for the neighborhood's gate and watched as it remained locked. Jesus fuck. They'd changed it. They'd changed the electronic system. Didn't take a genius to know who'd done it.

Samantha was the only person who'd given the key to an outsider.

Now, she was no longer a client.

What she was was pissed, vindictive, and no longer of use to me.

I parked my Harley in front of the gate. My foot was already on the first black railing when I heard someone behind me.

"Trespassing in broad daylight. If you want to buy your lawyer their next Cabo villa, just open a GoFundMe account," Vicious practically yawned.

I turned around, tipping my chin down to inspect him. He was tucked inside his silver Aston Martin One-77, one arm resting on the edge of his open window.

"Just open the fucking gate."

"Bane. Didn't recognize your face without the pube hair. Where you headed?" he said in a voice drenched with sympathy, and that's how I knew even he took pity on me. Wow. I must've looked like one pathetic piece of crap.

"The Morgansens'." It pained me to even say Darren's last name.

Vicious flicked his Ray-Bans down, scrutinizing me. "Business going well?"

"I don't want to talk about it." I was still hanging from the gate like a drunken monkey when he pushed his automatic button and the thing started moving. I hopped down. Vicious cocked his head to his right.

"Get in."

"I have my bike."

"They'll see you with it inside—they'll freak out. Samantha Haggins got a verbal spanking the other day for giving her boy toy the keys. Any guesses who he might be?"

Damn. I shook my head and got into his car.

Vicious didn't try to coax any details out of me on our ride to the house, and I tried not to think about how nervous I was to see Jesse. When he dropped me off in front of the colonial mansion, he produced a joint from his pocket, lit it, took a hit, and handed it over to me.

"No longer strangers," he said.

I stared at him impatiently but took the joint because I needed it. I shook my head. "I think I'm in deep trouble, Baron."

"Good. That means that there's someone in your life who's worth the risk."

There's a saying in Russian: Trouble never comes alone. I should have known when I left Darren's office that there was more to come. But I didn't because I was so fixated on the unfolding clusterfuck I'd gotten myself into, I hadn't even bothered to return Jesse's call.

She opened the door, her eyes and nose red, the rest of her face the palest I'd ever seen. Her hair was a mess, and her eyes lacked that mischievous zing that made my dick hard. I immediately forgot my long, elaborate speech and took a step in, jerking her into my arms.

"You okay?"

"Shadow died."

"Fuck," I breathed, clutching her harder, my nose buried in her hair. "When?"

"This morning. Pam found him but didn't call me. He had cancer. She's known for...a while."

Jesse delivered the news with the kind of detachment that showed me that she was still in shock. Now was not the time to drop another bomb on her ass and definitely not the time to drag her into my war with Darren. At the same time, I was aware that he was about to arrive home sometime soon, and I needed her out of there. I pulled back, running my fingers over her eyes, hair, cheeks, lips. Doing inventory, making sure everything was intact. That my Jesse was still mine. She was. For now.

"Where is he now?"

She looked up to the belly of her stairway. "I carried him up to my room. I...I didn't know what to do. Freaked out and didn't want to say goodbye yet. I need to bury him. But, Roman..."

She burst into tears again, and I held her for a few minutes, feeling the blood roar in my ears, before marching in and going up the stairs. Pam was coming down as I was going up. Her face told me she no longer wanted to fuck me, or if she did, it was with a broomstick up my ass. I flipped her the finger and continued to Jesse's room, wrapped Shadow up in a sheet, picked him up and carried him downstairs.

"Where are you taking the dog?" Pam barked from the kitchen, fixing herself a drink. I didn't answer. I wanted to kill her, her husband, and Dr. Wiese, who'd taken the shortcut and dropped the C-bomb on Pam just because he'd known it would be easier, that Jesse was fragile and sensitive when it came to her dog.

"Come on, Snowflake."

I hoisted Shadow to the trunk and climbed into the Rover. Jesse followed in silence. I drove to the reservoir on the outskirts of town, knowing there'd be plenty of land for me to bury him there. Snowflake sniffed and looked out the window. I didn't want to force a conversation, knowing how many things were going through her head. Sometimes she held my hand. I wanted so badly to squeeze hard and tell her there was more. That she needed to be strong for me because shit was about to get real complicated, real fast.

"Jesse."

"Mrs. B is dying. Her kids don't want to come to California to say goodbye," she said flatly, staring out the window, flicking the glass with her thumb and forefinger.

I bit down on a string of curses. "Is that so?"

"Yeah. They said I should stop contacting them. I wanted them to come here while she was still lucid, but that's not going to happen. Know what else is not going to happen? My going back to living with Pam. I've had enough of her bullshit. The only thing I really cared about in that house was Shadow, and he is gone now."

I knew I was cooking up a disaster, considering the shit I was keeping from her, but couldn't stop myself, anyway. "You'll stay with me." It wasn't a question.

"I was thinking of asking Gail. She needs a roommate."

"She needs better taste in music," I quipped. "If I hear My Chemical Romance blasting from her phone one more time, I swear someone will get decapitated."

I expected a snort, a laugh, anything. But nothing ever came. I reached to touch her thigh. "Hey. It will be okay."

"No, it won't. My dad's dead. My dog's dead. My best friend is dying. The only person I have left is you. Well, and Darren and Mayra, I guess, but they only care because they have to. One is paid, and the other is just embarrassed by his sorry excuse for a wife."

I didn't answer. I didn't think Darren cared for her. If he had, he wouldn't have pulled this type of shit. But hey, what the fuck did I know about love? A lot, apparently. For starters, I knew that it hurt like a motherfucker.

I parked her vehicle a few feet away from an old sycamore. The earth beneath it was loose and damp, easy to dig. I took out a shovel

I'd picked up from the gardener's shed from the trunk, flung my shirt to the driver's seat, and started digging. She watched my back all the while. I carried Shadow into his burial spot, covered him in dark soil, and then grabbed a pointy branch and wrote down his name in the sand. Shadow Dog Carter.

"Let's give him a eulogy." I tugged her to my side, wrapping my arm around her shoulders and dropping a kiss on the crown of her head. "He was a good dog. He deserves it."

She stared at the fresh pile of mud mounded under the sycamore, her chin shaking. I wanted to suck her agony into my own body until she felt better, even if it killed me. And the worst part was I knew I was wronging her by not telling her about my meeting with Darren this afternoon. About Artem. And still, I couldn't see her hurting more.

"Once upon a time there was a little girl," she started, crouching down and burying her palm inside the soil. "The girl was scared of the dark and loved Kit Kats. There were four fingers on every Kit Kat. One for her. One for her father. One for her mother, and one…" She paused. I knew she was smiling, even though she was looking down. "The girl wanted a companion, so her daddy gave her a puppy for Christmas. The girl named the dog Shadow because he followed her everywhere. In the pouring rain and the blistering heat. He was there for her when her daddy died. He was there for her when her mother reinvented herself and decided that the girl no longer fit into the picture. He was there for her when they took her soul and all that was left behind was her scarred body. He was there for her, even though she wasn't there for him. The girl was too scared to face the real world. To take him to the vet. To save him."

"Jesse."

She shook her head, a tear landing on the soil beneath her. "Why does the truth always hurt so bad?"

You tell me. I'm drowning in it right now.

When I was young and impressionable, Artem had given me a piece of advice I'd liked so much, I'd tattooed that shit onto my torso, just in case. A tribute to the man I hadn't known would be such a magnificent part of my downfall.

Don't fall in love. Fall off a bridge. It hurts less.

I liked it because it was funny. I'd had no idea it was also true. I picked Jesse up, and she buried her face in my chest. I wasn't much good at comforting, but I wanted to make it as easy as possible for her.

"Give me Mrs. Belfort's kids' numbers," I said.

I called them the same evening while Jesse was taking a shower. The next day, they were on a plane.

CHAPTER NINETEEN
JESSE

My mouth felt furry and dry when I woke up the next morning.

A dull, persistent pain had wrapped itself tightly around my head, like a turban. I wondered if I was experiencing my first hangover. My eyes fluttered against the rays of sunlight pouring through the naked windows of Bane's houseboat. Reality came in like a flickering light. On, off. On, off.

Shadow was dead. We'd buried him yesterday. Then we'd driven back to Bane's place—"Where is your Harley?" "Don't worry about it, Snowflake"—and I'd told him everything was dead, which was an *On the Road* reference that he picked up immediately because Roman Protsenko was both well spoken and well read. Probably the most well-read man I knew, save for my father. Roman told me it was time for a beer and a joint, and one beer turned into three. I hardly ever drank alcohol before the Incident and definitely not after, so it had hit me hard.

Now I was no longer drunk. I was sober and heavy with sorrow. I stirred in his bed that smelled like his cinnamon breath and heady skin.

I flung my arm over Roman's shoulder. It was hard as stone, and I loved how he felt like he'd been carved from the most resilient material in the world. The tough to my fragile. The sturdy to my frail. He groaned, and I peered at the clock beside him. It was eight o'clock. He'd skipped out on his surfing session, no doubt for me, and I had a shift I was already kind of late to.

"You think my boss will be mad if I'm late for work?" I hugged his midsection, trailing kisses up from his shoulder to his jaw. His skin was warm. Downy, almost. I'd been such a sour thing yesterday. Yes, I'd had my reasons, but I hadn't even acknowledged how amazing Roman had been. He whirled around and grabbed me by the waist, slamming me into his morning wood.

"Depending on what your excuse is. He seems like a reasonable dude."

Yesterday, he'd said he had spoken to Kacey and Ryan, and they were going to land in San Diego this evening. I wanted to be there when they arrived but dreaded to guess what method Roman had used to make them drop everything and jump on the first flight home.

"The excuse is me sleeping *with* said boss." I quirked an eyebrow. He smiled and brushed my hair out of my face.

"Hope that fucker gets slapped with a sexual harassment lawsuit by evening. How are we feeling this morning?"

"Torn." I kissed his lips. "Whole." I kissed his forehead. "Mostly, I'm just grateful to have someone to lean on."

I dragged my lips down to his neck, whispering, "I love you, Roman 'Bane' Protsenko. Not because you take away my loneliness, but because you give me strength."

I didn't wait for him to say it back. I kissed a wet path down his torso, flipping his blanket out of the way, and stopped when the metal of his cock ring touched my lips. I smiled up at him. His face was blank, hard, and unimpressed. I was momentarily confused, but not enough to pull away.

"We need to talk." He scrubbed his face with his big palms, looking pained.

I popped his shaft into my mouth and gave it a hungry suck. His head fell to his pillow, his forearm hitting his eyes. "Fuuuuck."

I licked him like a lollipop for a few minutes before he grabbed onto my hair and angled my head up to meet his gaze.

"If you want to suck me off, you'll need to do it my way."

I nodded silently.

"My way is not the kind of way you read in your books." He lowered his voice and chin, searching my eyes for signs of distress. There weren't any.

"You haven't read my books." I arched an eyebrow. "Don't make false assumptions."

He smirked like the cocky bastard he was, grabbing my head, angling it back to his cock. "Your safe word is antiestablishment."

"I'll never be able to say that word around your cock." My eyes widened.

His smirked broadened. "Good."

He pushed the back of my head, his shaft smashing into the back of my throat at once, and I wrapped my lips around it, sucking as hard as I could while controlling my gag reflex. I was hungry for it, and that confused me. I'd never wanted to do that to anyone else.

Slowly, he began to thrust into me with his pelvis, fucking my mouth rather than allowing me to set the tone. His strokes became faster, deeper, and more frantic, and I felt him growing in my mouth, his hand fisting my hair tighter.

"Shit. Your mouth is like a fist." His voice was husky with sleep and sex.

Two minutes later, I felt him jerk and twitch inside my mouth. He lifted my head up, his eyes dreamingly heavy-lidded. "Yes or no?"

I didn't need him to spell it out for me.

"Yeah."

I wrapped my lips around him again and felt as his cum shot into my throat in small, hot spurts. It was salty and thick and made every single part of me tingle.

After he finished, he dragged me to his living room, stark naked, and positioned me on the edge of his tattered couch. He threw my legs open and put his mouth on my already-dripping sex, my need for him running down my inner thighs. He began by licking my inner thighs, biting on them softly with a dazed smile. I tousled his hair in my fist, loving how soft and silky it felt under my fingertips. I gasped when he sucked both my lips into his mouth with force, pumping them in and out while casually sweeping his tongue along my slit. I stared down at his sunshine mane, my mouth puffy and the feel of his cock still lingering on my tongue, wondering if he realized he hadn't said it back to me. *I love you.* Maybe he didn't share the sentiment. That was okay, too. Soul-crushing but okay, I guess.

With loose, broad strokes, he flicked his tongue around my clit, making me squirm until I had to hold his hair and push him away because it got to be too much. He laughed into my core, my legs wrapped fully around his neck, knotted together by the ankles.

"Why the couch?" I nearly stuttered from pleasure.

"Better position for oral. Lie back and let me eat you."

"You're making me crazy." I writhed, my butt sliding down his couch as I thrust myself toward his mouth. I loved that I couldn't see his face. Loved that I could simply feel his smile on my sex as he licked me up and down now, using his thumb to rub my clit.

"I like your crazy. It makes you drip like a passion fruit." He looked up, and I should have been embarrassed to see just how wet and shiny his lips and chin were, but I was way past being self-conscious.

Just minutes later, I came hard, watching as his beautiful lips sucked me hungrily. He looked up, his green eyes menacing, wild, in every shade of green known in nature, and stood up fully, his erection leveling with my face. He pushed me down until I was lying flat on my back and kneeled between my legs, straddling my left leg.

"Pretzel position," he said, sliding into me bareback, his smirk dreamy and taunting all at once.

"Never heard of it," I murmured.

"Well, I'll make sure you never forget it."

By the time I arrived at my shift, sans Roman, who'd gone to pick up his Harley from El Dorado and train Beck, I felt normal. More like myself. Less like the monster I'd wanted to be yesterday.

Before we parted ways, Bane had kissed me in front of the entire café. It felt like a statement. A statement that lacked words but said the same thing that I'd said to him that morning.

He'd stroked my cheek. "We need to talk tonight. After you're done with Mrs. B. Promise me you'll go to her from here and then straight to the houseboat."

I nodded. I got it. He didn't want me to clash with Pam. I didn't, either.

"Pinky promise."

"Straight back home," he'd warned one last time.

I'd watched him as he jumped into Beck's car to pick up his Harley.

And I'd felt it. The strength to do what needed to be done. To overcome Shadow's death and everything else life had thrown at me the past few years.

What I didn't know was that this sudden strength was essential.

Because that evening, the princess had to wield her sword.

And finally slay all of her demons.

My shift zinged by. I was grateful to be occupied with work because it prevented me from obsessing over Shadow. But Shadow wasn't the only problem I had to deal with.

Where am I going to live?

Will I ever be able to forgive Pam?

Should I cut ties with Darren now, too?

Is Mrs. Belfort going to be okay?

And perhaps the biggest question of them all, the one that had been swimming in my head since the flashback had started: Who was the person who smelled of vodka? The one who made me subconsciously fill my room with Polaroids of people's backs.

When I finished my shift, I had four missed calls. Two from Pam, one from Darren, and one from Roman. I figured Pam wanted to apologize because she was scared I was going to kill myself and that would stain her precious reputation, and Darren was going to plead the "she ith jutht worried about you" case. I wasn't in the mood for the charade, so I only returned Roman's call.

"Headed to Mrs. Belfort's?" he asked.

"Yeah."

"Just remember, do your thing, give her kids grief for being assholes, and come straight home. This can't wait another day."

"You're making me nervous." He was. I couldn't bear any more bad news, but Roman was adamant we do this face-to-face. "Is it bad?"

He gave it some thought, not exactly what I was hoping for, before saying, "Straight back home."

Home. Like his home was mine.

"I'll see you tonight," he said.

"Bye," I said. *I love you,* I added to myself. *And I'm scared.*

I arrived at Mrs. Belfort's and headed straight to her kitchen. Kacey was holding a cup of tea, and Mrs. Belfort was eating an apple pie, crumbs adorning her chin and coat. Ryan sat opposite them, taking slow sips from a bottle of beer. They all looked up at me at once. I walked over and sat down in the spare chair.

"Hi. I'm Jesse."

"We know who you are. Your boyfriend's infamous, so getting a call from him was not exactly uplifting. This better be good," Ryan scolded quietly. Neither of Mrs. Belfort's kids resembled her. They were blond, tall, and completely unrelated to the warm woman I'd grown to love.

I stood up, folding my arms over my chest. "We need to talk in private. All three of us."

Mrs. Belfort looked up from her apple pie, her eyes wondrous and a little hurt.

"Imane"—I twisted my head, calling her housekeeper—"can you please keep Mrs. B company while we go to the dining room?"

Five minutes later, it was just Kacey, Ryan, and I. I sat across from them and felt grossly ill-equipped to help someone else—hell, I couldn't even help myself—but I loved Mrs. B too much to see her neglected by her kids.

"Your mother has Alzheimer's," I said flatly.

"She also has a lot of assistance, as you can see." Ryan waved his hand around at an invisible staff. I took a deep, measured breath.

"She has some lucid moments. She knows that she is dying. She knows that her disease is eating away at her ability to function. She knows her kids are all the way across the country, with their heads buried in the sand."

"We've been told that there's nothing we can do." Kacey, who wore a sharp suit and was a lawyer, jumped into the conversation, adding, "I can't take her with me. I have a kid at home and a sixty-hour job. I just can't."

"I have a family, and I work for the biggest advertising company in Boston," Ryan chipped in with his own sob story. I saw so many similarities between them and Pam. How they didn't want to take responsibility for their own families, even though Mrs. B had raised them. Even though Pam was my mother. And then I thought about all the responsibilities I hadn't taken, either. Refraining from taking Shadow to the vet sooner. Not reporting the men who did what they'd done to me and letting them get away with it, knowing that they were a ticking bomb waiting to explode on someone else. They'd gotten away with it once. They were going to do it again. I laced my fingers together and dragged my chair forward until my abs hit the table, drawing out the weapon I dreaded to use. The one that could have brought them over in a heartbeat if I'd had the balls to just tell them on the phone.

"Your mother changed her will."

"Huh?" Ryan scrunched his nose and slumped in his chair like a punished schoolboy. For the first time since we'd stepped into the dining room, his eyes were peeled off his phone screen.

I nodded solemnly. "She wants to give everything to me."

"She is not lucid!" Kacey jumped, standing up on her feet and slapping the table.

I shook my head. "She was when she changed the will. And her medical staff knows it."

"This is ridiculous!" Ryan screamed, still tucked snug in his chair. Kacey wagged a threatening finger in my face, leaning close.

"I heard all about you, Jesse Carter. I know you came from the slums. If you think you can cheat your way into my family fortune..."

"I don't want the money," I said wryly, because I didn't. I didn't care about anyone's money. The correlation between having money and being happy seemed to have the opposite effect. As far as I was aware, the most miserable people I knew were filthy rich. And maybe it was because of my complete lack of interest in money that everyone around me was so eager to throw it at me. Darren and Mrs. B seemed to have that in common. "I want you to take responsibility for the person who gave all of herself to raise you."

"So what are you suggesting?" Ryan huffed.

"I want her to move in with Kacey because I know her apartment is big enough." I turned from the woman in front of me and continued. "And you, Ryan, should take two weekends a month to drive down to New York and spend time with your mom. Let her see her grandchildren. And I want Imane and her nurse to move to New York with her. They already said yes."

They stared at me like I was the devil. To them, maybe I was. I was tired of people not owning up to what they needed to do, and that included myself. It was time for a change. It was time to stop sitting on the sidelines of my life, watching it pass. "I'm also happy to give up every single penny Mrs. Belfort wants to give me—I have only known her for about two years, since…" *It doesn't matter*, I tried to tell myself, only it did. I needed to start looking reality in the eye if I wanted to truly face it. "Since I went through something that changed my entire perspective about people and how you should treat them. I will give up all the money, reserving a very small budget for myself."

Ryan snorted, shaking his head. "Of course."

I continued, raising my voice. "A small budget that will go toward visiting her every other month to make sure that she is happy with you guys."

Stunned silence fell over the room. They looked at each other with such exasperation, I thought they were going to say no. And then what? The thought of moving in with Mrs. B occurred to me. But I wanted to put some space between Pam and me. Besides, Mrs. B didn't need me. She needed her family.

"I never realized things were that bad." Kacey's gaze dropped to her folded hands on the table. She sat back down, seemingly humbled by arguing with a twenty-year-old over her mother's fortune. "I mean, I would talk to her on the phone a few times every month and usually she'd talk like my dad was still alive. I didn't know she had any idea what was going on."

"She does." I sniffed, scraping an invisible stain from the table.

"Does she still go to the maze?" Ryan interrupted, his voice no longer hostile, although still edgy.

I shook my head. "I go there now."

"That's where they fell in love," Kacey commented, and my heart skipped a beat at her words. It was where I'd fallen in love, too. "She and my dad. This mansion belonged to his family. She was the gardener's daughter. He used to go there all the time. That's where they met. That's where they fell in love." Kacey took a shaky breath, a tear rolling down her cheek. "That's where I was conceived, and that's why we are all here."

I have no regrets. I loved fully, I remembered Mrs. Belfort saying.

I smiled to myself. "She is the best company I've had in years."

Ryan stood up and looked at his sister, who did the same. Something passed between them I couldn't interpret. They asked for an hour, which I was happy to give them. I spent the time sitting at the dining table, alone, thinking about everything and nothing.

After an hour, Kacey sauntered back into the room. Alone. She looked like she'd been crying. I wished I had a brother to hold me when I did.

"Yes. We will take her," she said and nodded curtly. "I'll make the arrangements ASAP."

I sucked in a greedy breath, realizing I'd been holding it for who knows how long.

One pin down.

Just a few more to go.

I hurried to my Range Rover like my butt was on fire. Mainly, I wanted to get to Roman as soon as I could and have this conversation that hung over my head. I light-jogged to my vehicle when I heard the familiar sound of Darren's Mercedes locking. I tried to slip into the driver's side, but then I heard his voice booming from behind the palm trees dividing the two mansions. "Jethy!"

I froze for a second. No matter how mad I was at Pam, Darren didn't deserve my wrath. I owed him at least an acknowledgment. I turned around from my door, plastering a patient smile on my face.

"Hey, Darren. I was actually just about to leave."

Darren rushed over to where I was standing, and I inwardly groaned. I really wanted to get to Roman as soon as possible.

"I need to talk to you, thweetie."

"Now's not a good time." I turned around, swinging my door open again.

"It'th about your boyfriend."

I paused, my back still to him. He had my attention, though, and he knew it.

"I wath hoping we could do it thomewhere elth. Maybe Mayra'th offith?"

Driving all the way downtown to have a talk with me? Why couldn't he do it at the house? *Because whatever it is, Pam doesn't know.* A terrible feeling came over me.

Why would Darren have a key to Mayra's office, anyway? Just how close were they?

I'm missing a chunk from my memory.

No, you're not.

"Darren, I want to leave."

I want to leave.

He gripped my arm and turned me around. It wasn't violent, and it didn't hurt. What it was was familiar. And it shouldn't have been.

"Jethy." This time it was a growl.

"What do you want?" I barked. A miserable feeling of a lack of self-control came over me. This felt dangerous. I wanted to take my imaginary sword and use it. I wanted to become the hero of my own story.

"You have to break up with Roman."

"Why?"

"Becauth he ith lying to you."

"Why?" I persisted.

"Because the only reason he slept with you was because I paid him to!" His words came out in an angry haste. The air in my lungs squeezed against my chest, and my mouth dropped open. I stared at him, wide-eyed, before the next splutter of words attacked me. He was so close to me, our faces so near, I could see things on his face I'd never seen before. Fury. Frustration. *Madness.*

"I knew he was the town's whore and that he was for hire. Knew that he had a café for you to work in. I paid him six million dollars to build his stupid SurfCity in exchange for spending six months with you. I didn't want him to touch you or seduce you, just bring you back to life. I meant well, Jesse, but he took the money and the girl, too. A girl who wasn't mine to give. He tried to blackmail me yesterday."

My back slammed against my vehicle. I cupped a hand over my mouth. "No."

"Yes. I bet he didn't tell you why I wanted to break the contract, right? I didn't even mind about you going out together. I only want what's best for you, sweetie." He was under the impression Bane had already told me.

I have something to tell you.

Is it bad?

Just come home.

He was about to.

Darren took a step toward me, even though we were already too close. "I ran a check on him to make sure he wasn't as dangerous as they said." He talked fast, in a hurry to get his point across. "And I found out that...sweetie, Roman is basically your stepbrother. Artem had an affair with Roman's mother."

An arrow of hot angry bile shot straight to my throat.

"You're lying." My voice broke.

Darren thrust his phone into my hand. "Call him and ask. He won't deny this. His mother was Artem's mistress. He is not the solution to your problems, Jesse. He is the *cause* of all of them."

"Why are you doing this?" I asked. I'd never seen him like this. Sweaty. Red. Angry. It's like he'd lost control over himself. His suit was wrinkly, his hair sticking out in every direction, and there were black circles under his eyes. Now that I thought about it—really thought about it—Darren never quite looked like he had his shit together. But lately...lately he looked even worse. The crumpled clothes. The fidgeting. The long hours in his office. He was falling apart.

Was he ever put together?

"Because I care about you, Jesse. All the things I did, I did because I care about you. I never knew he'd touch you."

"No." I pushed his chest, and he stumbled back, his mouth falling in shock. "Why did you marry my mother? You don't even love her. Hell, you hardly ever speak to her. Why do we live with you? I don't even acknowledge your existence most of the time. Why do you interfere with my life? Why would you hire Bane? And a private investigator? Why, Darren? Why, why, why?"

He stared at me, an ocean of emotions swimming in his eyes. There was something he wanted to say. Something he knew better than to utter aloud.

"Tell me!" I stomped my foot, allowing the tears to fall down now.

"Because I love you."

I sniffed, smiling bitterly. "Don't take it personally, Darren, but I hate you. I hate you, and I hate your mansion, and I hate El Dorado and Todos Santos. I hate the entitled assholes who rule this town and the fakers and the too-trimmed lawns and the too-shiny mall. I hate that you're trying to fix me. I hate that your wife is a bitch. I hate that your wife is my *mom*." But most of all, I hated Roman Protsenko for giving me hope and then taking it away. For giving me a false future but also for taking the one thing that mattered. My dad. I pushed Darren again so I could climb into my Rover and leave.

The slap came out of nowhere, landing square on my cheek. It was so hard it echoed in my ear for seconds later. I had to blink to make things blur back into focus.

"Oh. Oh, Jesse, I'm so sorry. I didn't mean to... I never meant to..."

He held his palms up, trying to peel my hands off my face so he could take a look at what he'd done, but it was too late. I was going to run over the bastard if I had to. I hopped into my vehicle, locked the door quickly, and started the engine. I bolted out of there like a bat out of hell, getting out of the neighborhood first, and rolling onto the main road leading into downtown Todos Santos.

It was only at the traffic light, when I stared at the bright-red circle on my face, that the penny dropped.

Darren hadn't had a lisp.

And he smelled of vodka.

CHAPTER TWENTY
JESSE

Fifteen missed calls from Darren.
    Eight missed calls from Bane.
    Five missed calls from Pam.

Darren: Sweetie, I'm so sorry. I snapped. I apologize.
    Please come back.
Bane: ?
Darren: We can work this out. Worse things have happened.
    My own father used to belt me when I was a kid. It's no
    excuse for what I did, but it happens.
Bane: Snowflake, where you at?
Darren: Jesse, please call back.
Pam: You're not ruining this for me, you little bitch, so you
    better drag your skinny ass back to El Dorado because
    Darren is going crazy and we need to sort this out.

I couldn't face any of them, but I also had nowhere to go.

Mrs. B was in El Dorado, the last place I wanted to be, so that was out of the question.

Instead, I crashed at Gail's. She lived in one of the pink-yellow villas on the promenade. Gail was understanding. She didn't call me a freak when I asked for her sneakers and yoga pants and announced that I was going for a run on the beach before I'd even dumped my backpack in her living room.

"I wish I had the urge to run every time I was anxious as opposed to polishing off an entire tub of Chunky Monkey." She sighed dramatically, smiling to herself.

Of course, I didn't tell her what it was about. I just turned off my phone and asked that if Bane called, to tell him I was not there. She thought my problems were boy stuff, so she wasn't too anxious.

"He's my boss, Jesse."

"I know," I said.

"And he's crazy about you. He would kill me. Do you want me dead?"

I looked at her flatly.

She rolled her eyes. "You better give me a hell of a eulogy, bitch."

Taking the stairs three at a time, I poured out into the salty-fresh air of the promenade and started running. I turned on my phone and plugged my headphones in, needing to drown the demons in my head. "Can You Feel My Heart" by Bring Me the Horizon poured through the earbuds. I put all the pieces together. Everything Darren had said and all the things Roman had probably wanted to explain before Darren beat him to it.

SurfCity.

Six-month contract.

Six million dollars.

To coax me out of my shell.

Like I was a fucking crab.

For him to throw into the boiling water while still alive.

Put on a plate.

Crack. Break. Devour.

Nausea crawled from the pit of my stomach up to my throat, but I didn't slow down. No. I ran faster, feeling my hot tears flying in the air beside me. They felt so hot on my cold face.

In the time after the Incident, I'd always wondered what it was in my judgment that had caused this disaster to happen. *She asked for it* was thrown in the air too many times. I'd guessed if I'd had my dad around, he'd have said that there was no such thing. He'd been a social worker, a poet, and a dejected drunk. But he was also smart. It wasn't anything I'd worn or said. It wasn't my quest to fit into a place that had decided that I was different—much like Roman—before I'd even opened my mouth. It wasn't because I'd been raped, and yes, I told myself, *I had been raped before.*

It was simply my messing with the wrong crowd. The wrong crowd who looked like the right one. Pristine white smiles, ironed clothes, good manners, and straight A's. Sometimes you just couldn't know, and I needed to let go.

Let go of the past. It's no longer yours, Mayra had said to me once, when I'd poked at my missing memory again.

But, of course, my past was mine—the only things that *were* mine were the moments that made me who I was. When Bane had come into my life, so had the flashbacks. I liked to think of it as a way for Artem—Pam called him Art, as she was embarrassed to admit she'd fallen pregnant by a Russian immigrant—to give me some of my sanity back.

I wanted to remember.

My feet hit the sand quietly, and I stared down at my own shadow, trying to regulate my breathing. *I miss you, Old Sport.*

Everything was falling apart around me, but I felt oddly tranquil. Free.

I looked up at the open sky, and it stared back at me. It was forming into a deeper and deeper shade of dark blue, like water spreading over a cloth, and I was trying to chase an invisible sun at the end of my track.

Why did you have to have an affair, Dad?

But it was obvious, and even I knew it. My mother had never been a good partner. They were never married. The way Pam had explained it to me one drunken night, when she'd stumbled back from her friend's wedding and come to my room to check that I was still alive, was that they'd met at a dive bar. She'd studied classical literature in college, and Artem knew all about Pushkin and Dostoevsky. They'd hit it off and ended up in bed the same night. They were both the wrong kind of wasted, and when morning came, so did their senses. He left her dorm, but then when she found out that she was pregnant with me, they'd tried to make it work.

I sometimes thought that my mom had her heart in the right place when all of this had happened, and maybe that's the worst part.

She'd tried to be a mother and a wife, but never consistently. She used to kick my dad out of the house for the smallest things. Because he hadn't taken the trash out or had accidentally cut my bangs wrong or was late from work because he'd gotten caught up on a demanding case. Then the small stuff became big stuff because he was just too frustrated. He'd drunk too much. He went MIA on us too much. He'd shown her that he loved her less and less. As with all loveless partnerships with children, they'd remained together hoping that someway, somehow, their problems would disappear.

It had rained the day he died. No, not rained, poured. I remembered thinking God was crying with me. I remembered thinking God was unfair because I was already unhappy and I hadn't even done anything wrong.

At his funeral, there'd been a redheaded woman standing a few graves across, hiding behind big glasses. She was staring at us. I didn't know why.

I now knew.

Then I remembered Darren stepping into the picture, conveniently close to the time Dad had died. The whole timeline of that year was a blur. Twelve is a bad age to lose a parent. You're on the verge of a hormonal revolution, your body is blooming, your innocence is wilting, and everything feels personal.

At first, I thrust myself into Darren's open arms willingly.

I'd been so thirsty for love, so unbearably lonely, I gulped up his attention like it was water in the desert.

And Pam had loved it. Us. For the first time since I was born, she'd looked at me with a smile on her face. Granted, it was because I'd played right into her second-family plan, but she'd enjoyed it nonetheless.

Then it happened.

It happened.

The flashback came and, with it, the terrible realization of how I'd gotten here, to this beach, at this hour, betrayed and stripped out of every meaningful relationship I'd ever had.

That night.

His back.

As he closed the door.

Locked it.

Put the key above the tall cabinet I couldn't reach.

Turned around and said, lisplessly, "Hello, Jesse."

I collapsed, my knees hitting the sand, my hands trying to grasp at it like it was ropes I could climb. Ropes leading to the entire flashback that was now so clear, so vivid, so real.

I shouldn't have been there.

But I was.

I remembered the vodka bottle he placed in front of me.

It'd had a snowflake on it.

CHAPTER TWENTY-ONE
JESSE

EIGHT YEARS BEFORE

Pam Carter just wanted to be taken seriously.

That's what she told me, anyway, in the rare moment when she'd decided to acknowledge my existence.

"I have *a lot* of potential," she said around the long cigarette tucked between her lips, looking at me in the rearview mirror of her crappy car. Her once-raven hair was now platinum blond, her dark roots telling the story of her empty pockets. "I went to college, you know. Almost finished it, too."

When Dad died, my mom looked almost relieved. He died in the stupidest possible way. He fell and broke his neck. The stairs leading to his office were wet. The last day of his life, I'd told her I needed new shoes, and she'd said, "We don't have the money. Your dad has a new family, you know. A second one. Maybe that's where all the money goes."

I'd turned around to him, looked at his helpless face. "Is that true?"

He didn't deny it.

Then, very calmly, with the tone I'd borrowed from her, I said, "I hate you. I never want to see you again."

I carried this moment in my life like the mark of Cain.

I didn't know when, exactly, Pam had met Darren, but I remembered the first time she told me about him. I believe it was akin to a royal wedding announcement. She'd said she'd fallen in love with a man and that he was wonderful and caring. That I would love him, too.

We moved in with Darren four months after Dad died, the weekend they got married in Todos Santos's City Hall. There wasn't much to tell about Darren. Everything he did, he did gingerly and neatly. He was harmless and would often expand his eyes when he was spoken to, as if he himself couldn't believe he was worth the attention. It was easy to see why he took a liking to Pam. She was a great actress and could fake emotions perfectly.

She made him feel powerful and important.

All the things he didn't believe about himself.

Darren laid the daddy stuff on real quick and real thick. When he found out I was into books, he set up an entire library in his living room. He would often take me on spontaneous shopping sprees and hold my hand.

"Would you like that, Jethy?" At first, his lisp embarrassed me. Then I grew to like it.

I would nod.

"Then it'th yourth."

He would actively try to engage with me in conversations every time we sat at the dinner table, and when I brought up the subject of wanting to visit my dad's grave and Pam almost fell over, Darren was there to tell her that it was a good idea. He was even there to buy the Kit Kat I wanted to place on Dad's grave, a token for all the Kit Kats we'd shared at the bus stop every morning while we waited. Me, for the bus to take me to school. Him, for the bus taking him to work.

"Two for you, two for me."

"But you're bigger, Daddy."

"Which means that you are growing. Remember: The journey is always better than the destination."

I'd been reluctantly happy. How could you not be, when you moved from a two-bedroom apartment in Anaheim to a mansion in Todos Santos and got a brand-new wardrobe and built-in dad who tried really, really hard to fill the impossibly large shoes your real one left behind? It wasn't Darren's fault that we'd been injected into each other's lives artificially. And it definitely wasn't his fault that I missed my real dad like an inner organ I couldn't function without.

Darren only had one vice. Just the one. And we were so accustomed to it from living with Dad for so many years that it blended into our lives like an ugly piece of furniture that's an heirloom from a dead loved one.

Every now and then, he would come back home from a business trip *fuming*. Anger issues didn't begin to cover his mood. But, like Dad, he always spared us his wrath. The first time he'd stormed into the house with a face like thunder was scary. Then again, he went straight to his office upstairs and didn't leave there for two days straight. It was odd, to say the least, but by no means terrible. When he finally came out, he was calm, serene, and polite. "I'm thorry I lotht it. I'd found out that I invethted a lot of money in a hotel that is not going to be built in the netht ten years. It was wrong, and it won't happen again." He would smooth his wrinkly tie.

Only it did happen again. And again. And then a-freaking-gain. I'd tried to block it out. It wasn't like he took it out on Mom or me. I sometimes heard him screaming at people on the phone—lispless, like losing his mind came with gaining his demeanor—but he was always soft-spoken when he talked to us. One time, a man came over to our estate a day after the anger started. A grandpa-looking lawyer in high-belted pants. I watched them from my bedroom window. Darren nearly punched him square in the face.

Darren only ever screwed up once, but that time was enough to tilt my whole world on its axis and rewrite the pages of my history and future. I really loved hanging out in Darren's office. I knew it was forbidden—it wasn't for me to enter and use—but I still liked it. He had three laptops, a library consisting of thousands of books, most of them untouched. "They look good, don't they?" he bragged once. "The interior dethigner really put an effort into buying all the clathics." It felt like a dark cave where I could be alone with my thoughts, the words. With Pushkin.

It was the time he came back from Honduras. I'd been in his office, lying on the deep-green-velvet couch, a Jane Austen book draped over my chest. I'd been sleeping. It was well after three in the morning.

Darren stormed in, slamming the door shut after him. I perked up immediately. He had a bottle in his hand. He *never* had a bottle in his hand. Vodka. I recognized the scent immediately because it reminded me of my dad. I slid the Jane Austen book back to its place above my head, tucking my hair behind my ear.

He turned around. Noticed me.

"Hello, Jesse."

He didn't have a lisp, and that worried me. It told me I was getting a Darren I didn't know. Darren who didn't necessarily want to be my dad.

He locked the door.

I blinked, and it felt like my eyelids were a camera, taking a picture of his back, memorizing the moment and cataloging it somewhere in my brain, like a flight recorder.

Remember this picture, Jesse.

I couldn't swallow the saliva gathering in my mouth.

"I need to leave." I thought I said it, but I wasn't really sure. I was frozen with a fear I'd never felt. I couldn't even explain it. He'd never been anything but nice to me. But everything felt different that night. Like the devil got the pen to write my script till morning.

He looked like hell in a crumpled suit, and for a moment, I pitied him. Pitied that he felt compelled to make so much money in order to be up to par with his deceased father. Pitied that he'd married a woman who actually *cared* about how much he was making. And that, even at his age, he still thought he had something to prove.

"Jesse," he croaked. Was he crying? Jesus. He *was*. I glanced around me. An irrational urge to hurt him washed over me. My survival instincts were making every nerve in my hands and feet burn.

"I'm so sorry," he apologized, his voice clear, strong, stable. "You shouldn't have come here tonight."

I finally managed to stand up. I watched him drinking for a few minutes, too afraid to make a move.

"You're really beautiful, you know." He took a step in my direction. I took a step back. My fear was like blood-sucking ants, rushing up my feet, *up, up, up.* They itched and burned until they covered my entire body.

"I'm going to go now," I said, advancing for the door. My suspicion and anxiety materialized into a reality the moment I felt his hand wrapping around my wrist. My hand was planted on the round door handle that I knew was locked, and still, he didn't let go. He looked down at the same time I looked up, and our eyes met.

He offered the bottle of vodka with the snowflake adorning its label. "Drink."

I didn't move. He twisted my wrist, my palm facing upward, and placed the bottle in it. "Drink until you can't feel it in your throat."

The best way to go about it was to squeeze my nostrils with one hand while holding the bottle in another. It was heavy. I remembered thinking *I might die tonight.* And I did, in ways I couldn't fathom at that age.

I walked back to the couch on order. It was still warm and dented with the shape of my small body. He hovered above me, leaned in, and pressed my wrists to each side of my head. The room swam out of focus, everything blurry and numb.

"You're drunk," I said. "My dad was drunk all the time. It doesn't have to be this way."

He shook his head. "Just this one time, Jesse. Give me this one time."

"No. Please. No."

He crawled on top of me, ignoring my plea. He smelled like a man, not like a boy. Boys smell spicy and sour, with too many hormones and deodorant. Men smell like violence. Bitter but subtle. "Oh, God. You're so beautiful. So beautiful, Jesse…" he said as he moved inside me. It probably hurt like hell. Sad thing was, I couldn't feel it at all. "Your tight, hot body against mine is just heaven. I want to *live* inside you, Jesse." His vodka breath burned against the shell of my ear.

I want to live inside you.

I want to live inside you.

I want to live inside you.

The words bounced inside my seemingly empty head. I kept on asking myself why I wasn't fighting, but I already knew. I was more scared of the alternative than what was already happening. First, I was scared that if I tried to push him away, he would become violent, and the plush, sincere approval he'd showered me with would evaporate. Second, I was afraid that it wouldn't matter anyway, and he would still rape me. He was so much bigger and stronger than me. Third, I was scared that if I told my mom, she wouldn't believe me—or, worse, would say something crazy, like I'd tried to seduce him. And fourth—even if I, theoretically, overcame all of the above-mentioned obstacles, where would it leave me? My mom didn't have a job. If she left Darren, we'd be homeless and poor and thrown back onto the streets.

I faintly remembered him tucking me into bed. The next morning, I woke up, slid my pj's down, and saw dried blood clustered on my inner thighs. The unnerving feel of wanting to throw up took hold of my stomach, but I wasn't sure what it was. I tried to pee, but nothing came out. I turned around, threw up into the toilet, and hugged it for a while, plastering my damp forehead to the edge of the seat and not caring much about the fact that it wasn't the most sanitary moment of my life. Pam strode past the open bathroom in the hallway, stopped, and looked at me, fixing her diamond earrings as she spoke.

"Not feeling well?"

"I think her thtomach upthets her," Darren called out from their bedroom, his tone casual. "I had to carry her upthtairs latht night." Pam's eyes dropped to the blood on my thighs. Her pupils dilated. I followed her line of vision down to them. Had I finally gotten my first period? That was the first thing that popped into my mind.

A lot of girls my age got it, and they always reported stomach cramps and other gross stuff I didn't want to deal with. Realization washed over Pam's face. She shook her head and turned her back to me. I blinked.

Click.

Remember this picture, Jesse.

"You can stay home today. Hannah will make you breakfast," she said coldly. "I have a session with my trainer and then lunch at the country club, but I'll be back to check on you after. Congrats," she snorted, her voice cracking a little. "You're a woman now."

That day, I started taking pictures of people's backs. Hannah's. Then Pam's. Then Mrs. Belfort's, when she went out to her maze and I watched her through my bedroom window.

And that night, my first nightmare occurred.

Click.

He plastered his forehead to mine.

I didn't move.

He stood up.

I didn't move.

He looked down.

I didn't move.

He said, "Fuck"—the first and last time I heard him curse.

I started to cry.

I tucked that memory somewhere safe and took a picture of Darren's office door.

Never remember this picture, Jesse.

CHAPTER TWENTY-TWO
JESSE

I crawled back to Gail's apartment later that night. I was covered in sand and tears and snot and looked less than picture-ready. Somewhere along the river of memories flooding in, I'd fallen to my knees again going up the stairs from the beach to the promenade. I was bleeding. I didn't even realize that I was until I scraped Gail's front door like a desperate stray cat, my throat burning with thirst. She swung it open and looked down, her eyes nearly bulging out of their sockets.

"Jesse!"

She dragged me in and threw me into her bathtub while my clothes were still on. I couldn't stop crying and clawing at my face. I wanted so badly to get back at them. All of them.

Darren.

Pam.

Emery.

Nolan.

Henry.

Even Roman. I wanted to make them suffer and watch as they did and not spare them the mercy they hadn't shown me. As I was planning the mass destruction of other people's lives, Gail was peeling the heavy, wet clothes off me and taking off my sneakers. Between gasps and sniffs, I could hear her talking on the phone. It was pressed between her shoulder and ear.

"...yeah. She won't be coming to work tomorrow."

Bane.

Pause.

"No. Don't come here."

Pause.

"Why? Because you're a fucking asshole, Bane. That's why. I don't know what you did to her, but she's a mess. You're not allowed to come here."

Pause.

"No. You can't talk to her, either."

Pause.

"If you come here, I will call the police, and I don't care that you're my boss. You're not allowed anywhere near her until she says so. I don't think you understand, Roman. She is *not* okay."

Pause.

"I'm not telling her that."

Pause.

"Because she needs to hear it from you."

She hung up, tossing her phone on the counter by the sink. I clung to her arms, pulling myself up to look at her. I couldn't see her through the curtain of tears. She was a shadow, much like all the other things I'd loved and lost.

"Thank you," I croaked.

She sat on the edge of the bathtub, running her hand through my wet hair. I pressed my face into her palm, naked and vulnerable.

"You need to tell me what happened," Gail said.

I did.

Jesse: I know.

Darren: ???

Jesse: About you. About Pam. About everything. I remember.

BANE

She knew.

Knew about Artem.

Knew about the deal. The contract. The betrayal. And everything in between.

She knew, and now it was my time to pull every fucking resource and connection I had to make sure that this shit was fixed.

I couldn't sleep that night, so I settled for driving to El Dorado, climbing that gate and knocking on Darren's door. I was half-wishing he'd call the police on me because I knew, beyond a shadow of a doubt, that fists would be flying. Pam opened the door, and I stared at her with a mixture of disgust and disdain.

"Out of my way." I brushed past her, rolling my sleeves up and shutting her door with my foot. Pam was feeling adventurous because she decided to throw her body at me. I raised my palms to make sure it was known and seen by every camera in the fucking house that I didn't touch her but stepped sideways to watch her tumble and fall on her ass.

She jumped up again, zipping after me.

"Wait! Where are you going? What are you doing? He's in his office! Don't go there." She wasn't the sharpest pencil in the pack because now I didn't even have to actively look for him. I headed up the stairs straight to Darren, Pam at my heels like an eager puppy. I gave her three warnings before turning around and pushing her against the wall. It wasn't violent or anything, but the message hit home like a grenade.

"Touch me again and I swear your husband will not have one tooth left in his mouth," I growled and then threw the door to Darren's office open.

He sat behind his desk, holding his head in his hands. He was shaking with violent sobs, and that threw me off. I'd never seen a man cry like this, even though I had seen men cry in general. Artem had cried watching Disney films, for God's sake.

I squeezed the doorjamb, slanting my head to the side as I watched him like a photographer studying his subject to get a perfect angle. Like a sniper ready to shoot straight to the heart.

"We need to talk, and you better save me the whole lisp charade because I don't have time for this bullshit. It's about Jesse."

He shook his head and then raised it, his eyes meeting mine. I've never seen more tears and snot on a human face. "I messed it up. It's over, Bane."

I had no idea what he was talking about, but if it was as bad as he looked, we had a problem.

"We need to fix this shit, man. We've both been assholes, but she wasn't. So let's come up with a—"

"Leave, Bane." He cut me off mid-sentence.

"Not before we help her."

"Jesse's done. I'm done. We're all done."

What was he talking about, done? Had he mistaken humans for steaks? I also resented the hopeless narrative he'd given us. *We* weren't done. Maybe *he* was. As for her and me? Jury was still out on that one.

"Do you know where she is?" He looked up, a sliver of hope passing in his eyes.

I gripped the molding above his door, my triceps flexing. "Somewhere safe."

"Where?"

"I'm sorry. Were you not awake for the past forty-eight hours? Why would I tell you anything that is not *go fuck yourself*?" I chuckled bitterly. "Now, tell me what she knows so we can clean this shit up."

The more I knew, the better I could prepare for my conversation with Jesse.

But Darren just shook his head again—his signature move—and

sighed. "She knows everything about everything. Which means that it is over for me."

There was a lot I didn't understand, and Darren looked about as cooperative and conversational as a fucking dildo-shaped candle. I wanted to slam his head against his desk until he gave me all the answers I needed, but it was futile. Dude was not making sense.

"I'm going to make it right," I said.

"It's too late." Some more headshaking. This asshole was about to break some boring Guinness record, and no one was here to give a shit. I darted down the stairs, back to the front gate and to my Harley, leaving Pam to run after me down the street in her little satin nightgown and yelling, "Whatever Jesse thinks she knows, tell her that I didn't know anything about it."

Whatever the hell that meant. As I said before—Jesse got all her wit and intelligence from Artem. This bitch had merely been a nine-month incubator. And when Jesse was born, she took away all of Pam's beauty and brains. Was it a wonder that Snow White's mother was such a devil?

I drove straight to Gail from there. I knew better than to try to convince my employee to let me in and see Jesse. Besides, I needed to start thinking about what was best for Jesse, and even I recognized that she didn't need to see me right now. But that didn't mean I couldn't text her. So I did that, just to cover all my bases.

Bane: You have to believe me when I say I didn't know about Artem. I had no idea. I would never keep something like this from you, Jesse. Ever.

Bane: Yeah, I signed a contract. But that was before. Before us. Before you. Before everything. I thought I was helping both of us. Then I got to know you and SurfCity didn't matter anymore.

Bane: You mattered. You MATTER. You're the only thing that matters, Snowflake. I went to Darren with the intention of

telling him the deal was off. He dropped the Artem bomb
on me that same day.

Bane: I'll be outside Gail's place if you want to talk.

No pressure, right?

I took a few power naps on Gail's front stairs, and then at six
in the morning I was awakened by Beck's text messages and phone
calls. Reluctantly, I dragged my ass back home to take a shower. I
needed another shave, and I needed not to deal with anything that
wasn't Jesse-related. I shot Beck a quick text.

Bane: Can't train today.

Beck: Fuckinghateyoubro.

I washed my hair and shaved, generally making sure I resembled
a real human being, and then hit the road back to Gail's. I knew she
had a shift, so that left Jesse alone. I rapped on the door as softly as
humanly possible, and when she didn't answer, I decided the next
best thing to do was to climb into the apartment through Gail's
window. Again—you should know better than to find the logic in
that. I just had a bad hunch things were a little shittier than the usual
my-boyfriend-is-a-shithead.

Don't get me wrong—Jesse had every reason to be mad at me.
Furious, even. But her reaction suggested something more was
happening.

I padded toward Gail's room in ground-eating strides and found
Snowflake lying in bed, her arm flung over a pillow, staring blankly
at the clock on the nightstand. I took a step deeper into the room,
making myself known. She didn't move.

"Hi," I said.

She didn't answer.

"I got you your check."

Nothing.

"Look, I fucked up…"

"Leave." Her voice was cold. I pressed my forehead against the wall, squeezing my eyes shut.

"Not before we talk."

"That's not for you to decide, Bane." *Bane.* "You betrayed me. Not exactly a concept that's foreign to me, but I'm getting real good at cutting my losses."

I moved over to her, losing control, losing *her.* That was the worst part. Knowing that I was losing her and that she had every right to kick me out of her life after what I'd done. I crouched down beside the bed so that we were looking at each other, only she was still staring at the clock. I flipped the motherfucker down and snapped my fingers.

Yup. Definitely losing my shit.

"Hey. Listen." I tried to grab her wrist so she would look at me, and that was a big mistake. She jumped up and out of the bed and pushed me. I didn't move an inch, but the second time she did it, I stood up and took a step back. She pounced on me, slapping me across the face.

Okay, I deserved that.

Jesse swiveled on her heel, stepped into her Keds, and grabbed her keys. She was wearing Gail's clothes, a floaty black dress that poured down all the way to her ankles. She turned and headed for the door.

I chased her, realizing that it was the first time I'd ever chased after something. *Anything.*

My whole life, people had come to me.

For pot.

For money.

For sex.

For networking. Hey, being the only guy who was from the wrong side of the tracks in a town that had no tracks had its appeal.

It was the first time I was desperate not to lose someone, and she was slipping through my fingers like dust. I decided to keep my hands to myself and not touch her unless she ran straight into traffic, but that didn't stop me from hunting her down. But as I was chasing her, it occurred to me that speaking would be a good idea at this point, too. But where would I start? The contract? Artem? Us? I didn't know which part bothered her the most.

"Jesse, fuck, Jesse. Stop. Just stop for one second. This bullshit thing with Artem wasn't my fault. He was my counselor for a while, and he used to come to our house to make sure my mom fed me and clothed me and didn't use me as a human ashtray. They hit it off. I had nothing to do with it. We didn't know that he was married or that he had a daughter or whatever..." *I said "whatever." Why did I say "whatever"?* It sounded...bad. Wrong. I couldn't take it back, and I hated that I didn't know how to get through to her. Jesse turned around at the door, the keys dangling in her fist.

"Not married. My parents were never married. I'm not mad at you for that."

Ten gallons of air hit my lungs at the same time. Okay. That narrowed it down to the deal with Darren. I could work with that. She got out of the apartment. I shadowed her movements, watching as she slammed the door and locked it.

"Darren tricked me. He doesn't even have a fucking lisp, dude."

"I know." She pocketed the keys in her backpack, and I waited for her to say something more, but she didn't. Instead of heading toward the main street, like I thought she would, she took a sharp turn into an alleyway. I hurried after her, running my fingers over my hair.

"Your stepfather knew I needed an investment. He made me an offer I couldn't refuse," I said, and then realized how fucking bad that sounded. "Okay. Yeah. I could have, and should have, but having sex with you was never a part of the plan. He wanted us to be friends, and I never thought I'd break that promise, anyway."

"Were we friends when I sucked your cock in your bed? When

we had sex in your shower?" She chuckled darkly, pacing faster, giving me her back. The alleyway was long and narrow. It sliced two rows of stores and was dark and full of huge-ass industrial garbage bins. It smelled like hell and felt a lot like it, too.

"Listen, you need to stop and turn the fuck around because I'm going to say it once and only once. I don't repeat myself, Jesse, and won't make an exception for you."

I didn't know where that came from. I just decided to mix shit up and try a different tactic. And *whaddayaknow?* It worked. Snowflake stopped and did as I asked. We were standing opposite from each other, panting hard.

Do this, motherfucker, or regret not doing it for the rest of your life.

I raised my hands to rub her arms before remembering that I'd lost that right about a day ago. I balled my fists beside my body instead.

"Look, I didn't know it'd be this way. I didn't know being this way was even a fucking possibility. This feeling shit? I'm new to it, Jesse. But I swear, at no point, before or after I knew you, did I ever mean you any harm. I love you, Jesse. I fell in love with your soul before I even knew who you were. With that Pushkin tattoo and that defiant stare and the way you carried yourself like a disobedient goddess who didn't belong here with all the snotty mortals of the beach. Even as I stand here now, I continue falling because you're a part of the only fucking person who resembled a father figure to me and also a part of the reason I quit doing the toxic shit that reminded me who I was made of. You're all my good parts wrapped together in a satin bow, Snowflake, and I can't lose you. Because if I lose you, I stay with all the bad parts. I stay *alone.*"

"You love me?"

"Whollytrulymadly," I mumbled, feeling like a dickless high school poem.

She smiled serenely. Like that part I was talking about wasn't there anymore. Then she turned her back to me and gestured with her arm like this place was her kingdom.

"This is where it happened."

I blinked a few times before I realized. *Shit.*

She turned back to me, stubbing her finger to my chest. "It doesn't matter if you love me or not. For the sake of argument—I believe you. You explained everything in the text messages. I know you're indebted to Darren now. Know that you got into a lot of trouble trying to save this—" She motioned between us. "Us. And there's one tiny part of me that is actually impressed with how you handled all this. I mean, at least you didn't take without asking or carve me like a Halloween pumpkin, right?" She snorted bitterly. "In my book, it counts for something. But it doesn't matter, you see? Because I'm done. I need space. I need to find me. And I need to do this alone. My life is such a mess that even if I wanted to forgive you, I couldn't, Bane. Not the way you need to be forgiven for us to be together. Consider this my official resignation from my job and from you."

She headed to the other side of the alleyway, and I spotted her Rover parked there. I wanted to chase her some more but knew that I'd be just like the other motherfuckers if I did.

Jesse stopped by her vehicle, unlocked her door, and slid in. She sent me one last gaze. There was more pity there than resentment. I was standing there like a tool, holding her unclaimed check, looking fifty shades of pathetic.

"Dad was right about one thing, Roman. The princess saves herself in this fairy tale."

CHAPTER TWENTY-THREE
JESSE

Let's talk about it at Mayra's office.

Mayra was helping Darren.

That much I was sure of. To what extent, I didn't know, but it didn't matter because she was my *fucking therapist* and therefore was breaking a gazillion codes.

I drove around in circles for a while. My thoughts were divided and split in the middle. Fifty percent of me wanted to make a U-turn and get back into Bane's arms, open up to him, beg him to help me, use his connections to make sure Darren and the boys would never get anywhere near an innocent soul again, and fifty percent debated whether I should march into Mayra's office and confront her.

The decision came to me when I finally parked my car, realizing that I'd parked it in the same spot as on the first day I'd met Bane. I stepped out and rehashed every single meeting I'd had with Mayra. Little snippets of our conversations chipped at my memory.

You could have lost your virginity in plenty of ways.

Best not to think about it.

You really should be moving on.

Darren is a lovely person, Jesse. You should let him take care of you and your mother.

Hypnosis? Oh, absolutely not, Jesse! You do not want to lose control. I'm afraid it will lead to a downward spiral.

I got back to my car, my foot bouncing as I looked left and right. I saw Bane's Harley parked a few rows down from my vehicle and knew that he was watching me. Somehow, I couldn't find it in me to be pissed. He was looking after me, but he knew better than to approach me.

I took out my phone. My messages were out of control.

Pam: Darren is missing. Come back home.

Pam: I really don't have time for this, Jesse. We need to talk about this ASAP. I have a manicure between three and four. Any other time is good.

Gail: Chunky Monkey and McMafia date when I finish my shift. Don't do anything stupid (like going back to your parents' house. Or...Bane, LOL).

Unknown Number (Maybe: Callum Beck): Have you heard from Bane? I'm trying to find the fucker everywhere.

Unknown Number (Maybe: Hale Rourke): Hey. It's Hale. Bane is not answering his phone and we have a business meeting in half an hour. Can you ping him?

I didn't answer any of them. Instead, I opened another text message.

Jesse: Hey, Kacey, it's Jesse. Some things came up and I can't visit Juliette this week. What are your plans?

She answered immediately.

Kacey: Booked our flight for Thursday. We'll be taking it from here. I'll come back to Todos Santos probably next month to bring Imane and her nurse with us and work out the details with you. Thank you, Jesse. For everything.

My heart was somersaulting in my chest, reminding me that I was still alive.

I loved that Mrs. B was finally going to get what she deserved—her family back. Even though a part of me, and not a small part, was dying a slow death trying to come to terms with the idea that I would no longer have her by my side.

I had nowhere to go. Nowhere to live. No job. No friends. No lead on what to do with my life. And that felt…oddly okay. Liberating, even. I was going to focus on building something of my own. Something that was completely mine.

The first thing I did was drive to All Saints High. It was the middle of a school day, so I had to ask for permission to take pictures with my phone.

"What for?" Principal Gabe Prichard sneered, not even bothering to lift his eyes from his paperwork, sitting behind his desk. He was ridiculously young for his position, and this was his first year at All Saints High. Tall, dark, handsome, and disgustingly stand-offish, the rumors said he'd completed his BA at the tender age of nineteen and was some sort of an educational maverick. As he asked me this, a trail of fangirls-slash-schoolgirls were standing behind me, waiting to be seen for whatever trouble they'd gotten themselves into purposely.

"A project." I remained vague.

"What kind of project?" He frowned, finally meeting my eyes. I nibbled at my lower lip, looking shy and wholesome and all the things I needed to be. He hadn't been here when I graduated. He didn't know how bad things had been for me.

"For a photography class," I finally lied.

He nodded. "No faces or students. No teachers. No staff. Nothing personal or intimate. Understood?"

Oh, it was going to be personal. But just for me. "Yes, sir."

I spent the rest of the afternoon squatting next to a bench under a tree, where *Jesse Carter is a SLUT* was carved into the wood, and in the gymnasium, where the mirror was still cracked at the edge from when Wren's friend, Ivory, tried to punch me and missed. I took pictures of every single piece of evidence there was. Most of it was still there, overlooked, much like my existence to the teachers after the Incident. High school is a great place to murder a soul. The deities don't care, and the mortals are too busy trying to survive.

I dug out the buried underwear Emery had stolen from my drawer and showed everyone, with the stain of my arousal from after we'd made out before things blew up. They were there, too, buried under a large pile of dirt.

The taunts. The laughs. The torment. It was all there, between these walls, in the courtyard. In my heart.

By the time I got out of there, it was close to six in the evening. I drove down to a taco shack and bought myself a foil-wrapped dinner. I knew money was going to be tight and was contemplating asking Mrs. Belfort for a little cash, even though the idea made my stomach toss. I'd refused Bane's check, trying to prove a point, but now I couldn't even afford a Kit Kat. I found myself driving to El Dorado despite my best intentions. I had to pack a bag. I couldn't walk around in Gail's weird clothes. Besides, after the text message I had sent Darren, I very much doubted he and Pam were going to give me more crap.

I parked in front of the mansion and opened the door. The only sounds noticeable were the crickets outside and the freezer producing some ice. I called Pam's name a few times, not wanting to be ambushed, and when no one answered, relief washed over me. I proceeded with caution straight into my bedroom and filled two bags with my stuff. I brought the bags down to my vehicle, about to climb behind the steering wheel before I slapped my thigh.

The Captain's Daughter. I needed to take the book with me. It had belonged to my dad, and who knew what those two would do to it? It was the only thing I had left of his.

The classics were all kept in Darren's office library because Pam believed "the staff" could get their hands on them and sell them to the highest bidder. Stupid, considering *she* was the staff not too long ago. No matter. I knew that there was no chance in hell Darren was in his office. He had a monitor that showed all the cameras recording around the house, streaming live. He would have seen me by now and tried to explain himself.

Debating only for a fraction of a second, I decided screw it. My dad was more important than Darren, Pam, and their bullshit. I headed back into the house, this time to Darren's office.

The problem, I realized seconds after I opened the door, was that you always feel sorry for yourself until you realize things could get much worse. They say it's better to be slapped with the truth than kissed with a lie. I wanted to drown in lies after I opened that door and saw him.

Darren.

Or what was left of him.

I gripped the door handle, struggling for breath. I'd wondered so many times over the past twenty-four hours what it would feel like coming face-to-face with him, but I never thought it would be like this.

He was lying face down on the floor, blood running like a river around him. At first, I was too shocked to react. I simply stood there, quivering like a leaf in fall. There was a Glock still clutched between his fingers. The scene looked fresh. And real. And tragic.

I pulled my phone out of my pocket and called nine-one-one. I delivered the news flatly, giving them all the details that they needed. They told me to remove myself from the room and not to touch anything. I went downstairs, swallowed down two Kit Kats (mainly so I could function—I had very little appetite), and downed a bottle of water. I sat in the living room, my foot bouncing, wondering where the hell Pam was. I thought about calling Roman and Gail but knew I needed to see this one through by myself. Gail was already doing too much for me, and calling Roman was inviting trouble.

He'd screwed me over so badly, the fact that I couldn't stop thinking about him frustrated me to no end.

The police arrived at the scene six minutes later: two detectives and a harem of badged staff. I was pretty much out of it, so I couldn't really distinguish who was who.

"I just want to leave here. I'm not his real daughter. We had a fight last time we spoke." Didn't they tell you in movies not to say anything without a lawyer? I wished I had someone as savvy as Bane to sit by my side and talk me through this.

The truth disturbed me. While I was shocked by Darren's death, I wasn't saddened by it. I felt no sympathy for the man who had ruined my future, not once but twice. Who had taken something so precious from me and hadn't even had the guts to admit it.

The cops deemed it a suicide from the beginning due to his position and the angle in which he'd been shot. There was even a suicide note—because, of course, Darren always had to do things right and proper.

I'M DONE.

They took my statement of what happened, and then Pam came in and started screaming. At this point, she had established herself as background noise, so I treated her as such and ignored her completely. A detective who looked like the human version of Peter Griffin from *Family Guy* asked me if I needed a ride anywhere, adding that it might not be the best idea to drive after what I'd seen, but I told him that I was okay because I was, even though I wished I hadn't been.

I wished I could feel sadness and compassion. I wished I hadn't prayed it had happened sooner, before Darren had ruined my life.

When I got to Gail's, I told her what had happened. She looked at me like I was a freak, her eyes wide and haunted.

"You must think that I'm the biggest jinx ever," I said. But Gail shook her head quickly.

"No. I think you had some really shitty things happen to you and that they're coming to an end sooner than you think. Good things are ahead of you, Jesse. You just need to look."

CHAPTER TWENTY-FOUR
BANE

It appears that a broken heart smells like rotten junk food and stale vodka. I know because I bathed in that rancid scent for a pretty long while.

Gidget, Beck, and Hale tried to visit me a few times over the next few days. I slammed the door in their faces when I even bothered to scrape my ass off the couch. After the third full day of my acting like an emo kid who'd just heard Fall Out Boy had broken up, they resorted to leaving me food outside my door. They would give it one knock and yell something along the lines of "Wake up, asshole, and don't forget to wash it down with water."

Water. Foreign concept. *I'll explain.*

After Jesse dumped my ass, I decided the best course of action was drinking myself into lengthy periodic comas, so I did that for, like, four days. Every time I would wake, I would text her something or try to call. Remind her that I was still alive-ish, even though she hadn't replied, and then go back to bleaching my liver with alcohol.

Bane: I love you.
Bane: Tell me if you need anything.
Bane: Hell, I NEED SOMETHING. You.
Bane: Is this what a spiral feels like? It looks much more

amusing when you're on the outside, judging it on other people.

Working and surfing weren't really a priority. Café Diem kept itself afloat thanks to Gail, and I was sure Hale was happy taking over the other side of my business. Beck, however, was rightly pissed. I'd dropped the ball on him and broken all his toes in the process.

I was wondering who was going to finally pull me out of my misery. I kind of gave up on Jesse answering me. Like, ever. Gail clammed up on me and wouldn't talk to me about her, so the front-runners to pull me out of bed and back into my miserable life were Mom, who'd stopped by twice and left me borderline psychotic voice messages, and Edie, who'd pulled the I'm-pregnant-and-hormonal card.

But in the end, it was Sheriff Diaz.

"Protsenko, open up before I kick this flimsy thing down." My door rattled to his knock, as if confirming the statement. If he thought I had fucks to give, he clearly hadn't checked in my fuck-bag lately because that shit was empty.

"Make me," I yawned from my bed. Mom had probably whined his ear off to come have a talk with me. She knew we'd gotten close since the police station had been my second home when I was a teenager.

"If you make me get a warrant, we're gonna have some trouble, kid."

I loved that he called me "kid" even though I was twenty-five and fucked his wife in five hundred positions on the reg.

"A warrant for what?" I snort-laughed, rolling onto my stomach and scratching my ass. "Drinking myself to death? This shit's still legal, sir."

He was silent for a second, calculating his words carefully. "There's a lot of new information about Jesse Carter. Might want to rethink the death part."

That's all it took to make me stand up and open the door. Diaz pulled up his pants over his beer belly, his mouth dropping open in astonishment. "Wow. You look like crap."

"Oh, shit. I was just on my way to an *America's Next Top Model* audition," I groaned. "Guess I'll have to wait for next year. Make yourself at home."

I offered him the only thing I had available—tap water and pot—and he politely declined both. With the state of the houseboat, I was surprised he agreed to sit down at the edge of my couch without draping a towel over it. I plopped on a beanbag opposite him, crossing my legs, giving him a wolfish, fake smile.

"Spill it," I ordered, and for the first time in days, I actually wasn't flippant and goddamn dead on the inside.

Brian took his hat off, always a good sign if you're looking for a dramatic announcement, and tipped his chin down. He was a short, balding man with freckles covering the better half of his face, lips included. Whatever was left of his fuzzy hair was the color of Cheetos. He looked tragic. "Where should I begin?"

"From the middle. I love stories that begin right in the middle," I deadpanned.

He rolled his eyes. "Goddamn millennials. Let's start with the freshest news I'm sure you've heard—Darren Morgansen is dead."

As evident from the way my jaw hit the fucking floor, it was not, in fact, something I was aware of. Sheriff Diaz's eyes bulged a little before he cleared his throat and rearranged himself on the edge of my sofa, nearly grimacing at the open Styrofoam take-out containers. I was normally on top of things. If I had interest in someone, I'd know where they were at any given moment and what time they took their daily shit. But I'd been too busy feeling sorry for myself for the past week to follow Darren.

"Yup. Suicide by gunshot. His stepdaughter found him."

"Jesse?" I perked just from hearing her mentioned. It was a whole other realm of pathetic, but at least I owned up to it.

Brian shrugged. "He only had one stepdaughter."

I sagged back into my beanbag and stroked my chin. Darren being dead was a blessing for my bank account. I owed the bastard a lot of money but literally no one knew, other than him, me, and Jesse, and the latter would never tell. But I was more concerned about how she'd taken it. She wasn't a fan of his—especially not near the end—but I guessed she was distraught as any other person would be.

"Do you know how she's handling it?"

Brian checked his phone, frowned, and tucked it back into his pocket.

"Her mother is in pieces."

"Her mother can go fuck herself in the ass with every dildo on planet Earth and I still won't spare her an ounce of lube. I asked specifically about the daughter."

Brian blinked a few times, scratched his bald head. "Now, now, Roman. You can't love a woman and not respect her parents. That's not how relationships work."

I stared at him, expressionless. "Rules don't apply to Jesse's folks. So what else is new with her?"

"The boys." He straightened his spine, flashing me a warning look that asked me not to act like a maniac. "They're coming back to town. I thought you'd want to know. Mr. Wallace had mentioned at the town hall meeting this week that they will all be flying back into Todos Santos to celebrate their former schoolmate's birthday next week. Wren Clayton?"

Didn't know. Didn't care. They were coming back. The plan was to deal with them myself. It had always been the plan. I didn't know how Jesse would feel about me doing it, but I wasn't planning on telling her until after the execution, anyway. I knew they were bound to return at some point and had bided my time mouse-quiet. Once they were here, they'd wish they weren't.

Brian was a mind reader, apparently, because he rolled his shoulders forward, tapping my knee and fishing for eye contact.

"I need to know what your plans are for them."

"Thanks for your time." I stood up. "And for the visit. And for not judging me for this." I motioned to the coffee table where all the half-eaten junk food was scattered, still in Styrofoam containers.

"Oh, I *am* judging you for this. And I still want to know what to expect. This is not the Wild West."

"Ever opened a map?" I sauntered over to the kitchen nook, lighting up a joint and then moving over to him. "And I pay you to give me information and to turn a blind eye, not to hear about my plans."

"I don't need a pile of dead, rich white kids in my jurisdiction," he said through gritted teeth. "There aren't enough trees in the world for that kind of paperwork."

I flicked his ear playfully. It annoyed and turned him on at the same time, my favorite reaction from people. "Zero body count. Trust me." And I meant it. But no one said anything about castration.

He stood at the threshold for a few moments, scanning my place, and then dragged his gaze to my face. "She must be real special."

I smirked. Such a fucking cliché. "Are we having a moment?" I arched an eyebrow.

He shook his head, laughed, and shut the door in my face.

I heard him mutter "Bastard."

Unfortunately, there wasn't a manual on how to react when your ex-girlfriend, whom you were crazy in love with, loses her stepfather to suicide abruptly. But if there was, suffice it to say texting would be low on the to-do list.

So here I was, showering, shaving, and making an effort to not look like a floating piece of shit. *Again.* I knew Jesse was still at Gail's because Gail had been acting like I molested fire extinguishers for a living and treating me like an untrustworthy prick, avoiding my calls and telling me she was busy every time I asked her if I could drop by for coffee (which I never drank, anyway).

So that's where I went, bearing a banana-strawberry-cantaloupe smoothie.

Gail opened the door and crossed her arms over her chest. I wanted to head-butt her just for sporting a smile that said that she knew something I didn't. But, of course, she did—she fucking lived with my girl.

Devil on my shoulder: *You mean your ex-girl. Forget that part where you betrayed her? Because she didn't.*

Angel on my shoulder: *Don't mind the asshole in black. You guys are on a break.*

"Where is she?" I leaned a forearm over her doorframe.

"At work." Gail applied dark-purple lipstick, her eyes still dead on mine.

"Work? What work?" I dropped the smoothie between us. Purposely. *Fuck.*

"The new job she got." She looked down, smirking. "You better clean that up."

"Do it yourself and I'll pay you extra."

"I hate you. No wonder she is dating someone else."

"What?" It came out as a snarl.

Gail waved her arm dismissively and laughed. "She's not, but God, you should have seen your face. Oh, how the mighty have fallen. And to think that you used to consider pool-banging multiple chicks as a water sport. Do you have a shrine for Jesse and everything?"

"Shut up, Gail."

There was more standing and looking at each other like idiots for a while as I tried to think of my next step.

"You sure she's not here?" I asked again. *Genius stuff, asshole.* I could feel her at my fingertips.

"Positive. God, you're rabid. It's kind of sweet but also kind of creepy."

"How is she handling the Darren thing?"

Gail shrugged. "You know. She's fine. It was traumatic to see, but after what he did to her, she is hardly heartbroken over it."

"What do you mean?" I asked absentmindedly, my eyes searching for stuff that belonged to Jesse behind Gail's shoulder in the apartment. Because, apparently, creepy outweighed the sweet by a few tons.

"You know, how he took her virgin—" She stopped there and stared at me like I'd slapped her. I looked down, something moving between us. Realization was a black fog through which I saw everything clearly. The pieces fell together.

What.

The.

Fuck.

"Repeat that," I ordered quietly. My blood simmered under my skin, bubbling with heat I was genuinely concerned could burn me to death.

Gail took a step back and covered her mouth with her hand. "I thought she told you."

"Why would she? She dumped my ass." This was new information because there was no way Jesse would keep it from me. She was always honest. The opposite of me.

"Yeah." Gail took a deep breath, rubbing her face, smearing the purple lipstick she forgot she'd just applied. "Yeah. Sorry. She is dealing with it, Roman. She is."

I looked at her expectantly, waiting for more, but she just turned around and rushed into the apartment. I followed her, kicking the door with my foot.

"What am I supposed to do, Gail? Tell me. Because I can't let her go, but I can't force her into being with me, either." She'd had enough of men forcing shit on her.

Gail looked up, munching on the edges of her fingernail, and I thought, *So much deep purple.*

"Time."

"What?"

"You've given her everything. A job, love, passion, your dick. The only thing you haven't given her is time."

"What if she decides she doesn't want me at the end of it?" I rubbed my face with my palm.

Gail smiled. "Then be happy for her, Roman. That's the essence of love."

CHAPTER TWENTY-FIVE
THE LETTER

My dearest Jesse,

This is the hardest and easiest thing I ever had to do in my life. Hardest because I know what I will be doing after writing this letter and dread the moment, even though I want it to be over and done with. Easiest because I've been keeping these feelings to myself for far too long, and there's nothing more liberating than the truth.

I wish I could tell you I regret what I did. But if we are being honest—and honesty is the only thing I owe you, really—I have given you and your mom everything that I have and will leave it to you, Jesse, after I die—the only thing I regret is you remembering. I thought you were too drunk. Completely out of it.

I wanted you.

So I took you.

Because it's always been you.

I remember the first time I saw you. You. Not Pam. Your mother was working the cash register at a diner in my accountant's building. It was by mistake that I'd gone into this branch. Rather than noticing the blond bombshell my age, I noticed the girl sitting next to her, with the inky ponytails and huge blue eyes. You were reading a book, your hair like feathers, your eyes like crystals. You were forbidden and luscious. From the shape of your eyes to your pillowy narrow lips, your beauty held so much power, and you didn't even know it yet.

The worst part was that you were easy.

A man of my position could lure a woman in your mom's situation into just about anything. Especially marriage.

I knew I didn't need much. One night, maybe two. I was going to be patient and good. I fell in love with you, Jesse. It was difficult not to. Your passion for books, for life, for love. And it was so easy to get near you, too. Your mother was recovering from losing Art. Both to another woman and to death.

I was quiet.

I was nice.

I was different.

I was evil.

No one knew.

No one suspected.

Still waters run deep.

My only regret is that you drowned in my sins.

I want you to know that it was never malicious. I had hopes. I did. Maybe you felt the same. Maybe I wasn't so crazy. Maybe for the first time in my life, someone didn't see me for the lisp-y loser that I was (or that I wanted people to think I am—oh, Jesse, it is so easy to manipulate people once they think you're weak). Maybe that person was you.

I will say this—I did feel sorry for what Emery and the boys did to you. When they hurt you, they hurt me. I never thought it would go this far. I didn't even think Wallace would notice. I definitely did not anticipate the rape, and for that, I apologize profoundly, although I have to believe that any levelheaded person wouldn't have acted the way he did.

I understand how hypocritical that sounds. I never thought that I was a levelheaded person. I'm saying Emery wasn't, either, and you were unfortunate enough to be a victim. Twice.

Jesse, I love you. I also hate you, in a sense. You made me put up with your mother, and I think we all know how difficult she can be.

It didn't surprise me one bit when they began to call you Snow White at school. I wondered—and more than once—whether your friends knew the whole truth. That you, too, had a wicked mother who was jealous of your beauty. That you, too, hid away from the world. Just with books instead of elves. That you, too, took a bite of the poisonous apple.

That apple was Bane Protsenko.

He was supposed to wake you up.

Not to steal you.

We had a deal. I knew he would pull you out of your misery, with his beautiful face and ugly reputation. I didn't know he would take it that far. I didn't know he would fall just like the rest of us.

Jesse, I am going to ask you for something very important now.

Don't forgive me.

Don't forgive them.

Break the cycle because there are too many bad men out there who need to be stopped, and the only way to stop them is to be a strong woman. So be one.

The truth is, Art was right to leave your mother.

The truth is, Bane was right to defy me and fall in love.

The truth is, this is the last thing I will ever say or write to anyone, and I will be remembered as the scoundrel.

But that won't matter to me in a few minutes. Nothing will.

A bullet to the head is my choice of suicide. It's messy and expensive, just like me.

Go to the police, Jesse. Tell them about Emery, Nolan, and Henry. Don't allow them to get away with what they did. God knows I got away with it for eight years, and I did not deserve one day.

With love, respect, and regret,
Darren Floyd Morgansen

CHAPTER TWENTY-SIX
JESSE

The crackling sound of thunder filled my ears and brought me up to Gail's rooftop in the middle of the night.

It was late September. Rain had no business running down the hot roofs and dusty windows of my South Californian desert town. Maybe it was all a part of something bigger. Maybe it was a sign. Maybe it was my dad. Or Darren. Or Bane. Or just the bag of evidence lying in my duffel bag, a ticking time bomb.

Maybe. Maybe. Maybe.

I let the drops lash against my face as I blinked at the sky. Darren's letter fell from my backpack not long after I came back to Gail's house. She'd asked if I wanted her to be there when I read it. I'd thanked her but said that the words were meant for me. I needed to face them alone.

The letter was a shock, but the simple, transparent plastic bag accompanying it was what shook every bone in my body. It was the evidence from the night of the Incident. My torn bra and panties. The semen- and blood-covered shirt. My old phone they'd stomped on, with their fingerprints on it. It was all there. A Post-it Note was stapled to the bag.

Kept it in my safe. Good luck.

My chest rattled as rain slipped between my lips. I let the last eight years sink in. I told myself that none of it was my fault. And for the first time in years, I actually believed that. I wanted to cry, but the tears wouldn't come. Replacing them were anger, rage, and a profound sense of injustice. Darren had been sick. Pam was sick. Emery, Nolan, and Henry were all sick. Bane wasn't sick, but he was a jerk, and the price of his mistake was divided equally between us.

And Mayra? Mayra was a manipulative bitch.

It felt strangely convenient that the only memory I'd blocked out of my mind was the one of what Darren had done to me. Sure, he'd forced me to drink until I'd passed out, but that couldn't have guaranteed a memory loss. That's where Mayra fit in, strolling into the picture mere weeks after Darren had raped me. She'd manipulated my reality, working relentlessly toward making me forget.

But now that I remembered, I was going to fight tooth and nail to rebuild my life.

This week, I'd walked into Book-ish, a local bookstore, and asked for a job interview.

"We aren't hiring," the dorky teenage girl behind the counter said flatly, her eyes stuck on the *Marie Claire* magazine she was flipping absently. I told her I was not leaving until I spoke with the owner. An older woman came out of the back room after a few minutes.

"You need to give me a job, and here is why."

I'd told her my story. Openly, candidly.

I'd shown her my tattoo, so she knew I wasn't just a poser. Books were my friends, my allies, my voice. They were my weapon of choice in the war I survived.

I got the job.

It felt good being employed again. And it felt even better to have gotten the job completely on my own. Darren had left me enough money to sustain myself and the next twenty generations, but I wasn't going to touch a dime of it. I fantasized about donating it to women's shelters and other good causes, but in practice, I was too sick to my stomach to think about it yet.

After I got hired, I went to Mrs. Belfort's to say goodbye. She was boarding a plane the same afternoon with Kacey. Ryan was staying in town to deal with the paperwork. We hugged, and cried, and I wondered what had taken me so long to take the initiative and help her. Help *myself.* But it was always there, plain and simple.

I wasn't alive before Bane came along.

Now I was present. I was feeling. My heart was an animal, caged and suppressed and *angry.* It was hungry. Restless. Out for blood. And I was going to feed it because new Jesse died. Her quiet, submissive corpse was left on the cool sand of the beach the evening I'd had the flashback.

I realized that I wasn't old Jesse just then. I was an even newer version, a *stronger* version, a version that was not to be messed with. She would make everyone pay. *Everyone.*

After visiting Mrs. B, the last thing I did while in El Dorado was knock on Wren's door. Her parents lived in a James Bond–esque compound on a hilltop. I knocked on her door and sported my best innocent smile. She answered, immediately scrunching her nose up in distaste when I came into view. She was wearing a sports bra and yoga pants. A Cardi B song was blasting from the home entertainment system behind her.

"What do you want?" She put her hands on her hips, looking down.

Last time I'd seen Wren, Bane had nearly killed her friends. The less-than-enthusiastic greeting wasn't surprising.

"To apologize," I said and batted my eyelashes, laying it on thicker than her makeup. "About the night at the track. I guess you've heard about my dad..." I referred to Darren as my dad, even though the only title he had truly earned in his life was that of a cunning rapist. But I had a plan.

Wren's eyes skimmed the length of me, her eyebrows finally relaxing, a look of sympathy washing over her expression.

"Yeah. I heard. Sorry." Her shoulders went slack.

"It's okay. It's been pretty crazy lately. I guess what I wanted to say was that I'm sorry about what happened with you, Henry, and Nolan. I overreacted." Each word was like a knife in my mouth.

Wren flipped her long blond ponytail and rolled her eyes. "It happens."

"And I also wanted to give you this. I know that it's your twentieth birthday in a second." I handed her a wrapped gift. It was nothing special. The same strong, flowery, nauseating perfume I remembered she liked from when we used to go to school together. The next part was tricky, but I knew I could pull it off.

"Aw, thank you." She took the gift but still didn't invite me in. "Yeah, I mean, it's kind of a big deal."

"Think about it. You're entering your twenties. That's huge." I leaned my hip against her doorframe, engaging her in an easy chitchat. We used to do this a lot, Wren and I, back when I'd dated Emery. I'd never really felt the connection with her, but I'd tried hard for my boyfriend. Emery only ever hung out with the popular kids, and Wren had been the perfect queen bee everyone loved to secretly hate.

"Oh. I should do something, shouldn't I?"

I widened my eyes. "You mean, you don't even have a party planned? Wren, it's the middle of the summer! Everyone is on a break. You *have* to do something."

She munched on her lip. "I'm going to a community college in San Diego. Everyone there is meh. All our friends are in real colleges."

Your friends, not mine.

"Invite them over, then." I did a half-shrug. My heart beat so fast, I was afraid it'd crack. I wanted to lure them back into town but knew that they weren't stupid. What they were was smug, and I was counting on them seeing me as helpless and vulnerable. Being newly orphaned worked in my favor.

Wren tapped her chin, her acrylic, candy-apple-red fingernails sparkling under the sun. "They said they were going to hang out in New York this summer."

"Aw, New York." I rolled my eyes, acting like them. Like *her*. "Home is the best place to be during summer vacation. Especially when it includes Tobago Beach and your family and friends."

"You mean, you won't mind if they come to town?" Wren shot me another suspicious look. My guess was Nolan, Henry, and Emery didn't want to rock the boat the minute they realized Bane was in the picture. Even in high school, we'd all known who he was, and nobody was stupid enough to mess with him.

"Dude, ohmigosh." I used her favorite phrase, reining in my gag reflex. "Everyone just needs to let go of this whole thing. I mean, it happened years ago, right? No need to dwell on it."

I wondered if Wren was toying with the idea of actually inviting me. I hoped, for her sake, that she wasn't because that would put her in the category of dumb as a rock. But by the smile spreading across her face, I knew that she'd totally bought every single lie I'd fed her and was coming back for seconds. I felt deceitful—lying isn't only about the people you lie to, it's mostly about your own integrity—but I could no longer stomach the idea that the boys could be planning another "orgy" with someone else. Plus, that plastic bag of evidence burned a hole in my duffel bag.

It couldn't stay unused.

"Ohmigosh, Jesse, you're right! I'm going to call them right after my private Zumba class. Hey, you should totally come."

I pretended to punch her shoulder. "Eeep! You're the sweetest, but I really need to get things prepared for the funeral and everything. Thanks, though."

Even though Wren had the intelligence of expired mayo, Emery and Nolan were pretty bright. I didn't want any of them to suspect I was pulling any tricks by declaring I'd be there. Wren pouted like an adorable puppy, her version of condolences.

"Prayers to you and your mom, Jesse." She rubbed my arm. We shared an awkward half-hug.

"Thanks."

Driving back to Gail's, I knew a few things:

1. Wren was going to throw a party.
2. She'd invited me because she was an idiot.
3. I was going to be there, but not in the capacity they were planning on.

Surprise.

I loved the feeling of my clothes, heavy and soaked with the unexpected rain, as I made my way down from Gail's roof. The tropic summer episode cleared my head, and I felt so alive I wanted to scream.

Gail had fire escape stairs leading straight down from the roof of her building to the entrance. I used them to get down and was about to hit the intercom to go back into her apartment when I noticed Bane leaning against his Harley, his head bowed down. He was standing in the rain, soaked to the bone, a look of sheer surprise at what he was doing—at how far he'd gone for a woman—crossing his face.

I turned my back to him and punched the intercom to Gail's apartment. She buzzed me in without answering because she knew my crazy self was out in the rain, thinking things over. Bane jogged behind me, scolding me under his breath.

"Are you going to ignore me forever?"

"That's the general plan." I pushed the building door open, and he strolled along with me, a trail of raindrops following him. I wanted to ignore his existence completely and go upstairs, but in reality, I couldn't tear my eyes from his beautiful face. Raindrops adorned his wet golden hair, dripping down to his boots.

"Crazy weather." He chuckled, but it sounded so sad, the words cracking like an egg. "When I was a kid, I thought God was flushing the toilet every time it rained. Made leaving SoCal virtually impossible. It rarely rains here."

"Thanks for the anecdote, Roman, but we're past chitchat, so you can keep the rest of your fun facts for your next client," I said viciously, twisting to the stairs and taking them two at a time. He caught up with my pace, and we were shoulder to shoulder, heat pouring through our damp clothes.

"Darren's dead," he said, mainly to show me that he knew.

"And this is your business because…?"

"He hurt you."

I stopped mid-step, turning around to face him.

"He hurt you, and you're my business." His eyes were lit and burning, and I knew there was nothing I could do to diffuse them.

"How do you know?"

"Gail thought you'd already told me."

I swallowed. I couldn't really fault Gail. Bane was after me, and she knew I wanted to hurt him. And that nothing would hurt him more than this piece of information.

"Why won't you leave me alone?" I pushed his chest.

"Because, unfortunately, I'm deeply in love with your ass."

"I bet you also love the fact that you don't have to pay Darren now."

"I do. Makes life easier, but I never gave a shit about the money, and I think we both know that."

I poked my lower lip up, tugging at it. The way he stared at it, like he wanted to catch it between his teeth, suck the rain from it, and bite it until it bled, made heat spread in my lower belly.

"You mean, you didn't care about the money so much, you signed a contract to make me your little toy project for six months?"

"That was before."

"Yeah, welcome to the 'after.' Sucks to be here, right?"

It wasn't until we made it to the second floor of the building, standing in front of Gail's door, that he spoke again. He looked broken, and I hated to see him like that. It made no sense at all. So many people had ruined me—him included—and yet seeing him suffer, seeing his emerald eyes turning droopy and miserable, made me want to stab my own chest with a fork. What the hell was wrong with me? Why couldn't I let him go the way I had Pam and Darren?

"Emery, Nolan, and Henry are popping in for a vacation," he said.

My fist hovered over Gail's door, and I halted. I wanted to push Bane into the hallway and slam the door in his face, but his words made me stop. I swiveled slowly, my mouth curving in disgust.

"How do you know?"

"I have eyes and ears everywhere. Especially when it concerns you."

"This McMafia stuff is not impressing me, Roman. Sorry to disappoint."

Plus, I was the one who lured them into town, I thought about adding but didn't. I only trusted one person in this operation, and that person was me.

"I'm not trying to control you. I'm trying to fucking *save* you," he growled, pushing me against the door with a soft thud. He boxed me in with his arms, his forehead dropping to mine. We were both wet and shivering, our breaths heavy and charged. Our hair stuck together, and I loved that we were yin and yang. Him, blond and whole and hidden by ink. Me, black-haired and broken and clean. He locked my chin between his fingers and tilted my head up. His eyes were hard and soft, honey-edged and flinty green. Cunning, like a snake's. But the way they looked at me, like I mattered, disarmed me. He pressed his lips to mine, and we stayed like that, in half a kiss, half a breath, for a few seconds before I pulled away and cupped my mouth.

"Don't touch Emery, Henry, and Nolan," I said.

"Like fuck I won't. I'm going to end the bastards," he snarled.

My phone beeped in my hoodie's pocket. I pulled it out. It was Pam.

She was on her tenth text message to me today. We were supposed to have a meeting with Darren's lawyer about the will. I wanted to drag it out for as long as I could before finally informing her that she was back to being dirt-poor. *God bless prenups.*

I thought that it was poetic justice that she didn't get to keep the thing she'd chosen over my happiness and mental health. *Money.*

I sent the call to voicemail and looked up at Bane.

"I have a plan," I said.

"Fill me in."

I shook my head. "It's mine."

He knitted his brows. "Who the fuck are you, Jesse Carter?"

"I'm the girl I need to be to save myself."

He clasped my arms in his hands, pinning me to the door. I wanted so badly to forgive him, to fall right into bed with him, to be in his arms. Safe. Sound. Protected. I knew, without a shadow of a doubt, that Bane was capable of giving me all the things the new Jesse needed. I wouldn't have to work hard for my justice. He would bring the prey to my doorstep, like a loyal, skilled hunter.

But I wanted messy. Bloody. I wanted wonky and imperfect. I wanted to drag them into justice my way, even if it lacked his force and finesse.

I rose on my tiptoes, darting my tongue and licking the outline of his Cupid's-bow lips. He stopped breathing, his eyes hard on mine, so engrossed in the moment he couldn't even close them to enjoy what I was doing.

"No." He pulled away.

"No?" I raised an eyebrow.

He shook his head. "You wanna kiss me, you do it fucking right."

His lips crushed down on mine, and before I knew it, he'd reached down, grabbing the back of my thighs and hoisting me up to wrap my legs around his waist. We were frantic, desperate. He shoved his tongue into my mouth, and I felt like he was filling me with much more than a kiss. With hope and with desire and with the ability to see the world a little brighter. He ground the bulge in his cargo pants against my clit, and I let out a muffled moan. We wrestled against Gail's door as my hands dug into his shirt and traced his glorious six-pack while he, once again, fucked me with our clothes on. I heard Gail from the other side of the door, about to unlock it and open up, before everything went silent, and she let out a yawn.

"Oh."

"What's up?" She was talking to someone on speakerphone. *Beck?*

"Nothing. Jesse and Bane are fucking against my door."

"Yet the dipshit still ain't taking my calls." *Yup. Beck.* "Can you slip him a note for me?"

"Hard no, Woody." She called him Woody? How had I not noticed it before? Oh. Right. I'd been too busy trying to get Bane to touch me.

"Think they're back together?"

"Who knows?" Gail chuckled, her slippered feet moving back to the living room. Roman groaned into my mouth, squeezing my ass tight with one hand while finding his way into the waistband of my jeans with the other. My fingers and toes curled in delight, heat gathering in my belly. He found my clit and toyed with it. Pinched it, flicked it with his thumb, and rubbed it between his two fingers like he was going to light it on fire.

"Missed you." He stamped my mouth with another searing kiss. Overlapping sensations of complete abandon and odd empowerment zinged through me.

And love. The kind of love that made me feel immortal.

"This doesn't mean anything," I growled into our kiss, rubbing into his big palm with my groin. "I still hate you."

"I know," he said, his mouth filling mine with the fresh taste of rain and cinnamon. We were grinding against each other in a rhythm that belonged to us, no one else's, in the kind of chemistry you couldn't fake or stage, like two pieces of an elaborate puzzle that only had one place: right next to each other.

"But I'm here for you, Snowflake. I'll be sitting on the sidelines cheering for you because you're the strongest girl I know, but I'll also be there if you need me. Needing someone wouldn't make you any less strong, Jesse. It would just make you human."

I planted one last kiss on his nose before I slid down the door and stood up, his hard-on between us nearly poking out of his cargo pants, the air saturated with what we'd just done. I took a deep breath, tilting my chin up.

"You gonna leave me like this?" He cupped his junk.

"How else would I leave my enemy?" I asked.

"Spent," he deadpanned. I shook my head and pushed the door open, hearing him taking a step back behind me.

"I can't wait to fuck the old Jesse." He sucked his teeth. "She seems like a fighter."

"Stay out of my shit, Protsenko."

But he was already going down the stairs, laughing like a maniac.

CHAPTER TWENTY-SEVEN
JESSE

The next morning, I pulled a pillow over my face and ignored the alarm clock yelling at me that I had a shift at Book-ish in an hour. Gail breezed into my room. Well, her room, really. We were sharing her queen-size bed without any trouble, other than that first night where she'd told me she found it gross to sleep next to a person who'd been in bed with Bane Protsenko.

"It's like secondhand smoking, but with prostitution." She'd pretended to gag. Secretly, I was happy I could still laugh about it and still remember how to breathe.

I knew that I needed to remove myself from Gail's apartment at some point because Gail was too nice to kick me out but decided to deal with the situation only after I'd dealt with Emery and his friends. One thing at a time. That was perhaps the only motto Mayra had taught me that had actually stuck.

"Good morning, sleepyhead." Gail splashed down on the bed, lacing her tattered black Chucks. I peeked at her from under the pillows, my eyebrows pinched.

"Hi."

"Have fun spreading STDs on my front door yesterday?"

"I think we missed a spot or two. Might revisit it tonight," I grumbled.

"Yeah. I don't care. I didn't come here to hear about Bane's dick.

That shit should have its own Wikipedia entry by now. I'm here to tell you that your mom's downstairs."

That made me jump out of the bed and fling away the blanket. I charged for my Keds, tightening the laces like they'd wronged me somehow. My hair was a mess, and my breath still had that after-make-out aroma—a little dry, a lot horny. I shot Gail a look from over my shoulder.

"How does she know I'm here? Did you have another slip of the tongue, like with Bane?" I immediately regretted the uncalled-for comment. Gail owed me nothing, and it really had been an honest mistake on her part. "Sorry," I muttered, untangling my hair with my fingers and taking a sip of water from a bottle discarded on the floor. Gail fell onto her bed and flicked chipped black nail polish from her nails.

"I didn't talk to her. I came back from the grocery store, and she was there, hanging out and asking questions. You really know how to channel people's inner creepers, know that, Carter?"

I didn't put it past my mom to have hired a PI to find where I was. I grabbed an apple from the fruit bowl in Gail's kitchen and jogged downstairs to face the Wicked Witch of the West. She was wearing sunglasses the size of Cyprus and enough Prada to open a store. Her hair was newly bleached, and she looked about as mournful as I looked like a respectable CPA. I dug one hand into the pocket of my black hoodie and took a juicy bite of the apple, leaning against the entrance of Gail's building. Last I'd directly spoken with Pam, she'd been flailing in the pool, spitting water. I doubted this was a social call.

"Lost your way to the plastic surgeon?" I arched an eyebrow.

"Save me the hilarious commentary, Jesse. I'm here because we need to go to the lawyer ASAP. Do you think this is some sort of a game?" She was trying hard not to bark, dangling over the edge of a breakdown.

I tilted my head, calmly producing Darren's letter from the back pocket of my jeans and handing it to her. "Is this why you're here? Because your pedophile rapist of a husband left me all of his shit and you're freaking out?"

She held the letter between her manicured fingers, not unlike it was a ticking bomb, and flipped her sunglasses to the top of her head. Her eyes skimmed the paragraphs, running in their sockets and widening with every passing second. I saw all the white around her blues. All the lies behind her fake-truths.

"Jesse…"

"Remember when I was twelve and had my first period? The one that didn't come back until eight months later? I was puking in the bathroom and there was blood on my thighs, and you saw it, because you asked Hannah to clean it afterward?" My voice was calm. Dry. The words slid from my mouth effortlessly, and even though I wasn't in a state of hysteria, I still felt them. They hurt, but they no longer burned.

I was healing.

"I didn't know. I mean, I wasn't sure," she stammered, taking a step in my direction. I took a step back, ripping another bite of the apple. It was shiny. Red. Beautiful, really. I understood why Snow White had fallen for the trap. But I was standing right in front of my very personal witch, refusing to make the same mistake.

"Yeah, you were." I sniffed, kicking a little rock between us. "So you found me. Mazel tov. Now it's time for us to go to the lawyer. You're acting like you should be looking forward to this meeting. Spoiler alert: You shouldn't."

"Jesse, baby, honey." She laughed, going for the hug—*going for the freaking hug*—and I sidestepped, avoiding what could have made me throw up the apple right on her glossy neon stilettos. I stuck up a hand between us, shaking my head.

"Get away from me, Pam. You want us to go to Darren's lawyer? No problem. Send me a text message with a time and a place. I'll be there."

"What are you planning to do with the money?"

I shrugged. "Burn it, maybe."

"Jesse, you're being ridiculous! This is *real* money we're talking about. Your father would be—"

I pushed her away before she could finish the sentence, smoke nearly shooting out of my nostrils. "Don't. Whatever you do, don't tarnish his name. He's not to be blamed for any of the bullshit that happened."

"Oh. That's rich. The drunk philanderer was a saint, huh?" She threw her arms in the air. I laughed. She didn't get it, and it occurred to me that she might never.

"Far from it. He was a cheater and an alcoholic. A savior and his own worst victim. He wanted to help people but was doing a spectacular job at ruining his own life. But all is forgiven, Pam, because he tried. He tried to be good. You?" I stepped toward the door, shaking my head. "You don't want to be good. You want to win. Maybe that's why you keep on losing."

"You need to leave me with *something*!" she called out.

"I am," I said, yanking the door open. "I'm leaving you with the consequences of your actions."

———

My father had once told me that Alexander Pushkin was born into Russian nobility and died in a duel with his brother-in-law, a French aristocrat, who'd tried to seduce his wife. I remembered thinking people had really crazy lives back then, but I didn't think that anymore. As I sat inside my Rover, outside the Todos Santos police station, strangling the steering wheel with my hands, I realized that his life had been no odder than mine.

Because we all had crazy stories.

I'd been raped *twice*.

Born to a mother who'd never really loved me.

Taunted and ridiculed in high school, manipulated by my own therapist.

All those things were true, but while they had happened, so had other things. Great things. I was blessed in so many ways:

Finding Gail.

Finding a job.

Finding literature and words and sentences that inspired me to be better, both to other people and to myself.

Finding Bane.

I threw the door to my vehicle open and walked into the station on autopilot, slinging my duffel bag across my shoulder. I couldn't believe I was doing it. It hadn't changed one bit since the time I provided a statement more than two years ago.

A sleepy receptionist with big dark curls and kind eyes looked over from the reception counter, scanning me. "How can I help you, sweetheart?"

"I need to amend a statement I gave two and a half years ago."

I told her my name.

She gave me a second glance, this time thorough and curious, and told me to wait. I watched her turn around and hurry over to her shoulder bag hanging from her office chair, taking out her personal phone and dialing a number. My palms began to sweat, and I regretted showing up here. What if Emery, Nolan, and Henry's parents had paid someone to keep me silent? What if I'd just walked into a lawsuit waiting to happen? Did I even have enough evidence?

Maybe she was calling Mr. Wallace right now. I couldn't face him. He was one of the most formidable men I'd ever met.

Two minutes later, the woman in the uniform was beside me again. "Coffee?" She smiled breezily.

I wiped my palms over my pants. My jaw was hurting because I was trying to keep myself from screaming.

"I'm fine," I clipped. "What's going on?"

The lady looked down, her gaze resting on the ample chest

covered by her khaki dress shirt. "I called Detective Madison Villegas. She said she was expecting you."

"She was?"

"Yes. Two years ago."

Villegas. The woman who'd cried when I gave my statement.

The woman who'd desperately tried to get a word with me, alone, but Darren, Pam, and the two lawyers they'd brought along with them had never allowed her to. They'd said my reputation would be tarnished and, therefore, so would my life. That I wouldn't be able to recover. That Emery's dad was going to destroy our family. They'd said that no one was going to believe me because it was their word against mine and they were the golden rich kids and I was some girl from Anaheim who'd made a stupid mistake and regretted it.

They'd said so many things that broke my heart that day.

I swallowed. "She knew I'd be back?"

The woman nodded, resting her hand on top of mine. "You're doing the right thing, Miss Carter."

A few minutes later, I was sitting in Detective Villegas's office. She was a petite woman with delicate bone structure and a fresh, short chocolate bob. Her movements were quick and efficient, but her eyes and mouth were full of crinkles and soul.

"Tell me everything from the start," she said. I did. I circled back to what had happened when I was twelve and continued until the moment I'd heard the ambulance picking me up after the guys raped me. I told her about the way Mayra covered up for Darren and about Pam turning a blind eye to all of this. And Darren's letter, I told her about it, too. Then I produced the plastic bag and slid it across her desk.

Her eyes bulged. "The evidence."

"Where did you think it was?"

Detective Villegas shook her head. "They said it disappeared somewhere in the hospital when you were admitted. It was my first clue something was fishy."

I gave her the original copy of his letter to me—I had a few more stacked in my backpack and saved in my cloud—along with all the evidence from school. All the pictures I'd taken when I'd visited All Saints High.

Villegas looked attentive, sympathetic, but most of all focused. "And you said they're now in college, studying on the East Coast." She scribbled something in her notepad, not looking up at me. I shook my head.

"They are here on vacation. There's a party tonight."

She looked up. Smiled. I smiled back. We shared something that was much more than words. I'd like to believe it was the realization that something bigger than us, justice, was about to take over the lives of those who'd ruined mine. I asked her what I should expect, and she said that I needed someone to lean on because the ride was about to get bumpy. I could only think of one man I wanted there, and I hoped that he wanted to be there with me.

Before I left Villegas's office, I asked her how she knew I was going to come back and tell her the truth.

She shrugged and took a sip of her Starbucks. "I knew you weren't telling the truth. Your parents were covering for them."

"But how?"

She grimaced, pulling at her collar. Great. She was hiding a secret, too?

I shook my head. "Please, just tell me."

"Well, this is hardly confidential. Your housekeeper, Hannah, came forward and said that your parents were not exactly what you'd call hands-on and that the boys hung out at your house often and she had a strong reason to believe that they were capable of doing such a thing. She even hinted that one of them came over when you weren't around, for your mother."

I thought about Emery's cockiness, about Nolan's sordid affair with Pam, but my stomach wasn't churning anymore. I ran my fingers through my hair. *Hannah.* The silent, blueberry pancake–making, birthday card–leaving housekeeper. Villegas took my file out of the cabinet and dropped it onto her desk, leaning back in her chair on a sigh.

"Then there was Juliette Belfort. She showed up at the station a couple of days after you were discharged from the hospital."

My eyebrows knitted. Mrs. Belfort and I weren't even close before the Incident. It was *after* what happened to me that I'd started hanging out with her. Before, I'd been the half-assed girl who visited her once a month or so, bringing whatever pie Hannah had made that day and sharing a piece with her, along with lemonade, in front of the maze, just to take some of her loneliness away.

"Mrs. Belfort had a lot to say about Darren and Pamela Morgansen. Especially the latter. Mrs. Belfort blamed her for not being around for you. Said that you'd kind of raised yourself since you'd moved into El Dorado, spending excessive time in her maze and by your window. Things added up, but you and your parents were cagey. Over the years, I thought about you a lot. I wanted to check in on you many, many times. But I knew it wouldn't be constructive for you. Knew that your parents were always going to guard you with their common yet mistaken belief that what had happened that night could ruin their business, stain their reputations, and affect your status forever."

We hugged after that, long and tight, like old friends who had missed each other. She wasn't a friend, but I had missed her. Before I walked away, I asked her, "What do you make of Darren? He raped me, but he also unleashed the plastic bag after his death."

"I think..." Villegas said carefully, rubbing her chin. "I think Darren was unbalanced. The writing was on the wall, but your mother didn't want to read it. There was too much at stake. Keep your phone turned on."

"You got it."

When I walked out of the police station, I could feel Emery, Nolan, and Henry's presence in the air. It sounded crazy, but I could.

It smelled of danger and the sour copper of my blood the night they'd tried to kill the old Jesse. For a while there, I thought they'd succeeded. The universe felt limitless all of a sudden. Big and wide in an unthreatening, the-world-is-my-oyster way.

I missed Bane like a limb but also wanted to punch him in the nuts. He'd betrayed me, before and after he knew me. Slept with me with the knowledge he was being paid. And yet I knew he wasn't the villain in my screwed-up story.

Artem, *Dad*, had given us each other, in the most unexpected way, and now I'd let Roman go. Only it seemed unfair that I'd have to give up someone who'd made me so happy just because of one mistake. I thought about the piled-up stack of mistakes and wrong-doings Artem had collected over the years, some of them behind our backs.

Bane wasn't perfect.

But he wasn't evil.

He deserved a chance.

I drove up to El Dorado. I promised myself I wasn't going to walk into the party and make a scene, but I wanted to know if my gut feeling was right. I parked a street away from Wren's house, pulled my hoodie up to cover the majority of my face, and walked down her street toward her house. I wasn't looking for Emery's Volvo SUV or Nolan's Ferrari. I was looking for an old beatdown red truck or a Harley.

Then I found the ugly red thing sitting right in front of the huge floor-to-ceiling window overlooking the street. A perfect spot to watch partygoers as they drank and laughed. I grinned to myself. Flippantly, I circled his truck from behind, opened the passenger door, and slipped in. He turned around from watching the party and almost punched my face on instinct before realizing who it was.

I tapped my chin thoughtfully, dragging my eyes over his beautiful face. "Hmm. Aggressive much?"

"Excuse me, Miss, did you lose your way to Hot Topic?" His eyes swept over my attire, and it occurred to me that Bane had never done this before. Teased me for my weird clothing. And…I kind of liked his teasing. Because I knew he admired every single thing about me. His corded muscles relaxed. I gulped. Roman "Bane" Protsenko was beautiful like a Pushkin paragraph. You could read his face a thousand times, and each time you'd find something new to admire.

"What are you doing here?" I squeezed his bicep. I already knew the answer but wanted to hear it anyway.

He looked away, smacking his gum loudly. "Figured you were gonna show up here. I respect that you wanna do this alone, but I can't justify these two gloriously big balls if I'm not man enough at least to give you backup." He cupped his groin, a dark zing igniting in his eyes. "Know what? Fuck it. It's not about you. I know you don't need backup. I came here because I was worried and I wanted to put my mind at ease. Are you mad?"

I shook my head, fighting a smile.

"Thank fuck. Gail says you're bringing out the creeper in me, and I can't afford a restraining order with my rich criminal record."

"I actually think that I'm done with creepers for this lifetime, if you don't mind. Can I get the cocky bastard version instead?"

Roman pretended to sift through an imaginary catalog in front of him, plucked a nonexistent page from it, and handed it to me. "Well, whaddaya know? It's the only version of me that's still in stock."

He pulled me into a kiss that made oxygen seem overrated. Our tongues lashed at each other, swirling together, at war over who was more in lust with the other. He jerked me into him, and I straddled his narrow thighs in seconds, fumbling with the buttons of his cargo pants while he unzipped my hoodie and pulled down the collar of my shirt, bringing one of my nipples into his mouth and biting it. He sucked his way up to my neck so hungrily I was sure he was going to leave purple marks all over me. His cock sprang free, and it was scorching hot in my hand as he pushed my jeans off and tugged my underwear to the side. I gave his PA a quick tug before I sank down onto his dick and closed my eyes, shuddering from the ripples of pleasure moving through me. He flipped us over, and suddenly, I was beneath him, writhing. I pulled his jeans down and scraped his lower back. We were moving in sync, like we always did. Like the waves he liked to ride. Knowing where to peak, where to soar, and where to break.

"Where have you been?" he asked, sinking into me, his weight on me. I should have been frightened to get caught. Especially with a reputation like mine. Like *ours*. But with Bane, I felt fearless.

The outliers. The rejects. We're free.

"Gail's," I answered. "Pam's. Mrs. B's. Just…around."

"No, Snowflake. Where have you been before? When I was lost. When I was a monster. When nothing made sense. Where have you been all my life?"

I pulled back to look at him. Some of his pain had melted away, but most of it was there, in his eyes, waiting for me to tell him that I didn't care that his family had stolen mine. That I wasn't too broken to love him how he so obviously and heartbreakingly deserved to be loved. "Iris" by the Goo Goo Dolls started drifting from the radio like a lullaby, and it was perfect, and *we* were perfect. Even though life was far, far from perfect.

"I was right here. Waiting for you." I pressed my palm against his heart, smiling.

My Whole Life Has Been Pledged to This Meeting with You

Bane. Roman. My sort-of stepbrother.

A con, a liar, and a thief. He was there for me at the end when no one else was.

He was there for me when I needed him and when I didn't.

And he was there for me even though I constantly pushed him away.

He thrust into me in long, punishing strokes, and I arched my back, forgetting where we were, whom we were surrounded by. His ass was bare and visible for everyone outside to see, but all I felt was pleasure and triumph as he snaked one hand between us, pushing two fingers into me, making me feel so full I could hardly breathe. Our sweat cemented us together, and his cock was so hard and thick inside me, I felt him everywhere. He kept sucking, biting, and nibbling at my skin. My breasts were exposed and pushed out of my bra, bouncing against his steel chest, the collar of my shirt stretched and ruined, and again, I found myself craving to be taken mercilessly but willingly. He circled his cock inside me, teasing every nerve end, and then hoisted one of my legs over his shoulder for better access, plunging into me harder than before.

I gasped his name over and over again. Then two knocks rattled the window above my head.

"Go the fuck away," Roman snarled, his face still buried in my chest, covering and licking me.

"Holy shit, dude, they're legit fucking!" I saw two guys I used to go to school with laughing and pushing each other excitedly.

"Go away!" It was my turn to yell. But my heart wasn't in it. I was so focused on the intense pleasure, on my pussy dripping and the wetness pooling between us, on the orgasm I was reaching just as they started hooting loudly.

"Shit, it's Jesse Parker!"

"Carter, dickhead, not Parker."

"Whatever, man. Orgy Girl strikes again. Call Emery. *Now.*"

"What?"

One of them punched the other on the shoulder. "Now!"

"Finish for me, baby, so we can get out of here. It's fucking Losertown. No wonder you moved out," Bane hissed, biting my shoulder. Just as he said that, I fell apart in his arms, feeling wave after wave of electricity slamming into my body. After I came, Bane raised himself on his forearms, picked me up, put me in the passenger seat, and revved up his engine. His dick was still hard, a pearl of white pre-cum welling along his cock ring. *He didn't come.* He rolled his window down.

"Hi." He smiled casually at the two guys.

"H...hi?" one of them said, confused. The other one was in the process of releasing a slow, recognizing *shit* when Bane sent his fist to both their faces in rapid succession, and the crack of their noses breaking filled the air.

Bane backed out of his parking space. The guys were standing at the curb, crouching down and screaming, holding their noses. I was zipping my hoodie up and covering as much as I could of myself when Bane stuck his head out from my window again, tucking his cock back into his pants.

"Warn Emery not to ask his daddy to bail him out. Because if I hear he's out and about tonight, I won't show him the same mercy my girlfriend did."

We took off just when the police cars started pouring in through the gate. There was a row of three of them. I saw Detective Villegas sitting in the passenger seat of the first one, looking serious and talking on her phone. Neighbors poured out of their doors and opened the curtains of their big mansions, watching intently as the line of vehicles stormed up to Wren's house.

It reminded me of the opening scene of *Blue Velvet*, when the seemingly perfect neighborhood was actually crawling with rustling beetles and hissing cockroaches. The perfect guys from the perfect families of All Saints High weren't so perfect anymore.

I felt Bane's hand wrapping around mine and looked up, watching the leaves shaking on the trees. And I thought that, if this was a fairy tale, this was how I'd end the chapter:

The princess's sword was bloody.

But she refused to sheathe it.

She wanted to leave a trail of their misery behind her so they could always find her.

CHAPTER TWENTY-EIGHT
BANE

Jesse asked if we could stop by her house first.

"Why?" I groaned, already frustrated with the prospect of meeting Pam again.

"I need to do something important."

Pam wasn't home—she was probably lawyering up and getting ready to dispute the will, according to Jesse—and I let out a sigh of relief as I took a seat on her bed. She crawled onto it on her knees and stood in front of the Polaroid pinboard, staring at it.

"Do you have a lighter?" Her eyes were still hard on the pictures.

What kind of question was that? I was a stoner from hell. I had two Zippos and a box of matches at any given time. Every pyromaniac's wet dream. I fished one from my pocket and tossed it over into her hands.

"Are we finally going to burn this ugly-ass place down?" I sniffed.

She turned around and smiled. "Not the entire house. Just the pictures."

We went to the backyard, where Shadow had died, by the Moroccan sunbeds, stacking the pile of pictures into a makeshift bonfire.

"The funny thing is I never took a picture of Darren's back. He was so good at blending in with his fake lisp and his B-grade suits." She flipped my lighter, began to burn the edge of a picture of some teenager's back, and dropped it down to the rest of the Polaroids, which caught fire quickly.

"Yeah, he kind of tricked me that way, too." I sat on one of the sunbeds, admiring her ass and pondering over her stepfather. "Hey, know what I was thinking?"

She twisted her head to watch me. "What?"

"I fucked my stepsister, and I didn't even know it. That's hot."

Jesse bit her lip. "I want to leave the Rover here. It's not even mine, anyway. Would you lend me your truck if I need it?"

Why not? I've handed you everything else I own, including my heart, which I don't want back.

I rolled my eyes, playing exasperated. "Knew you'd be a gold digger."

We drove around downtown a while after that, trying not to think about the scene that was playing out back in El Dorado.

We were supposed to wait until Villegas called to ask us to come to the station, and while I was glad Jesse had forgiven me—or maybe she was just making a habit of hate-fucking me and was still mad—I also knew we had a lot of loose ends.

"We're driving in circles," I pointed out after doing the fifth round from one point of the promenade to the other. People were no doubt starting to wonder what the fuck my problem was, going back and forth like my mission in life was to slow down traffic.

"I don't mind driving in circles." She looked out the window, munching on her hair again. It was a gross habit on any other girl, but I swear this chick could take a shit directly on my chest and I'd still think she was the cutest. I scratched my beardless chin. I was starting to get used to the smooth face. It made me look young, but that was good because I no longer felt like a pervert for pursuing Jesse.

"I do. Let's go somewhere."

"Where?"

"My mom's," I said, swallowing hard. Jesse may have been okay with leaving the Artem shit hanging in the air, but I wasn't. The two women I loved—the *only* people I loved—not only didn't know each other, but one of them actively saw the other as the villain. My mother wasn't the antihero of this story. She was the greatest fucking person in the world. Jesse needed to know that.

She whipped her head around, flinching like I'd clocked her.

"You want me to meet the woman who..." she started, before clamping her mouth shut and looking out the window again. I had to remind myself that for many years (four, to be exact), Jesse'd had to share the only thing good about her life—her father—with Mom and me. And that Artem had been at our place. *A lot.*

It was probably easier to pull shit like that off when you were a social worker and had to work your ass off and many of your cases got you on the road, but at the end of the day, he'd been with us days and nights. Entire weekends, sometimes. He'd told my mother he was married to his job and probably told Pam the same thing. He'd brought my mom and me over to his place plenty of times. Only it wasn't his place. It was his dead mother's place—the apartment he and his brothers never got around to selling. My mom found out about it after he died and she went over there to see if any of his living relatives needed any help. "Artem didn't live here," his brother, Boris, had said. "At least not in the last ten years," he huffed.

My suspicion was that she'd vowed to never let a man in again. And she hadn't.

Trent Rexroth had been a fuck buddy.

All the ones after him were more of the same shit.

It killed me that my mother had given up on love, but maybe that's why I owed it to myself to be less of a dick in general.

Snowflake's posture crumbled, her chin shaking slightly. "O... okay," she whispered. "I mean, sure."

"We don't have to." I was staring hard at the busy road and hoping my long internal scream wasn't audible to the outside world.

You need to give her a fucking chance, Jesse. For me.

I glanced at my phone every now and again. Saw something I'd been waiting for. Smiled.

"Why are you smiling?" she asked, shuffling in my peripheral.

"Beck won the competition. First place."

Her jaw nearly dropped. "That was today?"

I nodded.

"And you missed it, even though you trained him?"

I hadn't really thought about it like that. I just knew I couldn't be there when Jesse was dealing with so much shit. Even if she didn't let me be a part of that shit.

"No biggie. I've been to plenty of surf competitions before."

"Oh, Bane…"

"It's Roman."

"I want to meet your mom, Roman."

"What made you change your mind?"

"*You.*"

I spun my head to look at her. She let loose a bitter grin.

"You made me change your mind. Your sperm donor was obviously an asshole, and yet you're the best person I know. She must have done something very right to make that happen. So, yeah, I'd like to meet her."

I nodded, taking a sharp right toward my mom's place. It was the weekend. She'd be home. She'd be happy to see me. She'd be happy to see Jesse—even though I'd brought her up to speed with our issues. It's not like I'd wanted to, but she'd nearly kicked down my door when I'd been mourning my lost relationship—and had told me everything was going to be okay.

Possibly.

Probably.

Hell, hopefully.

I parked in front of my mom's house and rounded the truck to open Jesse's door. She kept on checking her phone, waiting for that phone call from Madison Villegas, and I had to pluck it from between her delicate fingers and tuck it into the back pocket of my pants.

"Don't worry. They didn't arrest them only to let them go because they forgot their weed at the party," I said. She crinkled her nose at me, which was adorable and also made my dick hard. Then again, there weren't very many things about Jesse that didn't inspire my blood to rush straight to my dick.

We walked into the house. I kicked my boots off against the wall, and Jesse slipped off her Keds and then arranged them neatly by the door. She wasn't the tidy type, so I took it as a good sign. She was trying to make a good impression.

"Mamul?" I called out from the hallway. I heard a thud coming from her bedroom and then a loud moan of pain. She came out a few seconds later, looking flushed and flustered, knotting a robe over her waist.

She wiped her hair away from her face and smiled through a suspicious blush. "Roman. My sun."

I took a sidestep and motioned for Jesse with my head. "This is Jesse. Jesse, my mom, Sonya."

They shook hands. I asked her if it was a bad time. She said it was never a bad time to see me. I had a feeling that there was someone in her bedroom, but I really didn't want to know, so I offered to go out and grab some take-out coffee while Jesse made herself comfortable. Mom sighed with relief while Jesse looked like she was about to stab me. I couldn't watch someone doing the walk of shame out of my mom's room without breaking both his legs on his way out.

"My phone, please." Jesse opened her palm and stared holes in my forehead.

I produced her phone from my pocket and put it in her hand, curling her fingers around it. "Take lots of pictures of him so I'll know who to stab later."

"*Bane*," she hissed. She called me that because I *was* acting like an asshole.

"What? He fucked my mom."

There was a line that seemingly started from the gates of hell at Starbucks. Then when it was finally time to order, I found out they had run out of the complicated shit my mom usually ordered, so I had to drive to another location, and before I knew it, it had taken me twenty minutes from the moment I'd left them to the moment I came back. I walked back into Mom's house worrying I'd find hair scattered on the floor as they'd beaten each other senseless, so I was pleasantly surprised to find them sitting in front of one another. My mom's hand was on Jesse's knee, and tears ran down Snowflake's face. They were silent and brave.

I stepped into the living room, dumping the Starbucks paper bag with the double-glazed donuts and sliding over a cup of coffee for each of them. My mom immediately took a sip. Jesse looked up and smiled through her tears.

"I hate coffee," she said.

I shrugged and took a sip of my latte. "Ditto."

My mom looked between us and laughed.

"Hey, Roman, what's the antonym of hate?"

"Jesse."

The call came an hour later. We were standing by the door in the hallway when I told Jesse she could do whatever she wanted. Take the truck if she wanted to do it all on her own or have me come with her if that was okay.

"For the record, I want to be there, but I know it's not my choice."

Mom stood next to us and smiled like we were exchanging our vows and not about to engage in a fucking war. It was the one battle I knew we didn't need any ammo for. Snowflake was equipped with the truth, and that was the strongest weapon on earth. Jesse looked over to my mom, took her hand unexpectedly, and squeezed it. "Thank you for loving my father when my mom couldn't."

"Thank you for becoming a girl he would be so proud of." Mom squeezed back.

Great. Now my mother was crying and Jesse was crying and I really needed a blunt, a drink, and a complimentary blowie in order not to feel like we were in a *This Is Us* episode. They hugged. My heart felt like two pieces locking back together into something whole.

My father had been a rapist.

My girlfriend had been raped.

And yet, somehow, I had managed to make the two women in my life stronger and proud.

I leaned against the doorframe, the keys dangling between my fingers. "So? What's it going to be? Every minute you spend here is a minute wasted on Emery not being thrown into jail."

That made her disconnect from my mom.

Mom wiped Jesse's tears and smiled. "You're stronger than your circumstances," she said to her, in English.

Snowflake said, "*Spasiba.*" Then she turned to me and held out her hand. "Can you be there for me? Just in case I need someone to hold my sword for me?"

I did a little bow with my head. "Why, my princess, I thought you'd never ask."

CHAPTER TWENTY-NINE
JESSE

Time stretched between the moment when we got into the truck and the moment my feet hit the asphalt of the police station's parking lot. Roman made some phone calls. I was too nervous to listen to them. My mind was elsewhere. It was like I was trying to remember why old Jesse had let it happen in the first place. Why I'd let them get away with it.

I didn't want to see their faces, their sneers, their anger. A part of me, a very ridiculous part, still wanted to please those who'd taken me under their wing when I was just the ex–poor kid from two towns over. A bigger part wanted them to pay for what they'd done to me.

"Hey, hang back for a sec," Roman said when we leaped out of his truck, lacing his fingers through mine, both of us watching the double glass doors of the police station open as a man in a sheriff's uniform walked out of them, yanking his belted pants up over his belly.

"Sheriff Brian Diaz." He shook my hand, and I returned the shake, like it was the most natural thing in the world, before realizing that six months ago I couldn't have done that. I would have turned around and run away. "Thank you for coming here today. It's a very brave thing that you're doing."

Bane squeezed my hand, still looking at the sheriff. "Bring us up to speed."

"Well, Miss Carter is going to be asked to identify the suspects from behind a window. They won't be able to see her, but she'll be able to see them." He turned his gaze back to me, smiling reassuringly. "You won't have to meet them or speak to them. After that, mainly more paperwork to supplement your amended statement, and you're done. Evidence is strong and sufficient."

"How long ago were they arrested?"

"Checked in forty minutes ago," Brian replied.

Roman nodded solemnly. "Bail?"

"A hundred K."

My teeth nearly snapped. Was that how little my innocence was worth? Roman massaged my back in circles, still talking calmly to Sheriff Diaz.

"Are they lawyered up yet?"

"Their parents and lawyers are on their way."

"Let me know if they're bailed." Bane's jaw hardened.

"Protsenko…"

But even Sheriff Diaz knew better than to argue with him over this point.

———

I wasn't supposed to come face-to-face with Emery, but somehow, I knew that I would. Like I couldn't truly move on unless our eyes locked together one last time. And they did. I was just passing through the hallway when Emery, Nolan, and Henry were being moved from the holding cells. The three of them were in handcuffs. My arms were swinging by my sides freely. *Free. I was free.*

The two large officers behind Emery exchanged annoyed looks, like it shouldn't have happened, and Villegas shook her head and stared at them blankly. It only took five seconds before Emery was pulled to the door next to the one I was entering, but it was enough.

Our eyes met.

His were empty.

Mine were full.

I knew that because of the way his gaze widened on mine when he realized, for the first time, that I wasn't the girl he'd left behind. I dipped my chin to my chest, smiling and muttering under my breath, "Pleasure running into you like this, Emery."

Bane waited out front while I was taken into a small white room where the paint job was chipped, rolling down from the ceiling. There was a window at the center of the room that showed us another room, still empty.

Detective Villegas explained the procedure, and the whole time, I thought about the first time Emery Wallace had asked me out on a date. I'd been so giddy and happy that day, I'd accidentally walked straight into a wall.

Looking deep into your rapist's eyes with them knowing you are on the other side of a tinted window was strange. When Emery walked into the room, I felt warmth spreading through my chest for the first few seconds before I remembered what we were here for. His pupils dilated when he stared back at the one-way window, like he, too, was able to look at me. Nolan and Henry were there, along with some men of different ages and attire. The three boys looked pissed and scared, their eyes bright, their jaws slack.

"Take your time. Breathe," Madison whispered into my ear.

I wielded my sword.

They couldn't hurt me anymore.

I pointed at the three of them calmly. "They were the ones who did it."

Villegas nodded and left the room.

I pressed a hand onto the window and smiled at them. Emery smiled back, as if he could see me. It was taunting, but it was there.

I took all of him in. His brown-blond hair styled in an expensive haircut and moussed to death. His pretty blue eyes. His slender body, Goody Two-Shoes polo shirt. Nolan, who looked like everything wholesome and American in the world. Henry, a WASP from hell, with his lanky frame and bony nose, looking like a classic trust fund baby. I looked at them, and they looked at me, and all they could see was black because that's who I was to them.

The darkness.

The stain in their history.

Not to be removed.

Not to be forgotten.

I would spread and conquer and be remembered so that other women would not end up like me.

I pressed my face to the chilly glass, laughing. Bane was outside. He couldn't be there with me when I identified them. He couldn't see how crazy they made me, and that was a good thing. That moment of insanity was mine. Not to be shared with others. Well, other than the officers, but I was sure they'd seen worse.

"You're not getting away with this." I rolled my head from side to side against the glass, realizing that my closure was going to be different. It was going to be made through lawyers and courthouses and documentation. I couldn't yell in Emery's face and bite Nolan the way he'd bitten me or kick Henry the way he'd kicked me.

And I was okay with that.

I turned around and asked, "Can I go now?"

They escorted me back outside to make sure I didn't run into any of the boys or their parents. The first thing I did was collapse into my boyfriend's arms and laugh and cry simultaneously, overwhelmed by emotions. Detective Villegas was there to stand outside the room, a smile tugging at her lips.

And I couldn't help but feel that justice had been served.

That the princess had won.

And that somehow, she'd even gotten her prince.

EPILOGUE
JESSE

A YEAR LATER

Slut. The whore of Babylon. Jezebel.

Emery, Nolan, and Henry are all in prison now, so these words no longer get tossed in my face when I walk down the street. Thirteen years each, the maximum the state of California usually gives a rapist. The judge had a lot to say about the boys' behavior when he gave the verdict. Especially after more girls came forward.

Two they'd met in college.

Emery's girlfriend, who admitted he'd forced her into doing things with him when they were together.

And Wren, who confessed they'd taken advantage of her one night when she was too drunk to drive home.

I say "boys," but chronologically, they should be men.

They'd never be men.

Men don't take without asking.

Men don't abuse women.

Men. Don't. Rape.

Mayra got her license revoked by the state, and she is now under investigation. Last I heard, she had to sell her house because she was no longer able to pay her mortgage. Comes with the territory of not being able to practice your profession, I suppose.

My bank account still says that I'm a millionaire, but it is my soul that feels rich these days. My mother is somewhere in Anaheim, couch-surfing with former friends and calling me every now and again, begging for a dime or two. I have yet to touch Darren's money, but when I do, I know what I'll be doing with it. I will help others in a way no one helped me when I needed it most.

I talk to Detective Villegas. A lot. Together we brainstorm ideas of what to do with the money. How to make sure it ends up in good hands. But here are the things I would never use it for: Clothes. Homes. Cars. Expensive gifts.

This money has meaning. I just haven't figured it out yet.

"Birthday pancakes!" Hannah yells from downstairs, and I grin into my pillow, cracking one eye open.

"I'm trying to watch my weight!" I call from my bedroom upstairs. Hannah only comes to work three times a week now, but I still pay her double what Pam did. *Thanks, Darren.*

"You have to have pancakes for your birthday, it's a rule."

"Well, rules are meant to broken!"

I take the stairs two at a time. I don't expect to see Bane there because I know he had some business downtown. Things have been hectic lately, with us sorting out our future in Todos Santos, Bane's career as a pro surfer and instructor, and the fact that I bought into a partnership at Book-ish, the bookstore where I still work.

Bane is not there, but everyone else is.

And there are balloons. Dozens of them. A huge "Happy Birthday" banner hanging across the dining room. I smile at my group, feeling loved and cherished and giddy. *Feeling loved.*

Hannah. Gail. Sonya. Edie. Beck. Mrs. Belfort. Kacey. Ryan. Everyone I know and love.

Gail and Sonya are the first to approach me. Gail unlocks herself from her boyfriend Beck's hug and walks over, scanning my pink pj's with amused mockery, and Sonya wipes the sleep from my eyes like the mother I never had.

"I thought long and hard what to get you for your birthday, and I decided I have just the thing for you." Gail laughs.

"Is it a new best friend? Because my current one is sassing around way too much," I say.

Sonya shakes her head and snakes her arm around me, gathering me into a hug.

Gail shoves a box of condoms to my chest. "Use them. My boss is an asshole, and I don't need more of him in this world."

Sonya shrieks in protest and wags her finger at Gail.

I take the box and put it on the granite kitchen counter.

I don't have the heart to tell her that it is too late for that. That I haven't taken my pills in months.

Besides, it's so early on, and I'm not even feeling nauseated yet. I've only missed one period, and I still haven't told Bane. But yesterday, when I took the test and it came out positive, I stood in front of the mirror and smiled.

My Whole Life Has Been Pledged to This Meeting with You

I hug Gail, and she puts her palm across my heart and whispers into my ear, "I'd have given you a sword, but you already own one."

BANE

"You fucked my fucking mom."

I drum my fingers over the glass separating me from jewelry that costs more than a five-bedroom house in Fresno. Hale rolls his eyes inside their sockets and waves me off. "I didn't know she was your mom. When you came in that day with Jesse, I was just as surprised as you were."

"I didn't know it was you in the bedroom. I'd have killed you," I say conversationally. This, by the way, is not an exaggeration.

"I know." He pretends to wipe invisible sweat from his forehead. "Dodged that bullet. And there are more to come."

"All set." The saleswoman behind the counter hands Hale a small green gift bag with his latest purchase. He spent his last ten paychecks on it. "Anything for you?" She smiles at me sweetly as she goes back to admiring the engagement ring in the catalog. The one Hale just purchased.

"Are you asking me if I feel like spontaneously spending thirty K today? Hard pass, woman." She laughs. I turn toward Hale and lift a finger in warning. "If you give me a sibling, I'll fuck you up."

He throws his head back and laughs. "You're nuts."

"That wasn't a no. Give me a solid, binding no."

"I'm marrying this woman, and she is forty-four. We may have a kid. We may not. Either way, you'll find out in the next few years."

So here is what happened: The day I came in with Jesse, my mom had decided to have a one-night stand with someone she had met at a bar the night before. Someone who had happened to be my business partner. She'd asked him what his name was. He'd said Johnny. He'd asked her what her name was. She'd said Ruslana. They both thought it would be nothing more than a one-time fling.

Then I came in, in the middle of their...*don't make me spell that out for you*, and she'd kicked him out. Well, Hale being Hale, he got super pissed. First, because of the unfinished business, but mostly because he'd messed with one of his best friends' moms. He swung by her house later that day to confront her about her lying to him. She pointed out that he was lying, too.

They told me the week after that they liked each other too much not to see where it would lead. They asked me, from a scale of one to killing myself, if it would hurt me if they pursued a relationship.

At first, I thought I was experiencing a heart attack.

"Snowflake, check my heart rate. It's as fast as a Ferrari." I'd drawn Jesse's palm to my chest. She'd said I needed to give them the chance to be happy with each other. With any other chick, I'd have told her to mind her own business and bend over.

With Jesse, I simply tossed Hale a look that said: Break my mother's heart and I'll break your teeth.

If everything goes according to this fucker's plan, my business partner is about to become my stepfather in the next few months or so. Weirdest part? He is two months younger than me.

But I promised I was not going to dwell.

I push past Hale as we both get out of the jewelry store and stop in front of my truck.

"Good luck today," he tells me.

"I'd say the same to you, but I really don't want you as family." I roll my eyes. I drive to where I need to drive to pick up what I need to pick up. Then I go up to El Dorado to meet the girl of my dreams.

We live in El Dorado. In a house that costs more than we'll ever make in our entire lives. It's not ours, and we don't pay rent. And it has a pool. And a tennis court. And a fucking bomb-ass maze.

I throw my truck into park and hop out. My gift follows closely behind me eagerly. It's Jesse's twenty-first birthday, and she can officially drink now. That's good. She might need some liquid courage to answer my next question.

"Come on, buddy. The maze is fun." I tug at the leash. "I did unholy things to your future mom there more times than I can count. Jesse!" I call out to her, which prompts her breathless giggles, the ones that float straight to my dick. I know where to find her. In the center of the snowflake maze. "Stay where you are. I'm coming to get you."

I'm praying the Labrador puppy behind me won't bark and shit all over my surprise. Especially literally.

"Are you panting?" She laughs harder, and I shoot the pup a you're-making-me-look-bad frown, trying hard not to crack up. Dude is killing my swag. For a cute thing, he sure sounds like a chain-smoking swine.

"Yeah." I smack my gum. "Gotta work on my cardio. I could use some help."

"You're getting help twice a day, sometimes three on weekends."
She hmmphs. I know what she is doing. She is reading one of her
smutty books. I've grown to love them almost as much as the classics.
Pushkin was the man, but recreating scenes from smutty books is
far better than trying to recreate his. Dude was fifty shades of crazy.

I find her in the center, like I knew I would.

No longer hidden by a hoodie, a walled-up expression, and
shapeless pants but with those dirty white Keds and ripped jeans
and the smile that could break your heart even from across the room.

I don't want you, Snowflake.

I need you.

I need you.

I fucking need you.

"Happy birthday." I unleash the pup on her, and he was a good
choice—I knew he would be, when I picked him up from the
shelter—because he runs straight into her arms and forces her to
put down the book and hug him. He licks her face all over, like he
is already hers. She squeals, her smile too big for her face. I take my
phone out and take a picture of it.

Click.

Remember this moment.

"Roman!" She stands up, holding him close to her chest, kissing
the top of his head. "This is perfect. *He* is perfect," she amends after
lifting him a few inches above her head, checking for his gender.
"I'm going to call him Pushkin."

"It's not all," I tell her. She raises an eyebrow, probably remembering the fact that these were my exact words last year when I gave
her the snow globe, and watches me. I decide on the spot, despite my
best intentions, to do the whole shebang.

Get down on one knee.

Produce the ring I bought for her a long, long time ago.

And bow my chin down, playing humble for once in my
goddamn life.

The ring was purchased after I realized I didn't need SurfCity or a mall or a fucking Vicious-styled secretary who looks like she is about to shit a brick every time I glance her way. I sold the hotel and bought the ring the same afternoon. It cost about the same. Zero regrets there.

"You'd better say yes because we're having dinner with my mom and Hale tonight, and he is going to pop the question, and I sure as fuck am going to beat him at his own game."

"So this is what our engagement is to you? A game?"

I huff. "I mean, you're an okay chick."

She giggles, plants another kiss on Pushkin. I like the name. It will feel good to hear it bouncing off the walls of our house. "Well, perfect timing."

"Why is that?" I grin.

"Because..." She lifts her shirt up. Jesse spent the last two months working on an elaborate tattoo to cover the marks the assholes left on her skin. It's a huge gladiolus, a flower that symbolizes strength and integrity, its name stemming from the word "gladius," an ancient Roman sword. I blink, ignoring her expectant stare.

"Because...?" I probe. She puts Pushkin down, grabs my hand, and flattens it against her lower stomach.

"Feel it."

"Feels tough."

"That's because your baby is growing there."

The air is knocked out of my lungs. I knew it was coming. Kind of. The birth control pills were gone, and Jesse asked me the other day how I felt about kids. I decided to be cautious and dodge it, not really sure if she would get freaked out by me wanting them or disappointed because I didn't. Truth was, I was impartial. What mattered was whom I'd have them with. "I wouldn't date one, but I guess they're cute," I'd said and shrugged. She said it normally took six months to get pregnant after you went off the pill. I'd responded, "Feel free to throw them in the trash bin, along with the memories of your asshole mom."

It took us less time than I'd anticipated.

Well, shit.

I'm still on my knee when Jesse cups her mouth. Mrs. B's kids let us stay in her house while they are looking for buyers. When a house costs twenty million dollars, finding a buyer is not that easy. So we house-sit for Juliette and hop onto a plane every now and again to visit her. Sometimes we invite friends over for dinner. Edie and Trent were here the other day with Luna and the baby, Theo. I love this house, but man, I can't wait to move into the yacht we purchased a few weeks ago. It's being painted right now, and that shit is huge.

"This is the part where you answer," I groan.

"Yeah. I mean, yes. Yes, yes, yes!" she yelps, and I slide the ring onto her finger. It's the wrong finger, so she tells me to do it right, and I roll my eyes and tell her I'm new to this love bullshit. She tells me I still do it very well, and we're happy.

So fucking happy.

And Pushkin is pissing on my boots.

And the sun is shining.

And I kiss her hard, my lips smashing into hers.

"I think we need matching ass tattoos," I say.

"Why? Do you have another cool story?" She grins into our kiss.

I pick her up by the ass and wrap her legs around my waist. "Yeah." I bite her lower lip and tug. Hard. "You."

BONUS SCENE
BANE

BANE TEACHING JESSE HOW TO COME AGAIN

"You don't have to touch me to ruin me." Jesse hopped back onto the large crate in my back office, pants off, spreading her milky thighs in front of me. Slowly revealing before me the path to heaven. Every ounce of self-control I possessed—and there wasn't much of it to begin with—evaporated completely. Seeing her stomach had ignited something in me. But the scar tissue didn't make me feel any pity or disgust, far from it; it highlighted how much of a lioness this girl was. She'd survived everything she had gone through and still had the courage to feel and experience the world all the time. Her bravery to seduce me with her gorgeous, curvy body took my breath away. I was a goddamn goner, and I had never thought anyone or anything could surprise me in this rotten world.

She strummed her clit with her long, lovely fingers, and I watched as the tiny pink bud swelled, glistening with the juices of her cunt. My cock was so painfully hard it was almost numb, precum leaking from the slit drop after drop. My palms were flat against the table, and I had to press them harder on the surface to ensure I didn't do something stupid, like take out my junk and rub one off right in front of her. Despite everything, I was still acutely aware of the trauma she had been through. She and I didn't play by the same rules.

"What the fuck are you doing, Jesse?" The words fell out of my mouth without permission from my brain. What a stupid question. I knew exactly what she was doing—killing me with desire. I was pretty sure my dick was about to fall off and run its way to her, begging for entrance permission.

"Seducing you." She spread her thighs even wider, giving me a better glimpse of that tight, shaved pussy. Every inch of her was smooth, sleek, and ready to be taken. She pinched her nipple through her shirt, and I was worried I was actually going to cream my shorts I was so fucking aroused. I'd never had a response this carnal to a woman before. I didn't know what it was about Jesse Carter, but she had a direct line straight to my fucking libido.

"Jesse." I slid my forehead over the cool surface of the table, strangling the edges to the point of white knuckles. I was panting like I was screwing her with everything I had in me.

"Do you want me?" Her voice floated over my head, across the room, on that stupid crate I was so jealous of because it got to feel Jesse's ass and her juices dripping on it.

"Want you?" I slapped the table with a growl. "I'm way beyond want. I'm somewhere between need and desperate. And I don't like that place, Jesse. I don't like it at all."

"Take me, then."

I raised my gaze to hers, searching for doubt, for fear, for anything to tell me not to go for it. I found nothing but determination and hunger in her irises. "You're not ready," I croaked out. I couldn't risk it. Couldn't hurt her. I'd die before inflicting pain on this woman after everything she'd been through.

"Who the hell are you to say?" she challenged, looking confident and happy with herself and whole, *so* whole. Cracked, but not broken.

"Your only lucid friend. And I'm not fucking up what we have for a fuck."

"You're a jerk," she groaned, still masturbating, still driving me mad, still tipping me over the edge of that red line I was desperate not to cross.

"Yeah," I choked out, my cock pulsating against my shorts, tapping them, begging to get out. *Thump, thump, thump.*

"*Bane.*" She went faster with her fingers.

"What part of the word 'no' don't you fucking understand?" I snapped.

She pushed two fingers into herself. They disappeared between the rosy folds of her cunt, and I imagined they were mine. Fantasized about her tightness as she clenched against me. Prying her open, working her body as I gave her pleasure and prepared her for my fat cock in the process. My throat bobbed with a swallow. I was losing the battle. The war. And my fucking sanity.

"Tell me you don't want to be the one doing this to me," she hissed out, and my eyes nearly rolled inside their sockets from delirious desire.

"Jesse…".

"I'm ready."

I shook my head, desperate to save her from me.

"Fine. I'm sure Hale will do what you are hesitant to," she murmured. "It's okay if you don't want to touch me, Roman. I can already feel you *everywhere.*"

I didn't know if it was the fact that she'd mentioned Hale— that fucker—or that she'd spewed out this nonsense about me not wanting to touch her, but that sprang me into action. I pulled my shorts down just enough to grab my shaft, squeezing it to calm it the fuck down. Jesse's wide eyes zeroed in on my Prince Albert. It twinkled like a star over my tip, moist from my precum. I started moving my fist along the length of my shaft, not taking my eyes off her. God, it felt *incredible.* Jerking off and watching as she touched herself. Imagining we were fucking. And we didn't break any rules. Not technically, anyway. I still wasn't touching her.

"Let's start over. Take your fingers out and push one in very. Fucking. Slowly. Now," I instructed.

She listened, but still stole a few strokes on her greedy, throbbing clit. "No one said anything about your clit," I grunted, pumping harder and faster. "Fuck yourself for me, but not enough to come. Because this is how I feel, Jesse, when you torture me."

"I don't enjoy torturing you." She stopped massaging her clit. "I'm inviting you to do anything you want with my body."

Sweet Jesus, she shouldn't have said that. Because I wanted to do *everything* with her body. Every. Fucking. Thing. Worship it and devour it. Kiss it and bite it. Lick it from head to toe. Fuck her so hard I'd put a dent in the mattress.

"Fuck," I hissed. I was close. Too close. "How wet are you?"

"Soaking."

"Show me."

She slowly pulled her fingers out of her cunt, and I closed my eyes, not trusting myself if I actually saw it. But I heard the whole thing. Her fingers were glistening with her juices. I wanted to feast on them like they were hard candy.

"Suck on it." I continued pumping my cock, incredibly close to the edge.

"You suck on it."

If only.

"If I come over there, I'll bite it off," I admitted. A confession, not a warning. As I said, I would never hurt this girl. "Just…for once in your life, do something you're asked to do, Jesse." I sounded as desperate as I was. Ready to go down on my knees if need be.

To eat her out, preferably.

She put her wet finger in her mouth and slurped, her eyes still trained on mine. Her cheeks hollowed as she sucked her finger nice and clean. Heat spread across my chest, and every muscle in my body tightened and arched. "Oh, Snowflake. What the fuck am I going to do with you?"

"Pounding me like the pavement would be a good start," she retorted.

"Three fingers," I ordered, refusing to let go, run over to her, and fuck her raw. Not because of her stepfather. Screw that loser. Because I didn't want her to regret us. Didn't want to go down in her history book as another stain of ink in her story.

Ever the overachiever, she inserted four fucking fingers into herself, going knuckle-deep, making my whole body tremble.

"Jesse." I was on the verge of ripping the walls apart.

"I'm so wet." She curved her back like a bow, an entire heaven sitting on a crate, up for the taking, and it was too much for me. I yielded to temptation, taking a few steps and stopping when I was between her legs. She was still fingering herself, and I was still rubbing myself furiously, but now we were so close the warmth of her fruity, sweet breath skated over my face and neck. I pressed my forehead against hers, squeezing my eyes shut, imagining that we were fucking. That my cock was inside her pussy. That this was all real. She could feel it, too. I knew because of the small whimpers she made each time she thrust her fingers deep inside herself.

"I can smell your pussy on your breath." My eyelids fluttered open, and I licked my lips, imagining her cunt dripping down my chin and neck as she came all over my face while riding it.

"Yeah?" she panted.

"Yeah. It doesn't smell like green apples or rain. It smells like a needy cunt. My favorite food category in the entire world. And I can't have you." I said that more to myself than to her. To remind myself she was still off-limits.

"But you want to." She ran her nose down the bridge of mine, and electric heat spread across my spine at that simple touch.

"I *need* to," I admitted. Snowflake was a need, not a want.

"What do you have to lose, then?" she coaxed.

Everything, sweetheart. Six million things, and more.

"Too fucking much. Come for me, Snowflake. Shit, I'm coming, too."

We fell apart at the exact same time. I could feel her entire body stiffening, then trembling against mine as strings of hot, thick cum shot down from my cock and onto her scarred belly. We were panting, shaking, melting into one another, and there was no denying what it was—not just crossing the line, but sprinting right past it into the hands of calamity.

"The queen is the most powerful piece," I groaned, my lips touching hers, but not quite kissing her. "Don't let the pawns bring you down."

PROLOGUE
DARIA/PENN

*It started with a lemonade
And ended with my heart.
This, my pretty reckless rival, is how our
screwed-up story starts.*

DARIA, AGE FOURTEEN

The tiles under my feet shake as a herd of ballerinas blazes past me, their feet pounding like artillery in the distance.

Brown hair. Black hair. Straight hair. Red hair. Curly hair. They blur into a rainbow of trims and scrunchies. My eyes are searching for the blond head I'd like to bash against the well-worn floor.

Feel free not to be here today, Queen Bitch.

I stand frozen on the threshold of my mother's ballet studio, my pale pink leotard sticking to my ribs. My white duffel bag dangles from my shoulder. My tight bun makes my scalp burn. Whenever I let my hair down, my golden locks fall off in chunks on the bathroom floor. I tell Mom it's from messing with my hair too much, but that's BS. And if she gave a damn—*really* gave one, not just pretended to—she'd know this too.

I wiggle my banged-up toes in my pointe shoes, swallowing the ball of anxiety in my throat. Via isn't here. *Thank you, Marx.*

Girls torpedo past me, bumping into my shoulders. I feel their giggles in my empty stomach. My duffel bag falls with a thud. My classmates are leaner, longer, and more flexible, with rod-straight backs like an exclamation mark. Me? I'm small and muscular like a question mark. Always unsure and on the verge of snapping. My face is not stoic and regal; it's traitorous and unpredictable. Some wear their hearts on their sleeves—I wear mine on my mouth. I smile with my teeth when I'm happy, and when my mom looks at me, I'm always happy.

"You should really take gymnastics or cheer, Lovebug. It suits you so much better than ballet."

But Mom sometimes says things that dig at my self-esteem. There's a rounded dent on its surface now, the shape of her words, and that's where I keep my anger.

Melody Green-Followhill is a former ballerina who broke her leg during her first week at Juilliard when she was eighteen. Ballet has been expected of me since the day I was born. And, just my luck, I happen to be exceptionally bad at it.

Enter Via Scully.

Also fourteen, Via is everything I strive to be. Taller, blonder, and skinnier. Worst of all, her natural talent makes my dancing look like an insult to leotards all over the world.

Three months ago, Via received a letter from the Royal Ballet Academy asking her to audition. Four weeks ago, she did. Her hotshot parents couldn't get the time off work, so my mom jumped at the chance to fly her on a weeklong trip to London. Now the entire class is waiting to hear if Via is going to study at the Royal Ballet Academy. Word around the studio is she has it in the bag. Even the Ukrainian danseur Alexei Petrov—a sixteen-year-old prodigy who is like the Justin Bieber of ballet—posted an IG story with her after the audition.

Looking forward to creating magic together.

It wouldn't surprise me to learn Via can do magic. She's always been a witch.

"Lovebug, stop fretting by the door. You're blocking everyone's way," my mother singsongs with her back to me. I can see her reflection through the floor-to-ceiling mirror. She's frowning at the attendance sheet and glancing at the door, hoping to see Via.

Sorry, Mom. Just your spawn over here.

Via is always late, and my mother, who never tolerates tardiness, lets her get away with it.

I bend down to pick up my duffel bag and pad into the studio. A shiny barre frames the room, and a floor-to-ceiling window displays downtown Todos Santos in all its photogenic, upper-crust glory. Peach-colored benches grace tree-lined streets, and crystal-blue towers sparkle like the thin line where the ocean kisses the sky.

I hear the door squeaking open and squeeze my eyes shut.

Please don't be here.

"Via! We've been waiting for you." Mom's chirp is like a BB gun shooting me in the back, and I tumble over my own feet from the shock wave. Snorts explode all over the room. I manage to grip the barre, pulling myself up a second before my knees hit the floor. Flushed, I grasp it in one hand and slide into a sloppy plié.

"Lovebug, be a darling and make some room for Via," Mom purrs.

Symbolically, Mother, I'd love for Via to make my ass some room too.

Of course, her precious prodigy isn't wearing her ballet gear today even though she owns Italian-imported leotards other girls can only dream of. Via clearly comes from money because even rich people don't like shelling out two hundred bucks for a basic leotard. Other than Mom—who probably figures I'll never be a true ballerina so the least she can do is dress me up like one.

Today, Via is wearing a cropped yellow Tweety Bird shirt and ripped leggings. Her eyes are red, and her hair is a mess. Does she even make an effort?

She throws me a patronizing smirk. *"Lovebug."*

"Puppy," I retort.

"Puppy?" She snorts.

"I'd call you a bitch, but let's admit it, your bite doesn't really have teeth."

I readjust my shoes, pretending that I'm over her. I'm *not* over her. She monopolizes my mother's time, and she's been on my case way before I started talking back. Via attends another school in San Diego. She claims it's because her parents think the kids in Todos Santos are too sheltered and spoiled. Her parents want her to grow up with *real* people.

Know what else is fake? Pretending to be something you're not. I own up to the fact I'm a prissy princess. Sue me. (Please do. I can afford really good legal defense.)

"Meet me after class, Vi," Mom says, then turns back around to the stereo. Vi *(Vi!)* uses the opportunity to stretch her leg, stomping on my toes in the process.

"Oops. Looks like you're not the only clumsy person around here, Daria."

"I would tell you to drop dead, but I'm afraid my mom would force me to go to your funeral, and you legit aren't worth my time."

"I would tell you to kiss my ass, but your mom already does that. If she only liked you half as much as she likes me. It's cool, though; at least you have money for therapy. And a nose job." She pats my back with a smirk, and I hate, *hate*, **hate** that she is prettier.

I can't concentrate for the rest of the hour. I'm not stupid. Even though I know my mother loves me more than Via, I also know it's because she's genetically programmed to do so.

Centuries tick by, but the class is finally dismissed. All the girls sashay to the elevator in pairs.

"Daria darling, do me a favor and get us drinks from Starbucks. I'm going to the little girls' room, then wrapping something up real quick with Vi." Mom pats my shoulder, then saunters out of the studio, leaving a trail of her perfume like fairy dust. My mom would donate all her organs to save one of her students' fingernails.

She smothers her ballerinas with love, leaving me saddled me with jealousy.

I grab Mom's bag and turn around before I have a chance to exchange what Daddy calls "unpleasantries" with Via.

"You should've seen her face when I auditioned." Via stretches in front of the mirror behind me. She's as agile as a contortionist. Sometimes I think she could wrap herself around my neck and choke me to death.

"We had a blast. She told me that by the looks of it, not only am I in, but I'm also going to be their star student. It felt kind of…" She snaps her fingers, looking for the word. I see her in the reflection of the mirror but don't turn around. Tears are hanging on my lower lashes for their dear lives. "A redemption or something. Like you can't be a ballerina because you're so, you know, *you*. But then there's *me*. So at least she'll get to see someone she loves make it."

Daddy says a green Hulk lives inside me, and he gets bigger and bigger when I get jealous, and sometimes, the Hulk blasts through my skin and does things the Daria he knows and loves would never do. He says jealousy is the tribute mediocrity pays to genius, and I'm no mediocre girl.

Let's just say I disagree.

I've always been popular, and I've always fought hard for a place in the food chain where I can enjoy the view. But I think I'm ordinary. Via is extraordinary and glows so bright, she burns everything in her vicinity. I'm the dust beneath her feet, and I'm crushed and bitter and *Hulky*.

Nobody *wants* to be a bad person. But some people—like me—just can't help themselves. A tear rolls down my cheek, and I'm thankful we're alone. I turn around to face her.

"What the hell is your problem?"

"What isn't?" She sighs. "You are a spoiled princess, a shallow idiot, and a terrible dancer. How can someone so untalented be born to *the* Melody Green-Followhill?"

I don't know! I want to scream. *No one wants to be born to a genius. Marx, bless Sean Lennon for surviving his own existence.*

I eye her pricey pointe shoes and arch a mocking eyebrow. "Don't pretend I'm the only princess here."

"You're an airhead, Daria." She shakes her head.

"At least I'm not a spaz." I pretend to be blasé, but my whole body is shaking.

"You can't even get into a decent first position." She throws her hands in the air. She isn't wrong, and that enrages me.

"Again—why. Do. You. Care!" I roar.

"Because you're a waste of fucking space, that's why! While I'm busting my ass, you get a place in this class just because your mother is the teacher."

This is my chance to tell her the truth.

That I'm busting mine even harder precisely because I wasn't born a ballerina. Instead, my heart shatters like glass. I spin on my heel and dart down the fire escape, taking the stairs two at a time. I pour myself out into the blazing California heat. Any other girl would take a left and disappear inside Liberty Park, but I take a right and enter Starbucks because I can't—*won't*—disappoint my mom more than I already have. I look left and right to make sure the coast is clear, then release the sob that has weighed on my chest for the past hour. I get into line, tugging open Mom's purse from her bag as I wipe my tears away with my sleeve. Something falls to the floor, so I pick it up.

It's a crisp letter with my home address on it, but the name gives me pause.

Sylvia Scully.

Sniffing, I rip the letter open. I don't stop to think that it isn't mine to open. Seeing Via's mere name above my address makes me want to scream until the walls in this place fall. The first thing that registers is the symbol at the top.

The Royal Ballet Academy.

My eyes are like a wonky mixed tape. They keep rewinding to the same words.

Acceptance Letter.

Acceptance Letter.

Acceptance Letter.

Via got accepted. I should be thrilled she'll be out of my hair in a few months, but instead, the acidic taste of envy bursts inside my mouth.

She has everything.

The parents. The money. The fame. The talent. Most of all—my mother's undivided attention.

She has everything, and I have nothing, and the Hulk inside me grows larger. His body so huge it presses against my diaphragm.

A whole new life in one envelope. *Via's* life hanging by a paper. A paper that's in my hand.

"Sweetie? Honey?" The barista snaps me out of my trance with a tone that suggests I'm not a sweetie nor a honey. "What would you like?"

For Via to die.

I place my order and shuffle to the corner of the room so I can read the letter for the thousandth time. As if the words will change by some miracle.

Five minutes later, I take both drinks and exit onto the sidewalk. I dart to the nearest trash can to dispose of my iced tea lemonade so I can hold the letter without dampening it. Mom probably wanted to open it with Via, and I just took away their little moment.

Sorry to interrupt your bonding sesh.

"Put the drink down, and nobody gets hurt," booms a voice behind me, like liquid honey, as my hand hovers over the trash can. It's male, but he's young. I spin in place, not sure I heard him right. His chin dipped low, I can't see his face clearly because of a Raiders ball cap that's been worn to death. He's tall and scrawny—almost scarily so—but he glides toward me like a Bengal tiger. As if he's found a way to walk on air and can't be bothered with mundane things like muscle tone.

SINNERS OF SAINT
CHARACTER INSPIRATION

Baron "Vicious" Spencer—Sean O'Pry

Emilia "Millie" LeBlanc—Emilia Clarke (with pink hair)

Jaime Followhill—Austin Butler

Melody Greene—Juliet Doherty

Trent Rexroth—Jesse Williams

Edie Van Der Zee—Dove Cameron

Rosie LeBlanc—Alexandra Daddario

Dean Cole—Chris Pine

Roman "Bane" Protsenko—Brock O'Hurn

Jesse Carter—Shailene Woodley

ACKNOWLEDGMENTS

As I write more books, my tribe continues to grow, and I find myself continuously and irrevocably humbled by the great talent in the indie community, a community that I am so grateful to take part in.

Firstly, I would like to thank my beta readers: Tijuana, Amy, Lana, Helena, and Paige. You've been my rock throughout this process, and I know how difficult it must have been to hear me obsess over a certain sentence or wording at three in the morning. Over. And over. Again.

To my editors, Tamara Mataya and Paige Maroney Smith, and the Bloom editorial team: Christa Désir, Letty Mundt, Gretchen Stelter, and Kylie Hagmann. Thank you so much for your feedback, attention to detail, and overall awesomeness. To my wiz graphic designer, Letitia Hasser at RBA Designs; my Bloom cover designer, Antoaneta Georgieva; and to my amazing formatter, Stacey Blake at Champagne Formatting.

A huge thank-you to my rock-star agent Kimberly Brower at Brower Literary and to Jenn Watson at Social Butterfly PR.

Special thank-you to my kick-ass street team. There is no one else like you. Blissfully unique and incredibly valued: Lin, Hayfaah, Sher, Kristina, Brittany, Julia, Summer, Vickie, Sheena, Sarah, Becca, Jacquie, Betty, Amanda, Erika, Leeann, Luciana, the two Vanessas (Villegas and Serrano), Tanaka, Avivit, and Galit. Thank you. Thank you. Thank you.

To the Sassy Sparrows, for being my safe place when I'm in need of a break from my crazy characters. And to the bloggers who push so hard and work even harder to make sure we indies have a voice. You're the best, and I love you.

Finally, to my readers, who never fail to stun me with your support. I will never take it for granted and will always try to give you magic. You deserve nothing less.

All the love,
L.J. Shen xoxo

ABOUT THE AUTHOR

L.J. Shen is a *USA Today, Wall Street Journal, Washington Post* and #1 Amazon Kindle Store best-selling author of contemporary romance books. She writes angsty books, unredeemable anti-heroes who are in Elon Musk's tax bracket, and sassy heroines who bring them to their knees (for more reasons than one). HEAs and groveling are guaranteed. She lives in Florida with her husband, her three sons, and a disturbingly active imagination.

Website: authorljshen.com
Facebook: authorljshen
Instagram: @authorljshen
TikTok: @authorljshen
Pinterest: @authorljshen